Michael Robotham is a former feature writer and investigative reporter, who has worked in Britain, Australia and America.

His debut thriller, *The Suspect*, introduced clinical psychologist Joe O'Loughlin and sold more than a million copies around the world, launching a nine-book series. It has been adapted into an ITV series starring Aidan Turner. Michael's standalone thriller *The Secrets She Keeps* has also been the basis of two BBC TV series.

He has twice won the prestigious UK Crime Writers' Association Gold Dagger Award for best crime novel, as well as the Ian Fleming Steel Dagger for *When She Was Good*, a Richard & Judy Book Club pick.

Michael lives in Sydney.

Also by Michael Robotham

Joe O'Loughlin series
The Suspect
The Drowning Man (aka Lost)
Shatter
Bleed for Me
The Wreckage
Say You're Sorry
Watching You
Close Your Eyes
The Other Wife

Cyrus Haven series
Good Girl, Bad Girl
When She Was Good

Other fiction
The Night Ferry
Bombproof
Life or Death
The Secrets She Keeps
When You Are Mine

MICHAEL ROBOTHAM

LYING BESIDE YOU

SPHERE

SPHERE

First published in Great Britain in 2022 by Sphere

This edition published in Great Britain in 2023 by Sphere

1 3 5 7 9 10 8 6 4 2

Copyright © Bookwrite Pty 2022

A CIP catalogue record for this book is available from the British Library.

ISBN 9-780-7515-8160-7

Typeset in Bembo Std by Palimpsest Book Production Ltd, Falkirk, Stirlingshire

Printed and bound in Great Britain by Clays Ltd, Elcograf S.p.A.

Papers used by Sphere are from well-managed forests
and other responsible sources.

Sphere
An imprint of
Little, Brown Book Group
Carmelite House
50 Victoria Embankment
London EC4Y 0DZ

An Hachette UK Company
www.hachette.co.uk

www.littlebrown.co.uk

'Tell me what you can't forget, and I'll tell you who you are.'

— Julie Buntin, *Marlena*

1

Cyrus

If I could tell you one thing about my brother it would be this: two days after his nineteenth birthday, he killed our parents and our twin sisters because he heard voices in his head. As defining events go, nothing else comes close for Elias, or for me.

I have often tried to imagine what went through his mind on that cool autumn evening, when our neighbours began closing their curtains to the coming night and the streetlights shone with misty yellow halos. What did the voices say? What possible words could have made him do the things he did?

I have tortured myself with what-ifs and maybes. What if I hadn't stopped to buy hot chips on my way home from football practice? What if I hadn't propped my bike outside Ailsa Piper's house, hoping to glimpse her in her garden, or coming home from her netball practice? What if I had pedalled faster and arrived home sooner? Could I have stopped him, or would I be dead too?

I am the boy who survived, the one who hid in the garden shed, crouching among the tools, smelling the kerosene and paint fumes and grass clippings, while sirens echoed through the streets of Nottingham.

In my nightmares, I always wake as I step into the kitchen, wearing muddy football socks. My mother is lying on the floor amid the frozen peas, which had spilled across the white tiles. Chicken stock is bubbling on the stove and her famous paella had begun to stick in the heavy-based pan.

I miss my mum the most. I feel guilty about playing favourites, but nobody is around to criticise my choices, except for Elias, and he doesn't get to choose. Ever.

Dad died in the sitting room, crouching in front of the DVD player because one of the twins had managed to get a disc stuck in the machine. He raised one hand to protect himself and lost two fingers and a thumb, before the knife severed his spine.

Upstairs, in the bedroom, Esme and April were doing their homework or playing games. April, older by twenty minutes, and therefore bossier, was usually the first to do everything, but it was April, dressed in a unicorn onesie, who ran towards the knife, trying to protect her sister. Esme had to be dragged from under her bed and died with a rug bunched beneath her body and a ukulele in her hand.

Many of these details have the power to close my throat or wake me screaming, but as snapshots they are fading. My memories aren't as vivid as they once were. The colours. The smells. The sounds. The fear.

For example, I can no longer remember what colour dress my mother was wearing, or which of the twins had her hair in braids that week. (Esme and April took it in turns to help their teachers differentiate between them, or maybe to confuse them further.)

And I can't remember if Dad had opened a bottle of home brew – a six o'clock ritual in our household – when he uncapped his latest batch with a brass Winston Churchill bottle opener. With great ceremony, he would pour the 'amber nectar' into a pint glass, holding it up to the light to study the colour and opacity. And when he drank, he would swish that first sip around in his mouth, sucking in air like a wine connoisseur, saying things like, 'Bit malty . . . a little cloudy . . . a tad early . . . half decent . . . buttery . . . quenching . . . perfect in another week.'

It is these small details that elude me. I can't remember if I knocked the mud off my football boots, or if I chained up my bike, or if I closed the side gate. I *can* remember stopping to wash the salt from my hands and to gulp down water, because Mum hated me spoiling my appetite by eating junk food so close to dinnertime. In the same breath, she'd complain about me having 'hollow legs' and 'eating her out of house and home'.

I miss her cooking. I miss her embarrassing hugs in public. I miss her spitting on tissues and wiping food off my face. I miss her trying to slick down my cowlick. I miss her nagging me about telling ghost stories to the twins, or leaving the toilet seat up, or the cap off the toothpaste.

I had nobody to nag me after the murders. My grandparents didn't have the heart. They were grieving too. I became the boy who was pitied and pointed at and whispered about. Befriended. Bullied. Cosseted. Counselled. The boy who did drugs and cut himself and turned up drunk at school. A hard child to love. Not a child at all, not after what I'd seen.

Monday morning, at a quarter to ten, and I'm sitting in the reception area of Rampton Secure Hospital, an hour's drive north of Nottingham. In fifteen minutes, a panel of three people – a judge, a consultant psychiatrist and a layperson, will hear an application from my brother to be released. It has been twenty years since my parents and sisters died. I am now thirty-three. Elias is thirty-eight. The boy is a man. The brother wants to come home.

For years, I have told people that I want what's best for Elias, without knowing exactly what that means and whether it extends to setting him free. As a forensic psychologist, I under-stand mental illness. I should be able to separate the person from the act – to hate the sin but forgive the sinner.

I have read stories about forgiveness. People who have visited killers in prison, offering sympathy and absolution. They say things like, 'You took a piece out of my heart that can never be replaced, but I forgive you.'

One woman, a mother in her sixties, lost her only son, who was stabbed to death outside a party. After the jury convicted the killer, a boy of sixteen, she forgave the teenager. Doubled over in shock, she kept repeating, 'I just hugged the man that murdered my son.' In the next breath, she said, 'I felt something leave me. Instantly, I knew all the hatred and bitterness and animosity was gone.'

A better me, a kinder soul, an empath, a religious man, would show mercy and give Elias the pardon he seeks. Unconditionally. Without question or hesitation. I am not that man.

Dr Baillie swipes a security card and comes to collect me from the waiting room. He is Elias's case worker. Fiftyish, compact, stern, a psychiatrist with a short-trimmed beard and a greying ponytail that seems to be dragging his hairline higher up his forehead.

'How is it going?' I ask.

'It looks promising.'

For whom, I want to ask, but I know whose side Dr Baillie is on. He assumes I'm with him. Maybe I am.

He waves to a security guard behind a Perspex screen. A door is unlocked and we are escorted along wide corridors that smell of pine-scented floor polish and phenol.

Rampton is one of three high-security psychiatric hospitals in England. According to the *Daily Mail*, it houses the 'worst of the worst', but reporters tend to focus on the high-profile patients, the 'rippers', 'butchers' and 'slashers' who make better clickbait than the bulk of inmates, being treated for personality or mood disorders; illnesses that don't involve a body count.

We have arrived at a large room where two dozen chairs, most of them empty, are set out in front of a long, polished table. A side door swings open. Elias enters. He is patted down one final time, before being told to sit. He waves to me. Relief in his eyes.

We don't look like brothers. He has put on weight over the years – due to medications and inactivity – and his hair is now flecked with grey above his ears. He has a round, blotchy face, a thin mouth, and eyes that are brown and intelligent yet strangely vacant.

Today, he is wearing his best clothes, beige chinos and a neatly ironed white shirt, and I see comb marks in his lightly oiled hair. Straight lines, front to back.

I shuffle along the row of seats until I'm close enough to shake his damp hand.

'You came.'

'Of course. How are you?'

'Nervous.'

'Dr Baillie says you've done well so far.'

'I hope so.'

Elias glances anxiously at the main table and the three empty chairs.

Another door opens and three people enter. The panel. Two men and a woman. They take their seats. Each has a name badge, but they make a point of introducing themselves. The legal representative, Judge Aimes, is a small rather plump man in a pinstriped suit, with greying hair swept back to form a wave that covers a bald spot. The psychiatrist, Dr Steger, is wearing a business shirt, rolled to his elbows, and an MCC tie. His hair is spiked with gel, and he has a heavy silver bracelet instead of a wristwatch. The lay member of the panel, Mrs Sheila Haines, looks like my old kindergarten teacher and I can imagine her jollying along proceedings and suggesting a mid-morning 'fruit break'.

Everybody new in the room must be identified. Their eyes turn to me.

'I am Cyrus Haven. Elias's brother.'

'Are you his closest family?' asks the judge.

I'm his only family, I want to say, but that's not quite true. He still has grandparents, aunts, uncles and a handful of cousins, who have been remarkably silent for two decades. I doubt if being related to Elias is one of their dinner-party stories.

'I'm his nearest living relative,' I say, and immediately wish I'd used different words.

'Are you a medical doctor?' asks Mrs Haines.

'I'm a forensic psychologist.'

'How fascinating.'

Judge Aimes wants to move on. He addresses Elias.

'Have you been given any medication that might affect your ability to participate in these proceedings?'

'Only my usual drugs,' says Elias, in a voice that is louder than the occasion demands.

'What are you taking?' asks the psychiatrist.

'Clozapine.'

'Do you know what would happen if you stopped taking your medication?'

'I would get sick again.' He adds quickly, 'But I'm better now.'

Judge Aimes looks up from his notes. 'We have received reports from two consultant psychiatrists, as well as heard oral submissions from Dr Baillie and the ward nurse and two resident psychiatrists. Have you been shown these statements?'

Elias nods.

'Do you have any questions?'

'No, sir.'

'This is your opportunity to make your case, Elias. Tell us what you'd like to happen now.'

Elias pushes back his chair and is about to stand when the judge says he should stay seated. Elias takes a piece of paper from his pocket.

'I would like to express my thanks to the panel for this opportunity,' he says, blinking at the page, as though he's forgotten his glasses. Does he wear them? It's been years since

6

I've seen him read anything apart from the comic books and graphic novels I bring him when I visit. Dad needed reading glasses when he turned forty and I expect it will happen to me.

Elias continues. 'I know what I did, and I know why it happened. I am a schizophrenic. What I experienced that day – what I saw and heard – the voices, the hallucinations – none of that was real. But I did unspeakable things to my family. Unforgivable things.'

He looks quickly at me and away again.

'I have to live with that stain on my soul. I broke many hearts – including my own – and every day I pray to God for His forgiveness.'

This is also new information, although I've noticed him dropping Bible quotes into our conversations on my fortnightly visits to Rampton. He wipes perspiration from his top lip.

'I have been in this place for more than seven thousand days and in all that time I have never left the grounds to visit the shops, or see a movie, or walk along a beach or ride a bike. I want to decorate a Christmas tree and wrap presents and go on holidays. I want to live a normal life, to make friends and get a job and meet a girl.'

I picture him practising this speech for weeks, looking at his reflection in the anti-break mirror.

'What job would you do?' asks the judge.

'I would continue to study law. One day I hope to be sitting where you are, helping people.'

'That's very noble,' says Mrs Haines.

Dr Steger seems less impressed. 'Almost half of all patients we release fail to keep taking their medication. Eighty per cent of them have relapsed within two years.'

'That wouldn't happen to me,' says Elias.

'How can we be sure?'

'I have worked on a recovery plan. I have coping skills.'

'Where would you live?'

'With my brother, Cyrus.'

The panel members look to me. I nod. Dry-mouthed.

'Do you have any questions for Elias, Dr Haven?' asks the judge.

Elias suddenly looks flustered. He didn't expect me to speak.

'How did it begin?' I ask. 'The voices.'

He blinks at me, as though unsure of the question. The silence fills every corner of the room and rises like water making my ears pop.

He finally speaks. 'There was only one. I thought it was my imagination at first.'

'What did it say?'

'I didn't think it was talking to me. It never said my name.'

'What did it say?'

'It . . . it . . . talked about someone else. "Can he stay awake all night?" "Can he skip school?" "Can he steal money from Dad's wallet?"'

'Was the voice telling you to do these things?'

'I didn't think so – not at first.'

'Why did you listen?'

'I thought it would make the voice go away.'

Nothing Elias has said is new. It has been documented, discussed and analysed. He is a case study now, taught to university students who are studying psychiatry and psychology and sociology.

'Do you ever think about them?' I ask.

Again, he blinks at me.

'Mum and Dad. Esme and April. Do you ever think about them?'

He shrugs.

'Why not?'

'It upsets me.'

'Did you love them?'

'I was sick. I did a bad thing.'

'Yes, but did you love them?'

'Of course.'

'Do you love me?'

'I barely know you,' he whispers.

'I appreciate your honesty.'

His eyes have filled with tears. 'I'm sorry.'

'What are you sorry for?'

'For what I did.'

'And now you've changed?'

He nods.

I glance at the judge and tell him I'm finished.

'Well, let's take a break,' he says, addressing Elias. 'We shall have a decision for you shortly.'

2

Evie

The manager has a moustache with waxed tips that curl at each end like frightened millipedes. It's the sort of facial hair you see on old-time villains dressed in black capes who tie women to railway tracks and cackle when they laugh.

His name is Brando, which could be a nickname, or a shortened surname. Maybe it's his only name, like Beyoncé or Prince. Brando is polishing a bottle of vodka with a soft cloth. He pauses and twirls each tip of his moustache like he's rolling a very long cigarette.

'What's your name?'

'Evie Cormac.'

'How old are you?'

'Twenty-one.'

'You look younger.'

I hold up my newly acquired driving licence, hoping he won't look too closely at my photograph, which resembles a mugshot. I don't know how to smile when people take my picture.

'Have you ever worked in a bar before?' he asks.

'Yeah, loads.'

'Any references?'

'No.'

'Can you make a Bloody Mary?'

'I can pour a beer.'

'I need someone who can make cocktails.'

'You could teach me.'

'We advertised for someone with experience.'

'Well, it's a chicken and egg thing, isn't it?'

'Huh?'

'What came first – the chicken or the egg? I can't get experience unless you give me a job.'

Brando wrinkles his nose. He's wearing jeans, a cotton shirt and a waistcoat that is too small for him. A tiny guitar dangles from a small golden hoop in his left ear. In my experience, people who wear colourful clothes are compensating for their lack of personality. I'm the opposite. I have no personality, but that suits me fine because I want to be invisible.

The bar is called the Little Drummer, one of those hole-in-the-wall places in the Lace Market, which is expensive and totally up itself. To be honest, I don't really see the point of bars, or alcohol. People have little enough control over their lives without getting shitfaced.

I need a job because Cyrus says I'm not 'pulling my weight'. What does that even mean? I weigh less than seven stone. He could throw me over his shoulder in one of those wife-carrying competitions and we'd win easily. Not that I'm his wife, or his girlfriend, and he treats me like a kid most of the time, which pisses me off.

I went back to school in September – part-time – doing my A-levels at Nottingham College because Cyrus says I should make something of my life. That's something else I don't understand. Why can't my mission be to do the bare minimum; to just scrape by?

I once saw this YouTube video about a Japanese soldier in the Second World War, who was sent to an island in the

11

Philippines to watch out for enemy aircraft. He was under orders to never surrender. When the war ended, he had no idea, so he kept hiding in the mountains for twenty-nine years, refusing to give up. That's my idea of a life well lived, hiding away on a tropical island, cut off from the world. Unreachable. Untouchable.

My new plan is to *pretend* to do something with my life. I will tell people that I'm writing a book, and if they ask me what it's about, I'll steal the plot from some Netflix drama and call it 'an homage'. I learned that term from Mr Joubert, my English teacher.

If that doesn't work, I'll tell people I want to travel and dreamily talk about the mountains I want to climb and the seas I want to sail across. Nobody ever questions a grand passion.

My third option is charity work. I'll volunteer for a week or two – so I can spend the next ten years banging on about my love for 'helping others' and 'giving back'. That should make my life seem worthwhile.

'Ever worked with customers before?' asks Brando.

'Yeah.'

'Doing what?'

'I was a waitress.'

I leave out the location – Langford Hall, a secure children's home – and the fact I was technically not an employee. He also doesn't have to know I got banned from working in the kitchen because I stole a month's supply of drinking chocolate. That was the old Evie. The angry Evie. The ward of the court. The girl in the box. Angel Face. The child who hid in a secret room while a man was tortured to death.

Brando turns over my single-page CV as though expecting to see something typed on the other side.

'Ever been in trouble with the police?'

'No.'

Another lie.

'Why do you want to work at the Little Drummer?'

12

'I need a job.'

Brando waits, expecting more.

'I'm a people person,' I say, lying through my arse. In truth, I'm a dog person.

'What is your best quality?' he asks.

'I'm unbelievably humble.'

He doesn't get the joke. Idiot!

Brando twirls his moustache. 'I can give you a job collecting glasses. Thursday, Friday and Saturday. You start at eight, finish at two. Nine quid an hour. The tips are pooled with the kitchen staff.'

'And that's all I have to do – collect glasses?'

'You smile. You clean up spills. You mop out the women's loo. You're the dogsbody.'

'A what?'

'It's a figure of speech.' He hands me a form. 'Fill this out.'

It's some sort of employment contract.

'Why do you need my address and phone number?'

'Tax.'

'I haven't earned anything yet.'

'That's how it works.'

I borrow a pen and take a seat at the bar, half watching him while he restocks the fridges. I like watching his shoulders move beneath his cotton shirt. I wish I knew more about men. Not the bad ones, but the good ones.

Ten minutes later, Brando studies the completed form, licking his thumb when he turns the page.

'Start Friday. Don't be late. And wear something decent.'

I'm dressed in jeans and a baggy sweater I stole from Cyrus's wardrobe weeks ago and he hasn't missed yet.

'I'm only picking up glasses.'

'We're a cocktail bar, not a local boozer. Our customers expect a little glamour. Wear a black dress. Show a bit of leg.' He looks me up and down. 'You do have legs, I suppose.'

All the better to kick you with. He turns away and puts a

13

six-pack of cider into the fridge. I'm still standing at the bar when he straightens.

'Can I get an advance – to buy a dress?'

'Yeah, right,' he laughs. 'Get lost before I change my mind.'

Outside, I zip up my parka and avoid being stampeded by a coachload of Japanese tourists who are taking photographs of the Adams Building, an old lace warehouse that is now part of Nottingham College. The tour leader is waving a folded yellow umbrella and counting heads to make sure she hasn't lost anybody.

I walk along Carlton Street and Long Row, heading for Old Market Square. A charity collector with a clipboard tries to make eye contact, but I keep moving. I don't like talking to strangers.

I check out the latest responses on my dating app. Someone has matched with me. I check their profile. Attractive, sporty, on the short side, but this isn't about me. I'll check out their other social media pages when I get home. In the meantime, I send a first message, trying for a casual vibe.

Hey, we matched.

A message pings back:

Obviously!

It's a little more sarcastic than I'd hoped for. I try again.

Nice pictures. You look great.

Don't say that or I'll find you boring.

Sorry

14

And don't apologise. I hate that even more.

Can we start again?

What would you like to know?

Dogs or cats?

Dogs.

Your thoughts on pineapple on pizza.

A travesty.

Coffee or tea?

Neither.

So, I can't invite you for a coffee?

We could have bubble tea

Sassy. Promising. I'm running out of questions.

What frightens you more – spinach or spiders?

Spiders. I'm a vegan.

Isn't that a cult?

I'm trying to save the planet.

Or to be extra annoying at restaurants.

TBH this isn't going to work out.

Have a nice life.

Another aborted romance. Maybe I'm too picky, but who knew that Nottingham would be such a shallow pool? I'm not looking for perfect, but I have some standards. No hats. No emo haircuts. No oversized sunglasses. No pouting. And keep your clothes on. A smile goes a long way.

My friend Morty is busking on the steps of the Council House. He's looking after Poppy, my Labrador. When she hears me calling her name, she stands to attention, pricking up her ears. Her entire body wags and she presses her head into my hands. I feel a surge of happiness.

'Has she behaved?'

'Totally,' says Morty. 'She earned more than I did.'

An upturned fisherman's cap is resting between his feet. Only a handful of coins are inside.

'This cashless economy is killing me,' he says.

Morty, whose real name is Mortimer, plays the harmonica and only knows four songs, all of them sea shanties. He likes making out that he's homeless even though he's couch-surfing at his sister's place. And he's always telling stories about people who were 'discovered' busking, like Ed Sheeran and Passenger.

I put a five-quid note into his hat.

'What's that for?'

'Looking after Poppy.'

'You don't have to pay me.'

'I know.'

He slips the money into his pocket. 'Did you get the job?'

'I'm officially a cocktail waitress.'

'Is that a euphemism?'

'Fuck off!'

I feel a drop of rain on my forehead and glance up into an ugly grey sky. I'd better hurry. Cyrus took the car today so I'm catching buses.

Morty tips the coins into his pocket and pulls the cap onto his head. The rain is getting heavier.

'You want a ride?' he asks.

'You're not going my way.'

'I can make a detour.'

His car is parked nearby, an ageing Mini with blue doors and a brown bonnet. A hand-painted 'for sale' sign is resting on the dashboard.

'You're selling it.'

'My sister is giving me her old car. She thinks this one is a death trap.'

'Is it?'

'No.'

'How much do you want?'

'Three hundred quid, but I'd knock off fifty for you.'

'I have ninety-two pounds.'

'I'm not a charity.'

'Shame.'

Morty drops me outside the National Ice Centre, and I run through the rain, late for my therapy session. Poppy leads the way. We dodge pedestrians, who are huddled under awnings and in shop doorways, or dashing between cover. A hatted man with a briefcase, head down against the rain, almost runs into me.

Pausing at a crossing, I wait for the signal to turn green. I step off the kerb. Brakes screech. Metal meets metal. The nearest car is bumped from behind and shunted forward. I jump out of the way and the woman driver looks horrified.

Out of her car. 'Are you all right? Did I hit you?'

She's in her fifties, maybe older, well preserved, dressed in black except for a brightly coloured scarf knotted around her neck.

'I can take you to hospital.'

'I'm fine.'

Poppy puts her body between us, either introducing herself or protecting me.

A second driver emerges from his van. A big guy. Fit once. Muscled once. Gone to seed. He looks at the front of his van and starts yelling at the woman, calling her 'a stupid cow'.

'You just stopped. No warning. No indication.'

'That's not true,' she says indignantly. 'I signalled.'

He looks at the damage to the front of his van and swears under his breath.

'Are you going to pay for this?'

'It wasn't my fault. You ran into the back of me.'

He mimics her accent and repeats the line, bouncing on his feet, crowding her space. I see her backing away.

Pedestrians have stopped to watch, and traffic is building up. Horns sound impatiently.

'He's lying,' I say, stepping closer to the woman. 'Don't let him bully you.'

The man glares at me, but I see the flicker of doubt on his face. The lie. I cannot explain how I know these things. I wish I could point to a twitch, or a facial tic, or a vein pulsing in his forehead; or say that he double blinked, or his voice changed, or his eyes looked up to the left. I just know he's lying. I always do.

'Are you calling me a liar?' he says, focusing his anger on me.

Poppy growls.

'Yes. Maybe your phone rang, or you changed the song on the radio, or you were checking out some woman who was walking across the road. It's your fault.'

The van driver isn't used to being challenged. He wants to bully me, or hit me, or shove a sock down my throat. He could,

I suppose, but I'd hit him back twice as hard. I'd bite and scratch and gouge. I'd fight like a girl.

I take a photograph of his van and the hatchback.

'You should call the police,' I say to the woman. 'I'll give a statement.'

In reality, I don't want to get involved. I hate being the centre of attention. The van driver starts making excuses, saying that we don't need to get the cops involved and we can sort this out ourselves.

'How about we pull around the corner and swap details,' he says.

The woman looks relieved.

'Can you come with me?' she asks.

'I'll go with him,' I say, nodding towards the van.

I follow the driver.

'Were you going to drive off?'

'No.'

He's telling the truth. He cocks his head to one side. 'Who are you?'

'I'm an eyewitness.'

3

Cyrus

Take away the twin steel fences, the razor wire and CCTV cameras, and Rampton could be mistaken for a health and wellness retreat, or an adventure sports centre with landscaped gardens and outdoor areas, a swimming pool, a shop, recreation rooms and a gym.

In all my visits, I have seen very few patients. They are kept apart, separated by gender and the acuteness of their illnesses. When Elias first arrived, he was in The Peaks, a unit for men with severe personality disorders, and spent eleven months in solitary because of his violent behaviour. For years, when moved around the hospital, he had to be chaperoned by four people. A lot has changed since then. He is medicated. Lucid. Placid as a winter pond.

Admittedly, he is not the brother I remember, the one I idolised and whose hand-me-down clothes I willingly wore because it made me feel closer to him. I didn't mind being mistakenly called by his name by teachers, or by relatives, who remembered him more readily than me. The firstborn child is always the most fussed over and photographed. I came second. And the twins had a genetic advantage because who isn't fascinated by an embryo splitting to form two perfect yet different halves?

Elias was a teenager, sitting his GCSEs, when the problems began. He drifted away from me like a Poohstick thrown from a bridge. Mum blamed puberty and raging hormones, but I knew it was something more serious. He hid away, spending hours in his room, where he sat on the window sill, smoking hash, blowing each depleted lungful into the night air, while he listened to 'headbanger' tapes on his Walkman.

When he did emerge, it was only to eat, or to argue, or to lift home-made weights in the garden. He lost his weekend job mowing lawns, but later bought a whetstone and bench grinder, and began sharpening knives and axes and mower blades. The neighbours were queuing up for the service and Elias would revel in how sharp he could make each tool.

Try as I might, I couldn't quite solve – or articulate – the mystery of what happened to change him. The slow disintegration. The whispered arguments through his bedroom door. 'Leave me alone,' he'd say to nobody but himself. 'I'm not listening.'

Once he told me that he could control the planets and that without him the moon would hurtle into the Earth and make humankind extinct, just like the dinosaurs. I wanted to believe him. Did it seem any more ridiculous than what I was being taught at Sunday School?

The diagnosis made things easier for a while. The drugs helped, although Elias called them 'zombie-pills'. By then, his grades were in freefall. A-levels were out of the question. Weeks passed. His silences grew longer. His isolation. Dad caught him sneaking out at night and not returning until the morning. Twice the police brought him home, his shirt torn and bloody.

We lived like that for two years – up and down – good weeks and bad, never knowing what to expect. Later, I told a counsellor it was like living with a time bomb that I could hear ticking, sometimes faster, sometimes slower, always ticking.

Until one day it stopped.

Dr Baillie finds me in the garden, trying to find warmth in a sun that offers nothing but pale, yellow light filtering through the high clouds.

'Sometimes I wish I was a smoker,' I say. 'It would give me something to do.'

He sits beside me. 'They're coming back.'

'Any indication?'

'No.'

We make our way to the conference room where Elias has been waiting patiently with his hands pressed together between his thighs. The three tribunal members enter in single file and shuffle between the long wall and the table, taking their allotted chairs. They are like a jury returning with a verdict.

Elias didn't have a trial. A judge found him not guilty on the grounds of insanity and ordered he be 'detained at Her Majesty's pleasure', which meant indefinitely. I remember wondering if the queen took 'pleasure' in detaining people. Did she even know Elias's name, or what he'd done?

My phone is vibrating in my coat pocket. I glance at the screen. Detective Superintendent Lenny Parvel has sent me a message:

You're needed. Call me.

I ignore it. Carrying a mobile phone still feels foreign to me. Until Evie came to live with me, I used an old-fashioned pager that meant people couldn't simply call me and talk. I didn't want to carry a computer in my pocket or be instantly contactable. My job involves human interactions, speaking face to face and reading body language and picking up on physical clues, which can't be done over the phone or in a text message.

Now, I have a phone that is smarter than me. It can calculate more quickly and knows where I am, and where I'm going, and when I'm looking at the screen. It keeps track of my likes and dislikes, and my Internet history, and can predict the words I'm about to type, which could be human progress or our surrender.

Judge Aimes pours himself a glass of water. He lifts the glass. Sips. Tastes. Sips again. Speaks.

'We are here to consider an application by Elias David Haven who has been detained under the Mental Health Act since 2001, after his role in the deaths of four people, namely his parents and twin sisters.

'Upon his arrival at Rampton Secure Hospital, he was diagnosed with paranoid schizophrenia, and found to be suffering from antisocial and narcissistic personality disorders. It has only been in the past five years that Elias has come to terms with what he did that night. Psychotropic drugs have led to a considerable improvement, according to the testimony of his psychiatrist and case worker. Elias has also learned coping skills and behavioural modification strategies, which have seen a moderation of his psychosis, so much so that he now presents little or no management problem.'

He raises his head to look at Elias.

'In the eyes of the justice system, Elias, you are innocent of any crime, and should only be detained until such time as the experts consider you are no longer a danger to the community. The question we must answer today is whether you have reached that point and if you are ready to take your place in society. The safety of the public is paramount, and our decisions must also respect the feelings and fears of those who were directly affected by your offences.

'We on this tribunal panel are very aware that any decision we make today will be subjective. We are attempting to predict the future behaviours of a latently dangerous mental patient, relying on recommendations from psychiatrists and psychologists who acknowledge that the sciences they study are inexact. Not everybody managing your case has been in agreement. Dr Reid, a resident psychiatrist, expressed the view that you could be cold, distant and unemotional, with a perverted arrogance that is the basis of your paranoid thinking.

'We have also heard oral evidence from two consultant psychiatrists and your case worker, Dr Baillie, who agree that your psychopathic disorder has been brought under control by medication and therapy.'

There is a pause and Judge Aimes glances along the table at his colleagues. Neither wants to add anything, but there is a trembling quality to the room, as though everything is poised to change. I'm nervous for Elias. I am nervous for myself.

The judge continues.

'Long-term leave under Section 17 of the Mental Health Act must be approved by the Secretary of State. Our recommendation to the minister will be that you be allowed to leave the hospital grounds on unescorted day leave.'

Elias interrupts. 'When can I go home?'

'Overnight leave is the next step,' says Judge Aimes. 'Weekends. Holidays. Every stage will be a test.'

'But I'm better. I'm no longer a danger.'

Dr Baillie leans forward, placing a hand on Elias's forearm.

He shrugs it away. 'They called me a model patient. You heard them. I'm cured.'

I hold my finger to my lips, urging him to be quiet. In the next breath, he cocks his head like a bird, watching something in the top corner of the room.

Judge Aimes finishes his statement.

'The minister will receive our recommendation by close of business today. This is usually a formality and, unless he decides otherwise, you will be eligible for day release once he signs the necessary forms.'

Chairs are pushed back. The panellists rise as one and walk in single file out the side door.

Elias doesn't react. Two orderlies appear. Big men in short-sleeved tops and dark trousers. They approach Elias carefully, telling him it's time to go. I expect him to react, but his entire body settles into stillness. He collects his papers, straightens the edges, and tucks them beneath his arm, before turning and bowing to an imaginary audience.

Sounding every inch a lawyer, he says, 'Thank you for coming. I appreciate your patience and diligence.'

4

Evie

My therapist, Veera Jaffrey, likes to be called by her initials, VJ, which gives me the giggles because I think of vajayjay. When I told her this, she couldn't see the joke at all.

Veejay is in her early forties with a wonderfully deep voice and thick dark hair. She still has the faintest trace of a Pakistani accent because her parents moved to England when she was seven. They were very strict and wanted her to marry a Muslim boy, but she eloped with a saxophone player called Nigel and went into hiding because her parents threatened to kill her.

I have no idea if any of this is true, but it's a good story. I like making up scenarios about people because the truth is either too boring, or I can't find out what really happened. Veejay doesn't talk about herself. I know that she has children because there are toys in her back garden. That's where Poppy is now, sniffing at her compost heap and drinking out of her fishpond.

Whenever I ask Veejay about her family, she steers the conversation back to me. Each session begins the same way. Have I been sleeping? Any dreams? Nightmares? Panic attacks? Random thoughts? Flashbacks?

Veejay is one of the few people who knows who I am and where I came from. How my real name isn't Evie Cormac; and that I was born in Albania and I came to Britain in the hull of a fishing boat with my mother and sister, who both died on the journey. Other people have fucked-up childhoods, but not like mine.

'Last week you were talking about your sister,' says Veejay, glancing at her notes. 'Agnesa. She was how much older?'

'Six years.'

'What do you remember about her?'

'She had lovely hair, a lot like yours, and she used to pay me to brush and braid it for her, or promise to buy me doughnuts.'

In that instant, I am transported back to my village, to a street-barrow beside the church, where a hanging spout is dropping balls of dough into hot oil. I can smell them cooking as they puff up and turn golden. The lady tosses them in icing sugar and puts them in a white paper bag, before squirting chocolate sauce over the top. Agnesa lets me have the top doughnuts, which have the most chocolate.

'Do you miss her?' asks Veejay.

'Yes.'

'How did she die?'

'She drowned.'

'Along with your mother.'

'Yes.'

'Were their bodies ever found?'

'No.'

'Tell me about your mother.'

'She used to be a seamstress, before she grew sick. Papa called it melancholia, but I don't know what that means. She spent most of the colder months in bed, but she cheered up when the weather grew warmer.'

These questions continue, but gradually Veejay focuses on what happened to me after the boat sank. Each time she touches on the subject, I find ways to deflect and divert her attention. It is like a game of cat and mouse, but I don't know which of us is the cat. I have no desire to relive what happened to me. People think that traumatic events should be laid out like a deck of cards and sorted into suits or four of a kind, because it looks neat and well ordered, but I want to shuffle the deck and deal again. I don't want 'closure', I want a new hand.

After fifty minutes my time is up.

'It's always good to talk,' says Veejay.

'Is it though?' I ask.

'Talking has the power to help.'

'And the power to harm.'

She puts a cap on her pen. 'Why do you keep coming?'

'I don't want to disappoint him.'

'Does Cyrus mean that much to you?'

I pause, wondering how to explain my relationship.

'I used to think I was the only conscious being in the universe. That everything existed because of me – physical objects, other people, animals, events – and that if I died everything would vanish.'

'Solipsism,' says Veejay. 'The idea that nothing exists outside your own mind.'

'Then I met Cyrus and I realised that I wasn't alone. I didn't just feel *my* pain. I felt *his*. His thoughts. His emotions. His experiences. I wasn't the only conscious being in the universe – there were two of us.'

5

Cyrus

As I walk to my car in the hospital parking area, the air seems saturated with oxygen, making the colours brighter and my senses sharper. I lean back in the driver's seat of my Fiat and feel my heart beating in my chest. Elias is being allowed out on day release. He expects to come home. The next step will be overnight stays.

The house is big enough. There are five bedrooms. Evie has one of them. I haven't even considered how she might react to having my brother come and live with me. I've been in denial. I've assumed that Elias's application would fail and the tribunal would kick it down the road for another two years, when he would try again.

Catching a glimpse of myself in my rear-view mirror, I see my thirteen-year-old self with freckles and curly hair and teeth encased in metal. My face is burning. I look again and he's gone.

My phone vibrates. I glance at the screen. There are two more messages from Lenny Parvel.

Beaconsfield Street, Hyson Green. Elderly deceased male. Blunt force trauma. Daughter missing. Call me.

And twenty minutes later: Where are you?

My heart slows and sinks. This is what I do now – I investigate violent and suspicious deaths. I am a criminal profiler, an expert on human behaviour – the worst of it, not the best – the sociopaths and psychopaths, the outliers, the mavericks, the deviant and the unhinged.

Most crimes don't require a forensic psychologist to unpack them. When two drunks get into a fight in a pub car park and one glasses the other in the throat, it doesn't require an honours degree in criminal psychology to explain what happened. I get summoned when the crime is beyond the comprehension of those investigating. When the police want someone to explain why one human being would do such terrible things to another.

I type a text message: On my way.

Lenny responds: About time.

My ageing Fiat doesn't have a satnav, so I use my mobile phone, which is suctioned to the dashboard, and has a female voice that sounds uncannily like a patient of mine, Ursula, an occupational therapist suffering from apotemnophobia – a fear of missing limbs.

Forty minutes later, I reach the outskirts of Nottingham, having skirted the eastern edge of Sherwood Forest, an ancient woodland that doesn't seem big enough to hold its own history; the folklore not the facts.

Police cars are parked at the ends of Beaconsfield Street, using the cross-streets to divert traffic. Two uniformed constables are manning the western barricade, which is threaded with police tape that twirls in the cold wind.

'DSU Parvel is expecting me,' I say.

The female PC makes a note of my name and points me to a parking spot. She's new – fresh out of training – and her face is full of excitement and gravitas. One day, crimes like this will sadden and horrify her; when she's seen too many bodies pulled from wrecked cars, or carried from bloodstained bedrooms, or collected from the base of cliffs, or cut down from rafters.

I study the houses. Most are detached or semi-detached. Red brick. Two storey. Built during the fifties and sixties. This is a working-class area, but clearly some owners are aiming higher, having renovated and added loft conversions.

'You took your time,' says Alan Edgar, a sergeant in Lenny's squad. His nickname is Poe, for obvious reasons.

'How bad is it?'

'Messy.'

A ghostlike figure walks from the house. Lenny Parvel is dressed in white forensic coveralls, latex gloves and a plastic face shield. She pushes back the hood and appraises me with hazel-coloured eyes. Warm. Intelligent. Judgemental.

'Where have you been?'

'Rampton.'

'Are they letting him go?'

'Yes.'

'How do you feel about that?'

'Nervous.'

'That's understandable.'

My relationship with Lenny is difficult to label. She was the young police constable who found me hiding in our garden shed, wearing muddy football socks and armed with a mattock, convinced that Elias was hunting for me. It was Lenny who coaxed me out and wrapped me in her coat and sat with me on the swings until back-up arrived.

Later, she chaperoned me during the police interviews and watched over me when I fell asleep on a foldout bed at the station. Over the next few months, she escorted me to the funerals and the coronial inquests and when Elias appeared in court. And later still, during my wilderness years, it was Lenny who came to find me when I was cutting, drinking, injecting, and vandalising my body with home-made tattoos.

Although only in her mid-forties, she has been like a mother to me, and maybe I'm like a son. Lenny didn't have children of her own, having married an older man and helped raise his two boys, who are not much younger than me. One is a doctor, the other a dentist. A credit to them both.

Lenny hands me a set of white polythene coveralls and I shimmy inside them, pulling elasticised plastic booties over my shoes.

'What do we know about the victim?'

'Rohan Kirk. Aged sixty-seven. Disability pensioner. His wife died in a car accident ten years ago. Rohan was at the wheel and suffered brain injuries. They have two daughters. Twins. Thirty-two. Maya lives with her dad and runs a mobile dog-grooming business. Melody is married with kids. Lives two streets away. Maya hasn't been seen since yesterday.'

A police siren approaches at speed. The car pulls up and a detective gets out. Dressed in a well-cut grey suit, he's about five-nine with a wiry muscularity that will defy middle age if he stays off the booze.

He spies Lenny and something passes between them. Not so much a smile as a smirk.

'I thought this was my case,' he says, patting his pockets as though he misplaced the note informing him of the change.

'I thought it might be something for SSOU,' says Lenny. She means the Serious Sexual Offences Unit, a new task force that Lenny has been running in Nottinghamshire.

'A man has been murdered,' says the newcomer.

'And his daughter is missing,' replies Lenny.

'That doesn't make it a sex crime.'

'Not yet.'

The stand-off lasts a few seconds and Lenny backs down. The detective turns his attention to me.

'I don't think we've met.'

'DCI Gary Hoyle, this is Dr Cyrus Haven,' says Lenny. 'He's our forensic psychologist.'

'Yes, of course, I've heard of you,' he says, pumping my hand. 'You shot that guy in Scotland.'

'In self-defence,' I say.

'Of course it was. His gun was empty, but you weren't to know that.'

I can't tell if he's criticising me or making a genuine attempt to sympathise. I wish Evie were here.

'Glad to have you on board,' says Hoyle. There is something very American about his smile, broad and quick and full of optimism. In the next breath, he says, 'I would prefer to limit contamination of the crime scene.'

'I'm suited up.'

We match each other's gaze for several seconds too long. Finally, he nods. 'I shall value your input.' Then he smacks his hands together, rubbing them as though ready to start work.

Scene-of-crime officers are carrying equipment into the house. Cameras. Lights. Biohazard bags. Back-up batteries. Swabs. Print kits. Evidence markers. Barrier tape. Duckboards. Hoyle signals to one of them that he wants a word and strides across the road.

'He seems very friendly,' I say.

'Yes, he does,' replies Lenny. 'He's the sort of friend I'm happy to follow.'

'Because you don't want him behind you.'

'Exactly.'

'Is he new?'

'Hoyle? No. He's been working with the National Crime Agency. Before that he was with SOCU. A star performer. Fast-tracked. Destined to rule us all.'

She's talking about the Serious Organised Crime Unit.

'A funny handshaker?' I ask.

'Not still a thing.' Lenny adjusts her face shield. 'He's one of those detectives who seems to enjoy this job too much. It's like he feeds off the suffering of others.'

'A soldier who thinks that war is glorious.'

'That sort of thing.'

I study the house, making mental notes. It fronts a quiet road, within line of sight of at least six other properties. No burglar alarm or security lights.

'What about the neighbours?'

'They heard nothing, for a change.'

'Meaning?'

'The daughter and father were known for their arguments. Rohan Kirk had a habit of calling the local cops and complaining that he was being mistreated. Said his daughters were stealing his pension payments.'

A blue van is parked in the driveway. The sign on the side says *Short Bark and Sides*. We have reached the entrance, which has an inner and outer door with a small porch in between designed to create a heat envelope in the winter. The outer door is double-glazed.

I step onto duckboards that are spaced along the hallway. Overcoats hang on pegs and boots are lined up beneath. The kitchen is directly ahead. The sitting room to my right.

I see his feet first, pale ankles sticking from flannelette pyjama bottoms. Dry hard patches of skin on the heels. Veins etched purple on his shins. He is curled on his side, with one arm twisted under his body. One side of his head has been smashed to a bloody pulp. He crawled no more than a few feet before dying in front of the gas fireplace. His right hand seems to be reaching out for a cushion, which has fallen from the sofa, as though he wanted something soft beneath his head.

A white duvet, speckled with blood, is lying on the floor beside him, along with a plastic Tupperware bowl.

A scene-of-crime officer is crouched beside the body.

'Craig Dyson,' says Lenny. 'He's managing the scene.'

'We've met.'

Dyson turns and nods. He's holding a moistened swab, which has been run over the victim's fingers, nails and around the cuticles. He slips the swab into a plastic test-tube which is sealed in a tamper-proof evidence bag. Labelled. Documented. Stored.

'Any sign of the weapon?' I ask.

Dyson motions to a decorative fireside toolset, which includes a hard-bristled broom and a shovel. 'The poker is missing.' He points to the blood spray on the wall. 'Looks like he was struck from the front as he came into the room. He kept coming and was hit again. He fell here and tried to cover his head with his arms, but the blows kept coming.'

'Fingerprints?'

Dyson points to a bloody smear on the nearest light switch. 'That was left post-crime, there are no loops or whorls, which suggests our perp was wearing gloves.'

More traces of blood were found on the kitchen floor and in the sink. Evidence markers indicate the locations. A single cupboard door is open next to the front-loading washer-dryer. Detergent and fabric softener are visible on a shelf.

I follow Lenny through the rest of the house, looking for signs of a disturbance, argument, robbery, or flight. A female technician is working on the stairs. We're dressed identically, but her hair is bunched under a hood and the suit looks better on her.

'Hello, I'm Cassie Wright,' she says, as though keen to introduce herself.

'I'm Cyrus Haven.'

'I know. We've met.'

'I'm sorry, I don't remember.'

She laughs, her eyes dancing. 'You will.'

Stepping back, she gives me room to squeeze past. Our suits brush and faintly crackle with static electricity.

There are three bedrooms upstairs. Rohan Kirk slept in the largest one nearest the road. The bedclothes are disturbed. His duvet thrown back. The pillow has a depression. He has a glass of water next to his bed. A bottle of sleeping pills.

A well-worn armchair is facing a large TV. Two empty beer cans are crushed on the side table, next to the TV remote and an ashtray full of wrapped sweets. Opening his wardrobe, I see a handful of sweaters, two pairs of jeans, and checked shirts, all with the same brand labels and similar colours. Clothes that are functional, but not statements.

Across the landing must be Maya's room, which is brighter and neater. Her double bed dominates the space, along with a wardrobe and a chest of drawers. Her duvet is missing. It must be the one downstairs. A dozen stuffed animals, including a Paddington Bear, are side by side on a shelf beside the window, arranged from biggest to smallest.

Several dresses are draped over a chair, beside a full-length mirror and a straightening wand that is still plugged into a socket. I picture Maya trying on clothes, deciding what to wear. Fixing her hair. Applying make-up.

'She was out last night,' I say.

I lift her pillow. A cotton nightdress is bundled underneath.

'Were there any traces of blood upstairs?' I ask.

'None yet.'

I turn slowly around, imagining Maya in this room, but I have little sense of her. I can't see her mind.

'Tell me about Rohan Kirk's brain injury.'

'Frontal lobe. It affected his attention and concentration. He couldn't hold down a job and drank too much.'

'Was he violent?'

'Impatient and impulsive.' Lenny glances down the stairs. 'It can't have been easy looking after him.'

'You think Maya did this?'

'Wouldn't be the first carer to lose her temper.'

'She didn't pack a bag or take her car.'

'She panicked.'

'Which means she'll turn up,' I say, sardonically. Lenny regards this as banter and doesn't get offended when I disagree with her.

'Does Maya have a dog?'

'No. Why?'

'It's just a little odd – having a dog-grooming business, but no dog.'

We descend, stepping over evidence markers in the hallway. I pause at the front door. Dyson is dusting for fingerprints. I

36

glance again at the hanging coats and the row of boots, which are slightly out of order, the right one where the left should be.

'Have you swabbed the uppers of the shoes?' I ask.

'We're very thorough,' says Dyson with a slightly arch tone.

Moving the coats to one side, I press my cheek close to the wallpapered surface.

'What is it?' asks Lenny.

'I'm not sure yet.'

6

Evie

The bus door hisses as it opens. The driver has a beard and a bright blue turban.

'Do you need a hand?' he asks.

'No, we're totally fine.'

I'm wearing dark glasses and Poppy has her harness. She leads me up the steps and I reach into my pocket, searching for my phone to tap against the reader.

'You're OK,' says the driver. 'No charge.'

'Thank you.'

I move down the bus. Two old people in the nearest seat immediately stand.

'This one is free,' says the woman, who wants to take my arm, but I don't like being touched. I pull Poppy closer, making her sit between my legs.

I'm getting quite good at being blind. I save money and get to watch people without them knowing. Cyrus would be furious if he knew, but it's not like I'm taking a seat from a properly disabled person or forcing a coffin-dodger to stand.

At the next stop, a young guy gets on and sits opposite me. He's my age, maybe younger; OK-looking in a pale underfed sort of way, wearing baggy clothes and a bomber jacket that's too big for him. I'm staring straight at him. He smiles. I don't smile back. He raises his hand and moves it back and forth. I ignore him.

'Nice dog,' he says.

'Thank you.'

'He your guide dog?'

'She.'

'I've always wanted to ask a blind person how they tell if someone is attractive or not.'

'I read their faces with my fingers.'

'You can do that?'

'Yeah.'

He is fiddling with his phone. Knees wide. One leg jiggling. 'How did it happen?' he asks.

'An accident. I was nine.'

'What do you miss the most? Is it watching TV, or going to the movies, or seeing a sunrise?'

'Porn,' I say.

His mouth drops open and he starts stammering. Blushing. It's cute.

'I'm shitting you, OK.'

He looks relieved although a little disappointed. I glance out the window.

'This is my stop.'

'How can you tell?'

'My dog tells me.'

'How?'

'Telepathy.'

I reach for the signal button. The boy does it for me. Our hands touch. I pull mine away as though bitten. Poppy stands with me. The boy closes his legs to give me more room. As I pass him, I lean a little closer before whispering, 'Nice jacket.'

His eyes widen, full of questions. Now he thinks I have some extraordinary 'other' sense that makes up for my sightlessness, which is ironic, because my real secret skill depends upon me seeing someone's face, looking for the lies.

The bus pulls away and I slip off my sunglasses.

7

Cyrus

A pretty, careworn woman answers the electronic door chimes. A toddler is balanced on her right hip, a little boy who is sucking his thumb with the brow-furrowing concentration of a symphony flautist.

'Have you found her?' asks Melody Sterling, whose eyes are full of hope and uncertainty.

Lenny shakes her head and makes the introductions. I touch the little boy's chin. Shyly, he turns his face into her neck.

'Yours?'

'One of my charges,' she replies, before leading us into her sitting room where three other children are sitting on the floor, playing with coloured plastic blocks. The entire lower floor of the house is a day nursery, full of children's toys, books, blackboards, painting easels, alphabet rugs and a big red reading chair.

'I didn't have time to let the parents know,' says Melody. 'They're coming as soon as they can.'

A little girl, aged about two, carries a book to Lenny, wanting her to read a story. Melody suggests 'Victoria' draw a picture instead. Lenny is happy to be distracted. She leads Victoria to the reading chair where she puts on her best storybook voice. Soon all four children are sitting on the rug in front of her.

In the kitchen, a child-sized table is covered with the remnants of lunch — sausages, mashed potato and peas, sauce-smeared and half-eaten. Plastic cups of water. Slices of apple. Melody begins clearing plates, incapable of sitting still because her mind is moving so quickly.

'I'm sorry about your father,' I say, helping her. 'Was he difficult to care for?'

'Sometimes. When he couldn't find a memory, or he forgot how to do a simple task, he became frustrated.'

'How did the accident happen?'

'A stolen car ran a red light. Mum died instantly. Dad had to be cut from the wreckage.'

'Where were you?'

'I was at university in Leeds. Maya was living at home and did most of the heavy lifting looking after Dad.'

'Was he ever abusive?'

'Maya knew how to handle him.'

She hasn't answered the question. 'Would she ever hit him?'

'No. Never. She loved him.'

Suddenly, she understands why I'm asking and immediately begins to backtrack.

'Before the accident, he was such a lovely, gentle man. A big softie. Later, he could try the patience of a saint, but we both learned how to stay out of his way.'

'When did you last talk to Maya?'

She tears a sheet of paper towel from a roll and blows her nose. 'Last night. She was going out.'

'Where?'

'On a date. She met some guy on a dating app. They were texting for a while, then talking on the phone. Finally, they arranged to meet.'

'Did she often use dating apps?'

'That's romance in the digital age,' she says. 'I'm glad I'm not single.'

'Where was she meeting him?'

'At a pub.'

'Would she have invited him home?'

'No. She knew what Dad might do. In his mind, we were both still sixteen. He used to joke about getting a shotgun to ward off any boys, but a part of him was serious. He was old-fashioned about sex and marriage. When we were growing up, he wouldn't let us go to parties or stay out late. We had to sneak out – Maya more than me. I was the good twin. She was the wild one.'

'Wild in what way?'

'She loved raves and music festivals and all the stuff that went with them.'

'Drugs?'

'Nothing hardcore, but that was years ago.'

'Are there any former boyfriends we should worry about?'

'No. Not really. Dean thinks Maya is a flirt, but I think she's friendly.'

'Dean?'

'My husband.'

'Where is he?'

'On his way home. He's been working in Leeds.'

Melody sits on one of the tiny chairs, her knees almost reaching her chin. 'There was one guy – he lives locally. Maya used to babysit him. A few months ago, she saw him in the garden. He was watching her getting undressed.'

Lenny has been listening from the doorway. 'Did she report it to the police?'

'Yes, but I don't think anything came of it.'

'What was his name?'

'Paulie Brennan.'

Lenny's eyes flare with recognition. 'Marlene Brennan's grandson.'

'You know him?' I ask.

'I know the family.'

The doorbell chimes. A parent has come to collect her child. Melody prepares to put on a brave face. She pauses at the kitchen door and asks, 'Where is my sister?'

She is hoping for comforting words; some reassurance that Maya is alive and well, but I don't believe in offering false hope. Equally, sometimes, silence says the wrong thing.

'We won't stop looking,' says Lenny. 'I can promise you that.'

A cold wind whips at my overcoat, pressing it against my knees. Lenny plunges her hands into the pockets of her Barbour jacket and walks with her head down, lips tight, deep in thought. She has pale, fine features and bottle-black hair cut short enough to brush against her shoulders.

'Did Maya run, or was she taken?'

'I think she was taken.'

Lenny doesn't ask for an explanation. I think she suspected as much, which was why she called me into the case.

'Somebody forced their way inside the house,' I say. 'When the door swung open, the latch hit the inner wall, causing a slight depression in the painted plaster behind the coats.'

'That could have happened at any time.'

'Yes, but the shoes were misaligned, which indicates it was recent. Rohan Kirk was probably asleep when he heard something downstairs and came to investigate. The intruder didn't expect anyone else to be in the house. He picked up the first thing that came to hand – a tool from the fireplace.'

The attack is played out in my mind. It was sudden and ferocious. The poker kept swinging long after the old man had stopped moving.

'The killer was angry and frustrated,' I say.

'Why?'

'He doesn't like making mistakes.'

We've reached the police car. Lenny radios the control room, asking for the latest intel on Paulie Brennan. Within minutes, the despatcher comes back with the details. Brennan, aged twenty-five, has a history of boosting cars and has served an eight-month sentence for malicious wounding. On the night Maya made the complaint, Paulie was stopped by a patrol car less than two streets from her house. He told police he was walking home from the pub and denied looking in her bedroom window.

Lenny puts the two-way radio back in the cradle.

'You said you knew the family.'

'His grandmother.' She glances at her watch. 'You should meet her.'

'I thought this was Hoyle's investigation.'

'We're in the neighbourhood.'

8

Cyrus

Marlene Brennan lives less than a hundred yards from where Rohan Kirk was murdered. Her house is an eyesore, with an overgrown front garden, a broken fence, and a disembowelled sofa perched on a builder's skip. The neighbours must love her.

Lenny has been filling me in on the 'Brennan clan', describing Marlene as the matriarch.

'She used to run a pub in Liverpool, down near the docks, one of those places with tiled floors so they could hose out the blood every morning. Old man Brennan was a union leader during the Liverpool Dock strike in the late nineties when Mersey Docks locked out their workforce in a dispute about overtime pay. The strike lasted two years. Failed.

'Brennan lost his job. He and a few mates bought a pub near the waterfront, but drank most of their profits, or gave it away on credit. When he died of a heart attack, Marlene took it over and managed it better.

'They had five children. Three girls and two boys. Both sons were shot dead in an armed hold-up of a bank in Manchester when they were still in their twenties. The manager triggered the alarm and police had the place surrounded within minutes. The gang was trapped inside. Twelve hours later, the police stormed the building and the boys died. One of them was Paulie's father.

'In the aftermath, Marlene sued the police, claiming her sons were murdered. She lost the case and sold the pub. Moved to Nottingham. Raised Paulie from the age of five.'

'What about his mum?'

'A junkie. Died of an overdose.'

'Sad.'

'Too common.'

Lenny presses her thumb to the old-fashioned doorbell. It echoes from inside. We wait. She sniffs the air. 'I smell cigarette smoke.'

Crouching, she yells through the mail flap. 'We know you're in there, Paulie. We only want to talk.'

Silence and then another sound. Slippers on wood. Locks and chains disengage. The door opens. Marlene Brennan looks like a small brown onion that has been pickled in vinegar. Eighty if she's a day, her eyes are like dark holes, and she has the sort of permed hair they seem to provide with every pension cheque.

'Hello, Marlene, you're looking well,' says Lenny.

'Do I know you?' asks the old woman.

'Detective Superintendent Parvel.'

'A female detective – are you a dyke?'

'Would it make a difference?'

Marlene shrugs. 'You see a lot of dykes these days. Dressed like men.'

An old coffee tin is hanging on a string around her neck. She dips her head and spits into it.

'Is Paulie home?' asks Lenny.

'He's gone to get my pills.'

'Will he be long?'

'Long enough.'

47

'I fancy a cup of tea,' says Lenny, stepping past Marlene, who is too slow to block her way. She starts to protest, but a voice interrupts her.

'I'm home, Gran.'

Paulie is standing in the doorway of the kitchen with the light behind him. He's dressed in old track pants and a moth-eaten sweater. Barefoot. Mullet-haired. Bum-fluff on his top lip. He's holding a miniature poodle with a head like a clump of cotton wool. The dog snaps at my elbow as I pass. I jerk away and Paulie smiles.

The kitchen smells of apples just starting to rot and cigarette smoke. It has a scrubbed pine table and mismatched wooden chairs. Unwashed dishes fill the sink, and the lone window has a yellowing net curtain.

Marlene lowers herself into a chair, mumbling under her breath. She fixes her rheumy eyes on me.

'Who are you?'

'I'm a forensic psychologist.'

'Most shrinks can't tell their arse from their elbow.'

'We must know some of the same people,' I say.

She cackles. Paulie fills the kettle. Lenny looks small beside him.

'Are you staying out of trouble, Paulie?'

He ducks his head as he nods.

'He's a good boy,' says Marlene, spitting into her can. 'He looks after me.'

'How does he do that?'

'I work,' he says truculently.

'And he gets my medicine,' adds Marlene. 'Council send a girl to clean up, but she's a lazy cow. She hasn't been around for days. I told Paulie to slap her or sack her.'

'I don't think he's allowed to do that,' says Lenny.

Marlene grunts.

Lenny is carefully moving plates in the sink, looking for mugs she can wash up. I study the room, the bric-a-brac magnetised to the fridge. Holiday snaps. Birthday cards. A post-card from Marbella. A child's crayon drawing.

'You have grandchildren,' I say.

'Eight of them,' replies Marlene proudly. 'Cops killed two of my boys, but I still got three girls, all good breeders. We grow through the cracks.'

'Like weeds,' says Lenny.

'Yeah, like weeds.'

Lenny returns to Paulie. 'Where are you working?'

'He's self-employed,' says Marlene. 'Buying and selling cars. Always been good with his hands.'

'Very light-fingered,' says Lenny.

The old woman scowls.

'I'm going to be a race-car driver,' says Paulie, jutting out his chin. 'Got myself a low-flying rocket.'

I pull aside the curtain and gaze into the rear garden where two car chassis are jacked onto blocks. A third vehicle, a souped-up Ford Focus RS, is partially covered by a tarpaulin.

'Street-racing?'

He grins. 'That would be illegal.'

'When was the last time you saw Maya Kirk?' asks Lenny.

Paulie looks at her blankly.

'You can't have forgotten already. You were peering through her bedroom window.'

'Weren't me,' says Paulie. The whiskers on his top lip barely move.

'You're barkin' up the wrong tree,' says Marlene.

'Where were you last night?' asks Lenny.

'He was here with me,' says Marlene.

'Is that true?'

Paulie lowers his head, but I'm not sure it's a nod.

'Why are you so interested in Maya?' asks the old woman.

'Rohan Kirk was murdered last night. Maya has disappeared.'

The old woman's face folds into creases, which could signify genuine concern or acid reflux.

'That poor mite.' She looks at Paulie. 'You seen Maya?'

'No, Gran.'

'Good.' She nods, as though the matter is settled.

'How do you know her?' I ask.

'Maya used to babysit for me when Paulie was little. She and her sister would ride their bikes up and down the road.'

'And they both worked in Powell's,' says Paulie, finding his voice.

'The bakery,' explains Marlene. 'On weekends. They used to slip Paulie an iced bun when the owner wasn't lookin'.'

'Did you fancy her?' asks Lenny.

Paulie looks shocked. 'I was seven years old.'

'I mean later, when you grew hair on your bollocks.'

'Nah, she was too old for me.'

'Yet you were seen peeping through her bedroom window.'

'It weren't me.'

'Did you take pictures?'

Paulie's eyes flash with anger and his fingers have curled into fists, causing a vein to bulge on his forearms, blue against white.

'Why are you picking on Paulie?' asks Marlene. 'Haven't we suffered enough? You lot killed his father and his uncle.'

'They were armed,' says Lenny.

'With starter pistols.'

'Replica handguns are regarded as illegal firearms.'

'They were *boys*!'

'They were twenty-two and twenty-five.'

The two women glare at each other. Lenny sighs and looks embarrassed for getting involved in the argument.

I motion to the yard. 'What are you driving, Paulie?'

'Depends.'

'What were you driving last night?'

He doesn't answer.

'We'll find out if you weren't at home,' says Lenny. 'We can track your phone using GPS.'

'I went out to the pub with a few mates,' says Paulie, making it sound like a God-given right.

'Which pub?'

'The Lord Kitchener.'

'What time?'

'About nine. We had a few pints then drove around a bit.'

'When did you get home?'

'I don't remember. Gran was asleep in front of the TV. She does that a lot.'

I can hear the rumble of engines in the street outside. The sound dies quickly and moments later the front door opens and two men enter. Both are about Paulie's age. One is tall and athletic and the other overweight and spilling out of his motorcycle leathers.

'Sorry, Mrs B, didn't realise you had company,' says the tall one.

'They were just leaving,' says Marlene.

'I smell pork,' says the fat one, who leans close to Lenny and sniffs.

Lenny doesn't react. She seems to be pondering her next move, not wanting to antagonise the Brennans, but also unwilling to back down.

'Were you gentlemen with Paulie last night?' she asks.

They glance at Paulie. 'I don't know – were we?'

'We went to the pub and drove around for a bit,' says Paulie, reminding them.

'Yeah, that's right.'

'What pub?' asks Lenny.

'Whatever Paulie told you. I'm not good with names,' says the fat one.

'Can you remember your own?'

He doesn't realise she's questioning his intelligence. Lenny asks to see his ID but he's not carrying one.

'I'm Boris Johnson,' says his mate.

'And I'm Harry Windsor,' says the fat one. 'I left Meghan at home with the baby in LA.'

Lenny gives them a tight smile. She turns to Paulie. 'You've been very helpful. I'll be sure to put that payment through. Same amount as last time.'

Paulie blinks at her, taking a moment to comprehend what she's saying. The penny drops. His mouth opens and closes.

'What? No. I'm not a fuckin' snitch,' he stammers, looking at his mates, almost pleading with them.

Lenny, blithely, 'Don't get up, Marlene. We can see ourselves out.'

9

Evie

How many ounces of flour make up a cup, and is a cup the same as a mug? Cyrus doesn't have any proper measurers; and he doesn't have a nine-inch cake tin, so this could be a disaster.

I want to celebrate my anniversary by baking a cake. It is a year since I left Langford Hall and came to live here. Cyrus rescued me when nobody else knew that I was drowning. This is the longest I've ever slept in the same room, apart from at the children's home, and when I shared a bed with Agnesa.

I try to crack an egg against the side of the mixing bowl, but it explodes in my hand. I dump the shell in the sink and fish broken bits out of the bowl with my fingers. They make it look so easy on *The Great British Bake Off*. Whisking, folding, blending, dusting. And that Nigella Lawson can make sucking a spoon look positively pornographic.

Half an hour later, I hear the door open and keys hitting the side table. Boots are kicked off. Mail is checked. An envelope is torn open. Cyrus appears in the kitchen. He looks at the bench, which is covered in flour, caster sugar and cocoa powder.

'I'm making a cake,' I say.

'Just the one?'

Sarcastic prick!

He tries to peer into the oven. I block his way.

'You're not allowed to look.'

'Why?'

'It's a surprise. And if I mess up, I'm throwing it away.'

He goes to sit down.

'Wait!'

I brush flour off the chair.

'How was the job-hunting?' he asks.

'I am officially a working woman.'

'Great. Where?'

'I'll be mixing cocktails at a bar.'

He frowns. 'Working nights?'

'Thursday, Friday, Saturday – eight till two.'

'Maybe you should have found a day job.'

'I don't need your permission,' I shoot back.

For the briefest moment, I see the hurt in his eyes.

'Do you know how to mix cocktails?' he asks.

'They're going to teach me. I already know how to make a margarita and a mimosa.'

'How about a Virgin Mary?'

'You're disgusting.'

'The drink,' he says. Normally, when he teases me, he laughs, but not this time.

'How are you going to get home?'

'I could borrow your car.'

'Are you asking?'

'Are you being a dick?'

He smiles tiredly.

'My friend Morty is selling his Mini. He wants two hundred and fifty quid. I'm going to save up – unless you lend me the money. I could pay you back.'

'It's probably a rust-bucket.'

'Fine. I'll find another way.'

I hate arguing with Cyrus. I hate that he's older than me and that he thinks he knows everything. I hate how he picks me up on my grammar and my vocabulary, like when I say literally when I mean figuratively (whatever the fuck that means). I hate how he laughs at me, but not in a cruel way. Cyrus thinks I'm a teenager, but I'm twenty-one, and I could be his equal, if he let me.

'So where is this bar?'

'In the Lace Market.'

'Is it a nice place?'

'Very classy. They want me to buy a dress.'

Cyrus knows my wardrobe consists of nothing but jeans and sweatshirts and oversized sweaters. It's another staring contest. Who will blink first?

'I'll lend you money for a dress,' he says. 'But I want you to go shopping the old-fashioned way. Choose a dress. Try it on. Make sure it suits you.'

This is another test. Part of my therapy is to interact more with people, rather than living like a hermit. He's challenging me to be 'normal', whatever that means.

'I could come with you,' he says.

'I don't need help,' I snap, annoyed with him.

Poppy has come in from the garden and sniffs at his socked feet. Cyrus tells her to sit. She obeys. She can also shake hands, and play dead, but only for Cyrus because he's the alpha male. Cyrus says I don't walk her enough; or brush her coat; or pick up her shit from the garden, but it's hard work looking after a Labrador.

'So why the cake?' he asks.

'It's my anniversary. I've been here a year.'

'That's gone quickly.'

I start to speak. Stop. Start again. 'I wanted to thank you for letting me stay, you know, and teaching me to drive, and other stuff.'

'You're welcome.'

How does he do that – accept a compliment so easily? I get embarrassed when people compliment me.

'What happened today with Elias – is he being released?'

'Day leave and then overnights.'

'Will he come here?'

'Yes.'

'Will he live here?'

'Most likely.'

I want more, but there's no point in pressing Cyrus. He says that secrets are important, and everybody is allowed to have them. That's why he doesn't ask me about my sessions with Veejay. He's chosen to be my friend, not my therapist. I wish he was something more, but I know that can't happen. Cyrus has made it very clear that he doesn't feel that way about me and it's not because I'm ugly or have cigarette burns on my back, or that I'm too broken. He thinks I'm too young, but the age difference isn't that big and it's not as though he has another girlfriend – not since Sacha Hopewell went back to London to look after her parents. I quite liked Sacha because she didn't treat me like a child.

'Did something else happen today?' I ask.

'A man was murdered. His daughter is missing.'

My stomach clenches. 'Is she in danger?'

'I don't know.'

Cyrus doesn't like talking about his police work because he's worried it will give me nightmares or trigger bad memories. I have enough of those already.

I suddenly remember my cake and rip open the oven door. 'Bugger!'

'Did you burn it?'

'It sagged in the middle.'

'That's perfect,' says Cyrus. 'We get more icing.'

10

Cyrus

The TV lights have bleached Gary Hoyle's face whiter than a wedding cake. He's wearing his dress uniform for the cameras – a pressed white shirt, black tie and polished epaulettes. His hat is resting on the podium.

Reporters have gathered in the conference room at Radford Road police station, a stark windowless space with plastic chairs arranged in rows. Media conferences used to be much bigger affairs, but nowadays the newspapers and wire services pool their resources and share stringers to save money, which means only the front seats are taken.

I recognise some of the faces. Latisha Davies of the *Daily Telegraph*. Bryan Madden of the *Nottingham Post*. Richard Holiday from Associated Newspapers. Holiday is a foot-in-the-door specialist, who covered the murders of my family. He was a young reporter back then, who famously spent days perched in the branches of a tree, until he snapped the first photographs of the boy who survived – images of me kicking a football in my grandparents' garden.

Hoyle reads from a prepared statement.

'We have grave fears for the safety of a young Nottingham

woman, Maya Kirk, who has been missing for more than twenty-four hours.'

A photograph appears on the screen behind him. It shows Maya laughing at the camera, with her head thrown back and her hair looking wind-blown. She looks like a woman in a shampoo commercial, or advertising toothpaste.

'Miss Kirk was living with her father, Rohan Kirk, aged sixty-seven, who was found beaten to death in the sitting room of a house in Hyson Green, early yesterday morning.'

Another image fills the screen. Rohan Kirk looks self-conscious, as though aware that he's being photographed and unsure of whether to smile or to look serious and is caught in between.

'We know that Maya Kirk went out on a date on Sunday evening, but we haven't identified the man she was meeting. Using mobile phone triangulation, we have traced Maya's approximate movements. She met her date at a pub near the river, the Canalhouse, at seven-thirty and later visited two more bars in the Lace Market. CCTV footage shows the couple crossing St Peter's Square shortly before ten o'clock.'

The grainy colour images were taken by a street camera. The male figure has his arm around Maya's waist, making them appear quite cosy, but neither face is visible.

'We are urging this man to come forward so we can discount him from our investigation,' says Hoyle. 'We know that Maya returned to her home shortly after ten-thirty and her phone ceased transmitting fifty-eight minutes later.'

Lenny has slipped quietly into the room and stands beside me, leaning her back against the wall. It's strange not seeing her on stage running the show. Hoyle has invited questions. Hands shoot upwards.

'What makes you think she was abducted?' shouts Latisha Davies, without waiting to be called.

'Maya hasn't answered her phone or contacted her family since Sunday evening,' says Hoyle. 'She also hasn't accessed her bank accounts or kept her work appointments.'

'Could she have killed her father?' asks Holiday.

'That's not our belief.'

Another hand is raised. 'What's taking you so long to iden-tify this guy in the footage?'

'Maya met him and communicated with him via a dating app. We are seeking that data from the company, which is based in America.'

Another reporter shouts, 'Could she be a hostage? Has there been a ransom demand?'

'Her family are not wealthy.'

'Do you have a murder weapon?'

'No.'

'Did Maya kill her father?'

'We don't believe so.'

Hoyle is growing annoyed by the questions. 'You will be issued with photographs of Rohan and Maya Kirk. We are asking for the public's help in tracing Maya's interactions on Sunday evening. Who did she speak to? Did she go home alone? Was she followed? If anyone saw her, please come forward. You can give information anonymously using the Crimestoppers' number.'

Hoyle picks up his hat and tucks it under his arm. The reporters are unhappy. Most are still looking for an angle – something that lifts this crime above the ordinary, tragic banality of another act of violence and puts it on the front pages of the national papers or the evening news bulletins.

Upstairs in the incident room, a task force of forty-plus detectives has gathered for a briefing. Some I recognise or know by name. DC Monroe gets called Marilyn, which she doesn't seem to mind. She shuffles sideways and offers me a corner of her desk.

'OK, what do we have?' asks Hoyle.

DS Edgar speaks. 'None of the neighbours saw or heard anything unusual on Sunday night. A little boy in the house opposite says he saw a ghost out his bedroom window, but his parents say he's always seeing monsters when he eats too much sugar.'

There are chuckles around the room.

'We're still collecting footage from home security cameras and CCTV; and checking vehicle movements in a four-hour window either side of midnight. So far, we've clocked fifty-eight vehicles in Beaconsfield Road, many of them cabbies using it as a short cut. A food truck was parked on the nearest corner for two hours. We're looking for the owner.'

Edgar hands over to another sergeant, Paul Lennox, whose nickname is Prime Time because of his love for cameras and his reputation for getting himself on TV.

'The Sex Offenders Register has thrown up eighteen possible suspects living within two miles of the murder scene. Twelve have alibis. We're looking more closely at the other six, but most are your garden-variety perverts and groomers.'

'Any of them have links with Maya Kirk?' asks Hoyle.

'None, but she made a complaint about a peeping tom a few weeks ago. Paulie Brennan lives two streets away. He was stopped by a patrol car, but denied he was watching her undress. Brennan was out on Sunday evening with two mates, both with biker connections. The Blue Angels MC.'

'Trace his movements. I want to know if they crossed paths. Where are we with former boyfriends?'

Monroe speaks: 'Maya had a two-year relationship with a local builder called Daryl Branagh, which ended acrimoniously. Branagh posted naked photographs of her on a revenge porn site but took them down within forty-eight hours. Police interviewed him, but no charges were laid because Maya declined to make a statement.' Dropping her voice, she mutters, 'We should have charged him anyway.'

Another detective, whom I don't recognise, delivers a back-grounder on Maya: 'She was born in Nottingham and educated at St Mary's Catholic Academy, which is in the same street as her house. Later she went to Nottingham Free, a co-ed secondary school in Sherwood, where she sat for her A-levels. She studied for a Bachelor of Science degree at Nottingham University and spent three years working for the National Health Service. After that, she drifted from job to job as a receptionist, office manager and sales rep. She set up her dog-grooming business two years ago. Most of her bookings are online or over the phone. Mainly cash. No receipts.'

'Customers ever come to the house?' asks Hoyle.

'Not usually.'

'What about her finances?'

'Solid. She took out a personal loan to buy the dog-grooming van but has almost paid it off.'

Hoyle has been pacing the floor in front of a whiteboard where Maya's photograph is displayed beside her father's. He scratches idly at his cheek with three fingers and examines the images. He turns suddenly.

'Any thoughts, Dr Haven?'

The question surprises me. I didn't expect him to ask for my opinion. Eyes weigh upon me.

'I don't think Rohan Kirk was the primary target. It's more likely he stumbled upon the abduction of his daughter.'

'You think she invited the killer home?' asks Hoyle.

'Or he forced his way inside. He isn't someone particularly close to Maya or he would have known she didn't live alone. More likely, he's a casual contact, or someone she met that evening who followed her home.'

'Why did he take her?' asks Lenny.

'I don't have enough information to answer that.'

A detective calls out from the far side of the room.

'The dating service has just sent us Maya's chat history. She arranged to meet someone called Alex Foley.'

Moments later, a webpage is projected onto the whiteboard. Foley's dating profile lists his age as thirty-six and says he works in IT. The main photograph was taken outdoors, showing blond highlights in his hair and muscled forearms sticking out of a T-shirt that is a size too small.

Pros: I'm not afraid of commitment. I love cooking. And my mum is the coolest person I know.

Cons: I don't like doing the dishes, or wearing white shirts when I eat, or ordering wine at restaurants because I know nothing about wine.

My motto: Be all in or be all out. There's no halfway.

There are two more photographs, casual shots designed to make him look like a relaxed, carefree, all-round nice guy, and a world traveller. In one he's pictured riding an electric scooter in Italy, and another shows him in Egypt, perched on a camel with the Sphinx in the background.

'He lives in West Bridgford,' says Prime Time, who has pulled up a street-view image of the house. Detached. Two storeys. A garage to one side.

Monroe has been typing. 'No rap sheet, but two years ago a woman alleged that Foley sexually assaulted her and held her against her will.'

'Was he charged?'

'She got cold feet and refused to sign a statement.'

Lenny studies the satellite images. 'Maya could be inside the house or the garage.'

'We don't have enough for a warrant,' says Hoyle.

'What about a gas leak? Probable cause,' asks Edgar.

'Any judge will see through that,' says Hoyle.

'Maya's safety is more important than a conviction,' says Lenny.

'Rohan Kirk might not agree,' says Hoyle. He addresses the task force. 'I want eyes on the house, around the clock, and I want Foley followed. We stick to him like goosegrass.'

'For how long?' I ask.

'Twenty-four hours. If Foley doesn't come forward, we'll know he has something to hide.' Hoyle claps his hands together. 'Let's get to work. Remember the ABC of being a detective. Assume nothing. Believe no one. Check everything.'

11

Evie

My English teacher, Mr Joubert, has a thick French accent and speaks through his nose, making him sound condescending even when he's calling the class roll.

'Cheryl Agostino?'

'Here.'

'Aaron Bailey.'

'Here.'

'Evie Cormac.'

'Yeah.'

He never looks up from his tablet, which means that anybody could answer. Half the class could be missing. He doesn't care. On our first day, he gave us a speech about treating us like adults not children, and that he wouldn't mollycoddle us. I still don't know what that word means.

Tuesday morning and I have two classes today, English and maths. I prefer numbers because letters sometimes get jumbled and start to move when I read them. Mr Joubert knows that I don't have the required GCSEs to be studying at Nottingham College and he probably thinks my father is somebody famous or influential, who bribed the admissions officer to let me in.

I don't really care. If it were down to me, I wouldn't bother with A-levels or higher education. I'm only here because of Cyrus.

There are about twenty of us in class today, a chocolate box of different ethnicities and colours. We're discussing one of our set texts, *Othello*. I don't understand Shakespeare, particularly the old-style language and the weird couplets and iambic penta-whatnots. The Bard couldn't rhyme for shit.

Everybody else is crowing about poor old Othello and what a tragedy it is; and how it's a play about human nature and relationships and sexual jealousy. I've been listening for twenty minutes, saying nothing, checking the time on my phone.

'What bollocks!' I mutter under my breath.

'Did you have something to say?' asks Mr Joubert.

I glance up and discover the entire class are staring at me.

'No.'

'Did you agree with Aaron?'

'No.'

'Why not?' He opens his arms. 'Share your opinion with us.'

'I'd rather not.'

'Class participation is a requirement.'

I roll my eyes and stare at the ceiling, knowing this is a mistake.

'Othello isn't honourable, or tragic,' I say. 'The whole play is nothing but toxic masculinity masquerading as art.'

'I think you're being a little harsh,' says Mr Joubert.

'Fine. I'll shut up.'

'No. I respect your opinion,' he says, lying through his arse. 'But the definition of a tragic hero is someone who makes a bad judgement that leads to his own destruction. As Aristotle said, tragic heroes are "doomed from the start".'

'Othello was dumber than a box of rocks,' I say.

Tianna gives me a filthy look. I scratch my nose, flashing her the finger.

She complains. Mr Joubert ignores her.

'Othello was an outsider, an outcast, who was manipulated by others,' he argues.

Paulo agrees. 'That's why Desdemona forgave him before she died. She understood his tragic flaws.'

'Dumb cow,' I say. 'They deserved each other.'

I must have piqued Mr Joubert's interest because he wants me to continue.

'I mean, she gets stabbed by her jealous husband and, as she's bleeding out, she wakes up and tells everybody that she did it to herself. She's dying and she's still protecting him. What does she want – a medal?'

'She made the ultimate sacrifice because she loved him,' says Mr Joubert.

'Call the Pope, we have a new saint.'

'It's a tragedy.'

'No, it's a travesty. A misogynistic prick kills his wife because he loves her too much. That's an excuse that violent men have been using forever – and everybody says it's a crying bloody shame. Poor old Othello. Pity the poor black guy.'

'You can't call him black,' says Tianna.

'But he is black. Shakespeare calls him an old black ram who is tupping a white ewe.'

'Yeah, but the way you said it was racist.'

'I don't care if he's black, white or turquoise. He's a pathetic loser.'

'You should be careful,' says Mr Joubert, who can sense other students growing restless.

Tianna points at me. 'I think she should apologise for bringing race into this discussion.'

'It's a play about race,' I say, growing exasperated. 'Othello is a black bloke in a white society who marries a white chick who is into black guys, which pisses everyone off. Happened then. Happens now.'

'He could have been any colour,' says Tianna.

'Yeah, but he wasn't, he was black. And you can't kill your wife and get a free pass because of your race.'

I look around the room expecting people to agree with me, but I'm preaching to the wrong audience, or maybe they're not listening.

'I think you should leave the classroom,' says Mr Joubert.

'Why?'

'You're upsetting people.'

'They're being snowflakes.'

'Another racist remark,' says Tianna.

'Snowflake isn't racist. It's like me calling you a stupid cow. You could be a stupid brown cow, or a stupid white cow. You're still a cow.'

'Report to the deputy principal's office,' says Mr Joubert.

I'm already halfway to the door.

12

Cyrus

Although I'm not a tenured academic, I have rooms on the fourth floor of the School of Psychology at Nottingham University. The corner office has two large picture windows that overlook Highfields Park, which has a boating lake and an arts centre and dozens of Canada geese grazing on the grass.

I was given the rooms because I guest lecture at the university and supervise postgraduate students who are writing their doctoral theses. In return, the chancellor allows me to see private patients on two afternoons a week.

As I unlock my door, I hear the sing-song voice from along the corridor. One of my colleagues, Henri Moretti, clearly wants a word. Henri is the Professor of Health Psychology and dresses like a caricature of a professor in corduroy trousers, an open-neck shirt and a tweed jacket with leather patches sewn onto the elbows. I sometimes wonder if he buys his clothes at a costume shop, rather than off the rack.

'You had a visitor. I told him to come back,' he says, whispering conspiratorially.

'I don't have any appointments until three.'

Henri follows me inside, keen to chat. 'Strange chap. Nervous.'

'Did he give you a name?'

'No.'

Henri's accent is pure Yorkshire, but he clings to his Sicilian roots. His parents own the oldest and best Italian café in the city, one of those bustling, noisy places staffed by an inexhaustible supply of aunts, sisters, cousins and more distant relatives.

Henri's father, Arturo, operates the espresso machine, a belching, farting contraption that he plays like a church organ. At the same time, he argues incessantly with his wife, Rosina, always in Italian, hurling mysterious insults at each other. The melodrama is unmissable, and customers visit Moretti's not for the food or coffee but the floor show.

Another reason is because of Henri's sister, Candelora, a rare beauty, with flashing green eyes and a wardrobe of tight clothes. Despite the male attention, Candelora has remained stubbornly single, which has prompted Henri to suggest I ask her out. The thought appealed to me until I woke one night in a cold sweat, imagining that I had married Henri's mother.

'He didn't look like a druggie,' says Henri.

'Who?'

'The chap who came to see you. I'm always worried you'll invite someone round who will chew off your face.'

'I don't treat meth addicts,' I say, which isn't completely true.

A knock interrupts me. A man is standing in the doorway. I hope he didn't hear what I just said.

'That's him,' says Henri.

'I have an appointment,' says the stranger. 'My parole officer contacted you.'

I glance at my phone and see a missed call.

'Take a seat. I'm sorry, I didn't get the message.'

I signal to Henri that he should leave. He reluctantly departs, whistling down the hallway.

'What's your name?' I ask.

'Mitch.'

He hands me an envelope. I take a moment to read the

contents. Summarising. Mitchell Coates, aged thirty-six, convicted of sexual assault and actual bodily harm. Released from prison after six years of an eight-year sentence. Struggling to readjust to life on the outside.

Mitch is sitting up straight, clasping a woollen hat in his hands, pressing it into his lap. He ducks his head – a legacy of his time in prison, when making eye contact can be a revolutionary act, or a stupid one.

'When were you released?'

'Ten days ago.'

'How has it been?'

He inhales and holds the breath for a few moments. 'Terrible.'

'Any particular problem?'

'I'm innocent.'

'By that you mean . . . ?'

'I didn't attack anyone. It wasn't me.'

'You were convicted. You served six years.'

'I pleaded not guilty.'

'Yes, but to be granted parole, you must have accepted your guilt and told the parole board that you were sorry—'

'I told them what they wanted to hear. I couldn't survive another day in there. If I was guilty, maybe, yes, but not when I'm innocent. Do you know what that's like? It eats you up inside. It's wrong . . .'

He wants to explain but can't find the words. He begins again.

'I thought I could pick up my life where I left off. That I could forget what happened, but I can't. It's like having a boulder on my chest. I struggle to breathe, to sleep, to talk to people. I want my old life back.'

'That might not be possible.'

'Maybe if I could prove my innocence?'

'What do you expect me to do?'

'Hypnotise me. Learn the truth.'

'Hypnotism doesn't work that way and the results aren't admissible in court.'

'What about a lie detector test?'

'The same.'

His shoulders are shaking. I find him a box of tissues. He pulls out too many and clumsily tries to shove them back inside.

'I'm happy to discuss what happened to you, Mitch; and to help you come up with some coping strategies, but your guilt is a matter of public record. You have served your time. Earned your freedom. Now you have to pick up the pieces.'

He doesn't respond.

'Where are you living?'

'A boarding house. I have a month to find somewhere else.'

'Are you looking for work?'

'They gave me some numbers, but nobody is hiring.'

'What do you do?'

'I used to be a film editor. Now I'd take anything.'

My phone beeps. It's a message from Evie.

I've been arrested by the truth police. I need you to come get me.

'I have to make a phone call,' I tell Mitch, stepping into the corridor. Evie answers on the second ring.

'What have you done?' I ask.

'Why do you assume it's me?' she replies belligerently. 'It might not be my fault.'

'What is it then?'

'The deputy principal wants to see you.'

'Why?'

Evie starts to answer but is instructed by somebody to hand over the phone. She does so reluctantly, yelling, 'It wasn't my fault,' before the handset is with someone else, the deputy principal.

I've met Richard Thorndyke before. He's one of those tall, square-shouldered types with a crushing handshake and a brusque manner. He might be ex-military, or an army reservist.

When I applied to enrol Evie at the college, she didn't meet the entry requirements, but I promised Mr Thorndyke that she was very bright, and she'd get to class and be no trouble. Famous last words.

'Dr Haven, I'm sorry to bother you, but Evie has upset some of the students and faculty. Under our short-term exclusion policy, she is being asked to stay home for the next week.'

'What did she do?'

'She expressed opinions that were deemed to be racist and triggered other students.'

'I did not,' interjects Evie.

'We are very inclusive at the college and aim to provide a safe and nurturing environment where people can feel free to express their opinions without being harassed or made to feel uncomfortable.'

'I understand.'

'I want to make sure her behaviour isn't repeated. Perhaps we should consider a multi-agency assessment.'

'She will write a letter of apology.'

'Like hell I will!' says Evie.

'I'll make sure it doesn't happen again,' I say. 'I'll come and pick her up.'

Mitch is still waiting in my office where he's managed to put all the tissues back in the box.

'Are you any good at odd jobs?' I ask. 'Gardening? Painting?'

'Yeah.'

I write my address on the back of a business card. 'Come around tomorrow. Early as you like. Wear old clothes.'

He looks at the card. 'That's all I own.'

13

Cyrus

'He's a fascist,' says Evie, who is sulking in the passenger seat. She has unlaced her boots and put her socked feet on the dashboard, which annoys me, but I let it go. For most of the drive she's been quiet. Her silences can sometimes last for days and be so inexplicable and impenetrable that I can't find out what I've done, or not done.

'You can't call people fascists because you don't like what they're saying.'

'What if they *are* fascists?'

'You have to respect other people's opinions.'

'They don't respect mine. They laugh at me.'

'I'm sure that's not true.'

'Whenever I'm in trouble, you immediately say, "What have you done, Evie?" You never think that I might be right and they're wrong.'

We're driving around the edge of Wollaton Park where the trees are a blaze of red and orange leaves.

Evie opens a new line of defence. 'You told me that I'd make friends. You said I'd become more independent, and confident. You said school would offer me all these new opportunities and I'd be doing what I love. Well, I haven't made friends and I don't love it.'

'I thought it might help you break out of your shell,' I say.

'I like my shell.'

'And find a new direction.'

'Why do I need a new direction?'

'To expand your career choices.'

'I don't want a career.'

'What are you going to do with your life?'

'I'm going to be a professional nihilist.'

'I'm being serious.'

'So am I. Worry about your own life.'

'What does that mean?'

'You're single. You have nightmares. Your brother is a nutcase. You lift weights like you want to punish yourself. You're the shrink who can't find a cure for what's wrong with him.'

'This isn't about me.'

'It never is.'

The car is stopped at a set of traffic lights. Evie's fingers are hovering near the handle as though she's contemplating an escape. We are silent for a while. I'm angry, but also regretful. I shouldn't get into these arguments with Evie. I forget how young she is – and how damaged.

When we reach the house, she jumps out of the car and goes inside without waiting for me. She'll be in the back garden playing with Poppy, the only creature in her life who seems incapable of disappointing her. I would like to be another one, but I'm caught between being her friend and her protector.

14

Evie

Some strange guy is mowing the lawn. He's wearing jeans and a checked shirt and a red woollen hat that makes him look like a gnome.

'Who is he?' I ask.

'Someone who needs the work,' says Cyrus.

'But I'm supposed to mow the lawn.'

'Really?'

Only Cyrus could put that much sarcasm into a single word or turn a question into a statement. We're in the kitchen, looking out the window, as the mower guy does the edges of the garden. He's mid-thirties and walks with a limp.

'His name is Mitch,' says Cyrus. 'He'll be doing some odd jobs around the place. He can fix up the side gate and paint the window frames and maybe sort out your bedroom door.'

'Where did he come from?'

'He's been in jail.'

'For what?'

'Does it matter?'

'It matters to me.'

'He was convicted of sexual assault.'

'And you want him fixing my bedroom door?'

'You said it was sticking – and he's served his time.'

Mitch notices us watching him and stops the mower. He makes a drinking motion with his hand.

'Make him drink from the hose,' I say, feeling anxious.

'He won't bite.'

'That's not what I'm afraid of.'

Mitch comes to the door. His boots are caked in grass clippings. He slips them off. There are holes in his socks. Cyrus introduces us. Mitch nods shyly.

'Are you going to rape me?' I ask.

'Evie!' scolds Cyrus, who glares at me. He starts apologising to Mitch, saying I should be ashamed for asking a question like that, but it's the only question that matters because I'll be able to tell if he's lying.

Mitch is holding his hat in both hands. 'I'm no threat, Evie. I didn't hurt anyone.'

Cyrus is looking at me, waiting for me to apologise. I suddenly wonder if this is a set-up. Mitch fills his glass again and is drinking. I move out of earshot, and whisper to Cyrus, 'How can both of you be telling the truth?'

'What do you mean?'

'You said he was a rapist.'

'He was convicted of sexual assault.'

'Well, if he's guilty – nobody told him.'

I can see Cyrus is troubled by this. Mitch rinses his glass and leaves it on the drainer.

'I'll get back to work.'

'Evie will make you a sandwich later,' says Cyrus.

'I can walk to the shops.'

'She doesn't mind,' says Cyrus, nudging me.

'Yeah, no trouble,' I say, when I mean the opposite.

Cyrus hates me lying, then forces me to do it.

The doorbell sounds. Cyrus motions with his head, expecting me to answer it. What am I – the maid and the butler?

I check the spyhole — force of habit — and see a fish-eye view of some guy with a crewcut that makes his head look like a bowling ball. I open the door.

'Does Cyrus Haven live here?' he asks, looking me up and down. I'm still in my pyjamas, which makes me feel self-conscious.

'Who are you?'

'Detective Chief Inspector Hoyle.'

'What's this about?'

He pushes past me into the hallway and calls out for Cyrus, who tells him to come through. It's like an open house today — everybody is welcome, cops *and* criminals.

Cyrus pours Hoyle a coffee. I grab a bowl of cereal and pretend not to be listening. Mitch has gone back to the garden, where Poppy is following him around. Dogs are good judges of character.

'Foley showed up at a police station first thing,' says Hoyle. 'He says he heard a report on the radio about Maya Kirk going missing.'

'Has he lawyered up?'

'Came with a solicitor. And here's the thing — his real name is Anders Foley.'

'It was a fake profile?'

'He has multiples; as well as different social media pages.'

'The man is a player.'

'Or a predator.'

'What's he said?'

'Nothing yet. I'm letting him stew. I want you there for the interview.'

Hoyle glances out the window, and Mitch chooses that moment to look back at the house. He and Hoyle seem to stare at each other.

'You've hired a gardener. Had him long?'

'No,' replies Cyrus.

'Where did you find him?'

'He pushed a flyer through the door.'

Another lie. And he complains about me.

Hoyle has a car waiting outside. Cyrus puts on his jacket and prepares to leave.

'What are your plans?' he asks.

'I have to buy a dress – for the new job.'

He opens his wallet and takes out a fifty-quid note. 'And you pay me back.'

I slip the money into the pocket of my pyjamas and watch him walk down the front path to the gate and the car. Hoyle opens the back door as though arresting him.

Upstairs, I get dressed into jeans and a sweatshirt. Afterwards, I sit on the back step, holding a mug of tea and watching Mitch at work. He pauses and cuts the engine, tipping the mower on its side and scraping wet grass from the blades.

'Did you call the police on me?' he asks.

'Huh?'

'The detective in the kitchen.'

'Oh, him. Cyrus works with the police as a consultant. Profiling. Sherlock Holmes stuff.'

Mitch wipes his hands on his jeans and tips the mower back onto its wheels.

'You recognised that detective, didn't you?'

He doesn't answer.

'He recognised you.'

Mitch shrugs. 'Ancient history.'

Pulling on the cord, the mower splutters to life and roars, drowning out my next question.

15

Cyrus

Radford Road police station is a three-storey red-brick building separated from the River Leen by a car park and waste ground. The interior of the building matches the façade – solid and functional, rather than welcoming. The interview suites are on the lower floor, adjacent to the charge room and holding cells.

Anders Foley has been waiting for two hours. I can hear his solicitor complaining to the desk sergeant about the delay, explaining that time is money and that she's due in court at ten o'clock.

'You're free to leave any time,' says the sergeant.

'My client will leave with me.'

'That's his prerogative, madam.'

The word 'madam' is delivered with just the right amount of faux respect to infuriate the lawyer.

Anders Foley is sitting alone in the interview suite. I spend a few moments studying him through the one-way mirror, comparing him to the man described on his various dating profiles. Most people massage the truth when they create these personal online billboards. Foley's three profiles were each worded differently, with carefully curated images designed to interest different women and cast the widest possible net.

His Anders Foley persona is an 'action man', or alpha male, who loves outdoor pursuits such as rock-climbing, windsurfing and triathlons. 'Andrew Foley' describes himself as shy and thoughtful and his ideal romantic evening is to prepare a home-cooked meal and to curl up on a sofa to watch a movie with a glass of wine. 'Alex Foley' – the one Maya responded to – is a traveller and adventurer, who 'loves getting lost in nature' and 'exploring different cultures'.

None of these descriptions seems to equate with the figure I see on the far side of the glass. Dressed in skinny-legged jeans and a tight-bodied shirt, he is a decade older than the ages listed on his profiles. His hair is receding, creating a wasteland on his forehead, and his cheeks are pockmarked with old acne scars.

Lenny has joined me in the viewing room.

'Did he lie about his job?' I ask.

'No, he's a freelance IT contractor. Works mainly for the university.'

'Any links to Maya?'

'Only the dating app.'

Hoyle enters the interview room, accompanied by DS Edgar. The solicitor follows them. Tall and thin, with hair pinned tightly to her scalp, she is dressed in a dark grey trouser suit and a white blouse.

Foley gets to his feet, smiling and holding out his hand, as though this is a social engagement. Neither detective takes up the offer.

'I don't know how much I can help you,' he says. 'I barely knew Maya.'

'Why have you referred to her in the past tense?' asks Hoyle.

Foley blinks at him. 'Pardon?'

'Is Maya Kirk dead?'

'I have no idea . . .'

'Yet you referred to her in the past tense.'

Foley begins to stammer. 'It was a slip of the tongue.' He looks at his solicitor, hoping for instructions.

Giana Camilleri introduces herself. 'My client is here voluntarily. He heard Maya Kirk's name mentioned on a radio report and has come forward. He wishes to help the police in any way he can.'

'Is that why he brought you along?' asks Hoyle.

'He has a right to legal counsel.'

'We only met once,' says Foley. 'On Sunday night. We had a drink. We chatted. We parted ways.'

'Where did you meet?'

'A pub near the river. The Canalhouse.'

'How long did you stay?' asks Hoyle.

'About an hour. Then we walked into town and went to a few other bars. One of them was on Low Pavement. I can't remember the names.'

'Who arranged the date?' asks Hoyle.

'We both did. We were texting each other and we talked on the phone.'

'About what?'

'Usual stuff. Likes. Dislikes. Family. Work. Music. I thought she was very chill and down to earth.'

'Did Maya tell you where she lived?'

'No.'

'Apart from messaging on the app, did you communicate any other way?'

'Texts, but I deleted them.'

'Why?'

'I liked Maya, but the chemistry wasn't there, you know? You can tell, can't you – if there's a spark – but I just didn't feel it with Maya.'

'When did you decide that?' asks Edgar.

'Almost immediately. We had a few drinks. We didn't click. We said goodbye.'

'Maya left by herself?'

He nods resolutely.

'And that was the last time you saw her?'

'Yeah.'

Hoyle signals to Edgar, who produces a laptop and turns the screen to face Foley. 'This is CCTV footage taken by a security camera on Sunday evening.'

Lenny points me to a nearby desktop computer and calls up the same footage. Although grainy and poorly lit, it clearly shows Maya standing on a footpath, struggling to get her arms through the sleeves of her coat. Foley helps her. She stumbles. He holds her up.

Hoyle continues, 'We also have CCTV footage taken of you and Maya crossing St Peter's Square shortly before ten o'clock.'

Foley grows agitated. His relaxed, eager persona has been replaced by a prickly defensiveness.

'Yeah, OK, I was hoping we might kick on. I offered to buy Maya dinner and said we could go see a mate's band. They play covers – Dire Straits, Oasis, Blur, that sort of stuff. Maya wasn't interested.'

'Earlier, you said there was no chemistry. No spark.'

'We could still have a fun night.'

'Hook up, you mean?'

Foley doesn't answer.

'Why is she stumbling?'

'She'd had a few drinks.'

'Are we going to find her fingerprints in your car?' asks Hoyle.

Foley hesitates and comes to a decision. 'I offered to drive her home. It was the least I could do in the circumstances.'

'What circumstances?' asks Edgar.

'She was drunk. I was concerned.'

'Maya was in your car?'

'Only for a minute. She vomited. I kicked her out.'

'Charming,' says Edgar.

'Hey! I was trying to do the right thing.'

'When did you last see her?'

'She was walking towards the taxi rank on Wheeler Gate.'

'And then what?'

'I went home.'

'What about your mate's band?'

'They're pretty shite.'

Edgar smiles, but Hoyle doesn't find it funny. Lenny scrawled something on a piece of paper, which she hands to a female constable. Moments later, the same constable knocks on the door of the interview suite and passes the note to Hoyle. He glances at it quickly and crushes it in his fist. Instead, he opens a green manila folder and reads from a single page.

'Tell us about Alice Shelley.'

Foley frowns and looks at his solicitor. 'Who?'

'August two years ago, you took Alice for a drive to Sherwood Forest. You pulled up at a secluded spot and unzipped your trousers. Alice said she wasn't interested. You didn't listen. You began masturbating. When she tried to phone for help you threw her handset out the window.'

Foley's face reddens and his shoulders grow rounded. He looks to his solicitor, expecting her to intervene.

'My client has come here voluntarily to talk about Maya Kirk,' she says. 'Any other material is irrelevant unless you'd like to charge him.'

Hoyle ignores her. 'Alice was held against her will and sexually assaulted.'

'That was consensual,' says Foley.

'You locked the car doors. You soiled her clothes and afterwards gave her a tissue to clean herself up.'

'It was a misunderstanding.'

'You kept her prisoner.'

Camilleri gets to her feet. 'I think that's enough. We're leaving.'

'Did Maya Kirk say no to you? Did that make you angry?'

'My client will not be answering any more questions,' says Camilleri. 'Come on, Anders.'

Foley gets to his feet.

'We're going to find more CCTV footage,' say Hoyle. 'And we're going to pick apart your life. If we discover that you've been lying to us, I will personally kick down your door and put you in handcuffs.'

Solicitor and suspect have gone. Hoyle looks at his reflection in the mirror and shrugs, aware he has an audience.

'Any thoughts?' asks Lenny.

'He doesn't like women very much,' I reply.

'Are you talking about Foley?'

'No.'

16

Evie

I don't own any dresses. They belong to my past life, when men and women would bring me clothes and dress me up, making me pretend to be a daughter, or an orphan, or a waif, or a schoolgirl, or some other character from their sick fantasies.

Before that, my dresses were mainly hand-me-downs from Agnesa, which were always too big because I was small for my age. The runt of the litter, according to Papa, who said it in a nice way. Agnesa had the curves and the cheekbones. I got the funny elbows and llama eyelashes.

For the past hour I've been looking in dress-shop windows, and wandering between department stores in the Victoria Centre, trying to summon the courage to actually try something on. Posh shops intimidate me. I don't know what it is exactly. The peacock-like assistants. The choice of clothes. The feature-less mannequins. The perfumed air. Some of the boutiques are so classy that I feel like I'm trespassing.

Normally, I love shopping malls – the escalators and the fountains and the food court, the unlimited things to buy. I once saw a film about a man who got trapped in an airport, unable to return to his home country, so he lived in the terminal building. He had everything he needed – shops, cafés, arcade games, friends. I couldn't understand why he wanted to leave. I would have stayed there forever.

My mobile sends me an alert. It's a message from my dating app. A Constable Lowry wants me to contact him urgently. He's given me a number. It's probably spam. I delete his message.

I continue walking past the same boutique, but this time I turn left and enter the hallowed ground. The clothes are displayed like works of art. Colour-coordinated and accessorised. The two assistants look emaciated and bored shitless.

'Are you lost?' asks the older one.

'No,' I reply, spying myself in the mirror. I see what they see – my torn jeans and hooded sweatshirt, my botched attempt to put highlights in my hair. They'll think I'm a shoplifter, or a timewaster.

'I'm just looking,' I mumble.

Her colleague is younger, wearing sling-back heels that make her butt stick out in a tight black dress. I couldn't wear something like that. I wouldn't want to.

'I'm Riviera,' she says. 'I'm your fashion advisor. If you need any help with sizing I can—'

'No, I'm good,' I say, pushing back hangers and pretending to read the labels. They're watching me.

After a while, I unhook a simple black dress with a nipped-in waist and short sleeves.

'That's a ten. You'll need an eight,' says Riviera.

I put it back. She chooses another.

'This one is more a cocktail dress. Mid-thigh length. Satin with pleats. Sleeveless. Very sexy. You could try it on.'

Before I can answer, she drapes it over her arm and leads me to the changing rooms. For a moment, I think she's going to follow me inside and watch me undress, but she points me to a booth. I latch the door. I'm alone. I sit on the bench and unlace my boots to pull off my jeans, which seems to take an age. I can picture the two women talking about me. Sniggering. Stripped down to my bra and knickers, I avoid looking at myself in the mirror. I don't like seeing myself naked, or in underwear. I don't like my pale blotchy skin and the cigarette burns on my back.

Unzipping the dress, I lift it over my head. The fabric slides over my shoulders and down my sides. I reach behind me to pull up the zipper before brushing my hands down my hips and turning to the mirror.

For a moment, I don't recognise the girl who is staring back at me. I blink. She blinks. Her feet are turned inwards. So are mine. I brush a strand of hair from my right eye. So does she.

An image flashes into my mind – a dress laid out on a bed – a man stroking my cheek, telling me to try it on. I can feel his fingertips crawling on my skin, his breath on my neck. My chest tightens. It's like bands of iron are being wrapped around my torso and riveted into place.

I seize the hem of the dress and pull it over my head, forgetting to undo the clasp or the zipper. It's caught. My arms are trapped inside. I'm blindly struggling to pull my head from the neckline. I smell my breath. I feel his hands touching me.

'How are you getting on?' asks Riviera.

I grunt a reply.

'Are you all right?'

I'm fighting with the dress, clawing at the fabric. Bouncing off the walls of the changing room. The lock rattles.

'Can I come in?'

I don't answer her. I can't. I'm locked in hand-to-hand combat with the dress, ripping at the collar, screaming in frustration.

Someone has a key. The door swings open. I can't see the women, but I hear them trying to calm me down. Someone has grabbed my shoulders. Someone else is trying to unzip the dress. I am no longer fighting them. My skin has gone clammy. My limbs are loose.

Suddenly, I'm free and I slump down onto the bench, holding my knees.

'I broke a fucking nail,' says the emaciated manager, sucking her finger.

'Maybe she's on drugs,' says Riviera. 'Should we call an ambulance?'

'We should call the police. Look at this dress. It's ruined.'

'I'm sorry,' I whisper. 'I couldn't get it off.'

'Well, you'll have to pay for the damage.'

'How much is it?'

'Ninety pounds.'

'I don't have that much.'

'Well, why were you trying it on?'

'She suggested it.' I point to Riviera.

If they call the police, they'll contact Cyrus and I'll have to explain it to him – and he'll treat me like a child and never look at me like I want him to look at me.

'I have fifty pounds,' I say. 'I can pay off the rest in instalments.'

'You'll have to fix the zip,' says the manager.

'That's OK,' I say, but I know that I'll never wear the dress. She gives me one of those buy-now-pay-later forms, but I put down a fake name and address and tell her that I don't have a card. I promise to come back tomorrow with my bank account details, but that's never going to happen.

She takes the fifty and folds the dress in tissue paper, before placing it in a polished paper bag that is more valuable than the contents.

'Enjoy your purchase,' she says.

'Have a nice day,' adds Riviera.

I walk out of the boutique and through the Victoria Centre, planning to toss the bag into the nearest rubbish bin. Feeling guilty, I consider the Hope Church charity shop, but I doubt if any poor people are looking for size-eight cocktail dresses with a broken zip.

Thirty minutes later, I step off the number 36 bus at Wollaton Vale roundabout. The shopping bag is in the footwell between the rear seats, waiting for a better owner than me. Someone who can look pretty on the outside without feeling ugly on the inside.

17

Cyrus

The Crown Prosecution Service in Nottingham has offices in King Edward Court, which is twenty minutes' walk from the Crown and District Court precincts. I see barristers heading that way, carrying their horsehair wigs, and wearing open-fronted black gowns that make them look like extras in a Harry Potter film.

I'm waiting for Clara Siganda – a girl whom I knew at secondary school, although we barely spoke for the first four years. She was one of the few people who didn't treat me differently after the murders. One day in biology, students were supposed to choose a partner, and everybody avoided picking me. It became a running joke, until Clara tapped me on the shoulder and asked to be my pair.

'Are you trying to be funny?' I asked, angrily.

'No. They're a bunch of arseholes. Are we doing this, or not?'

Clara went on to study law at a different university to me, but we've stayed in touch. She calls my name from the top of the stairs and click-clacks down the polished marble before kissing both my cheeks. She still looks impossibly young to be a trainee barrister, with bee-stung bottom lip and hair braided close to her scalp.

'I have to be in court in forty minutes,' she says, pulling me into a nearby meeting room. For the first few minutes we talk about mutual friends and enemies and people we remember from school. Who's come out. Who's moved overseas. Who's married and had babies. Clara asks if I'm seeing anyone. I wonder if she's making small talk, or interested, but she's out of my league.

Gossip exhausted, she folds her hands in her lap. 'How can I help?'

'I'm looking for information about an historic sexual assault.'

'How long ago?'

'Seven years.'

'Was it appealed?'

'No.'

She taps her front teeth with her finger as she thinks. 'You might not find anything. People often assume that court records are kept forever, but that's not the case unless the trial is historically significant or was the subject of an appeal. Other than that, there's no need to hold on to the evidence or transcripts. I can check.'

She pulls a keyboard closer and logs in. 'What was the name of the defendant?'

'Mitchell Coates.'

The page refreshes.

'Convicted of sexual assault and actual bodily harm.'

'That's him.'

We're looking at the original charge sheet, which gives his full name, place of birth, occupation and age, as well as the date of his arrest. Clara types in the case number, pulling up more records.

'It was a jury trial. The defendant pleaded not guilty. I can't see any transcripts, but here is the original statement from the victim.'

I pull my chair alongside her and read the scanned handwritten document. The author, Lilah Hooper, aged twenty-eight, was attacked as she arrived home after a night shift.

I reached for the light switch, but nothing happened. I thought a fuse might have tripped. I called for Trevor, my dog, who usually made a fuss when I came home. I heard him whimpering from the bedroom and knew something was wrong.

The fuse box is in the kitchen. I keep a torch beneath the sink and a box of candles. I should have used my phone, but I didn't think. As I reached into the cupboard, I heard someone behind me. Before I could react, he pulled a pillowcase over my head and shoved me onto the floor. He was kneeling on my back, dragging my hands behind me. I felt the rope winding around my wrists and arms. One loop went around my neck. When he pulled tighter, I couldn't breathe. I kept begging him to let me go, but he didn't say anything, not a word, but every time I made a sound, he tightened the ropes, cutting off my air.

I must have blacked out because when I woke again, I was lying on the bed, naked, with the pillowcase still over my head and more ropes around my arms and legs. I managed to roll off the bed and kick at the walls until my neighbour heard me.

Lilah had spent nine hours bound and gagged. Mitchell Coates lived upstairs. He freed Lilah, called the police and accompanied her to the hospital. Mitch wasn't named as a suspect until weeks later, when Lilah amended her statement, saying she recognised how her attacker smelled because she had slept with Mitch once, calling it a 'drunken one-night stand'. The police claimed this was the motive for the attack.

I can picture how the investigation unfolded. Eighty per cent of all sexual assaults are committed by people who are known to the victim. Friends. Acquaintances. Neighbours. Ex-partners. Family members. Mitch would have come under suspicion immediately because he had access to Lilah's flat. He fed her dog. He left her door unlocked because she often forgot her key. His DNA was discovered on the pillowcase and other bedding. His fingerprints were in her bedroom and elsewhere in the flat. He admitted to watching Lilah's TV when she was working, because she owned a flat screen, and he felt sorry for her dog.

Clara checks her phone. 'I have to go. I'm not allowed to leave you here.'

'That's OK.'

'Why are you so interested?'

'I met this guy. He says he's innocent.'

She laughs. 'They all do.'

'Yeah, but my friend thinks he might be telling the truth.'

'And she's never wrong?'

'Not yet.'

'How did the shopping go?' I ask, when I find Evie curled up in a corner of the sofa, watching TV, while playing a game on her phone. Multi-tasking in the digital age.

'Fine,' she says.

This is her universal reply and could mean that she almost died, or that she had the most amazing day of her life, or anything in between.

'Did you buy a dress?'

'No.'

'Why not?'

'Dresses are stupid.'

'What about your job?'

'What do you care?' she snaps. 'You didn't want me working at a bar.'

Something must have happened, but Evie won't talk about

it. If I press her too hard, she'll accuse me of prying, or nagging, or not trusting her. This is the tightrope I walk when I offer her advice, balancing my desire to protect her with giving her the space to make her own mistakes and to learn from them.

Tonight is 'takeout Tuesday', which is happening on a Wednesday because Evie wasn't talking to me last night. Once a week we order Uber-Eats and explore different cuisines. The foremost attraction of takeout Tuesday is that Evie doesn't have as much to clean up. Again, I pick my battles.

'What are we having tonight?' I ask.

'Fish and chips.'

'That's not exactly international cuisine.'

'Fish don't have borders.'

'Did you have fish suppers in Albania?'

'I don't remember.'

'Did you have a favourite dish?'

'No.'

The tone of voice is clear. She doesn't want me prying.

When the fish and chips arrive, we eat off the paper, which is 'traditional', according to Evie, but also means fewer plates to wash. The silence weighs on both of us. Normally, Evie has two verbal settings – one-word answers, or stream of consciousness monologues that seem to require her breathing through her ears.

Suddenly, she breaks.

'I couldn't find a dress that I liked. One that didn't make me feel like some man's fantasy, or make me feel self-conscious, or that people would be staring at me.'

'I see.'

'What does that mean?'

'Nothing.'

'Don't you have something else to say?'

'No.'

Poppy is sitting patiently, waiting for a chip. Evie drops one on the floor.

I make a comment about Labradors being prone to putting on weight and Evie accuses me of fat-shaming her dog.

'Do you have to wear a dress?' I ask.

'He said something classy.'

'Want me to help you?'

'No, I'll look for another job.'

I can't tell if she wants me to change her mind or agree with her. Instead, I choose another subject.

'Elias is coming this weekend for a day trip. Rampton sent me an email. He'll be chaperoned by two members of staff. You don't have to be here.'

She looks at me sideways. 'Do I embarrass you?'

'No.'

'Well, why can't I meet him? You said he was better.'

I did say that, but I don't know if I could make the same words form in my mouth. The closer it gets to Elias's release, the less certain I am that I want him back in my life. I have counselled people in my situation. I have told them that forgiveness can be cathartic and set them free. Hatred, bitterness and animosity can disappear, like a weight that is lifted from their hearts. At the same time, forgiveness can be premature. It can protect someone from the absolute horror of what they've done. Instead of being a form of grace, it becomes a disguise, a panacea, not a cure.

'Is that your phone?' asks Evie.

It is ringing from the hallway table.

Lenny's name lights up the screen.

'Have the police been in contact?' she asks.

'You *are* the police.'

'Don't fuck with me, Cyrus. You *knew* Maya Kirk.'

'What are you talking about?'

'Your name came up in her recent contacts.'

18

Cyrus

Lenny's bungalow was built in the 1930s and backs on to Colwick Wood, a local nature reserve in the east of the city. Her husband Nick answers the door wearing an apron that looks like it belongs to a child because he's a big lumbering man with forearms like a pro wrestler. He's also the hairiest man in the world, according to Lenny, which is why she calls him 'Bear'.

Nick is older by fifteen years and recently retired. He's taken up brewing beer, which Lenny complains about because their garage reeks of fermenting hops, but she's one of those women who complains with such softness and motherly chagrin that I know she's not properly angry. She would forgive Nick almost anything except infidelity or murder, and I'm not sure about the second one.

He yells over his shoulder and up the stairs. 'It's for you – I told you.' And then to me, 'Hi, Cyrus.'

I follow him into the kitchen, where he's washing beer bottles in the sink.

'My father used to brew beer,' I say, which triggers lots of questions, which I can't answer. Did he brew stout or lager or brown ale? Any flavourings? Was his keg stainless steel, copper, or plastic?

'You're asking the wrong person,' I say. 'I didn't like beer at thirteen.'

'But you do now,' he says. 'Fancy a taster?'

Already he's setting up a row of small glasses on a polished wooden paddle.

'This isn't a social call,' says Lenny, who has come down the stairs.

Nick looks disappointed. 'Maybe later. I'll chill the glasses.'

Lenny takes me into a sitting room where one wall is entirely filled with vinyl albums. Pride of place is a record player with a hinged glass lid, and expensive speakers on either side.

She points to one of the matching sofas. There are graduation photographs of her stepsons on the mantelpiece. Black gowns. Mortar board hats. Smiles for the camera.

There are no smiles for me. Lenny's voice is hoarse and harsh. 'DCI Hoyle has you under investigation.'

'For what?'

'Do you know Maya Kirk?'

'No.'

'Wrong answer.'

I feel myself growing annoyed. Lenny swipes her phone and turns the screen towards me. I'm staring at a photograph of myself. I'm in our back garden washing Poppy under the hose. My shirt is drenched and clinging to my chest, showing the outline of my tattoos beneath the cotton.

I remember when it was taken. Poppy had rolled in something rotten in the park. Evie kept gagging at the smell, so I washed the Labrador.

There is a caption beneath the photograph.

Cyrus 33

· 2 miles away

I'm six foot tall, emotionally available, and the last time I was someone's type I was giving blood. I think I'm funny, but not everyone agrees. I spend my life rescuing people, but occasionally I need to be rescued. (I also write lame profiles)

There are two more photographs. One shows me cooking a barbecue with tongs in one hand and a beer in the other. Another has me dressed in a blazer with my hair gelled. The image has been cropped to remove the other person in the photograph – my most recent girlfriend, Sacha Hopewell, who is back in London, caring for her elderly parents.

Lenny opens her laptop and turns the screen to face me.

'The dating service has given us complete access to Maya Kirk's profile, including matches and direct messages. You direct messaged her twice.

I read the texts.

Maya typed:

> What star sign are you?

Sagittarius

> They can be hard to read. How will
> I know if you're falling for me?

That's easy. I'll trip.

> OMG, how cute are you.
> What do you like to do for fun?

I run. I read. I go skydiving.
(Not true, I'm scared of heights)

> Did you just lie to me?

Last time. CMHAHTD

I am staring at the screen, speechless. Baffled.

'After the second exchange, Maya suggested you meet. You fobbed her off,' says Lenny.

'That didn't happen.'

'Which bit?'

'Any of it. That isn't my profile. I didn't set it up.'

'They're your photographs.'

'Yeah, but they could have been lifted from Instagram or Facebook.'

'Do you use either of those?'

'No. But it isn't me. I wouldn't use a dating app.'

'You're saying someone stole your identity,' says Lenny.

'Clearly.'

'Why?'

'I don't know.'

Lenny gets wearily to her feet and walks to the gas fireplace. My mind is racing ahead of her, trying to put the pieces together. I look again at the exchange. The text messages are corny and flirtatious and young. A thought occurs to me. I want to push it away, or erase it completely, but it keeps bobbing back up like a rubber duck in a bath.

Evie took the photograph of me in the garden washing Poppy . . . and the one of me cooking the barbecue. She has access to my phone . . . my laptop. She guessed my password within twenty-four hours.

'Where are you going?' asks Lenny. I'm halfway across the room.

'To sort this out.'

'I need you to give me your phone.'

'Take it,' I say, tossing it onto the sofa.

Lenny's own mobile is chirruping in the back pocket of her jeans. She wants me to wait but I'm already out the door and halfway to my car. She doesn't follow.

On the drive home, I try to calm down, telling myself that Evie doesn't understand the rules of friendship or relationships because of what she's endured. At the same time, I'm tired of making excuses for her. She wants to be treated like an adult, yet she keeps acting like a child.

I'm almost home when I see the flashing lights behind me. A police car. For a moment I wonder if I've been speeding or if Lenny has had me arrested for leaving her house without permission.

I pull over opposite Wollaton Park. Blue lights strobe across the iron fence and shrubs and ivy-covered walls. I wait with my hands on the wheel, looking in the mirror. Instead of a uniformed officer, I watch Hoyle get out of the passenger seat, hitch up his trousers and walk towards me, growing bigger in the mirror. I lower the glass. He leans his forearm on the door.

'Cyrus Haven. I'm arresting you for wasting police time and obstructing a criminal investigation.'

19

Cyrus

A hand protects my head, as I slide onto the back seat of the police car. Handcuffed. Protesting. Ignored. Hoyle maintains his silence on the journey to Radford Road where I am taken through the charge room to the interview suites. A public parade – part of my humiliation. Alone in the spartan room, I wait for Hoyle to return. He must know that I didn't abduct Maya Kirk, or murder her father, but he will use this as a way of sidelining Lenny or deflecting attention away from his own failings.

My issue is how much I should tell him. Evie has stolen my identity and faked a dating profile. She sent messages to Maya, pretending to be me. If I tell that to Hoyle, he could have her charged with catfishing or identity theft.

The door opens. He enters with Edgar. The two detectives sit opposite me.

'Do you require the services of a lawyer?' asks Hoyle.

'No, sir.'

He names everybody in the room and turns on the recording device.

'Before you go on, I can explain,' I say. 'Somebody stole my identity. I didn't set up the dating profile. I didn't communicate with Maya Kirk. I have handed over my phone to Detective Superintendent Parvel and will fully cooperate.'

'Where were you last Sunday evening?'

'At home.'

'Alone?'

'I have a housemate. She was with me.'

Hoyle consults his notes. 'Evie Cormac?'

'Yes.'

'She's a bit of a mystery, isn't she? I couldn't find any details about Miss Cormac. No birth certificate. No passport. No previous school records.'

'She was a ward of the court.'

'But she's no longer a child.'

'The protection order is ongoing.'

'Why?'

'That would rather defeat the purpose of the protection order,' I say. 'People aren't supposed to know her background.'

'Does DSU Parvel know?'

'Yes, sir.'

'Then you can tell me.'

'No, sir.'

This seems to light a fire under Hoyle, but he keeps it under control.

I hear Lenny's voice before she arrives. She enters the room like an acorn and spreads like an oak. Suddenly everything seems smaller. I think she's here to rescue me, or launch a spirited defence, but she doesn't bother to make eye contact. 'A farmer has found a body near Newstead Abbey. Early indications are it's Maya Kirk.'

Hoyle and Edgar react instinctively and suspend the interview.

Lenny motions to me. 'You're coming.'

'He's under arrest,' protests Hoyle.

'Last time I looked, stupidity wasn't a crime,' says Lenny. 'Otherwise we'd be short-staffed.'

'This is *my* investigation.'

'And I outrank you. Take it up with the chief constable.'

Early November and the overnight temperatures have dropped into single figures. A light rain is falling from a starless sky as a convoy of police cars travels along narrow country lanes, snaking around blind bends and over humpback bridges, the headlights forming a tunnel through the landscape.

Turning onto a farm track, the lead car lurches into a pothole, bottoming out, rock against metal. The constable at the wheel apologises but doesn't slow down. Instead, we buck and weave along the muddy track, which follows the raised bank of a drainage ditch. Occasionally, I catch a glimpse of ploughed fields and patches of trees and the light of a distant farmhouse.

A lone tree appears ahead of us, lit from below, as though someone is camping beneath the branches. Figures create shadows. Police officers. Crime scene investigators. Pulling through another farm gate, we cross a culvert and stop at the edge of the lighted area. The tree is an ancient oak, turned white by the spotlights.

Matching strides with Lenny, I walk along the eastern bank of the ditch. A fetid chemical smell rises from the water — a mixture of fertiliser and faeces. Hoyle is ahead of us, still grumbling.

'Are they sure it's Maya?' I ask.

'She has a tattoo of a bluebird on her shoulder,' says Lenny.

We reach the tree where the blades of a plough have left a teardrop-shaped section of compacted earth around the trunk. Bare branches reach out across the drainage canal, where the water looks black as sump oil and refuses to reflect the light. A shuffling figure encased from head to toe in pale blue coveralls is moving gingerly through the mud and reeds towards a bundle of rags.

'I need more evidence bags,' he yells, turning towards the brightness. His John Lennon glasses blink when they catch the light. He is attached to a safety harness, which is looped around the waist of another technician, who is letting out rope, or pulling in slack. She is the woman I met on the stairs at the murder house, Cassie Wright.

The SOCO in the water lifts a camera and focuses on some detail. The flash leaves a white dot dancing on my retinas. Someone hooks a clip onto the safety rope and the evidence bags slide into his hands. Crouching down, he collects a soft drink can between his gloved fingertips and slips it into a bag.

We're joined on the edge of the ditch by Robert Ness, a senior Home Office pathologist, who gets called Nessie behind his back, but never to his face because he's six-three and over two hundred pounds. Until I met him, I expected him to be Scottish, but he has Jamaican parentage and a Scouse accent.

'I'd have done it myself but it's a body mass issue,' he says, motioning to the water. 'We sent Voigt. He's expendable, but if he drops that camera I'll have his guts for garters.'

Voigt struggles to keep his balance in the mud, his legs braced apart, squatting to lower his centre of gravity.

'He's going to need more than a tetanus booster if he falls in there,' says Lenny.

My eyes study the water ahead of him and settle on a dumped car tyre and the bundle of rags, which now appears to be a discarded tarpaulin. Voigt carefully pulls back the tarp, revealing the body. He calls out details.

'Caucasian female. Thirties. She doesn't have any hair.'

'Say that again,' says Hoyle.

'Her head has been shaved.' Voigt moves around the body. 'Stud earrings. Polish on her fingernails. Soft colour.'

'To your left – next to your knee,' calls Ness.

Voigt follows his instructions, bending to pick up a crisp

packet, which he seals in a plastic evidence bag. Each time he moves, he searches for his centre of gravity before he takes a photograph or collects a sample.

The crime scene manager, Craig Dyson, is hovering near Ness's shoulder, awaiting instructions.

'We'll need a stretcher and guide ropes to move the body,' says the pathologist. 'Use the branches of the tree as a tether point. You might want to get a winch.'

Dyson begins making the arrangements.

Ness looks at the terrain. 'It's been raining, which will make it harder to find footprints or tyre tracks.'

'Who discovered the body?' I ask.

'A local farmer.' He points to lights on a distant ridge. 'He saw a vehicle on the track last night. Thought some local teenagers had come out to party. Forgot about it until this afternoon. He was checking fences when his dogs started barking.'

I peer into the darkness, knowing that I might need to return and study the location in daylight, to understand the landmarks and the lines of sight.

'Where does this track lead?' I ask.

'An abandoned barn.'

'What about those buildings?' I point to the far side of the field where I can make out the sloping silhouette of rooftops.

'Piggeries,' says Ness. 'Hence the smell.'

I can picture the history of this area – the mum-and-dad smallholdings swallowed up and turned into a mega-farm. High-intensity agriculture, the changing face of the British countryside.

Below us, in the ditch, Voigt has leaned forward to shoot a close-up of Maya Kirk's face.

'There's something around her neck,' he yells, asking for Cassie to let out more line. Voigt shifts his weight. Cassie is too slow. One foot slides out from beneath Voigt. He tries to correct himself and seems to be running on the spot, arms flailing, pitching forward and then back. There is no recovering. Gravity wins. He plunges into the water, sliding beneath the putrid surface and emerging again, coughing and spluttering.

'Fuck!' says Ness. 'Pull him in.'

People clamber down the bank. Hands grab hands, forming a human chain, hauling Voigt from the water. Dripping with wrack and weed, he spits and coughs and wipes his eyes, before glaring at Cassie.

'It wasn't my fault,' she explains, trying not to laugh. 'You slipped.'

'And contaminated my crime scene,' says Ness, who examines the ruined camera.

Voigt looks aggrieved as he peels off his coveralls and is wrapped in a foil blanket. Mud has smeared his glasses and his teeth are chattering. A second technician volunteers to go into the water, while a third wades to the far side and secures a guide rope, which is pulled taut. Ness looks at the sky impatiently, worried about more rain.

I have wandered away from the light, trying to put together a sequence of events. The killer made little attempt to hide Maya's body. He knew it would be found. But why this place? And why dump her like a piece of garbage?

The shearing of Maya's hair interests me. He may have been removing traces of his DNA or taking it as a souvenir. In the history of gendered violence, cutting off a woman's hair has often been a tactic for dehumanising or humiliating a victim, setting her apart.

Lenny interrupts my thoughts.

'There's nothing more we can do here,' she says. 'I'll take you home.'

She's right. The scene belongs to the scientists. As we reach the car, a voice makes us turn. Voigt is jogging towards us, still wrapped in the foil blanket.

'Any chance of a lift into town?' he asks, calling Lenny 'Ma'am'.

'I'm not a madam,' Lenny replies. 'You call me boss, guvnor, or DSU Parvel.'

Voigt stammers an apology.

'What's your name?' asks Lenny.

'Stephen Voigt.'

'Are you going to mess up my nice clean police car, Voigt?'

'No, ma'am, sir, boss . . . I could sit on this blanket.'

Four corners of the car flash yellow. Voigt climbs into the back seat alongside me, apologising about the smell. Lenny cracks a window and we drive in silence until we reach the tarmacked road. The journey back to Nottingham has less urgency than the one that brought us here.

'How long have you been a CSI?' I ask.

'Twelve years.'

'You don't look old enough.'

'I was still at school, studying for my A-levels when I managed to get a week's work experience with a CSI team. I went to burglaries and break-ins – nothing gruesome – but I was hooked, you know. They tease me because I'm so keen, but it shows they like me.'

Not in my experience, I think to myself. Voigt reminds me of an overenthusiastic red setter that bounds around thinking everybody loves dogs.

'Shame about your clothes,' I say.

'That's OK.' He hums to himself and then asks, 'Do you think Cassie minded that I got angry? I thought she did it on purpose. I didn't mean to blame her. Did she look upset?'

'I didn't notice,' I say.

'Where can we drop you?' asks Lenny.

Voigt hesitates and seems to be silently debating the issue.

'Home might be an idea,' suggests Lenny.

'Yes, of course, but I don't want Mrs Whitby seeing me like this.'

'Mrs Whitby?'

'I'm between properties right now. Staying with a family

friend. I used to call her auntie, but we're not really related. She and Mum were at school together.'

Voigt glances at me briefly, aware that he's sharing too much with complete strangers.

'If you could drop me at the office, I'll have a shower before I go home.'

He means the Arncliffe Centre, an annexe of the East Midlands Forensic Services, which is based in a business park in Hucknall, north of Nottingham.

'Just before you fell over, you found something around her neck,' I say. 'What was it?'

'It looked like a thick rubber band, but I might be wrong.'

After dropping Voigt at his office, Lenny drives me back to my car, which is parked a few streets from the house. As I slip a key into the ignition, my thoughts return to Evie. What am I going to do about the fake dating profile? It's illegal to steal someone's identity.

Letting myself into the darkened house, I kick off my shoes and quietly climb the stairs. Evie will be in bed, asleep, or watching TikTok videos on her phone, ruining her posture and possibly her mind. Our lecture, the confrontation, the stern words, the recriminations, can wait until tomorrow. By then, I might have calmed down and be less likely to say something I regret.

I know what to expect. Evie's natural defence mechanism is to push back, rather than surrender or apologise. And the only time she ever walks away from a fight is to set up an ambush.

20

Evie

I hear him come home. His key in the lock, the security chain, his boots being kicked off. He's on the stairs now. The third one from the top creaks like an old rocking chair. Cyrus wants to get it fixed, but I like hearing him come home.

I sit up in bed, expecting him to knock and say goodnight. He does that sometimes when he sees the strip of light beneath my door. He knocks and asks if I'm awake. Then he comes into my room and perches on the end of my bed, leaning on his outstretched arm. I always look at his hand and want him to move it closer to me, to touch my covered foot. Nothing else would have to happen. It would be enough.

I know where he's been. It came up on my news feed. The police have discovered a woman's body near Mansfield, half an hour from Nottingham. Her name hasn't been released, but everybody seems to know that it's Maya Kirk.

Cyrus doesn't stop outside my door. Instead, he goes to his bedroom and gets changed. Minutes later, he returns. I imagine his knuckles tapping on the door, but nothing happens. He continues downstairs to the basement. That's not a good sign.

When something is troubling Cyrus, he lifts weights. I have watched him some nights, spying on his sessions, fascinated and fearful of what he does, how his ink-stained arms tremble as he raises the bar from the cradle, his breath coming in short bursts. He does it again and again – each lift slower than the last. This is not exercise. This is self-abuse. This is punishment.

I don't know how long I lie awake, listening to the sound of weights being dropped into the cradle, imagining his groans of pain. This is how I fall asleep, wishing I could make him stop.

In the morning, Cyrus is up and gone before I get downstairs. There is a note on the kitchen table.

> Take down the dating profile.
> It's against the law to steal someone's identity.
> Stay out of my life, Evie, or you can't be part of it.

My legs go hollow and my heart drops to my feet and further. I read the note again. I want there to be an 'x' at the end, or an 'o'. Even his initials would do. I want to read between the lines and see that he's angry, but not finished with me.

How did he find out? Somebody must have recognised his photograph on the dating profile. I was going to tell him, but only when I had found someone who was perfect for him.

When I suggested that he join a dating site, he laughed, saying that he'd meet someone 'organically', whatever that means. Nobody meets organically. It sounds creepy. And I know Cyrus. He doesn't go to parties, and he is completely hopeless at flirting or realising that someone fancies him.

Sacha went back to London four months ago and there hasn't been anyone since then. He needs someone, now more than ever. Elias is getting out. It's going to bring back memories of his parents dying, and his sisters. Nobody should have to go through that alone.

'Knock, knock,' says a voice.

Mitch is standing at the laundry door, holding his cap in both hands. He's wearing the same clothes as yesterday.

'Bus broke down. Sorry I'm late.'

It sounds like a lie, but he's telling the truth.

'I had to walk the last half-mile.'

He leans down and massages his knee.

'What happened to it?' I ask.

'Broke it in prison.'

'How?'

'A misunderstanding.'

Not the whole truth.

'You were attacked,' I say.

His shoulders rise and fall.

'Why?'

'I was a sex offender. The lowest of the low. Not as bad as the nonces, you know, the paedos and kiddie-fiddlers, but still a bottom feeder.'

'What did they do?'

'Two guys held me down, while another one jumped on my leg.'

I flinch and Mitch apologises. Why do people do that – say sorry for something they didn't do?

'Does Cyrus have any paint?' he asks. 'He wanted me to fix the side gate. Thought I'd give it a few coats.'

'Did you check the shed?'

'Some half cans that weren't sealed properly.' Mitch scratches his chin. 'I could pick up some paint from a hardware store. Do a colour match.'

'Do you need money?'

'He can fix me up later.'

Mitch limps back into the garden to get his jacket. Watching him, I feel guilty. Cyrus's car keys are on the hall table.

'I could drive you,' I say, twirling the keys on my finger.

'If it's no trouble, miss.'

'Please call me Evie.'

The once red Fiat, now a faded pink, is parked beneath trees, and pigeons have been using it as target practice. I sweep leaves off the windscreen and Mitch struggles into the passenger seat, lifting his damaged leg into the footwell. Poppy jumps into my side and scampers onto the back seat.

The engine coughs, complains and spits out a cloud of smoke.

'Nice car,' says Mitch.

'Are you being sarky?'

'No. It's very retro. When did you get your licence?'

'Who said anything about a licence?'

I stamp on the accelerator and roar away from the kerb, aiming at the cars parked opposite before swerving back to the centre of the road.

Mitch is clutching the door handle. 'I don't think this is a good idea. I don't want you breaking the law.'

'Relax. Cyrus works for the police.'

I'm speeding towards a busy roundabout; Mitch braces both his hands on the dashboard and closes his eyes.

I slow the car and start laughing. 'The look on your face.'

It takes a few moments before Mitch cracks a smile. I'm driving carefully now with both hands on the wheel, at positions ten and two, along Derby Road past the Wollaton Park Golf Club, before taking the exit onto Clifton Boulevard, heading south towards the River Trent.

'I used to ride my bike around here,' says Mitch.

'You had a motorbike?'

'No. A racing bike. Fancied myself as a road cyclist for a while. Joined a club, wore Lycra and went cycling every Sunday morning. A group of us went to Paris one year and watched the final leg of the Tour de France.'

I think that's a bike race, but I don't want to show my ignorance.

'Did you live around here?'

'I was renting a one-bedroom flat near the Arboretum.' He's talking about a park, which has lots of old trees. 'I bought the bike to save money. I wanted to buy my own place.'

'Is that where it happened – the attack?'

He goes quiet. 'I shouldn't talk about it.'

'Why not?'

'You're too young.'

'I'm twenty-one.'

'Even so.'

I want to tell him that nothing that happened to him could be as bad as what happened to me. If this were a competition, I'd get the stuffed giraffe on the top shelf of the coconut shy.

'Did you know her?' I ask.

'She lived downstairs. We dated for a while. Well, it was one date, the classic one-night stand.'

'You were drunk.'

'Maybe, just a little, but I fancied her. Some people say that a man can't be friends with a woman without contemplating what it would be like to sleep with her.'

'Then we must *never* be friends,' I say.

Mitch looks horrified and starts to apologise. 'I didn't mean you. I would never . . . you're too . . .'

'Ugly?'

'No. Can we change the subject please?' He tugs his hat over his eyes, embarrassed. The silence grows uncomfortable. He adds, 'You're not ugly, by the way.'

'Good to know. What happened after you slept with her?'

'We both realised it was a mistake and decided to be friends.'

'You decided, or did she?'

'Lilah did. She was having problems at work and didn't need me to complicate things. After that we hung out as mates. I minded her dog when she worked nights. She had a poodle called Trevor. Stupid name for a dog, I know, but Lilah thought it was hilarious.'

'Cyrus said she was sexually assaulted.'

Mitch sucks in a breath between his teeth. 'Someone must have followed her home from the hospital. He put a pillowcase over her head. Tied her up.'

'Did she see his face?'

'No.'

'Hear his voice?'

'No.'

'Why did they arrest you?'

'I lived upstairs. I had keys to her flat. The police said there was no sign of forced entry, so they figured that whoever attacked her must have been waiting for her.'

'There must have been other evidence.'

'They found my fingerprints in her flat and traces of my DNA on the pillowcase. Some nights I'd hang out at Lilah's flat because I felt sorry for Trevor being all alone. And she had this big-arse TV screen in her bedroom. I'd watch football or road cycling. That's how my DNA got on the pillow.'

'And you told that to the police.'

'They didn't believe me. They said I attacked Lilah out of revenge because she dumped me after one date, but it wasn't like that. We were mates.'

He sounds frustrated rather than angry. I pull into the parking area and circle twice before I find a spot. Reversing isn't my strongest skill, but Mitch helps direct me. I clip a lead onto Poppy's harness and follow Mitch towards the large automatic doors.

'You can't bring her in,' he says, pointing to a sign. 'Only guide dogs and assistance dogs are allowed.'

I put on my sunglasses. 'She's my assistance dog.'

Mitch starts to argue, but I'm already inside the store, walking down a wide aisle where shelves reach to the ceiling.

'There must have been stronger evidence,' I say, when we reach the paint section and begin looking at colour charts.

'DNA is pretty convincing.'

'But you could explain that.'

'Lilah lost an earring. They found it in my flat.'

'How is that possible?'

'My barrister argued that the earring must have got caught in my clothing when I untied Lilah.'

'You found her?'

'I heard her kicking at a wall and went downstairs. She was in the bedroom. Bound and gagged. Naked. Someone had shaved her head.'

'Why?'

'I don't know.'

I step in front of him, looking directly at his face. 'Tell me again that you didn't attack her.'

'I didn't.'

'I wish I'd been on the jury.'

'So do I.'

21

Cyrus

The Nottingham Mortuary is in the Queen's Medical Centre, one of the largest hospitals in the UK. The receptionist acknow-ledges me by name, which is depressing because that sort of familiarity leads to circumspection rather than contempt – I've been here too often.

Cassie Wright comes to collect me from the waiting area.

'We meet again,' she says, smiling as though we're old friends. I suddenly wish we were. I'd like to spend more time with her. Today she's dressed in proper clothes, instead of a hazmat suit. Black jeans, black shirt, black shoes. She's my age, maybe younger, with an upturned nose and a slight overbite which reminds me of the actress Liv Tyler, who played Arwen in *The Lord of the Rings* – daughter of Elrod, wife of Aragorn, Queen of Gondor. As a teenager, I had a poster of Arwen on my bedroom wall, with her dark hair pushed back behind elfin ears, and her eyes swimming with tears.

We are walking along a wide, brightly lit corridor and I feel my gaze drift down to her figure. Some far-flung part of my brain tells me that I shouldn't be objectifying her, but another part of me wonders if she's single.

'Do you remember where we met?' she asks.

'No.'

'You gave a lecture to my forensic science class at university. I was in my second year, and you were a postgraduate psychology student, specialising in criminology. I queued up afterwards to ask you a question.'

'I remember.'

She laughs. 'No, you don't.'

'It was a very intelligent question.'

'Really? What did I ask?'

'You asked me if I thought that psychology was a science.'

Her eyes widen. 'Not bad. That was my friend Meredith, but not bad.'

We have reached the post-mortem suites.

'Are you going to watch?' she asks.

'Does that surprise you?'

'A little. A lot of people are upset by the sight of dead bodies, but I guess you've seen it before.' She stops herself. 'I didn't mean . . . I'm sorry, that was a terrible thing to say. Awful.'

She's referring to my family.

'It's OK. I'm not offended.'

Cassie pushes her hair behind her ears in a gesture that I've always found appealing. She leads me to a small auditorium overlooking the post-mortem suite. The rows of tiered seats are designed to allow students the opportunity to watch as post-mortems are conducted below.

'This adjusts the volume,' she says, showing me the controls. 'If you need to talk to us, you can press that button.'

Below us, Robert Ness is making the final preparations. Dressed in green scrubs and a mask, he reaches to adjust an overhead light. The pale, thin body of Maya Kirk has the dull whiteness of a marble statue, laid out on the stainless-steel slab. Despite being naked, she has more dignity now than when I saw her body in that muddy, fetid ditch. In life she had been young and vital, but death has bruised her eyelids and blood has settled at her lower parts.

Ness touches her cheek, as though apologising for what he's about to do to her.

'At approximately 2200 hours on the tenth of November, at the request of Nottinghamshire Police, I attended the scene of a death near Newstead Abbey, north of Nottingham. I was logged into the outer cordon of the scene and approached via a farm track. Senior crime scene manager Craig Dyson gave me a short background briefing.

'The body of a young woman was lying partially submerged in a drainage canal. Photographs were taken under my direction. She was curled on her left side with her head resting on her left shoulder.

'The deceased is a Caucasian female, of slim build, approximately 170 centimetres tall with brown eyes. She was found wearing a knee-length dress and black lace underwear. No shoes. Her wrists and arms were bound with rope, secured with slipknots that would have tightened the more she struggled. Her hair had been removed roughly, causing abrasions and cuts to her scalp.'

As Ness recites these details, he is assisted by a photographer, a technician, and someone I assume is a trainee pathologist. Craig Dyson and Stephen Voigt are also watching. Voigt has cleaned up since I saw him last but is wearing the same round glasses that make his eyes float and bobble.

Cassie Wright joins them, having changed into medical scrubs. She adjusts a plastic face shield and acknowledges Ness and the others. Voigt steps aside to make room. Cassie ignores him and smiles instead at Dyson. I sense some male rivalry, although I think Cassie has made her choice.

Ness is still talking. 'Post-mortem lividity is reddish-purple in colour, fixed on the neck, shoulder, back and buttocks, and the outside of her left thigh. Rigor mortis appears fully developed. No signs of decay are apparent. Her ears are pierced. Her fingernails are painted. She has two inoculation scars on her upper arm and an old curving scar around the outer aspect of the right elbow. There is a tattoo of a bluebird – approximately an inch square – on her left posterior shoulder.'

Ness begins to itemise her external injuries, every scrape, scratch, contusion and fracture. Moving gloved fingers over her skin, he makes special mention of rope marks that have formed a pattern on her chest and upper arms. He also mentions brick dust found embedded in her knees and beneath her fingernails.

'Bluish discoloration of cyanosis is present on all nail beds and fingers, mouth, lips, gums, including the face. The mucous membranes of the upper and lower eyelids appear reddish. Petechial haemorrhages have appeared on the inside of the eyelids, in the whites of the eyes and in the mouth.'

He traces his finger along her arms, before examining her neck, where a thick rubber band has created a groove in her skin. He takes measurements and photographs before using a scalpel to cut the bands, which he places in an evidence bag.

When he turns on the oscillating saw, I leave the viewing room because I don't want to watch the internal examination. I know that it's necessary in forensic terms, but I don't need to see her being defiled in death as well as life.

An hour later, I'm sitting in Ness's office. The pathologist has changed out of his hospital scrubs, but there is still talcum powder between his fingers and a smudge left on the side of his nose.

'How did she die?' I ask.

'The rubber band around her neck would have deprived her of oxygen, but not enough to kill her.'

'How then?'

'Her neck is broken.'

'She was hanged?'

'No.'

Ness begins drawing a sketch on a piece of paper.

'Maya had four distinct external injuries. Fractures to her

skull, left upper shoulder, right frontal rib bones and severe bruising to her lumbar region. All of these indicate that she fell or was pushed from a height, most likely falling down a set of stairs. That explains the cement dust embedded in her knees.'

I picture the scene. Maya's arms were bound behind her back. Once she lost her balance, there was no way of shielding her head, or stopping her fall.

'She was trying to escape,' I say, thinking out loud.

'Possibly,' says Ness.

'When?'

'She was alive for forty-eight hours after she was taken.'

'DNA?'

'Unlikely. The risk of contamination from the ditch is too high.'

My mind drifts back to the rubber band around her neck.

'He was keeping her alive. He had plans.'

'Your area of expertise, not mine,' says Ness.

At some point, the police will ask me for a psychological profile. I need to understand the killer's behavioural parameters and triggers. To do this properly, I have to put myself in Maya's shoes – to see the world through her eyes. The bindings suggest sexual intent, but she wasn't raped or sodomised. She was kept somewhere for two days. Given food and water. Slowly deprived of oxygen. We're looking for a planner. Someone forensically aware, who is prone to making mistakes when put under pressure.

But I still don't know his motive. Did he mean to kill her or to keep her?

22

Evie

Veejay is dressed like a hippy today in a linen top with an embroidered neckline and white harem pants. The first streaks of silver are showing up in her thick dark hair, but she hasn't tried to hide them. Maybe this is her statement about ageism, or she could have lousy eyesight.

'How is the new job?' she asks.

'I'm going to find another one.'

'Why?'

'They want me to wear a dress.'

'And that's a problem?'

I lift my shoulders and drop them. 'I don't have any dresses.'

'I see.'

What does she see? She doesn't have a clue.

'What else is happening in your life?' she asks.

'Nothing.'

'How are your studies?'

'Pointless.'

She asks me about my dreams. Nothing seems to make her happier than when I have a dream to share, something she can analyse and write in her notes. I make them up sometimes, like when I dreamt that my hair turned into spaghetti, or that I could bake puppies using pancake batter. Veejay wrote that down.

We fall into another silence. She and Cyrus are both experts at letting time drag out. I can feel my life ebbing away. Tick . . . tick . . . tick. Veejay gets paid by the hour, so it doesn't matter to her. Maybe that's what I should be – a therapist. I'd know when people were lying.

I want to talk about what I did to Cyrus – faking his dating profile – and how angry it has made him, and how maybe he doesn't want me living with him any more, but I was only trying to do something nice for him. Maybe I could convince her that my heart was in the right place. Maybe I'd be lying.

Instead, I ask her about Mitch.

'If someone is found guilty of sexual assault and they didn't do it, what happens?'

'They can appeal.'

'What if they've already served their sentence?'

'They've missed their chance.'

'So that's it? What if they can't get a job, or find a place to rent, because everybody treats them like a criminal?'

'I'm sure there are welfare agencies. Who is this person?'

'Someone I met.'

'He could be lying.'

'He's not. There must be some way to prove he's innocent.'

'Perhaps if the guilty person confessed, or if your friend found new evidence.' Veejay seems to stop herself. 'Have you talked to Cyrus about this?'

'He's not very happy with me just now.'

'Why?'

'I don't want to talk about it.'

That's the one thing I like about Veejay. When I choose to avoid a subject, she doesn't pressure me, or act like I'm wasting her time.

'His brother is getting out of the loony bin,' I say.

'It's a secure psychiatric hospital.'

'Whatever.'

'Does that concern you?'

'Yeah. He killed his entire family – everyone except Cyrus.'

'That was a long time ago.'

'If I had a brother who did that, I wouldn't be visiting him in hospital, or letting him back into my life, but Cyrus is acting like everything is OK.'

'Maybe he forgives him.'

'Yeah. Right.' My sarcasm has no effect on her. 'What if Elias is faking it?'

'What do you mean?'

'Being better. I mean, I once pretended I could hear voices. I was hoping they'd send me to some posh country house where I'd get to do art classes and make pottery and play croquet.'

Veejay smiles. 'How did that work for you?'

'I spent a night on suicide watch in a psych ward, hearing teenage girls moaning and screaming. Some were being force-fed. Others had bandaged wrists. Next morning, I told them the voices had gone.'

I don't know why I'm telling her any of this, but it's the truth.

'Is this about Cyrus's brother or about your sister?' asks Veejay.

'What do you mean?'

'You lost your family and you found Cyrus. Maybe you're worried that he will get close to Elias, and you will feel left out.'

'No. I don't care.'

Veejay hears the harshness in my answer. She's playing devil's advocate, trying to push my buttons to see how I react. She wants me to be kinder to people, and by extension, gentler on myself.

'You're not a bad person, Evie,' is one of her favourite lines, but she has no idea what I've done. I don't deserve to be happy.

I don't deserve to be loved. If I was a good person, I'd want Cyrus to find someone to love. The truth is, I don't. I created a dating profile for him, but I did everything I could to push the women away who swiped right. None of them were good enough.

'What if they're wrong about Elias?' I ask. 'What if he's not better?'

'He deserves the benefit of the doubt.'

'No. There shouldn't be *any* doubt. They *have* to be certain. I don't want Cyrus to get hurt.'

'I'm sure he can look after himself.'

I snort, 'He can't look after a dog.'

'I thought Poppy was *your* dog.'

'She is, but that's not the point.'

23

Cyrus

Melody Sterling is seated in the mortuary waiting area with a tote bag resting on her lap. She reacts to every movement and sound like a frightened animal that has wandered into a clearing. Her husband is with her. Unshaven and solidly built, he has a round, flushed face with a sun-damaged nose. Calluses on his hands.

'Call me Dean,' he says, delivering a crushing handshake which feels like a test. I try not to flinch. I fail.

'The post-mortem has just finished,' I tell Melody. 'They won't be long.'

'They cut her up,' says Dean, screwing up his face.

Melody goes pale.

'They're gathering evidence,' I reply.

Dean cocks his head to one side and begins clicking his fingers. 'I remember you. We were at school together. Chilwell Comprehensive.'

'I'm sorry, I don't recall you.'

'Yeah. I was a few years ahead. You're that kid whose family got killed by your brother – the schizo.'

Melody suggests he be quiet. He ignores her.

'You found the bodies, yeah? That must have been rough. I heard it was a bloodbath.'

'I don't think he wants to talk about it,' says Melody.

'What are you now – some sort of a shrink?'

'A forensic psychologist.'

'Like Cracker?'

He's talking about a BBC series from the nineties. Robbie Coltrane played a chain-smoking, gambling-addicted psychologist who helped police solve crimes.

'I'm nothing like Cracker,' I say, embarrassed for Melody more than myself.

'What happened to your brother?' asks Dean. 'Is he still banged up?'

'Yes.'

'Thank God for that, eh?'

He retakes his seat and picks up a glossy fashion magazine, leafing through the pages, looking at the models. Almost as an afterthought he asks when they 'get the house back'.

'Pardon?'

'Rohan's house. I left some tools there. I wanted to pick them up.'

'Dean retiled the bathrooms,' explains Melody.

'It's a crime scene,' I say.

'Yeah, but that won't be forever,' says Dean. 'I need my tile cutter and laser level. Won't take me a minute to get them.'

'That's not possible.'

Dean wants to argue but changes his mind. I offer to get Melody a tea or a coffee from a machine outside, but she wisely chooses to stick with water. I take the chair next to her and ask if she minds answering a few more questions.

She nods and seems to steel herself.

I begin with gentle queries, building up a picture of Maya's life. Her likes and dislikes. Passions. Relationships. Schooling.

'Did she own a dog?'

'No. Why?'

'Having a dog-grooming business, I just assumed . . .'

'Dad was allergic to them. Maya always loved dogs. She used to work in an animal shelter after school and talked about becoming a vet, but she didn't get the A-levels. She studied science and worked as a nurse for a few years. I really thought she'd found her vocation. She made great friends and moved out of home.'

'Why did she stop?'

'Something happened. A medical mix-up. Maya didn't feel the same about nursing after that. She quit her job and went travelling – backpacking through South-East Asia and fruit picking in Australia. She came back for my wedding and to help look after Dad.'

'Did she have many boyfriends?'

'Compared to me, yes, but I've always been easy to please.' She says it in a teasing way, knowing that Dean is listening.

'When was her last serious relationship?'

'A while back. Daryl Branagh. He worked at the building company.' Melody drops her voice to a whisper. 'Before that, she was seeing a married man for a while, which embarrassed her, because she didn't want to be a home-wrecker. He promised to leave his wife, but Maya didn't come down in the last shower. She knew he was lying.'

'But she stayed with him?'

'He took her away on nice weekends – to Scotland and the Cotswolds.'

'You described Maya as outgoing and friendly. Did she make eye contact with people when she passed them in the street? Men, I mean. Would she smile, or say hello?'

'She was friendly.'

'Did she like to draw attention to herself? Was she flirtatious, or sexually provocative?'

'She liked wearing nice clothes, but nothing too revealing.'

'Oh, c'mon,' says Dean, who seems bored at being left out of the conversation. 'She was a party girl. Remember at university?

She would change boyfriends more often than she changed her underwear. That's when she wore underwear.'

Melody gives him a death stare. 'That's my sister!'

Dean realises his mistake and reaches out to take her hand. Melody brushes it aside angrily. 'You didn't have to come.'

'I'm sorry. I didn't mean—'

'I know you don't want to be here. Just leave.'

I'm trapped in the middle of a domestic, where the anger feels practised and tired and worn into a familiar groove.

A bereavement counsellor arrives and saves my discomfort. Maya's body is ready for viewing.

'If you'd rather not see her directly, I can show you photographs,' she explains.

'No, I'm here now,' says Melody.

'I should warn you that she doesn't have any hair.'

'Why?'

'She was found that way.'

The counsellor knocks gently on an adjoining door, which is opened by Cassie, who is still wearing her medical scrubs. She steps back to allow Melody into the spartan room, which has a trolley-bed and a body outlined beneath a white sheet.

Cassie takes the corners of the shroud and pulls it back, revealing Maya's face. I hear an intake of breath.

'Your beautiful hair,' whispers Melody, who reaches out and touches her sister's cheek. 'You silly old thing. You've left me all alone.'

24

Evie

Cyrus has been in the library all evening. I know he's looking at crime-scene photographs and other grisly things, which is why he has the door closed.

I heat up leftovers and knock on the closed door, asking if he's hungry.

'I'll eat later,' he says from within, sounding impossibly far away.

'It will get cold.'

I wait, leaning my head against the painted wood. I raise my hand and knock again.

'Are you going to ever talk to me again?'

'Yes.'

'When?'

Silence. I feel a desolate wind sweep through empty spaces inside me.

'Do you want me to leave? I mean – move out – live somewhere else.'

'I want you to stop interfering in my life.'

'Ditto,' I whisper, but not quietly enough.

'I heard that,' he says.

The door opens and I stumble inwards, off balance. Cyrus reaches for me, but I correct myself and brush his hand away, surprised by his touch. He apologises and I wish I could do the same, but the word sorry has never rolled easily off my tongue. It's such a small word, but it gets caught in my mouth, or my throat, or my brain.

'Why did you do it, Evie?'

'Because you were lonely, and I wanted to find someone nice for you.'

'I'm not lonely.'

'Yes, you are. I hear you at night, lifting weights, moaning, hurting yourself.'

'I'm exercising.'

'You're punishing yourself when you've done nothing wrong.'

'That's not your concern.'

I show him my phone. 'Look at all the people who swiped right for you.'

'I'm not interested.'

'Some of them are really nice. I've been vetting them.'

'Catfishing is a crime.'

'I'm not catfishing. It's matchmaking.'

Cyrus sighs in frustration. He never raises his voice. Sometimes I wish he'd shout at me or hit me because I understand that sort of treatment. I've been beaten, starved and denied affection by people who used cruelty and small acts of kindness to make me feel grateful and compliant, until each new bruise became another merit badge.

Cyrus speaks softly. 'One of the women you *chose* for me was abducted and murdered. My name came up on her dating history. My photographs.'

I feel my mouth open in surprise. I want to close it, but I can't be sure unless I cup my chin and make my lips meet.

'That's not my fault,' I say.

'You sent messages to Maya Kirk, pretending to be me.'

'I didn't know she was going to be murdered.'

Cyrus is shaking his head, as though he doesn't know where to start with me. 'We can't go on like this, Evie. I have too many other things to worry about.' He means his brother being released. 'Why can't you be . . . be . . . ?'

'Someone else?' I ask.

'No.'

'Normal? Less fucked up?'

'That's not what I mean. Every day I seem to be putting out fires. I'm called to the school, or I get a complaint from the neighbours.'

'It won't happen again,' I say. 'I'll try harder.'

Cyrus gives me a pained smile. He's heard my promises before. I glance around the room and my eyes rest on a polished paper shopping bag sitting on a spindly wooden chair in the corner.

'That's for you,' says Cyrus.

'What is it?'

'Look.'

Tentatively, I approach and peer into the bag. Reaching inside, I pull out a delicate bundle wrapped in tissue paper. The garment unfurls across my hands, slipping over my fingers. It is a tailored black jumpsuit with pleated trousers and a V-neck. The sleeves are long and buttoned.

'I heard you had some trouble finding a dress. I thought this might make it easier,' says Cyrus.

I am holding my tears at bay. Crying on the inside. 'Why don't you hate me like everybody else?' I whisper.

'Not in my nature.'

'I don't deserve this.'

'No.'

'At least be angry.'

'I am.'

'I hate you.'

'Ditto.'

25

Cyrus

Evie has gone to bed and the house is quiet apart from the wind rattling the windows and radiators creaking as they begin to cool. I have decorated the library with photographs, propping them on the mantelpiece and the window sill, against the spines of books, and desk lamps, and an antique vase my grandmother insists is valuable, but could hardly be uglier.

Sitting in my swivel chair, I turn slowly, taking in the images of Maya Kirk, in life and death.

When I chose to study forensic science, I thought I'd be employed in prisons or psych hospitals, treating people like Elias. Instead, I have found myself working in the field, identifying sociopaths and psychopaths. Explaining their actions to police. Stopping them when I can or catching them when it becomes necessary.

Maya's disappearance and death wasn't a random abduction, or a spontaneous act. Whoever took her came prepared, which suggests a degree of planning and deliberation. But he didn't expect to find Rohan Kirk in the house, which means he can't have been watching Maya for any length of time. Although Rohan rarely left the house, there was ample evidence of him — his shoes were in the entrance hall, and his clothes were drying on the radiators.

Every sexual predator is different. Some pick out the weakest in the herd, the young, the sick, or the vulnerable. Others are drawn to their prey by some perceived slight or misread signal. Maya might have smiled at him in a supermarket aisle or across a petrol station forecourt. Or perhaps the opposite happened, he smiled, but she looked away or ignored him.

I go back to the photographs and concentrate on the marks on her wrists and ankles, along with those on her neck. There are similar chafing marks across her back and in the centre of her chest. There is an odd symmetry to them, diamond patterns on her skin. Whoever tied her up had wrapped the ropes into a harness that passed above and below her breasts, wrapping around her back and over her shoulders before being secured by a large bulbous knot in the middle of her back. A dark purple lividity mark shows where the knot was pressed against her spine, while further ropes criss-crossed her hips and were pulled between her legs.

Opening a web browser, I call up images of rope bondage until I come across a rope dress that matches the pattern on Maya's body.

I reach for my phone and call Ness. He's watching TV. I can hear the theme music for *Newsnight*. He mutes the volume.

'The bindings you found on Maya Kirk's ankles, what were they made of?'

'Woven hemp. Why?'

'She was bound in a particular way and the ropes formed a pattern on her chest. It's called Shibari – a form of rope bondage that originated in ancient Japan. It began as a form of torture but has morphed into performance art; or a form of subjugation.'

'Should I ask how you know this?'

'I studied fetishes and paraphilias at university.'

'And I wasted my time on medicine.'

Ignoring his chortle, I ask if he's had any more results back on Maya.

'We found traces of semen on her dress, which was highly degraded but gave us a partial DNA profile. There was also semen on the sofa in the living room, next to where we found Rohan Kirk.

'We did an analysis on the dust and grit found beneath Maya's fingernails and embedded in her knees. The samples contained traces of sand, lime and oyster shells, suggesting some sort of mortar, but nothing modern.'

'How old?'

'Nineteenth century, maybe earlier. And the paint chips had a lead carbonate pigment, which dates from the same period. She was held somewhere old.'

There are lots of historic buildings in Nottingham, which could narrow down the search.

'What about the toxicology report?' I ask.

'Nothing in her bloodstream, but some drugs aren't detectable after twenty-four hours. We're testing her hair follicles, which should tell us more.'

Ness wishes me a goodnight, and I go back to studying the photographs, turning slowly clockwise and then anticlockwise on my chair. The ropes, the shaving of the head, the slow suffocation – all are indicators of someone using control to subjugate and humiliate. The question is why? Sexual gratification? Revenge? Jealousy?

During the Spanish Civil War and the Second World War, women were often punished by having their hair removed, particularly if accused of collaborating with the enemy. It is a gendered form of violence, targeting their identity and sexuality. Maybe we're looking for an incel (involuntary celibate), who blames women for their failures. Someone who believes that feminism has gone too far and that men are owed sex and servitude and unquestioning respect from women.

If this were the case, drawing up a profile would be relatively straightforward. I would be looking at someone with a high sex drive, who has struggled to form intimate relationships – a man who falls in love easily, but who lacks the social skills to woo the women who attract him and, ultimately, begins to resent what he can't have, and to fantasise about punishing those he believes are responsible.

But this is different, and I don't know enough to understand why. The violence, the control, the elaborate bindings, the shaved head, all suggest a sexual psychopath, but it's almost as though the killer has ticked off the relevant boxes.

I know what Lenny would say: 'If it walks like a duck and quacks like a duck . . .' But this little duck is trying so hard to be a duck, maybe it's not a duck at all.

26

Evie

My feet are hurting. I wore flats but I'm not used to doing so much standing or weaving between tables. The bar is packed with people, who are getting drunker and louder. I've forgotten how much I dislike crowds and the possibility of strangers touching me.

Every table is taken and they're standing two-deep at the bar. I recognise the different groups. The football fans who have been drinking since before the game and are celebrating a win or a loss with equal amounts of alcohol. By the early hours they'll be eating doner kebabs or greasy food-truck burgers and picking fights with anyone wearing a different coloured shirt.

There are single guys on the pull, who act like roosters eyeing off the hens – young women in clingy dresses, sparkly tops and tight jeans. Some are here to flirt, or be seen, or find love, or to blag a free cocktail before they go dancing at one of the clubs, which aren't worth visiting until after midnight.

There are other groups. Husbands and wives, boyfriends and girlfriends, first dates and last dates. Brando calls them 'punters' and acts like he owns the bar instead of managing the place. He's working alongside two bartenders, Eric and Grady, who are bantering as they mix cocktails, pour wine and pull pints.

My job is to collect glasses, wipe tables and direct people to the loos. A trained monkey could do it. I'm also supposed to be on the look-out for pickpockets and bag snatchers.

Most of the people treat me like I'm invisible unless they want something.

'We don't do table service,' I say for the umpteenth time.

A drunk guy in a red football shirt tries to hug me. I duck under his closing arms and navigate my way to the kitchen, carrying a tray of empty glasses. Backing through the swing doors, I enter an oasis of quiet, not calm. The chef is a big-bellied Geordie, who uses swear words like adjectives. Mostly, he yells at the small Filipino man who is packing and emptying the dishwasher.

I take a moment to catch my breath, slipping off my left shoe and massaging my toes. The chef yells across the kitchen. 'Put yer fookin' feet away. This is not a fookin' foot spa.'

I give him the middle finger and smile, before pushing back through the doors. On the far side of the bar, I notice the bouncer signalling to Brando. Moments later, four police officers enter and move between tables. Three are in uniform. The fourth is in a rumpled suit. A detective.

Brando meets him halfway. After a short discussion, the officers continue to mingle, stopping at each table. They're showing people photographs. Out of the corner of my eye, I notice a guy slinking through the kitchen doors. I hear the chef telling him the kitchen is off-limits, but he disappears out the fire door into a side alley before anyone can react.

I continue collecting glasses, until a constable steps in front of me. He's holding a photograph.

'Hi, sorry to bother you, miss.'

'Don't then,' I say, stepping around him.

'Do you recognise this woman?'

My automatic response is to shake my head, but I know that it's Maya Kirk.

The constable has a dimpled chin and is standing so close that I can see the black hairs in his nose.

'We're trying to trace her movements. She was in this area on Sunday night.'

'This is my first shift,' I say, collecting another empty glass.

He turns to a woman at the nearest table.

'How about you, miss, were you in the Lace Market last Sunday?'

The woman waves to her friend. 'Hey, Toni. Have a look at this.' Toni slides off her stool and tugs her dress down over her thighs. 'Oh, aren't you the handsome one,' she says, eyeing the officer up and down.

Her friend shows her the photograph. 'It's that woman who got murdered near the abbey.'

'She was at the Lace Market last Sunday,' says the officer, who shows her a second photograph. 'What about this man?'

'Is he the one who killed her?' asks Toni.

'I know that guy,' says her friend. 'He's always hanging around here like a bad smell. He told me he was a TV producer. Fat chance!'

'Is he dangerous?' asks Toni. 'You'll protect us, won't you?' She squeezes the constable's forearm. 'You're very strong.'

A half-full glass of wine topples from my tray and spills over her tits. She lets out a squeal and flaps at the front of her dress, giving me the stink eye.

'Oops!' I say, smiling apologetically.

Brando turns up, bringing paper towels. He offers Toni a free drink and all is forgiven. Clearly, he wants the police to leave because they're killing the buzz of the place.

Five minutes later they're gone but the energy level isn't the same. Around midnight, I take a break, sitting on a step in the alley, rubbing my feet. The police are still on the footpath, showing photographs to late-night diners and people heading home.

Brando finds me. 'You're needed in the women's loo. Take a mop and bucket.'

'I don't get paid enough for this.'

'You haven't been paid at all.'

Stepping back into the kitchen, I fill a bucket with hot soapy water and carry it to the loos. The pool of vomit is just inside the door. Someone must have tried and failed to make it to the toilets. Breathing through my mouth, I start mopping, but hear a retching sound. One of the cubicle doors is closed.

'Hello?'

No answer.

'Is everything OK?'

I crouch and peer beneath the lower half of the door. A woman is kneeling with her head over the toilet bowl. She has bundled up a jacket beneath her knees, but her tights are torn. One sandal is lying next to her.

'We're closing soon. You can't stay here. Do you have friends outside?'

'They left to go dancing,' she slurs. 'I'll catch up with them.'

She retches again and spits into the bowl before getting unsteadily to her feet.

The door unlatches. She's older than I imagined, with short dark tousled hair and smeared make-up.

'I'll be fine now,' she slurs, embarrassed. She picks up her jacket and walks unsteadily to the sink. Reaching out, she grips the sides and scoops water into her mouth. Spitting. Wiping. Adjusting her hair.

'I'm such a lightweight. I barely drank a thing.'

Her words are slow and slurred, but she's trying hard to pronounce them clearly.

'Maybe it was the pizza we ate. Someone ordered anchovies.' She shudders and begins patting at the pockets of her jacket. 'My phone. I had it with me.'

'Where did you have it last?'

'It was on the table. I would have picked it up.'

'Don't panic. Where were you sitting?'

'At one of the booths.' She turns too quickly and stumbles. I catch her before she falls, letting go of the mop, which bounces loudly onto the tiles.

'What's your name?' I ask.

'Daniela.'

'You sit down. I'll look for your phone.'

I lead her into a cubicle and go back into the bar, where the crowd is thinning out. I peer under tables and chairs, looking in the darkest corners. I'm reluctant to get on my hands and knees – not on this floor. Botulism, Ebola, the plague, anything is possible.

I yell to Eric, 'Did anyone hand in a phone?'

He relays the question to Grady, who answers with a shrug.

'Who lost a phone?' asks Brando.

'The woman in the bathroom.'

'The one who puked?'

'Yeah. Her friends left her.'

'Get her out of here.'

'How do I do that?'

'Call her a car.'

'She doesn't have her phone.'

'I don't care how you do it.'

I want to argue but Brando has already turned away. As I walk back to the loos, I hear Eric yelling my name. He's holding up a mobile phone.

'It was next to the cash register. Someone must have handed it in.'

I swipe the screen, but it needs a passcode. Back in the bathroom, I hand the phone to Daniela, who looks relieved, but still pale and shaky. She slides off the back of the phone's case and checks that her driver's licence and credit card are still tucked into a small compartment.

'I'll order a car,' she says, but her fingers won't do what she asks. I take the phone from her and finish the task. A map appears on screen, showing the nearest available drivers. One of them accepts the request.

'Five minutes,' I say.

Daniela stands and leans against the cubicle door. When she sways forward, I grab her around the waist to stop her falling. It makes me feel uncomfortable, but I don't have a choice. Side by side, we navigate the narrow corridor and up the short flight of stairs, before reaching the bar. Empty glasses need collecting and tables need wiping. Brando wants me back working.

I signal that I'll be two minutes and steer Daniela towards the main door. The bouncer, Hamid, holds it open for us and I help her outside where the cold air seems to revive her and she stands on her own, gulping in each breath. She keeps thanking me and making excuses.

A car appears, travelling too quickly down the one-way street. The driver brakes hard when he sees us. He lowers the passenger window. 'Car for Daniela.'

I open the rear door and Daniela ducks her head as she slumps onto the seat. I lean inside and clip on her seatbelt.

'Do you have the address?' I ask.

'Stapleford,' says the driver. He taps the phone on the dashboard.

'Make sure she gets home,' I say.

'Consider it done.'

For the briefest moment, as the door closes, I feel something flutter in my stomach. Moments later, the car is moving away, disappearing around a corner.

Back in the bar, I continue working until a bell signals last orders. After a final rush, the bell rings again and the stragglers are coaxed and cajoled and bullied into leaving. The doors are locked. Glasses are collected. Dregs emptied. Tables wiped. Chairs stacked. Brando checks everything I do and points out things I've missed.

My final chore is to dump the rubbish bags into wheelie

bins in the alley. Brando hands each of the staff an envelope. Mine contains eighty quid, including tips. I send a text message to Morty, which he won't read until he wakes.

I'll buy your car. Give me until Monday.

27

Cyrus

Mitch is working inside the house, repairing one of the stairs to the attic, which has been sagging since my grandparents left me the place. He's trying not to make too much noise because Evie didn't get home until the early hours. I lay awake waiting for her, only falling asleep when I heard her bedroom door close.

Mitch isn't much of a talker. He arrives at eight each morning and leaves at four. When I pay him, he lowers his head, as though embarrassed about taking my money.

At midday he breaks for a sandwich and sits on the back step with Poppy. I offer to make him a cup of tea.

'I'd rather have a shower,' he says.

I notice a bulging rucksack that is sitting beside the back door. Unlacing the top, he looks for a clean shirt, sniffing at several before pushing them back inside.

'Do you want to do a load of washing?' I ask.

'Tomorrow maybe.'

A sleeping bag is strapped to the rucksack.

'How are things at the boarding house?' I ask.

'The landlady asked me to leave.'

'Why?'

'The police came round. They were asking questions about that murdered woman.'

'Did you know her?'

'No, but I guess I'm on some list of sexual offenders.' Mitch has found a clean shirt. 'My landlady doesn't like coppers. She says it makes her other lodgers nervous.'

'Where are you staying now?'

'Here and there.'

'Where did you sleep last night?'

'There's a fire station on London Road that offers emergency shelter if the temperature drops below zero.'

'And if it doesn't?'

'The car park on Queen Street is warm enough.'

'You should have said something.'

'Why? It's not your concern.'

'You're welcome to stay here for a few days,' I say, 'until you finish the job.'

'You've done enough.'

'This place has five bedrooms.'

He chews on the inside of his cheek. 'You should check with Evie.'

'If it makes you feel better.'

Mitch nods and climbs the stairs to the bathroom. Later, he reappears with damp hair, and razor marks on his neck. This time he accepts a soft drink, which he barely touches, running his finger through the condensation on the can.

'I did a bit of reading on your case,' I say. 'Who was the arresting officer?'

'Your friend.'

'Who?'

'He came here the other day and saw me working in the garden, but I don't think he recognised me.'

'Gary Hoyle.'

He nods. 'He treated me like a scumbag rapist from the very beginning.'

'What do you mean?'

'Usual stuff. You're walking, hands cuffed behind you, and a boot trips you up. Face first. Nothing to break your fall. Either that, or they spit in your food, or leave the cell lights on all night, or wake you every few hours for a strip search.'

'Your DNA was found in Lilah's flat.'

'She was my friend.'

'How did her earring get into your washing machine?'

'Maybe it was planted.'

'You think you were framed?'

'It's the only thing that makes sense.'

I want to argue, but I'm aware that police will sometimes tilt the scales against a suspect. It might be a sin of omission – disposing of evidence or burying a detail that could muddy the minds of a jury. At other times it involves forcing the facts to fit a particular narrative.

I hear the side gate open. Evie has been walking Poppy in Wollaton Park. She's wearing jeans and a large woollen coat that makes her look even smaller. Poppy drinks noisily from a metal bowl beneath the tap, and Evie hangs the harness on a hook in the laundry.

'Mitch is going to be staying with us for a few days. Is that OK with you?' I ask.

'Why wouldn't it be?'

I glance at Mitch, who smiles and says, 'Thank you, Evie.'

'No problem.'

She heads upstairs, but returns almost immediately, yelling, 'Your phone was ringing.'

She shapes to throw. I yell no, but the handset is already tumbling through the air. Mitch plucks it out with his left hand, like he's fielding at first slip.

'Good catch,' yells Evie.

Lenny has sent me a message.

Maya Kirk's brother-in-law has been arrested for breaking
into the crime scene. Meet me at the house.

Dean Sterling is sitting in the back seat of a police car, resting
his eyes, or asleep. When he hears my voice, he blinks at me
and raises his handcuffed wrists. 'Hey, Cracker, explain to these
guys that it's all a mistake.'

Ignoring him, I join Lenny at the mobile incident room, a
police-liveried caravan parked in the driveway, where officers
have been guarding the scene and quizzing locals who might
have seen or heard something that night.

'Sterling was caught coming out the back door,' she says.

'How did he get inside?' I ask.

'He had a key.'

Sterling shouts from the car. 'I was picking up my tools. I
left them in the cupboard under the stairs.' He motions to me.
'I told him.'

'And I said it was still a crime scene,' I reply.

'Yeah, but I got bills to pay; mouths to feed.'

He gives me a locker-room grin, as though we're both the
same, working stiffs trying to do a job.

Lenny looks at me. 'Did he mention the tools?'

'At the hospital.'

She seems to chew over this detail. She nods to the constable.
'Cut him loose.' And then to Sterling. 'Next time, do as you're
told.'

'There won't be a next time,' he says. 'Sorry to waste your
time.'

The cuffs are keyed open. Dean rubs his wrists, before walking
quickly to his van, which he deliberately parked further along
the street because he knew the police were guarding the house.

'What was he carrying when you arrested him?' I ask the
constable, who has orange hair and freckles.

'Nothing. I mean, he had the house keys and a small screw-driver.'

'What about the tools he came to collect?'

'Told me he couldn't find them.'

I look at Lenny. 'Does that make sense to you?'

She takes the keys from the constable. 'Time for a look.'

The house has been locked up since the forensic teams departed, but the signs of their presence are still everywhere – evidence markers and fingerprint powder and a missing section of carpet that once lay beneath Rohan Kirk's body.

Moving along the main hallway, I check the cupboard beneath the stairs. Inside is a wine rack and a spill-over pantry with canned goods, boxes of pasta and jars of preserves.

'Not the sort of place you'd put tools,' I say. 'A tile cutter is a heavy piece of kit.'

I move up the stairs to Maya's en-suite bathroom, which smells freshly painted. The bath has been recycled but the folding glass shower screen looks new, along with the tap fittings. I crouch to examine the floor drain and notice scuff marks on the edge of the bathtub. A faint pattern has been left behind by the soles of work boots. Someone was standing on the bathtub. I glance up at the ceiling light, which doubles as a room heater. There is also a smoke alarm with a round plastic cover.

Lenny has joined me.

'What sort of screwdriver was he carrying?'

'A small Phillips-head.'

'About yea big?' I ask, pointing to the smoke alarm.

'Yeah.'

Leaning one hand on her shoulder, I stand on the edge of the tub and reach up, twisting off the cover of the alarm, which would normally be secured by two small screws. Both are missing.

I turn the cover over in my hand. There is a battery, but no smoke detector.

'What is it?' asks Lenny.

'Best guess – a spy camera. The battery has been unplugged but the camera has gone.'

I put the cover into a plastic evidence bag while Lenny uses her phone to photograph the ceiling and the edge of the bath. She calls Hoyle, asking for a search warrant for Dean Sterling.

Meanwhile, I go to Maya's bedroom and look for other likely hiding places. Eventually, my eyes settle on the shelf of stuffed animals near the window. The toys are lined up in order of size, but one of them, the Paddington Bear, is slightly askew. I pick it up and discover that the back has been ripped open and one of the glass eyes is missing.

'In here,' I shout.

Lenny appears.

I hold up the bear. 'Another camera. It was most likely hooked up to the home Wi-Fi and accessed using a phone app, or a laptop. The batteries would have to be replaced every so often, but other than that, he could have been watching Maya from anywhere.'

'Where are the cameras?' asks Lenny. 'He was searched when he left the house. He was only carrying a screwdriver and the house keys.'

I take a step towards the window and feel something small and brittle snap beneath the heel of my shoe. Bending to investigate, I find a shard of black plastic. The sash window is pulled shut but unlatched.

I'm moving. Out the door. Down the stairs. Lenny follows. We reach the kitchen and take the side door, along a short path to the garden. Stepping onto the muddy grass, I look up at Maya's bedroom window, estimating the trajectory. I pull aside the branches of a shrub. Lying in the dirt, amid the dead leaves, are broken pieces of plastic, glass and circuit board.

'We need to get hold of his computers and his phone,' I say.

'I'm on it.'

28

Evie

Mitch has been working inside, fixing my bedroom door, which doesn't lock properly because this house seems to shift with the seasons, creaking and groaning as it inhales and exhales. Someone can close a door downstairs and my bedroom rug will ripple and bulge. It terrified me at first because I thought the place was haunted.

Having unscrewed the hinges, he lowers the door and props it between two chairs. Then he uses a tool that shaves off slivers of wood that curl and flutter to the floor like party streamers.

'What was jail like?' I ask, watching him from the attic steps.

'Slow.'

'What does that mean?'

'Everything comes down to time, but you learn to make it pass.'

'How?'

Mitch pauses and blows wood shavings from his wrist. 'We humans are the only animals that worry about time. Other animals live in the continual present, with no sense of the past or the future. That's what I learned to do in jail. I ate. I slept. I breathed. I worked. I lived in the continual present.'

'What job did you do?'

'In the laundry. It was OK in the winter, but a sweatshop in the summer. I also studied for a degree. Almost finished.'

'What degree?'

'English Literature.'

'My least favourite subject.'

'Why?'

'I'm dyslexic.'

Mitch planes off another sliver of wood. 'Did you hear about the dyslexic bank robber? He walked in and shouted, "Air in the hands, mother, this is a fuck-up!"'

I laugh, even though dyslexics don't mix up words when they speak.

Taking a square of sandpaper, Mitch rubs at the base of the door and checks it with a spirit level, before lifting it back into place. I hold it steady while he attaches the hinges.

'Where did you learn to do this?' I ask.

'My dad was good with his hands.'

'Where is he now?'

'Dead. Lung cancer. Smoked two packets a day.'

'How about your mum?'

'She remarried. Lives in Scotland.'

'Did she ever come and visit you?'

'Twice a year. I think she was embarrassed by me. I was the black sheep, not the prodigal son.'

'The who?'

'It's a Bible story.'

'I like stories.'

'It's about these two sons of a wealthy man. One of the brothers asks for his inheritance early and then parties hard, having a good time, living the high life. When the money runs out, he goes home, where the other brother has been working hard, looking after the farm and his old father. Instead of being treated like a waster for pissing away his inheritance, the son gets welcomed home like a hero, and they throw a party in his honour. The good son is working in the fields, and nobody bothers to tell him about the party. He's forgotten.'

'That's an awful story.'

'Yeah, I used to think like that,' says Mitch, smiling, 'but I think I understand it now. The father said that his son was lost and now he'd been found. It's about redemption and absolution.'

'I don't believe in forgiving people who hurt me.'

'Has anyone ever hurt you?' he asks, raising an eyebrow.

Suddenly, I want to change the conversation because I don't want Mitch treating me like I'm damaged goods.

'Tell me about Lilah,' I ask.

'She was nice. She worked as a nurse. Neonatal intensive care, looking after the premmie babies. It was a tough job.'

'But she saved lives.'

'Yeah, but she also had to watch some babies die, you know – the ones they couldn't save. She said it was nature's way, part of natural selection, but you can't say that to grieving parents, can you?'

'I guess not.' I have no idea what natural selection is, but I don't want to interrupt him.

'She talked about quitting nursing because someone made a mistake at the hospital and she took the blame, but I can't imagine her doing anything else.'

'Where is she now?'

'Don't know. Don't care.'

He tests the door, making sure it closes properly. 'She used to own the flat where the attack happened. Her parents helped buy it for her. Maybe she moved back home, although I doubt that. She didn't really like her old man. Said he was too controlling.'

'Are you angry at her?'

'No.'

'But if only she'd realised.'

'Do you know the two saddest words in the English language?'

I shake my head.

'If only.'

Later, when Mitch is putting another coat of paint on the side gate, I take a can of Red Bull to the library, where I open my laptop and type in his name.

There aren't many stories. One from the *Nottingham Post*:

A 30-year-old film editor has appeared in court charged with sexually assaulting a Nottingham nurse. Mitchell Coates of Portland Road confirmed his name, date of birth and address, but no pleas were entered. He was granted bail with conditions and his case was sent to Nottingham Crown Court, in Canal Street, to be heard on February 12.

I look for more stories. Seven months later, there was a trial.

A neighbour who terrorised a young nurse, cutting off her clothes and sexually assaulting her, has been sentenced to eight years in prison.

Mitchell Coates, 30, lived upstairs from the victim and had a key to her flat. Traces of his DNA were found on her bed and on a pillowcase used to cover her head during the attack. An item of jewellery, lost during the struggle, was later found in his washing machine.

The jury at Nottingham Crown Court was told that Coates was lying in wait for his neighbour when she arrived home shortly before midnight. She was attacked from behind and lost consciousness, before waking hours later with her arms and legs bound, her head covered, and her clothes lying on the floor.

In sentencing, the judge set a non-parole period of six years, and described Coates as a violent, arrogant, and controlling bully who had terrorised and humiliated a young woman.

'Your lack of remorse and refusal to admit your crimes has ensured you will spend a considerable period behind bars.'

I can't imagine Mitch being violent or arrogant or controlling. Why can't people see what I can see?

The only other mention of the crime is a feature article about the most dangerous streets in Nottingham. Home Office figures had named the Arboretum as the worst area, with more than four hundred violent crimes in the previous twelve months. Among those highlighted was the sexual assault of a young nurse, who lived in Portland Road. It must be her.

29

Cyrus

Melody Sterling is singing a nursery rhyme to the wet-cheeked child on her lap. Her daughter. Victoria. Around her, the police are at work. Belongings are being picked up and examined. Books feathered. Drawers opened. Furniture moved. Carpets peeled back.

Something falls and breaks above our heads.

'They'll be gone soon,' I say apologetically.

'But what are they looking for?'

'Electronic equipment. Computers. iPads. Phones. USB sticks. Memory cards.'

'Is this about Maya? What has Dean done?'

'We found evidence of spy cameras in Maya's bedroom and bathroom. We believe your husband placed them there.'

Melody's mouth opens, ready to argue, to defend him, but something makes her stop. Instead, her shoulders sag and her head drops as the air leaves her lungs. I wait as she processes this new information, watching her face change as she moves from denial, to shock, and to cold hard anger.

'Where were the cameras?' she asks.

'One was in the smoke alarm in Maya's bathroom and the other was in a teddy bear on a shelf in her bedroom.'

'The Paddington Bear?'

'Yes.'

'Dean gave that to Maya for her last birthday. He used to tease her about her collection of stuffed toys, saying she'd never grow up.'

'Is teasing all that he did to her?'

Melody doesn't answer immediately. The light fitting on the ceiling shakes as detectives move from room to room.

'When Dean and I first started dating, he would joke about how he couldn't tell Maya and me apart. He had this fantasy that one night we'd switch places and Maya would be in his bed and not me.

'He always laughed, as though he was teasing me or trying to make me jealous, but I knew that a part of him wanted her . . .' The words dry up and she wets her lips. 'It's not as though we were ever identical. I've always carried more weight, particularly since the pregnancy.' She pushes hair from Victoria's forehead and kisses her cheek. 'I once saw a documentary on twins. Even though we share the same genes, some of those genes can be influenced by outside events, getting turned on or off. Illness. Stress. Exercise. Nutrition. Smoking. Maya had pneumonia when she was four and I had a staph infection when I was eight. Maybe that's why she was skinny and I'm like this.'

I want to tell her to be kinder to herself, but depression is part of the grieving process. She rocks Victoria in her arms. The toddler is struggling to stay awake.

'Dean seemed to lose interest in sleeping with me after Victoria was born. I tried to spice things up, arranging date nights and romantic dinners. Maya would come and babysit, but Dean was more interested in talking to her about *her* sex life – living vicariously through her adventures – imagining that he was single and available.

'I guess we all want that sometimes, but I hated how it made me feel – like he'd married the wrong twin.' The words get caught in her throat. 'But he isn't a killer. He would never hurt Maya.'

'He filmed her.'

'That makes him a sleaze – and if he had ever tried anything, Maya would have sent him packing.'

'You trust your sister.'

'More than my husband.'

Something else topples upstairs.

'They'll pay for any damage,' I say. 'And put everything back.'

'Not everything,' says Melody, talking about more than furniture.

Hoyle walks into the kitchen like a gunslinger entering a saloon. Unbuttoning his suit jacket, he pulls up a chair and sits on it backwards, propping his elbows on the backrest.

'Where was your husband on the night your father died?'

'In Leeds. He drove up on Sunday afternoon.' Melody looks from face to face, wanting us to believe her. 'He's working on a big project. A block of flats. A dozen bathrooms. Kitchens. Laundries. He's been staying in Leeds during the week and coming home on weekends.'

'Where does he stay?'

'At a pub near the railway station. The Clayton.'

'Does your husband own a computer?'

'Yes. A laptop.'

'Where is it?'

'In the third bedroom. We use it as a study.'

'We didn't find a computer,' says Hoyle.

Melody hesitates, clearly surprised.

'He also seems to have misplaced his phone,' says Hoyle.

She looks miserable. 'I can't help you.'

'Right! We'll just keep looking,' says Hoyle, who bounces to his feet and smacks his hands together, making Victoria jump and begin to cry. Melody quietens her quickly, rocking her gently until her eyes close and she falls asleep with her head resting against her mother's chest. Behind them, the refrigerator is covered in crayon drawings and finger paintings. A tap drips. The clock ticks. The searchers have gone quiet.

'Does he have a secret place?' I ask.

Melody blinks at me.

'Everybody has one,' I explain. 'Somewhere they put personal items of special value.'

She shakes her head.

'A workshop. A lock-up. A caravan. A shed. A lower drawer. A shoebox. That's where he'll be hiding the memory card, or USB stick. He's been watching Maya undressing, showering, sleeping.'

Melody wants to block her ears.

'Where is he?' she whispers.

'Outside, sitting in a police car.'

'Can I talk to him?'

'No.'

She bites her bottom lip, leaving carmine tooth marks on the soft pinkness of her skin.

'I can't help you.'

Dean Sterling is in the back seat of the police car, eyes closed and head back, acting like he doesn't have a care in the world. When I open the door, he raises his cuffed hands and scratches his nose. 'We have to stop meeting like this.'

I slide alongside him and take a stick of chewing gum from my pocket, offering him one.

'I'm going fishing tomorrow with my mates. Should I cancel?' he asks.

'I would.'

He nods, trying to appear unconcerned, but I can see the uncertainty in his bloodshot eyes and smell it on his skin.

'Lying to the police isn't going to help you,' I say.

'Don't look so serious. I didn't kill anyone.'

'You keep saying that. I hope that alibi in Leeds holds up.'

'I was there,' says Dean, growing circumspect. 'But I wasn't staying at the pub.'

'Where were you staying?'

157

'With a friend.'

He watches me, waiting for the penny to drop. 'Who is she?'

'A single mum, making ends meet. She's a good girl. Decent. She's had a tough time. Fella walked out on her when she was pregnant.'

'How did you meet?'

'Online.'

'Through a dating app?'

'Not exactly. She was looking for a sugar daddy. I know how that sounds but she's not a prostitute – not really. She has a few regulars. Guys who help her out.'

'Out of the goodness of their hearts.'

A rictus smile creases his face.

'You should tell the police,' I say.

'I don't want Melody knowing.'

'You either tell the truth, or they'll charge you with obstruction, or worse.'

He blows some air into his cheeks and exhales. 'If I give you her address, you could talk to Tessa and confirm my story. You could keep her name out of this.'

'Sounds like you care more about Tessa than you do Melody.'

Again, he grimaces. 'If I admit to filming Maya, what happens to me?'

'You'll be convicted of voyeurism and put on the sex offenders' register.'

'Will I go to prison?'

'The maximum sentence is two years, but if you cooperate and if you haven't disseminated the footage—'

'I wiped the files.'

'What about footage from the night of the murder?'

'All gone.'

'That's a shame,' I say. 'You might have been able to do a deal.'

Dean seems to weigh up this information. His thoughts are self-serving, and he cares more about his own fate than Melody, or Tessa, or Maya for that matter. There is a long silence during which we watch police officers carrying bags of his clothes from the house.

'I've always fancied Maya, you know – the *other* sister. The forbidden fruit. I used to wonder if everything else was the same, you know. Underneath. Naked.'

My stomach churns.

'Maya was the naughty one, the sexy one. Melody was nice and neat and polite, but she never really did it for me, not in the sack. Know what I mean?'

You're an arsehole, I want to say, but I keep listening in the hope that he might say something incriminating or less self-serving.

'When did you start filming Maya?' I ask.

He acts surprised. 'Me? I didn't film her.'

'You just said you wiped the files.'

'Which means you have no proof.'

'We have the broken cameras.'

'No idea what you're talking about.'

He smiles, thinking he's so clever.

'Are you going to give me Tessa's name?'

'Will you keep her out of it?'

'I can't make that sort of deal.'

'Well, find me someone who can.'

30

Evie

Elias is late. Rampton called and said his transport was delayed, making him sound like a package they're delivering. Cyrus has been walking from room to room, adjusting a book on a shelf, or a photograph in a frame. Now he's checking the fridge.

'Are you nervous?' I ask.

'No.' He shuts the fridge door. 'A little.'

'Do you like him?'

'He is my brother.'

'Yeah, that's a given, but do you like him? You don't have to. There's no rule. At Langford Hall there were kids who had shitty brothers and sisters.'

'It's not about liking him,' says Cyrus. 'I'm the closest family he has left.'

'Whose fault is that?'

Cyrus gives me a look.

'It's what my parents would do,' he says. 'They'd want me to forgive him and help him make something of his life.'

'Are you sure?'

'Elias is still young. Not even forty. He could go on to lead a good life. Surely that's better than having him die in a psychiatric hospital.'

'That was his punishment.'

'It was never meant to be that.' Cyrus leans against the kitchen bench. 'Schizophrenia is a mental illness.'

'What causes it?'

'Nobody knows for certain. Most likely it's a combination of genetics, environment and altered brain chemistry.'

'Can you catch it?'

'No.'

'You said genetics – does that mean you could get it?'

'Yes.'

'How would I know?'

'My behaviour would change. My thoughts and speech would be disorganised. I'd become isolated and lose touch with people.'

'You do that now.'

'Very funny.'

'What if Elias hasn't changed?'

'He has. He's a lot different.'

'But people can be born bad, can't they? Under the wrong sign.'

'I don't believe in signs or omens or fate. I stick to the science.'

A horn toots and I watch from the library window as a van pulls up and Cyrus opens the front door and waves. I've seen photographs, but I didn't expect Elias to be so fat. Not obese, but just big all over, with a double chin and blotchy skin and a terrible haircut. He's wearing baggy jeans and a sweater that stretches over his midriff.

Two hospital orderlies are with him, black guys who are built like bouncers and move like basketball players.

Cyrus and Elias embrace. It's not the most convincing hug, but I guess they're out of practice. Soon they're into the kitchen, talking about the weather and the drive into Nottingham.

'So many new buildings,' says Elias. 'You'll have to take me on a tour.'

The senior orderly is Roland, and his colleague is Oscar, and they look more like brothers than Elias and Cyrus. Oscar makes me think of Oscar Wilde because I'm reading *The Importance of Being Earnest* as one of my English texts.

Five people make the kitchen feel small.

'You don't have to stay,' says Cyrus, who is smiling more than usual.

'That's not how it works,' replies Roland. 'On the first visit we have to remain here.'

'Of course.' Cyrus turns to me. 'Evie, this is Elias. And Elias this is Evie. She lives here.'

I don't move. Am I supposed to shake his hand? I don't want to touch him.

'Is she your girlfriend?' asks Elias.

'No,' we answer in unison.

Cyrus calls me his housemate, hesitating over the word, as if unsure of how I should be labelled. Elias is still staring at me. Maybe he hasn't seen many women my age.

'She's *not* your girlfriend,' he says again, as though wanting to be very clear.

'I'm nobody's girlfriend,' I reply.

There is a beat of silence. Cyrus suggests making tea and says that he's bought a carrot cake because he knows how much Elias loves it. There are comments about the kitchen and the garden. Small talk. Minuscule talk. Blah, blahing.

Elias asks about their grandparents.

'They're good,' says Cyrus. 'Living in Weymouth. Granddad golfs. Grandma plays bridge.'

'They never came to visit me,' says Elias. 'I got birthday and Christmas cards.'

Cyrus doesn't respond.

'And now you're living here – in their house – I always loved this place.' Elias has walked to the kitchen window. 'The beech tree is still there. Remember that summer we built the treehouse? And Mum said, "If you fall out of that tree and break both your legs, don't come running to me"?'

They both laugh and I think it's weird they're talking about a woman that Elias stabbed to death. People often misuse the word surreal, using it when something is unreal rather than bizarre, but this is just fucking weird.

'You made that ladder out of knotted rope,' says Cyrus.

'And you weren't strong enough to climb it.'

'I made it eventually.'

'Only with my help.'

'You were older.'

'And you were a weakling.'

There is an edge to the banter. Maybe it's sibling rivalry, which is something I never really had with Agnesa because I knew she was prettier and cleverer and nicer than me.

'But look at you now,' grins Elias. 'You've been pumping iron?'

'I built a gym in the basement. You're welcome to use it.'

'I used to be able to bench-press you.'

Not any more, I think. Now you're a salad dodger.

I can picture them growing up. Elias being older. Cyrus trying to compete for his attention or affection, but he's the one in control now and Elias looks like the ugly fat friend who makes people feel more attractive by standing next to them. He begins to walk from room to room, remembering certain stories and anecdotes from their childhoods. Roland and Oscar stay in the kitchen eating carrot cake, while Cyrus gives Elias a tour of the house. I hang back when they go upstairs but I can hear them talking.

'You can't go in there,' says Cyrus. 'It's Evie's room.'

'How long is she staying?'

'As long as she wants.'

They've reached Mitch's room. His rucksack is on the bed. I half climb the stairs. Eavesdropping.

'Someone else is staying for a few days,' says Cyrus.

'When I come home, where will I sleep?'

'You can have this room.'

'But Evie has the one with the view over the park.'

'You'll choose another.'

Elias goes quiet for a while.

'I could ask Granddad and Grandma.'

'Ask them what?'

'About which bedroom is mine.'

'They gave the house to me,' says Cyrus. 'I get to decide.'

There is another long silence. 'What about Mum and Dad's money?' asks Elias.

'It went into a trust fund.'

'For you?'

'It paid for my education and my living expenses. And I sent you money every month – so you could buy things at the Rampton shop.'

'What's left?'

'Nothing.'

Elias doesn't reply. They're in Cyrus's room and I can't hear them any more, but I wait on the landing, crouched out of sight. When they reappear, Elias is telling Cyrus why they were never allowed in the attic.

'That's where Granddad kept his *Playboys*. He had hundreds of them. I used to sneak up here and look at them.'

Cyrus laughs. 'Did Grandma know?'

'I don't think she cared.'

'Reckon they're still there?' asks Elias.

'They're not.'

'How do you know?'

'I know.'

There is a moment of silence and I hear their footsteps getting closer. I retreat downstairs. I don't want anyone touching the attic. That's my place. It's where I hide when I have my nightmares. I squeeze between the crates and chests, and curl up on the floor, making myself small, trying not to make a sound.

★　　★　　★

The van has gone, but Cyrus is still standing at the gate. A gust of wind sends leaves tumbling across the lawn, pinning them against the fence. Three hours with Elias has felt like a year. At least I didn't say the wrong thing. Normally I don't care, but this is different.

I start tidying up the kitchen. Cyrus returns.

'Why didn't you tell Elias that I was living here?' I ask.

'I did.'

'Yes, but only now. I've been here a year.'

'He must have forgotten.'

Cyrus scoops cake crumbs from the table and tips them into the pedal bin.

'Don't you think it was weird, how he talked about your family, as though nothing had happened? Like that stuff with the treehouse and your mum.'

'He was nervous, that's all. He's not used to socialising.'

'Is he going to come and live here?'

'Yes.'

'Do you want me to move out?'

'No.'

'Look at me when you say that.'

We're face to face. Eye to eye.

'I want you to stay.'

31

Cyrus

Morning cold. I walk through Wollaton Park on my way to the university. The sun is a pale yellow ball behind the grey clouds that won't shift all day, or month, or perhaps until the spring. Three gardeners are planting bulbs but seem to break regularly to brew up mugs of tea in their shed, sternly gazing at the sky, discussing the weather.

On the edge of the park, a group of students are holding up placards and chanting. They're protesting about student loans and the rents charged during lockdowns but look half-hearted or half frozen.

Henri meets me in the corridor. He's holding a soiled nappy, wrapped in a tight bundle, treating it like an unexploded bomb.

'She's very nice, but that toddler shits like an espresso machine.'

I have no idea who he's talking about until I discover Melody Sterling in my office. Victoria is sitting on the floor, playing with crayons and a blank piece of paper.

'You gave me your business card,' says Melody, sounding embarrassed. 'I know I should have called, but I didn't know if I could do this. I've been sitting in the car for the past hour, summoning the courage.'

She's wearing cargo pants, a cotton blouse and loose sweater.

'They won't let me see Dean. I don't know if he's been charged, or if he's appearing in court. Can the police do that – tell me nothing?'

'Yes.'

'But he didn't hurt Maya. He was in Leeds.'

'He wasn't staying at the pub,' I say.

It takes a moment for the information to register and the implications to become clear. Her eyes cloud before growing bright and hard. 'Who is she?'

'Someone he met.'

'Someone he paid for?'

I don't answer.

'I knew it. I do the accounts. I see where the money goes.' She walks to the window, muttering to herself, 'The bastard! The lousy, fucking bastard!'

Victoria looks up from the floor and babbles something incomprehensible. Melody understands and pulls a rusk from a plastic Ziploc bag. The toddler grips it in both hands and gnaws on the edge.

'I feel stupid.'

'It's not your fault.'

'I wanted to give him the benefit of the doubt. He's a good father. He works hard. He's never raised his hand to me.'

I don't know if Melody is trying to convince me or herself.

'Who is she?' she asks.

'A single mother. Tessa. He won't tell police her full name.'

'He wants to keep seeing her.'

It's a statement, not a question. Melody seems to reach a decision. She unzips a side pocket of her bag and retrieves a cork that looks like it belongs in a wine bottle. Squeezing it in her fist, she twists it in half, revealing the silver plug of a USB stick.

'I found a bottle of red wine in our wine rack. The plastic seal had been broken. Dean drinks beer. It made me wonder . . .'

167

She hands me the thumb drive.

'Have you looked?'

She shakes her head. 'I don't want to see what he filmed. I won't lie for him. I won't wait for him.'

Melody gets to her feet and takes a few minutes to gather the toys and crayons and baby paraphernalia that has found its way into every corner of my office. She looks at the soggy biscuit crumbs on the floor.

'Do you have a dustpan?'

'I'll clean up,' I say.

I walk mother and daughter along the corridor to the stairs. Victoria reaches up and takes my hand, swinging her legs in the air between us.

'Will he be charged?' she asks.

'Yes.'

'Will he go to prison?'

'Not if he tells the police everything and expresses remorse.'

Melody smiles sadly. 'Dean has only regretted one thing in his life. Marrying me.'

Returning to my desk, I plug the USB into my laptop and wait for it to be recognised. I expect to need a password or a code, but the files appear automatically. Hundreds of them, each with a letter and seven-digit number.

I randomly right-click a file and ask for information. It gives me the size and the date it was created. When I double-click to open the video, my computer doesn't recognise the formatting. I try several versions until finally a window pops up and I see Maya Kirk's bedroom, her double bed and dressing table. This was taken by the Paddington Bear camera.

A woman walks into frame. Maya. She's wearing exercise gear and looking at her phone. She sits on the bed and kicks off her shoes, smiling at something on screen. Flopping backwards, she holds the phone above her head and continues watching. After a few minutes, she sits up, peels off her top and begins to shimmy out of her leggings. I close the file, not wanting to see any more, but at the same time I feel strangely compelled.

The word 'voyeur' seems old-fashioned, as though it belongs to an era of peepshows and Victorian erotica, of women in stockings and giant panties. Either that, or it conjures up images of men with binoculars or telescopes, training their gaze on neighbouring windows, seeking gratification by spying on someone else's life.

The media have softened the word by linking it to reality TV shows where people agree to be filmed, playing games of survival, or deception, but that isn't true voyeurism. Permission cannot be granted. A voyeur watches in secret, peering through keyholes, up-skirting or watching through windows as someone undresses or bathes or has sex.

The files on the thumb drive are arranged in chronological order. I choose the most recent. When the screen opens, I'm looking at footage of Dean Sterling's face, as he reaches up towards the smoke detector with a screwdriver in his hand, removing the spy camera. The next file shows him reaching for the Paddington Bear and turning it over. The image shakes as he retrieves the second camera, pulling out the eyeball lens.

I keep searching. Some of the footage only lasts a few seconds and nobody appears in frame. The motion sensor has a time lag, which means someone can enter the room and leave again immediately, without being recorded. I open a new file and see a forensic officer, wearing coveralls, working in Maya's bedroom, dusting for fingerprints and collecting fibres from the bedding. Cassie Wright. She calls to someone. Craig Dyson appears. They discuss something on the dressing table. Cassie takes strands of Maya's hair from her hairbrush, sealing it in an evidence bag.

The next file shows Stephen Voigt using a spray bottle to coat the bath and sink with Luminol, searching for the presence of haemoglobin, which will turn blue under an ultraviolet light if even the faintest traces of blood are left behind.

Working backwards, I watch as the first responders arrive at the house. A young constable appears in the bedroom, looking for Maya, making sure not to touch anything. Rohan Kirk is lying dead downstairs in a pool of his own blood.

Growing impatient, I jump backwards to an earlier timecode and discover footage of Maya getting ready for her date. Dressed in a bra and panties, she opens her wardrobe door and searches for something to wear. Again, I feel like a voyeur, but this has become necessary. Maya holds a dress against her body . . . a second . . . a third. Having chosen one, she lifts it over her head, arms raised, and shimmies as the fabric slides over her shoulders and falls to just below her knees. This is what she was wearing when they found her body.

Taking a seat on a padded stool in front of her dressing table, Maya applies vermilion lipstick, uncapping the silver applicator and painting it over her lips. She pops her thumb in her mouth and pulls it out again, removing any residue. Then she brushes her hair, before sliding a tortoiseshell clip above her parting, holding it away from her face.

Afterwards, she opens a small clutch-bag and checks the contents. Her car keys. Lip gloss. Tissues. One last look in the mirror and she leaves, turning off the light. Her bedside lamp remains on, and her duvet is turned down at one corner, waiting for her to return.

The screen goes dark when the motion sensor turns off the recording. I press play on the next file. It is the same room, darker, but still lit by the bedside lamp. A figure crosses the room. A man, wearing jeans and a jacket. He drags the duvet from the bed and bundles it under one arm. He hesitates and walks to the dressing table, opening the top drawer. He sorts through Maya's underwear, holding up pieces against the light. He puts a pair of knickers into his pocket and turns towards the door, revealing his face.

Anders Foley lied about leaving Maya outside the bar. He brought her home. He searched her bedroom. He took something away.

32

Evie

'The handbrake is a bit dodgy, so make sure to keep it in first when you park,' says Morty, as he shows me around the Mini.

'You're not much of a salesman.'

'You should know what you're buying.'

I sit in the driver's seat and hold the wheel. Practising. Pretending. I have a sudden, jarring memory of being six years old and sitting on Papa's lap as he drove. I turned the wheel, while he changed gears and worked the pedals. The truck smelled of tobacco and diesel fumes and the windows would sometimes drop into the doors when we hit a pothole.

Every Sunday, after Mass, we'd drive into the mountains – Papa, Mama, Agnesa and me – and picnic among the wildflowers eating sandwiches and honey and nut cake. Papa would fall asleep with his head on Mama's lap, while Agnesa showed me how to make daisy chains which we draped around Papa's neck and across his face. He was only pretending to be asleep and would wake with a roar and tickle us until we begged him to stop. I know that's a real memory, but sometimes I wonder about other parts of my childhood. I feel like one of those science-fiction robots that gets programmed with a past to make them feel more human.

'Do you want to take it for a spin?' asks Morty.

'I'm sure it's fine.'

'If anything goes wrong, I'll feel guilty.'

'Good.'

I hand him the envelope with the money that I've earned over the past two nights, plus my savings, and the shrapnel I stole from Cyrus's bedside drawer and his car. Morty slips the envelope into his back pocket without bothering to count. I have no idea why people like Cyrus and Morty trust me, but it gives me all the feels inside.

Poppy instinctively takes the passenger seat, as though she knows that she's riding shotgun from now on. We have our own wheels and that means freedom. We can go anywhere we want. Well, maybe not anywhere. The tank is only a quarter full, and I just gave Morty all my money.

'Where shall we go?' I ask Poppy. 'London? Paris? New York might be a stretch.'

I wonder if it's possible to drive to Albania. I picture myself arriving in my village in the mountains – the one I struggled to find on a map. I would drive down the main street, waving to the girls I knew at school. I still picture them being small with pigtails and hair ribbons and school tunics, but they'd be grown up now. Some will have jobs or be married.

'Look at me, I have my own car,' I'd say. 'And this is my dog. And I live in a big house in England.'

In reality, there is only one person I want to see – my best friend, Mina, who lived in a shack beside the railway yards with the other Roma families. Nobody else would remember me except Mina. I wouldn't tell her the truth about what happened – how Mama never set foot in the promised land and Agnesa didn't get to marry a prince and live in a castle, which is what she'd dreamed about since she was old enough to dream.

I drive carefully, getting used to the mirrors and positioning the Mini on the road. Cyrus thinks I'm an anxious driver, but I get nervous when I'm with him because I want to prove myself. I'm more confident when he's not watching me. Poppy has her nose to a crack in the window, navigating the world through scent.

I try the radio and get nothing but static. The aerial is broken. I'll get that fixed and buy car seat covers and floor mats and air freshener because Poppy just let one rip and almost suffocated me.

After crossing Lady Bay Bridge, I pull over and type Portland Road into my phone, asking for directions. The posh voice reminds me of Mrs McCarthy, the manager of Langford Hall.

Portland Road isn't very long. Mostly it is full of old terraced houses with bay windows and tiny front gardens. I drive along it slowly, looking for any obvious blocks of flats.

Towards the far end, near the T-junction, there is a modern-looking building made of concrete and brick. Rubbish and recycling bins are lined up outside, each painted with numbers and letters that must correspond to flats.

I climb the stone steps and come to the front door. There are five post-boxes. Mitch said Lilah was on the ground floor, one of the low numbers. Poppy is sitting at my feet, looking at me expectantly.

I try one of the intercom buttons. Nobody answers. I try another.

'Yeah?' says a male voice, sounding annoyed.

'I'm looking for Lilah.'

'Wrong address.'

He hangs up. I buzz again.

'It's really important I find her,' I say. 'It's about her dog.'

'Flat two. She works shifts.'

I try to thank him, but he's gone again. Prick!

Nobody answers the buzzer.

'We'll come back,' I tell Poppy. 'Let's go for a walk.'

As we turn back onto Portland Road, I notice a food truck

parked near the corner. A picture of a sombrero and a cactus are painted on the side, next to a menu of Mexican street dishes. My stomach gurgles. I haven't eaten since yesterday. A man is lifting the sides.

'Are you open?' I ask.

'Not yet.'

'When?'

He's about to answer when I notice a woman turning the corner. She's walking on the far side of the road. Her overcoat is unbuttoned. Underneath, she's wearing dark blue trousers and a light blue tunic – a nurse's uniform. Her long hair is pinned to her scalp and she's chatting on her phone.

Retreating to the stone steps outside the flats, I take a seat and pull Poppy between my knees. The woman appears. She ends her phone call and searches in her shoulder bag for her keys. She's not looking as she climbs the steps and doesn't see me until the last moment, when she lets out a squeak of alarm.

I act equally surprised.

'I'm sorry,' she says. 'I didn't mean to startle you.'

'That's OK. We surprised each other.'

She steps around me and stops. 'Are you waiting for someone?'

'My uncle Mitch.'

As I say the words, her eyes widen, but she pretends that she didn't hear me.

'Mitch Coates. He lives here,' I say.

She turns away and puts a key in the lock. 'No, he doesn't.'

'This is his address. I came here once, years ago.'

'He left.'

'Where did he go?'

'Away from here.'

She doesn't want to say he went to jail. Poppy is trying to be friendly, wagging her tail. Lilah gets tangled in her lead and has to unwrap it from around her legs.

'I have to find him,' I say. 'It's really important.'

'I can't help you,' says Lilah, who pushes open the heavy

door. I let out a moan and rest my head on my knees and pretend to cry. I have no idea if she's watching, or if she's gone inside, but Poppy seems to find me convincing. She puts her head on my lap, wanting to comfort me.

After an age, I hear Lilah's voice. 'What's your name?'

'Evie.'

'Where do you live?'

'London.'

'How did you get here?'

'I caught the train and I walked from the station. I don't have enough money to get back and I don't want to go. I'm going to stay with Uncle Mitch.'

'That's not a good idea.'

'Do you know where he is? Can you call him?'

'No,' she says. 'You should go home.'

'I can't.'

She frowns. 'I'll give you the money for a train fare. You can pay me back.'

'It's not that. My mum has this boyfriend, Barry, who's always trying to walk in when I'm in the shower or getting dressed.'

'Sounds like a creep.'

'Totally. Gives me the ick.'

'Did you tell your mum?'

'She doesn't believe me or she can't be arsed.'

'Go to the police.'

'It's Barry's word against mine and Mum is going to side with him.'

Lilah is standing on the landing, hands on hips, deciding what to do.

'Your uncle can't help you.'

'Why not?'

She sighs. 'Come inside. I'll make you a cup of tea, but then you have to leave.'

'What about Poppy?'

'Does she get on with other dogs?'

'Loves them.'

'Well, she can come and meet mine. I'm Lilah, by the way.'

I wipe my nose on my sleeve and follow her inside. As the door opens, I hear scampering sounds, claws on hardwood, and a large poodle appears around the corner, wagging a tail which is tipped with a ball of fur.

'How are you, old boy?' says Lilah, crouching to hug the poodle, who seems to creak a little with age. Trevor is more interested in Poppy. The two of them circle and sniff and circle some more.

Lilah dumps her bag on a chair, before pulling the pins from her hair and shaking it loose. She looks at herself in the hall mirror and touches the skin beneath her eyes. She's come from a night-shift and is clearly tired.

'You have lovely hair,' I say. She looks at me oddly and touches it protectively.

'I didn't know Mitch had a sister.'

'Just the one. I'm his only niece. That makes me his favourite. Uncle Mitch said that if I ever needed somewhere to crash, I could stay with him.'

'When did you last see him?'

'Not for a long time. I know he went to prison, but he's out now.'

'Do you know why he was there?'

'It was a mistake. Mum said he was innocent.'

'Did she?'

We're in the kitchen. Lilah fills the kettle and puts teabags into two mugs. She wraps the string tags around the handles to stop them falling into the tea. Papa is the only other person I've ever seen do this. She takes a carton of milk from the fridge and puts a bowl of sugar on the table.

'I'd offer you a biscuit, but I refuse to have them in the place.'

'Work of the devil according to my mum,' I say, even as my stomach rumbles. 'Uncle Mitch was given parole, which is some sort of early mark for good behaviour. I thought he might come back here.'

'I hope not!' she says. 'He's not supposed to come anywhere near me.'

'Why?'

She gives me a strange look and I act surprised, saying, 'You're her! The woman who said she was attacked.'

'I *was* attacked. And I think you should apologise or leave.'

'Don't take it the wrong way. I'm only saying what Mum said. She called you a . . .' I stop myself.

'Go on. What did she call me?'

'She said you lied and stitched him up.'

'I did no such thing.'

'Maybe you made a mistake.'

'No. He left me naked, bound and gagged on the bed. He shaved off my hair.'

'But you didn't see his face.'

'How do you know?'

'Mum told me.'

'She's wrong. Your uncle deserved to go to jail.'

There it is – the flicker of doubt. It's in her eyes or her voice or shimmering in the air between us. Sometimes it's not a lie I see, but an absence of truth, or the illusion of truth, rather than certainty.

Poppy hears the raised voices and comes padding into the kitchen, putting her velvety head on my lap. I scratch behind her ears and say, in a childlike voice, 'Have you been playing with Trevor?'

The moment the question leaves my mouth I realise my mistake.

Lilah is staring at me coldly. 'How do you know his name?'

'Who?'

'Trevor. How do you know his name?'

'You called him that when we came inside.'

'No.'

Lilah is on her feet, standing over me. 'You're not supposed to be here. My identity is a secret. I'm protected.'

I start to stammer an excuse.

'He's not your uncle. Who are you?' she asks.

'I'm trying to help him.'

'Did he send you?'

'No. I'm nobody. I shouldn't have come here. I'm sorry.'

Taking Poppy by the collar, I pull her towards the door, but Lilah pushes ahead of me and blocks our way. She has a phone in her hand. Holding it to her ear. She's talking to the police.

'Yes, she's here now . . . Mitchell Coates sent her. He attacked me six years ago. Now he's on parole. I'm frightened.'

I take a step towards her. 'You're making a mistake.'

She braces herself. 'What are you going to do? Attack me?'

'Mitch had nothing to do with this.'

'Explain that to the police.'

I glance at the door, knowing I should run.

'You're not sure, are you?' I say, pleading with her. 'You think it had to be Mitch because he had a key to this place, but what if you're wrong?'

'I'm not,' she says, but I see her doubt. I taste it on my tongue, metallic and sticky like blood.

'You have no idea what I've been through,' says Lilah. 'What it's like to live in fear.'

I want to laugh. Fear is all I've ever known. I've been abused, beaten and burned. I've hidden in walls. I've listened to men die. I've faced down guns. And it happens again and again each time I close my eyes.

33

Cyrus

Applause breaks out among the detectives when I arrive in the incident room.

'The man of the moment,' says Lenny. 'You caught the bastard.'

'He caught himself,' I reply, as my back is slapped and hand pumped. Everybody wants to hear the details, to bathe in my reflected glory, but it doesn't feel very glorious. Two people are dead. A man is in custody. Nothing will turn this tragedy into a triumph.

'Back to work,' says Lenny. 'We have forty-eight hours to charge Foley or cut him loose.'

I go to her office. She sits on the wide window sill where several African violets are growing in clay pots. Velvety leaves. Pink and purple flowers.

'You proved yourself to Hoyle,' says Lenny.

'Was that the aim?'

'No, but it will make things easier, going forward. I can't always be here.'

'Where is Hoyle?'

'Claiming his share of the glory.'

Lenny turns on the TV that is bolted to the wall. Sky News

is reporting the arrest. Forensic officers are shown entering Foley's house and examining his van. The footage cuts to Foley arriving at Radford Road station, hidden beneath a tartan blanket, flanked by Edgar and Prime Time. The walk of shame.

Hoyle appears on screen, microphones thrust towards him like swords.

'Thanks to the hard work and skill of my task force we have a suspect in custody who has serious questions to answer. Our job is only half done. Maya and Rohan Kirk deserve justice and I will not rest until their killer is behind bars.'

'Fifteen seconds,' says Lenny. 'The man knows how to deliver a sound-bite.' She turns down the volume. 'The toxicology results are back. Maya Kirk had traces of GHB in her hair follicles.'

Gamma-hydroxybutyrate. A party drug that has become a date-rape drug. Clear. Odourless. Easily dissolved in a drink.

'The semen found on the sofa has been matched to Foley's DNA; and the sample we took from Maya's dress, although degraded, has enough markers to put him in the frame.'

These two details seem to jar because they don't fit with how I pictured the abduction or the murder. Why would the killer be so careful about wearing gloves, but leave something so incriminating behind?

'Where is he now?' I ask.

'Downstairs. His solicitor has arrived.'

'Who's interviewing him?'

'Hoyle. You want to watch?'

'Not really.'

'Come on. Enjoy your moment.'

We walk down the internal stairs. Everybody we pass seems to be smiling and nodding to me, aware of the breakthrough. The viewing room is also crowded, but a seat is found for me, as though I'm the guest of honour turning up at the awards ceremony.

Through the glass window, Anders Foley is sitting beside

Giana Camilleri, who has none of the aggression and bravado I witnessed in the original interview. This time she looks ready to wave a white flag. Foley has also changed. His eyes are puffy and red and his nostrils flare each time he exhales.

'My client wishes to correct the record,' says Camilleri. 'Some of his previous answers were not entirely correct.'

'He lied,' says Hoyle, who is standing behind his chair, gripping the backrest.

'He wishes to make a full statement.'

'A confession?'

'I didn't touch her,' says Foley. 'I'm being set up.' He has a plaster on his forehead that has a pink tinge of blood at the centre.

Hoyle takes a seat and folds his arms, acting like a man with a closed mind. Edgar starts the recording equipment and announces the date, time, and those present.

'What would you like to tell us, Mr Foley?' asks Hoyle, ready to disbelieve him. 'We're all ears.'

'Ah . . . well . . . what I said the other day wasn't entirely true, but I didn't hurt anyone.' Foley wipes his nose with his sleeve. 'I drove Maya home because she could barely stand up. She kept apologising and saying that she'd get a cab, but I didn't think a driver would take her because she was so drunk.'

'You went into her house.'

'She couldn't get the key in the door. I had to help her.'

'What happened then?'

'I put her on the sofa in the front room because she couldn't get up the stairs. I took off her shoes and put a pillow under her head and got a bowl from the kitchen in case she vomited again.'

'That's very gallant of you,' says Hoyle, sardonically. 'Was she conscious?'

'Yes. No. Maybe.'

'An unconscious woman – and you didn't think to take her to hospital,' says Edgar.

'She was conscious,' says Foley. 'She wanted to sleep.'

'Did you go upstairs?' asks Hoyle.

Foley hesitates, as though sorting the lies into an orderly line, deciding which one is more believable. 'I needed to use the bathroom.'

'There is a toilet downstairs.'

'I didn't know that.'

'Did you go into Maya's bedroom?'

'I'm not sure . . . maybe . . . yeah, that's right, I grabbed her duvet – something to keep her warm.'

'Did you take anything else from her room?'

'No.'

'You're still lying,' says Hoyle.

'I'm not. I didn't hurt her. I wrapped her in the duvet, and I left. I never saw her father.'

'You undressed her.'

'No. I . . . I . . . took off her shoes.'

'Your semen was found on the sofa and the inside of her dress.'

Blood drains from Foley's face. 'That was . . . It's not what you . . .'

'You sexually assaulted her.'

'No. No.'

'How did your semen get on her dress?'

Foley begins to stammer and drops his head into his hands. Hoyle and Edgar wait. The invisible clock is ticking, building pressure. Foley breaks.

'I had a wank, OK? I'm not proud of the fact.'

'You took off her dress.'

'No. I . . . I . . . I pulled it up. I didn't hurt her. She was sleeping, and I thought . . .'

'Is that when her father interrupted?' asks Edgar.

'No. I didn't see anyone else.'

'Oh, come on, Anders,' says Hoyle, sighing tiredly. 'Your semen is on her dress. Her DNA will be in your car. We know you stole her underwear.'

Foley frowns, wondering how the police could know what he took. Hoyle has a folder of photographs. Eight-by-tens, colour images. He begins laying them out on the table. They show Maya's body, lying at the bottom of a ditch.

'Why are you showing me these?' asks Foley.

Hoyle talks over him. 'Why did you shave her head?'

'I didn't touch her.'

'You broke her neck.'

'No. I left her on the sofa.'

'Let me tell you what I think happened,' says Hoyle. 'You drugged her. You drove her home. You raped her and she cried out, waking her father, who came downstairs. That's when you beat him to death with a fire poker. And you abducted Maya because you couldn't leave her behind. She was a witness.'

Foley looks to Camilleri, hoping for support, but the solicitor is bending a paperclip, twisting it into different shapes.

'We need an answer for the tape,' says Hoyle.

A different kind of shine comes into Foley's eyes. 'None of that is true.'

'The rape or the murder?'

'I didn't touch her.'

'Why did you clean your van?'

'She vomited.'

'Where are the clothes you were wearing that night?'

'They had sick on them.'

'Did you burn them, or throw them away?'

'I washed them at the laundrette.'

'You took her somewhere. You bound her in a rope corset. You cut off her hair. You broke her neck.'

'No, no. I left her on the sofa. I drove home. I went to bed. That's the truth. I swear to God.'

'You swear to God,' says Hoyle, barking a laugh. 'You should be praying, not swearing.'

Foley chews his bottom lip, and a bubble of snot inflates and breaks in his right nostril.

Even as he argues, I remember the rope marks on Maya's pale skin and her hacked hair. Foley's social media pages and his dating history reveal his casual misogyny and predatory nature, but nothing overtly sadistic. Whoever took Maya chose her for a reason, and most elements of the crime and aftermath showed planning and design, yet Foley made some avoidable mistakes.

Hoyle gets to his feet, having heard enough. 'Anders Foley, you will be charged with the murder of Rohan Kirk and the abduction and murder of Maya Kirk, between the seventh of November and tenth of November. You do not have to say anything, but it may harm your defence if you do not mention now something that you later rely upon in court. Anything you do say may be given in evidence.'

The recording equipment is turned off and Hoyle signals to a waiting constable. Foley is forced to stand and handcuffs close around his wrists. He sniffles and wipes his eyes with his raised hands, before glimpsing himself in the mirror, disgusted at what he sees.

34

Evie

In my limited experience – I've been locked up five, maybe six times – all police station cells smell the same. It's a mixture of boiled cabbage, sweat and bleach, and some mystery ingredient that might be tears or sorrow.

A police patrol car stopped me two streets from Lilah's flat. I saw the blue flashing lights in my mirrors and heard the burst of a siren. For a half-second, I thought about trying to make a run for it, but the Mini is hardly a getaway car. They would have laughed all the way to the station.

As it is, I've been arrested for refusing to give them my name and address; or produce a driver's licence or registration papers for the car, which is still in Morty's name.

'Are you old enough to drive?' one of them asked.

'Are you old enough to shave?' I shot back. His female partner laughed, which made things worse.

Since then, I've been staring at the same square light for so long that it's still there when I close my eyes, shining inside my eyelids. Occasionally there are footsteps. The observation flap slides open. Eyes peer at me. I raise my middle finger. Seconds later, the flap shuts and I go back to staring at the light.

I don't want Cyrus finding out what I've done, but I know they'll trace the car eventually and talk to Morty, who will tell them my name. At some point, Cyrus will be contacted and come to collect me. In the meantime, the station sergeant says I should think about what I've done. That's always been my problem. I leap before I look. I play with fire. I skate on thin ice. But why can't those other clichés apply to me, like fortune favouring the brave, or he who hesitates is lost?

They confiscated my phone, along with my belt and shoelaces and my earrings, although I don't know how they expect me to harm myself with two platinum studs shaped like bolts of lightning.

I hear steps outside. The cell door unlocks. A woman enters. She's wearing a tweed skirt and matching jacket, and if it's possible a harmonised hairdo.

'Hello, sweetie,' she says in a sing-song voice, talking to me like I'm in kindergarten. 'I'm here to make sure you're OK.'

Oh shit! She's a social worker. They think I'm a minor. Her name is Mrs Beaumont, and she reminds me of the bleeding hearts who worked at Langford Hall where the do-gooders annoyed me more than the sadists because they smothered every conversation with syrupy smiles and sad-eyed tuts. Shoot me now.

'The police want to ask you a few questions,' she says. 'What's your name?'

'I don't have to tell them that – not unless they tell me what offence I've committed.'

She giggles rather than laughs. 'My, you do seem to know your rights. Have you been arrested before?'

'That's none of your business.'

'Well, I'm your designated adult. If you want anything, you ask me.'

'I'm twenty-one. I don't need a designated adult.'

'Really?'

Clearly, she doesn't believe me. Moments later, a police officer shows up and I'm taken to an interview room where my two arresting officers are waiting. They have taken off their black stab vests and don't look anywhere near as scary. We're being recorded so they're extra polite, offering me a soft drink and asking if I want to call my parents.

'I don't have any parents.'

'What about a guardian?'

'I'm an adult.'

'OK, where do you live?' asks the female officer. She has thick blonde hair, which was bundled under her cap when we first met. I've always wanted to be blonde, regardless of the dumb jokes.

'Is your hair natural?' I ask.

The question surprises her. 'Yes.'

'It's lovely. Makes you look Swedish.'

'People say that.'

'Can we get on with this?' whines her partner, the impatient one, who has a pimple on his neck that I want to pop.

'What is your name?' asks PC Blonde.

'I don't have to tell you that.'

'Yes, you do,' she says, speaking softly. 'I'll accept a first name.'

'Evie.'

'Well, Evie, you have committed a serious offence. Victims of sexual offences are given lifelong anonymity under British law. They cannot be approached, harassed or identified.'

'I didn't mean to do any of those things.'

'Did Mitchell Coates give you the address?'

'No.'

'Why did you go there?'

'I wanted to talk to Lilah, that's all.'

'You're not allowed.'

'I know that now,' I say, as though it should be obvious.

'The car you were driving – who does it belong to?'

'I bought it from my friend Morty. It's not stolen, if that's what you're asking. This is my fault. It has nothing to do with Mitch, or Morty.'

'Where do you live, Evie?'

With each question they're getting closer to Cyrus. I want to magic myself away, to disappear, to slip through the cracks. I need a Cloak of Invisibility like Harry Potter. With one of those, I could sneak past them.

'Where's my dog?' I ask.

'We called animal control. They're coming to pick her up.'

'You can't do that. They'll put her in a gas chamber.'

'No, they won't,' says Mrs Beaumont, looking alarmed. 'Where do you get such ideas?'

'I want to see her.'

'Not unless you answer our questions,' says PC Pimple.

'If I tell you my name – can I see my dog?'

'If she's still here.'

I nod in agreement.

'Is Mitchell Coates really your uncle?' she asks.

'No, he's a friend.'

'You lied about that,' says PC Pimple.

'People lie all the time,' I reply. I motion to his partner. 'Do you fancy her?'

'No.'

'See? You're lying.'

I watch him blush. Cute. I still want to pop his pimple.

'Let's get back to the subject,' says PC Blonde, who is hiding a smile.

Finally, I give them my address and she jots down the details. The officers leave. They'll be typing my name into a computer, looking for information, but they won't find anything about me. I'm a non-person, a ghost, a shadow. There are court orders that protect my identity, which is ironic given what I'm being accused of doing.

I hear voices in the corridor outside. One of them sounds familiar.

'Please don't tell Cyrus,' I whisper under my breath, but Mrs Beaumont hears the words.

'Who is Cyrus?' she asks.

'My conscience.'

'That must be nice.'

'It's a pain in the arse.'

35

Cyrus

The viewing room clears. I'm alone with Lenny, who begins clearing the plastic coffee cups and torn sugar sachets, scooping them into a wastepaper bin. It's not her job, but she does it anyway, out of habit or because she hates seeing the mess or feels sorry for the cleaning staff.

My silence seems to irritate her.

'Foley is good for this,' she says.

'Absolutely.'

'He had the motive, the opportunity, the means.'

'Open and shut.'

There is another long pause, which could be a pregnant one, but I've never understood that term.

'OK, what's bugging you?' she asks.

'Nothing. You've taken out the trash. You've cleaned up the gene pool. We can all sleep more easily tonight.'

A beat of silence. Now she's even more annoyed.

'Out of interest – did they find any evidence of Maya Kirk at Foley's house?' I ask.

'No, but she vomited in his van.'

'Which he's admitted. Have you tracked his phone?'

'Of course.'

'Where did Foley go after he left Maya's house?'

'Back to his house. Most likely, he dumped his phone then took Maya somewhere else.'

'Where?'

'We're still looking.'

'What about his computer – any evidence of violent pornography? Ropes? Knives?'

'He seemed to prefer the revenge-porn sites.'

'Anything sadistic?'

'That's sadistic enough for me.'

I'm following her, along the corridor and up the stairs. We pass two constables on the landing, who are arguing about an arrest. Lenny gets a jump on me and I have to jog to catch up.

'I'm not saying you're wrong. All the evidence points to Foley. He drugged Maya. He took her home. He sexually assaulted her. Rohan Kirk woke up and found them. Foley panicked and killed him. Everything fits except . . .' We have reached the double doors.

'Except what?' asks Lenny.

'I can't understand why he'd wear gloves to avoid leaving fingerprints, but not care about leaving his semen on the sofa and on Maya's dress. Isn't that a bit amateur-hour?'

'It's like you said, he panicked.'

'Yes, but he didn't run. He stayed in the house. He cleaned himself up. He managed to get a semi-conscious woman to his van. He went home, dropped off his phone, and then took Maya somewhere quiet, where he kept her for two days. Somewhere secret, where he bound her in a very particular way. He fed her. He gave her water. He cut off her hair. Was that always his plan, do you think?'

'I don't know if he had a plan,' says Lenny, through clenched teeth. 'I think he made it up as he went along.'

'Or he's telling the truth.'

Lenny scoffs, 'You think someone else showed up at the house and took her away? How unlucky can one girl be? Meeting a pervert and a killer in the same night.'

She's right – it defies logic – yet so many aspects of the crime make no sense.

Upstairs, Hoyle addresses the task force, knowing the job is only half done.

'Important questions have to be answered. Where did Anders Foley keep Maya Kirk? Where did she die? Was he acting alone? Fumigate this guy. I don't want him crawling away and hiding under some rock. Am I understood?'

The affirmation is unanimous and then someone shouts, 'Who's buying?'

'Who do you think?' says Hoyle, and another cheer goes up.

Lenny looks at me and makes a drinking motion.

'Next time,' I say, glancing at my phone. I promised Evie that I'd be home. I feel like I've been neglecting her; and I know that she's worried about Elias coming to live with us.

When I reach the top of the stairs, I hear Hoyle calling my name.

'Before you go, I want to apologise about some of the things I said earlier – my behaviour. Arresting you. It wasn't my finest moment.'

'That's perfectly OK. It was understandable.'

'You did good work today.'

'Thank you.'

I descend the stairs and pass through the charge room, glancing up to see a girl sitting on a plastic chair with a Labrador lying at her feet. I carry on for two more steps before I realise who it is.

Evie raises her head and groans.

36

Evie

I hate the way Cyrus looks at me when he's disappointed. He has these wet brown eyes like those baby harp seals that get clubbed to death in Canada because rich women like to wear dead things. I wish someone would club me.

Without a word, he takes the chair next to me. Poppy sniffs at his pockets, hoping he's brought some food. Cyrus cradles her head in his hands and rubs behind her ears. I want him to do that to me – not rub my ears, but look at me like that, with nothing but love, without asking questions.

'I made a mistake,' I say.

'OK. I'm listening.'

'I was trying to help Mitch, but I misjudged the situation.'

'How?'

'Well, I thought if I could find the person who accused him. And if she changed her story . . . If she realised . . .'

At that moment I look up and see Mitch being led into the charge room. Handcuffed. Head down. He has a bruise on his cheek. The officer pushes him roughly towards a bench, telling him to sit.

Without thinking, I'm on my feet, shouting, 'Let him go! He didn't do anything wrong.'

Cyrus wraps his arms around me, pulling me back.

'No! Please. This is my fault,' I yell.

Mitch glances up and away again. The arresting officer talks to the sergeant, 'Mitchell Coates. Resisting arrest. Breaching parole. He's going back inside.'

Cyrus has lifted me off the ground, my feet are wheeling in mid-air. He's talking in my ear. Telling me I'm making things worse.

'It wasn't Mitch. It was me. Please. Help him.'

'Not like this, Evie. Quiet now.'

My legs stop churning and my muscles relax and my eyes splinter with tears.

'You wait here,' he says, making me sit on a chair.

He crosses the room to where Mitch is being processed. I hear some of their conversation and lip-read the rest, or maybe I'm putting words into their mouths.

'I don't know what they're talking about,' says Mitch. 'I haven't been near Lilah. I don't even know where she lives now.'

Cyrus glances back at me. I can't meet his eyes.

Mitch is photographed and fingerprinted. An officer yells that the prison transport is coming. Cyrus returns. He expects me to make excuses or to push back, but I have no defence.

'Mitch didn't send me there. I found the address. I wanted to see if she was lying.'

'That doesn't matter, Evie. It's not allowed. You can't identify or approach the victim of a sexual assault.'

'But she only *thinks* Mitch attacked her. She's not sure.'

'She is protected. Nothing changes that.'

Mitch is being led away. His boots still have grass stains from our garden. His jeans are speckled with paint from the side gate.

'What's going to happen?' I ask.

'He'll serve the rest of his sentence.'

'Can he appeal?'

'There is no appeal process. All he can do is make representations to the parole board.'

'When?'

'I don't know.'

'What if I make a statement?'

'It won't matter.'

'Because nobody believes me.'

Cyrus wants to deny it, but he knows that it's true. Nobody trusts what I tell them because 'I can't lie straight in bed' – his words not mine. What if I don't want to be straight? I'm not an arrow, or a road or a ruler. Being bent is less boring.

'Come on,' says Cyrus, taking Poppy by the collar.

'Where are we going?'

'Home.'

Sometimes, when my world is washed in grey, I go to dark places in my mind. Lonely places. Cruel places. The only way to escape this is to hide; to discover somewhere no bigger than a crawlspace, where nobody can find me. I push boxes aside and squeeze between crates and old furniture in the attic, before curling up on a bedspread that smells of mothballs and mildew. Closing my eyes, I listen to the ticks and wheezes of the radiator, the cars that pass outside, the voices of children in the park. Time slows down. Time stops. And my skin registers the fall in temperature as it grows dark outside.

Next to me, on the narrow sill of the attic window, I have my most precious things – the button from my mother's coat and my collection of coloured glass that looks like gemstones. When I hold the button in my fist, I can remember what my mother looked like and the sound of her voice and how she smelled.

She was wearing that coat when I last saw her. I clung to

her, and they had to prise my fingers apart. It was only later, when I opened my hand, that I saw the button, which must have come loose in the struggle.

A creak on the stairs. A gentle knock.

'Are you hungry?' asks Cyrus.

'No.'

'I made pasta.'

Silence fills every corner. I wait to hear his weight on the stairs, but he's still there. A moment later, a box slides aside and I see his face.

'Leave me alone, please.'

'This is cosy,' he replies, squeezing in beside me. He sits with his back against the wall, hugging his knees. His socked feet almost touch mine. We sit like that for a long while, listening to each other breathing.

'What's with the button?' he asks.

'It belonged to my mother.'

'You don't talk about her.'

'It won't bring her back.'

Silence. Breathing.

'Cyrus?'

'Yeah.'

'How long will Mitch have to serve?'

'Another two years.'

That's how much I have cost him. Two years of hating me, of cursing my name.

'Sometimes I wish I was dead,' I say.

'Don't say that.'

'Everyone would be better off.'

'Not me.'

'Why?'

'Because I think you are the most fascinating, challenging, infuriating, exciting, unknowable person that I've ever met, and I want to see how you turn out.'

'What if this is how I turn out?'

'Well, that would be just fine.'

I gaze into his face, looking for the lie, but can't see one. Maybe I'm not so good at picking them. Maybe he's getting better at hiding them.

I am weeping now, head down, hands over my eyes.

'Evie?'

I can't answer.

'Evie, listen to me.'

I feel him shuffle closer and his hand touches my head and strokes my hair.

'You are the bravest person I've ever met. You have been forged by fire. Don't give up, OK? Never give up.'

He leans forward and wraps his arms around me, pulling my head against his chest.

'You deserve to be loved, Evie Cormac. Believe what I say.'

37

Cyrus

It is still early when I arrive at the Arncliffe Centre, where the East Midlands Forensic Services shares laboratory space with a private company that does CSI analysis for five different police forces across the Midlands.

Cassie Wright meets me at the reception desk. She's dressed in jeans and a fitted white blouse and cowboy boots that make her almost as tall as me. Her hair is pulled back into a ponytail and she's wearing tortoiseshell glasses. She touches them self-consciously.

'Usually I wear contacts, but I forgot to take them out last night,' she says.

'You were celebrating.'

'Where were you? I thought you'd be there.'

'I'm not much of a drinker.'

'Neither am I.'

I notice the paracetamol on her desk and a can of fizzy drink. At that moment Craig Dyson puts his head around the door but doesn't see me.

'Hey, where did you disappear to last night?'

Cassie hushes him and nods towards me.

'Oh, Dr Haven. I didn't realise you were here.'

'Officially, I'm not,' I reply. 'And call me Cyrus.'

Dyson nods and addresses Cassie. 'How are you feeling?'

'Like death.'

'Me too. Have you seen Voigt?'

'No.'

'He was supposed to finish up those tests on Foley's van.'

'Maybe he's still in the garage. Do you want me to fetch him?'

'Thanks.'

'Dr Haven was looking for some information – can you help him?'

Dyson nods and takes a seat at Cassie's desk. We both watch her through the open door, as she walks along the corridor and pushes through swinging doors.

'Are you two together?' I ask.

'Not really. It's complicated.'

'You're married.' I motion to his wedding ring. He looks at his left hand.

'Separated. Waiting for the papers to be signed.' He glances again at the door, as if worried that she might be listening. 'Cassie's sister died a few weeks ago. Cancer. She's putting on a brave face, but I know she's hurting. Sometimes you wonder why the best of people get the worst of luck.'

He borrows her soft drink and takes a swig.

'How can I help you, Cyrus?'

'There was a sexual assault case seven years ago. A woman was attacked in her flat. Her neighbour was convicted. Portland Road, Nottingham.'

'I remember,' says Dyson. 'I was the crime scene manager.'

'Would you still have the photographs?'

'Maybe.'

He snaps his thumb and forefinger. 'Is this about the hair?'

'Pardon?'

'The victim had her head shaved.'

I must be looking at him blankly.

'The victim – I can't remember her name – had her head shaved, just like Maya Kirk. They arrested the upstairs neighbour. His fingerprints were all over her flat and we found his DNA on the pillowcase. From memory, we also found evidence in his flat – a piece of jewellery.'

Dyson has been typing at a computer. He pulls up another series of files, which contain the photographs. There are general pictures of the bedroom, entrance hall and living areas. The images show the bed and the pillowcase used to cover Lilah's head, as well as her nursing uniform, which was cut from her body.

'These were taken at the hospital,' he says, pulling up a new series of images. They show Lilah's injuries. Without hair she looks like a vandalised shop mannequin, with overly large eyes that are bruised and red-rimmed. Maya's hair had been removed using clippers, shaved close to her scalp, but Lilah's locks were hacked off crudely, so that tufts remain above her ears.

'What did he use?' I ask.

'Scissors or a blade,' says Dyson. 'We didn't find the implement. He must have disposed of it, or hid it too well.'

'But not the earring.'

'That could have been an oversight.' Dyson is still reading. 'Coates was sentenced to eight years' jail. He should still be inside.'

'He was released on parole two weeks ago.'

The information ignites Dyson's interest. 'Do you know where he is?'

'He was rearrested yesterday and sent back to prison for breaching his parole conditions.'

Dyson is calculating the dates.

'Does Hoyle know? He ran the earlier investigation. It was before he went to the NCA.'

'I don't think Mitchell Coates is involved in Maya's death,' I say.

'Yes, but you can't ignore the similarities. The hair. The ropes . . .'

I pull my chair closer to the screen. 'Do you have a record of the exhibits?'

Dyson types in another search. 'This is a list of the items that were tendered to the court by the prosecution.'

It includes the pillowcase, a length of rope, the earring and the nurse's uniform.

'Where was the earring found?' I ask.

'In the filter of the washing machine.'

I look again at the list. 'The rope used in the attack. Where would it be now?'

'The trial was eight years ago. The exhibits were most likely destroyed unless RRD protocols deemed them necessary.'

'RRD?'

'Review, retention and disposal. If they were kept, they'd be at an archive in the city.'

'If we could find that rope, could you compare it to the one used to bind Maya Kirk?'

He nods. 'We can test the organic make-up, along with the weave and fibres. There's even a knot expert in Oxford, who can tell if the knot-tier was left- or right-handed.'

My phone is vibrating. It's a call from Dr Baillie at Rampton. My heart sinks.

'I have to take this,' I say, excusing myself and walking into the corridor.

Dr Baillie is quick to reassure me. 'Elias is fine. I wanted to make an appointment to visit your home.'

'Why?'

'Your brother has requested a weekend visit.'

'Has it been approved?'

'Yes, but I wanted to talk to you first. Can you be home this afternoon? Four o'clock?'

'You know my address.'

'Of course.'

38

Evie

Another cruel morning. People stop talking when I enter the classroom. It's like someone has flicked a switch. I walk between desks to the back of the room, knowing they're pulling faces and sharing some inside joke at my expense. Despite what Cyrus thinks, I've tried to make friends, but whenever I say something, they look at me like I'm stupid or speaking another language. Somehow, instinctively, they know that I'm different. That I haven't had the same experiences.

I barely slept last night. I kept thinking of Mitch lying in a prison cell, hating me with all his strength, wishing he'd never met me. They shattered his leg last time. Now he faces two more years of trying to stay safe. Cyrus told me about something called Blackstone's ratio, named after some dead English judge, who said it was better for ten guilty people to go free than for one innocent person to be wrongly imprisoned. I bet you couldn't get ten people to agree on that. Most would choose to lock them all up because they can't imagine that sort of mistake would ever happen to them. Everybody gets what they deserve, even the unlucky ones.

Miss Harmsworth, my maths teacher, is handing back our

test papers. In the bottom right corner of the last page, circled in red, is an 'A'. There is a message: *Well, done, Evie*, and a smiley face. I've never had an 'A' before. I'm usually a shaky D or a fail.

'Only one student answered question twelve correctly,' she says. 'Well done, Evie.'

People turn to stare at me. Someone mutters 'muff-diver' and I hear the guffaws. Someone else says 'bean-flicker'. I don't know what that means, but some of the boys think Miss Harmsworth is gay because she shares a house with Miss Bottari, the head of drama, who is really pretty. I've seen them arrive at school together, car pooling. Maybe they're just housemates, but the boys like making crude comments.

After my classes, I avoid hanging around because nobody wants to talk to me. My car is in the teachers' parking area because I was running late this morning. I've given the Mini a name – Mouse – and managed to fix the radio by using a coat hanger as an aerial. As I unlock the door, I hear Miss Bottari.

'Excuse me, but you're a student and you're not supposed to park here.'

'I have special permission,' I say, tossing my bag onto the passenger seat. 'On account of my disability.'

Her eyebrow lifts. 'Really? And what would that be?'

'I have macular degeneration.' I have no idea what that means, but it sounds like a serious medical condition.

'Should you be driving?' she asks.

'Yeah. It's totally fine.'

'You don't wear glasses.'

'My oncologist says I don't need them.'

'You mean your ophthalmologist?'

'Yeah.'

'Or maybe your optometrist?'

She knows I'm lying now, but I decide to distract her by

asking her about the school musical which I know she's casting because she's been pleading for volunteers at every school assembly.

'*Little Shop of Horrors*. Are you thinking of auditioning?'

'Oh, I can't sing.'

'You could dance.'

'I'm a triple non-threat.'

'Oh, I think you can act, Evie,' she says. 'You're very convincing.' She turns away. 'Tomorrow, park somewhere else.'

'Yes, miss.'

I drive straight home, eager to show Cyrus my maths paper because I don't normally have anything to brag about. As I come through the front door, I yell his name, but stop abruptly when I reach the kitchen. We have a visitor, a skinny guy with a short-trimmed beard and a retro ponytail that makes him look like a paedo.

'This is Dr Baillie,' Cyrus says. 'He's from Rampton.'

Another shrink.

Poppy is whining and scratching at the door.

'Why is she locked outside?'

'I'm allergic to dogs,' says Dr Baillie, getting to his feet. I'm not used to gentlemanly gestures and immediately step back.

'This is Evie,' says Cyrus. 'She is my lodger.'

That's a new one. My status seems to be changing by the day.

'Elias said you had a young lady staying,' says Dr Baillie.

'How was school?' asks Cyrus.

'Same old,' I reply. I'm not going to boast about my maths paper in front of a stranger. I dump my tote bag on the table, rattling cups.

'Elias is going to visit again,' says Cyrus.

'For how long?'

'The weekend, maybe longer.'

'When?'

'He'll come on Friday,' says Dr Baillie. 'I'm checking on how things went last time. Did you get to meet Elias?'

I nod.

'What was your impression?'

Creepy as fuck, I want to say, but Cyrus is listening. 'He was OK. A bit intense.'

'Did he make you feel uncomfortable?'

'Not especially.'

'Elias will take time to adjust. We have female employees at Rampton, but he hasn't spent much time with them, certainly not someone your age, not one-on-one.'

'Will I be one-on-one?' I ask.

'Elias won't be chaperoned on his next visit. He will be wearing an electronic monitor and be subject to geographic limits and a curfew.'

'What curfew?' asks Cyrus.

'He won't be able to leave the house unaccompanied, and he will have to be at this address by ten every evening. There will also be mandatory drug and alcohol tests. He'll be expected to collect his medications and look after his own meals, laundry and other chores. Up until now, these things have been done for him.

'The main thing is to prepare yourself for the long haul,' says the doctor. 'These first few visits are just one small part of Elias re-entering society. He might need further counselling and he will face lifelong hurdles to readjust, to find a job and a place to live. For him to succeed, he'll need your support.'

'He has that,' says Cyrus.

I don't say anything.

'You should brace yourself for some degree of conflict,' says Dr Baillie.

'What sort of conflict?' I ask.

'You may find that Elias struggles with the simplest things. He's been out of society for twenty years. The Internet was in its infancy when he went into Rampton. Smartphones and streaming services and social media didn't exist. The world has changed, and he hasn't been part of that change.

'This may frustrate him, at first, and upset his routines. At Rampton, his life was very regimented – he knew where he had to be at any given hour – but he will find freedom more difficult. Making decisions. Bearing the consequences. I suggest you make sure he gets plenty of rest and that he continues taking his medications.'

'And if he doesn't?' I ask.

'That would not be good.'

Dr Baillie doesn't elaborate. Instead, he continues, 'Loneliness could be another issue. Right now, Elias is surrounded by people, but when he gets here, he will find that sometimes he is home alone. The absence of people and the silence will be deafening to him.'

'How do we fix that?' asks Cyrus.

'You should try to keep him busy. Give him chores. Talk to him. Make him feel needed.'

A part of me wants to push back. Why should Cyrus have to do these things? Why should I be included?

'You should also avoid creating any trigger events. Elias knows exactly what he did, but I suggest you remove any photographs or items that might remind him of his past actions.'

'Like sharp objects,' I say, trying to make a joke. It falls flat.

Dr Baillie presses on. 'Elias will have idealised what being released will be like. And he will have forgotten how hard day-to-day life can be. You need to remember that he will always be a schizophrenic. Properly medicated, he can lead a relatively normal life; his behaviour can be tempered, his triggers deactivated, but there will be bumps along the way when his anxiety and paranoia may spike. Bumps, not cliffs.'

'Good to hear,' I say, earning a look from Cyrus.

Dr Baillie smiles and stands. 'All being well, we'll deliver him at four on Friday afternoon.'

Cyrus walks him out, while I go to the back garden and

throw a ball to Poppy, bouncing it off the wall. Later, I carry my schoolbooks upstairs and do an hour of homework, not bothering to show Cyrus my maths paper. It doesn't seem to matter any more.

39

Cyrus

The police property stores warehouse looks like something built during the Second World War with red-brick chimneys and iron downpipes that are rusting in patches where the paint has bubbled and peeled away. The cavernous interior has been broken up by rows of shelves reaching to the rafters where cobwebs glow silver beneath the skylights.

The property officer is a sergeant who introduces himself as Theo. He has ginger hair and a tattoo of a tiger on his right forearm where his shirt is rolled to his elbow. We're both wearing hi-vis vests and hard hats and I've had to sign a safety disclaimer in case a box falls on my head.

I get the impression that Theo doesn't get many visitors as he eagerly escorts me down a long aisle, triggering lights as we pass, telling me how he helped design the system.

'How long have you worked here?' I ask.

'Sixteen years. Other police forces are following us – they come here to learn.'

This section of the warehouse has cages of meshed steel that are chained and padlocked.

'Everything must be labelled and packaged properly,' he

explains. 'Banknotes in a money envelope. Sharp instruments in knife tubes. Hypodermic needles in a sharps' container. Drugs in a self-seal drug bag. Clothing, bedding and footwear are kept in paper sacks, unless they're stained with body fluids, which means they're marked with health hazard tape.'

We turn a corner and I feel as though I'm getting lost in a maze.

'We have regular audit checks to make sure nothing impor-tant has gone missing – the dangerous and valuable stuff, firearms or drugs.' He turns to talk over his shoulder. 'We once had a diamond in here worth over half a million pounds. Belonged to a duchess who had it nicked from her stately home. Turned out to be her daughter. Families, eh?'

Theo doesn't wait for me to answer. We have reached his office, which is tucked in a corner of the warehouse and smells of sugared biscuits and coffee grounds. On a large table beneath the window there is a miniature landscape of papier-mâché hills and valleys, upon which there are legions of hand-painted lead soldiers doing battle. There are knights, archers, axemen, pikemen, vassals, retainers, swordsmen, mercenaries and cross-bowmen.

'I collect them,' says Theo. 'I don't have enough room at home, and nobody bothers me here.'

I lean over the table. 'What battle?'

'Hastings.'

'Where's King Harold?'

He points to a figure who is standing defiantly, brandishing a shield and an axe, surrounded by his enemies.

'He's a goner,' I say.

'You can't change history.'

Theo goes to his computer and types in a search, using the information I've given him.

'OK, we have the statements, CPS briefing papers, photo-graphs and – yes – the exhibits,' he says, pulling up the reference numbers. 'One item was returned to the victim – a piece of jewellery.' He pauses to read on. 'An application was made to dispose of the rest two years ago. Nothing was done.'

'Who made the application?'

'Doesn't say. The police most likely.'

Theo prints out the reference sheet and leads me back into the warehouse.

'We have an eponymous law in this place, you know, like Murphy's Law?'

'Anything that can go wrong, will go wrong.'

'Exactly. We have Theodore's Law. The box you want will be on the highest shelf, in the hardest place to reach.'

He has been counting down the aisles, before pulling a ladder into place. He climbs. I watch from below. Theo has clearly done this before. When he reaches the highest shelf he asks me to push the ladder a few feet to the right. It moves on wheels. He reaches for a box and checks the label.

'This is it.'

Lifting the sealed box onto a platform next to his feet, he lowers it with a pulley, before climbing down to join me. He slices it open with a retractable blade.

'What exactly are you looking for?'

'A length of soft hemp rope.'

He consults the printed page. 'Exhibit eleven.'

One by one, he takes items from the box, setting them out on an empty lower shelf. A pillowcase. Bedding. The remnants of a nursing uniform, trousers and a blouse that were cut from Lilah Hooper's body.

'That's odd,' he says, gazing into the empty box. 'It's not here.'

'Why would that be?'

'No idea. It's on the list. Exhibit eleven. It was tendered in court.'

'Who else has access to the archives?'

'Police. Lawyers. People like yourself.'

'When was it last opened?'

I follow Theo back to his office, where he sits at his computer screen, calling up the visitor logs.

'You're the first person to request these files since they arrived here.'

'Maybe somebody entered the wrong details,' I say.

Theo looks aggrieved. It's as though I've found a flaw in his perfect battle plan – a missing soldier in the massed ranks of his infantry and history might have to be rewritten.

Suddenly, he has an idea and rolls his chair across the floor to a different computer.

'Gotcha!' he says, triumphantly. 'My colleague Derek is notoriously slow at updating the visitors' log. He made a note but didn't complete the application form.'

I lean closer. 'You're telling me someone took the rope.'

'It happened yesterday. Another request. They viewed the material but there's no record of them removing any item.'

'Who was it?'

'Hold on. It was someone from the East Midlands Forensic Services.'

'Craig Dyson?'

'No. Stephen Voigt.'

40

Evie

I'm ten minutes late for work and Brando treats it like a hanging offence, threatening to dock my pay if it happens again. The others seem pleased to see me. Eric is unpacking glasses from the dishwasher. I reach past him and take a packet of peanuts from the shelf and tell him to put it on my tab.

'You don't have a tab.'

I blow him a kiss. 'Start one.'

'Is that the only outfit you own?' asks Brando. I'm wearing the same black jumpsuit that Cyrus bought me.

'What's wrong with it?'

'You wear it every night.'

'Maybe it's a different one.'

'Is it?'

'You shouldn't make demands on female staff that don't apply to the men. Look at what Eric is wearing.'

The bartender is dressed in stone-washed jeans and a Rolling Stones T-shirt.

'That's different,' says Brando.

'Why?'

He tries to think of an answer but isn't quick enough or

can't be bothered to argue. Instead, he tells me to check the loo rolls and soap dispensers. I pick up supplies from the kitchen, stealing a taste of the tapas meatballs that are simmering on the stove. The chef swears at me. He swears at everyone. He says I remind him of his daughter, who lives in Scotland, but she doesn't visit him very often because her boyfriend is terrified of him. I don't blame him.

Back in the bar, I notice a middle-aged woman pushing her phone under Eric's nose.

'No, love, I haven't seen her,' he says. He yells to Brando. 'There's a lady here who is looking for her daughter. Says she was in here on Friday night.'

Brando is carrying a crate of beers up the basement steps. He pauses to look at the phone and shrugs. The woman is wearing a mumsy floral dress and trainers. She looks vaguely familiar.

'It's my daughter,' she says. 'She was here with some friends. Nobody has seen her since.'

Brando is restocking the fridge.

'The police aren't interested because she hasn't been missing for long enough,' says the woman.

'Long enough for what?' I ask, moving closer.

'To be called a missing person.'

I look at the picture on her phone and my heart somersaults.

'Daniela,' I say. Even as the word comes out, I want to catch it in mid-air and swallow it again. I look at Brando. 'She threw up in the loos. Remember?'

Brando seems to find the memory. 'We sent her home.'

'She ordered a car. I saw her leave,' I say.

'Who was she with?' asks the woman.

'Nobody.'

She looks like she's going to cry. 'She was supposed to come to lunch on Saturday. She hasn't called. And she didn't go to work on Monday. She never misses a shift.'

I see similarities between mother and daughter, the eyebrows

214

and hairline, the shape of her nose. She talks quickly. 'She lives with a couple of her friends. Nurses. They were together on Friday night. They were going dancing. The others went ahead. Daniela was supposed to join them. Did you talk to her? Was she sick? I've called the hospitals. The police think Daniela must have gone home with someone she met – a date, I mean – but she has a boyfriend and she wouldn't miss work.'

I tell her about finding Daniela's phone and helping her outside. As I'm talking, she calls someone called Harriet and relays the information word for word.

'Do you remember anything about the car?' she asks.

'No. It was a normal car. The driver took her to Stapleford.'

'Why?'

'That was her address.'

'No. That's where I live. Daniela hasn't lived at home for two years. She shares a house in Rylands with Harriet and Alissa.'

'But her driver's licence,' I say, less certain than before. The fluttering in my stomach has become a sick feeling.

'I'm going to call someone. Wait here.'

Brando follows me into the kitchen. 'What are you doing?'

'Her daughter is missing.'

'She's probably run off with some guy.'

'That was the same night as the police came in, asking questions about Maya Kirk.'

'Who?'

'The woman who was murdered.'

'That had nothing to do with us,' says Brando. 'And they caught that guy. This is a random drunk girl who didn't call her mum.'

'She was here.'

'And then she left.'

We're speaking in loud whispers. Faces close. Arguing. My finger is hovering over the phone.

'I don't want any cops. It's bad for business.'

He grabs my wrist. I jerk my hand away and summon the first name on my contacts list – the only one that matters. I press the green button.

Moments later, I'm outside on the crowded footpath alongside Daniela's mother.

'Did you just lose your job?' she asks, shocked.

'He's an arsehole.'

'Who are you calling?'

'A friend. He'll know what to do.'

41

Cyrus

Lying on a padded bench, my feet braced apart, I grip the bar above my chest and concentrate on a small water mark on the ceiling that is shaped like an elephant. Three short breaths and I lift. The bar doesn't want to move at first, but slowly it begins to rise until my arms straighten. Three more breaths and I lower it towards my chest and lift it again. Sweat prickles, beading the birds that are tattooed on my skin.

Eight . . . nine . . . ten. When I cannot hold the weight any longer, I force myself to go on. I will not break. I will not fail.

This is what I do when I need to think, or to forget. Elias is getting out. I keep saying that he's 'coming home' but this isn't his home. It belonged to our grandparents. They gave it to me. Does he deserve half of this? Half of me?

I grew up without a family. I was the boy who survived. Set apart. Shunned. And when I grew tired of people pitying me, or whispering behind my back, I gave them something else to talk about. I drank. I took drugs. I cut myself. I stole. I vandalised. That's why I can forgive Evie her mistakes. I have been in the back of that police car, being delivered home after some new destructive misadventure.

My phone is vibrating. Speak of the devil.

'I need you,' she says. 'Someone else is missing.'

Headlights reflect on the dew-covered lawns of Stapleford. The two-storey brick houses all look the same, especially in darkness, each with a small front garden fenced off by hedges or wooden pickets. I find the number. Evie answers the door. A woman is standing behind her under the light.

'This is Mrs Linares,' says Evie. 'Her daughter is Daniela.'

The small sitting room has too many pieces of furniture competing for space with a large flat-screen TV. The curtains match the sofa, which are matched by the cushions, which are the colours of the cut flowers on the mantelpiece.

Mrs Linares apologises about the mess. The place looks spotless.

'I had to downsize after my husband left me,' she explains. 'I couldn't decide what to leave behind, or to sell.'

'When did you separate?' I ask.

'Oh, we've been divorced for eight years,' she says, looking around the room. 'I guess that makes me a hoarder.'

Evie tells me about meeting Daniela in the bar and helping her outside. Mrs Linares picks up the story, speaking in a rush. I make her slow down. Relax. Remember. Daniela hadn't come home on Friday night. She missed work on Monday, without calling in sick; and she hasn't answered her phone in four days.

'I called the police first thing Monday morning. They said I should go to my nearest police station and file a missing person's report. A sergeant took down my details, but I don't think they're taking it seriously. He said I should call her friends. I've done that. I've contacted the hospitals, clinics, shelters . . .'

'Does she have a boyfriend?'

'Martyn. He's lovely. He keeps asking her to marry him, but Daniela says she's not ready. I don't know what she's waiting for. Good men don't come along like buses.'

Aren't buses supposed to come all at once, I think, but say nothing.

'Where was Martyn on Friday?' asks Cyrus.

'On a rugby tour in Wales. He came back on Tuesday. Since then, he's been helping me make phone calls.'

'Has Daniela ever gone missing before? Dropped out of sight for a few days?'

'Never.'

'You talked to her housemates.'

'Harriet and Alissa. They all work together at St Jude's. They're worried sick. They were with Daniela on Friday night, but they left the bar early to queue outside the nightclub. Daniela said she'd be right behind them.'

'And you told the police this?'

'Of course.'

I've been making notes on my phone. Evie is hovering, waiting for some sign from me that she hasn't panicked for no reason. Everything Mrs Linares has said must be the truth, or Evie would know otherwise.

'I'll need a photograph of Daniela,' I say. 'More than one, if you have them.'

She opens a cabinet and pulls a photo album from one of the drawers. As she turns the pages, old memories surface and she grows more distressed.

'This was taken at a friend's birthday last year.'

The photograph shows Daniela raising a glass of champagne towards the camera, smiling cheekily.

'How do I get in touch with Harriet and Alissa?'

Mrs Linares provides me with their numbers. The photo album is still open on the coffee table. One of the images shows Daniela in a nurse's uniform, alongside two colleagues.

'That was taken on her first shift at St Jude's,' she explains. 'I keep thinking of poor Maya. It was dreadful what happened to her and her father. But they caught him, didn't they – the man responsible?'

I blink at her in surprise. 'Did you know Maya?'

'Daniela did.' She points to the photograph. 'That's Maya there. They studied nursing together.'

I look more closely at the picture. Maya is in her early twenties, with blonde highlights in her hair and laughter in her eyes. She's standing, hands on hips, pointing her toe at the camera and pouting.

Mrs Linares has found another photograph – a birthday celebration with Daniela kneeling on a chair, leaning forward to blow out candles on a cake. Maya is next to her, filming on her phone.

The room seems to suddenly tilt.

'Daniela was so upset when she heard the news,' says Mrs Linares. 'We all were.'

'When did she last see Maya?' I ask, stunned by the connection.

'Not for ages.'

'Months?'

'Years.'

The Swiss psychoanalyst Carl Jung coined the term 'synchronicity' to describe events that seem more than coincidental. We've all experienced them. Thinking about someone we haven't thought about in years and suddenly the phone rings, or we bump into them in a supermarket, or we hear the news that they've died, or been hurt. We often see these events as having special meaning, somehow believing they are beyond cause and effect. It's the reason that some people believe in God or star signs, or that our fates are predetermined.

I am not one of them. We do not live in a supremely ordered world where every occurrence or action serves some purpose. The pattern of a bird through the sky, or a beam of light breaking through clouds at a critical moment, or the overhearing of a chance remark – these are only significant because we give them meaning or imagine they're part of some greater grand design. Sometimes, an unlikely event is just a coincidence, or God's way of remaining anonymous.

Not this time.

42

Evie

I'm jogging to keep up with Cyrus as he crosses the lawn, leaving footprints in the dew.

'Where are we going?'

'The police.'

'Now?'

'I wish it were sooner.'

Cyrus calls Lenny Parvel on the journey. The shadows of streetlights slide across the bonnet and over my face.

'Another woman has gone missing,' he says. 'Daniela Linares. Nobody has seen her since Friday night when she left a bar in the Lace Market. I have a witness who says Daniela's drink may have been spiked.' Cyrus glances at me.

'People go missing all the time,' says Lenny, who sounds half asleep.

'This one knew Maya Kirk.'

Now he has her full attention. Lenny is thinking out loud. 'Foley wasn't arrested until Monday afternoon. Where are you now?'

'On my way to Radford Road.'

'I'll meet you there.'

'What about Hoyle?'

'I'll wake him.'

The call ends and Cyrus keeps asking me questions, wanting the whole story – right down to what Daniela was wearing, and who she might have met or spoken to.

'She was sitting at a table near the front windows. There was a group of them.'

'Women or men?'

'I can't remember. The place was crowded.'

'What time did her friends leave?'

Again, I can't tell him. Daniela had vomited in the loo. I was sent to clean it up. She said it was something she ate.

'Who ordered her a car?'

'She had an account. I helped her.'

'She could walk steadily?'

'Yes.'

'And she could talk?'

'Of course. Otherwise, I would have called an ambulance. I helped her outside. When the driver arrived, he used her name. I asked him if he knew where to go. He said Stapleford. That was the address on her driver's licence, but not where she lived.'

'You think someone took her phone and read her licence?'

'Yes, but how would he know Daniela was going to order a car?'

'Perhaps he didn't. Maybe he planned to follow her home.'

At the police station, Cyrus buys me a machine hot chocolate that tastes of sugar rather than cocoa. The sergeant in the charge room recognises me and raises an eyebrow, as if to say, 'Back again so soon?'

Lenny is equally surprised, until Cyrus explains that I'm the witness. Before he can explain, a male voice booms down the corridor, shouting at a cleaner for leaving a mop and bucket in the middle of the floor.

Hoyle appears. Pillow marks crease his face and he's dressed in a khaki shirt, baggy jeans and boat shoes that reveal bare ankles below the cuffs.

'This had better be good,' he announces.

We meet in Lenny's office. I sit nearest the door, hoping to hide, and only look up when my name is mentioned. Hoyle turns out to be one of those loud, opinionated men, who uses swear words as adjectives and punctuation marks. Mr Joubert would be proud of that analogy. He'd be proud that I know what analogy means.

'You don't even know if this woman is missing,' says Hoyle. 'She could be shacked up with some new bloke.'

'Daniela has never missed a shift at St Jude's,' says Cyrus. 'Monday was the first time. She hasn't answered her phone in four days. No calls. No texts.'

'Give it to the uniforms to investigate.'

'Daniela and Maya knew each other. They studied nursing together.'

'Maya wasn't a nurse.'

'She used to be.'

Hoyle dismisses it as a coincidence.

'Maya Kirk didn't disappear from a bar. She was taken from home. And you have no evidence Daniela Linares was drugged.'

'She told Evie that she'd barely had anything to drink.'

Hoyle swings his gaze to me. He takes a moment to size me up and I can feel his eyes on my skin. 'A little birdie tells me that you approached and harassed a sexual assault victim.'

I know he's baiting me. I bite my tongue.

'I also hear that you stole someone's identity and catfished women on a dating app.'

Cyrus tries to interrupt, but Hoyle isn't finished.

'Is it true you're a pathological liar?'

'Is it true you're an arsehole?' I reply.

Hoyle smiles.

'Can we get back to Daniela?' says Lenny, who has been quiet up until now. 'Look at the timeline. Foley wasn't arrested until Monday.'

Hoyle seems to chew over the details, reluctant to decide. 'Contact the rideshare company. See who picked her up and where he dropped her off.'

'What about the task force?'

'I'm not committing resources until I'm sure that she's missing.'

Cyrus interrupts. 'Maya Kirk was alive for two days before she was killed. What if Daniela is in the same place?'

'If she is, we'll find her, but right now, you don't have enough.'

'You want to see her body?'

Hoyle's top lip curls and his face reddens. He takes a deep breath. Maybe he's silently counting down from ten, or repeating some mantra in his head. That's what Cyrus does when he's angry.

'You know the problem with psychologists,' says Hoyle. 'They always assume they're the smartest person in every room when they're not even the smartest in their own family. How is your brother? Poorly, I hope.'

Hoyle gets to his feet and strides down the corridor, his loose-fitting boating shoes flapping against his heels. The silence he leaves behind is like a smell.

'Who put a chainsaw up his arse?' I ask, earning a look from Cyrus. 'What? The guy is a muppet.'

Lenny tries to stop herself smiling. 'I won't criticise Hoyle for wanting more evidence.'

She picks up a spray bottle, aiming the nozzle at the leaves of an African violet on the window sill.

'Tell me, Evie, what did DCI Hoyle mean when he said you approached a sexual assault victim?'

I glance at Cyrus. He holds a finger to his lips, wanting me to be quiet. He answers.

'Do you remember a case a few years ago – the sexual assault of a nurse in Portland Road? Her neighbour was convicted – Mitchell Coates.'

Lenny pauses, bottle in hand. Her mouth opens in surprise. 'She had her hair cut off.'

'Same as Maya Kirk,' says Cyrus. 'The rope bindings, the hacked hair.'

'Where is Coates now?' asks Lenny.

'He was released on parole in late October. Now he's back in prison.'

'When?'

'Monday.'

'Shit!'

'Mitch is innocent!' I blurt, ignoring my promise to Cyrus. 'He's done nothing wrong.'

Lenny ignores me. 'You should have told Hoyle.'

'Forensics are comparing the rope used to bind Lilah Hooper with the rope found around Maya Kirk's wrists. That could establish a link between the two cases.'

'And put Mitchell Coates in the frame.'

What is Cyrus doing? He's making things worse.

'Did you ever have doubts about the Lilah Hooper case?' he asks.

'No.'

'She didn't see her attacker's face or hear his voice.'

'His DNA was all over her flat.'

'Because he looked after her dog, and he found her the next morning. He called the police. He gave a statement. He provided samples.'

'Because it made him look innocent.'

'Or he *was* innocent.'

The statement hangs in the air between them.

'Hoyle ran that investigation,' says Cyrus. 'He should have seen the similarities between the attack on Lilah Hooper and the murder of Maya Kirk – the hacked hair, the ropes . . . He didn't say anything.'

'The offences are eight years apart.'

'Even so, don't you think it's odd?'

'No. You're suggesting that a senior police officer withheld information, or deliberately misled an investigation.'

'I'm suggesting that Hoyle made a mistake.'

'A jury took less than twenty minutes to convict Coates.'

'And juries *never* get it wrong.'

The comment lights a fire in Lenny, who swallows her first attempt at a reply.

'Go home, Cyrus. We start again tomorrow.'

43

Cyrus

I wake before dawn with a warm body next to me. Evie's hair has fallen across her eyes and her lower lip trembles as she breathes. I don't remember her coming into my room and crawling into bed.

I try to move without waking her, but her eyes open.

'You can't keep doing this, Evie.'

'You were having a nightmare.'

'What?'

'Last night. I heard you moaning. I was going to wake you, but I couldn't remember if you're supposed to wake people or not.'

'That's sleepwalking.'

'Oh, yeah. Well, you were moaning in your sleep.'

'Are you making this up?'

'No.'

'Well, you shouldn't get into bed with me. We're friends, that's all.'

'Friends can share a bed. You're dressed. I'm dressed. Nothing happened.'

'Yes, but you shouldn't tempt people.'

She half sits up. 'Were you tempted?'

'No! Definitely not!'

'Why? Am I that disgusting?'

'That's not what I mean. But there's an age difference and a power imbalance and I don't want Elias thinking we're sleeping together.'

'What power imbalance? You're not my guardian, or my therapist, or my boss. You told Elias I was your lodger.'

'It's not up for discussion, Evie. Stay in your own bed.'

'Even when you have a nightmare?'

'Yes.'

My phone is buzzing on the side table. I reach for it. Fumbling. Answering.

Lenny in my ear. 'The rideshare service says Daniela Linares was a no-show.'

'But Evie put her in the car.'

'The driver turned up outside the bar, but nobody was waiting. He called Daniela's number and she didn't answer.'

Swinging my legs to the floor, I sit with my back to Evie, who rolls into the warm spot.

'Where was Foley?' I ask.

'Playing poker with his mates.'

'How solid is his alibi?'

'Pictures were posted on Instagram.'

'Someone else picked up Daniela. He knew her name.'

'Hoyle is talking about an accomplice,' says Lenny.

'It doesn't feel like two people,' I say, but logistically it might make more sense. Someone spiked Daniela's drink and took her mobile phone. A second person could have been waiting outside to pick her up or follow her home.

'We're looking at Foley's search history and social media feeds. He might have met someone in an online chatroom or forum,' says Lenny. 'Where was Mitchell Coates?'

I try to remember what Mitch told me. His landlady kicked him out of the boarding house. He was sleeping at a homeless shelter or on the streets. Either way, it makes him a suspect.

'You can trace his phone,' I say.

'We will be. Hoyle is briefing the task force at ten.'

'I can be there.'

'I think you should stay away. You antagonised him last night.'

'Not on purpose.'

'Really?' she asks sarcastically. 'Is Evie with you?'

'Yes.'

'Did she get a good look at the driver?'

Evie has been listening. She rocks her hand from side to side.

'Maybe,' I say.

Lenny puts me on hold. A few minutes later, she returns. 'There is a police sketch artist at the Arncliffe Centre. He'll be waiting for her.'

Twenty minutes later, I'm showered and shaved and yelling up the stairs for Evie to hurry. After ten more minutes she appears with a blob of pimple cream on her forehead.

'Why didn't you tell me?' she asks accusingly.

'You can barely notice it.'

'Don't look at me.'

'I used to get pimples when I was your age.'

'Fuck off!'

Evie is not a morning person, or an afternoon person, or an evening person. I think her sweet spot is possibly late at night when she's sleeping or playing with Poppy. Sometimes I think living with her is like playing a game of pass the parcel, peeling off another layer, never knowing what I'm going to find hidden inside.

Taking a box of cereal from the cupboard, she noisily sets down a bowl and spoon, before drowning Bran Flakes in milk.

'Tell me about the driver,' I say.

'I only saw him for a second. He didn't look at me.'

I pull out my phone and call up an image of Anders Foley. 'Was this him?'

'No.'

'And it wasn't Mitch.'

'Of course not.'

'What can you remember?'

She pushes out her bottom lip and thinks for a moment. 'He was wearing a baseball cap. He had tufts of hair sticking out.'

'What colour hat?'

'Red.'

'And hair?'

'Dark brown maybe.'

'What about the car? The make? The model? The colour?'

'It had four wheels.'

'You're not trying.'

'It was a car!' she says, sarcastically, her frustration spilling over.

'I could hypnotise you.'

'No!'

'It can help you remember.'

'No! Never! You're not poking around in my head.' Her voice is rising. 'You're itching to get inside there . . . to find the broken pieces. There's nothing wrong with me.'

'OK. I'm sorry. I didn't mean to upset you.'

She goes back to her cereal, which has grown soggy. She adds more to the bowl.

I begin again. 'What do you remember about the bar that night? Did anyone stand out?'

She shrugs.

'What about men acting strangely – hassling women, buying them drinks?'

'That's what men do, isn't it?'

Someone had to get close enough to Daniela to slip something in her drink.

Evie wipes milk from her chin. 'When the police showed up to ask questions about Maya Kirk, I saw a guy sneak out through the kitchen. The chef tried to stop him, but he used the fire door that leads into the back alley.'

'Any cameras out there?'

Evie shrugs.

'What did he look like?'

'Tall. Skinny. Thick eyebrows.'

'Could it be the driver?'

'No, he was different.'

'Would you recognise him again?'

'Yeah, I think so.'

Ten minutes later, we're on the road, heading north along Bilborough Road on the western edge of Nottingham, where newly ploughed fields are visible through the trees and the hedges are broken by farm gates and walking tracks. Rain threatens.

'How long does she have?' asks Evie, who has been quiet on the drive. 'You said Maya was held somewhere – before he, you know . . .'

I want to lie to Evie, to reassure her, but that's not possible. 'She was alive for forty-eight hours.'

'Then we're already too late.'

'Every case is different. Every victim. She could have found a way to make a personal connection, he may begin to care about her and keep her alive.'

'How?'

'By talking to him and pandering to his ego or being compliant.'

'Is that what he wants – someone compliant?'

'There is a time to fight and a time to retreat. Strategise. Placate.'

'What does placate mean?'

'To soothe or pander to his ego.'

Evie goes quiet for a while and then whispers, 'I don't know how you can do this.'

'What?'

'Understand why people do horrible things.'

'Sometimes it's the only way to stop them.'

44

Evie

A woman in a white lab coat collects us from the reception area. Her name is Cassie and she's flirting like crazy with Cyrus, which annoys me because she's clearly not right for him. I can tell the ones who are needy, or controlling, or want an errand boy not a boyfriend.

'Back again so soon,' she says, flashing him a smile. 'And who's this?'

'This is my friend, Evie.'

'I'm his lodger,' I say.

'How old-fashioned.'

'Yeah, Cyrus is that sort of guy.'

Cassie takes us to an open-plan office, where workspaces are separated by shoulder-high partitions. Another room, visible through glass, is full of people wearing white coats, face masks and hairnets.

Cassie points out some of the technology, like she's a tour guide. 'This one we call the beast. It's a liquid chromatograph with a time-of-flight mass spectrometer. It can analyse drugs, blood, alcohol, fibres, skin cells . . .'

In between the talking, Cassie asks questions, wanting to

know what we're doing here. Cyrus tells her about Daniela Linares going missing and how I got a look at the driver.

'Only for a second,' I say.

'That's a shame.'

'Why?'

'A poor identikit can deflect attention away from the real perpetrator.'

'I don't want to do that.'

'You won't,' says Cyrus, who is annoyed with Cassie, not me. Serves her right. I've decided that I don't want Cyrus finding a girlfriend. Nobody is good enough for him. Certainly not me. I'd be the worst. And he refuses to look at me like that, not with my pimple. No wonder he treats me like a child.

Cassie has stopped at an office. Inside, an old man is sitting on a high stool in front of a drafting table. He has shaggy grey hair and thick-lensed glasses that exaggerate the size of his eyes, making them bobble when he moves his head.

'Hi, Frank. This is Evie Cormac.'

He gets to his feet and bows at the waist. 'Hello, Miss Cormac.'

I laugh.

'Did I say something to amuse you?'

'Nobody ever calls me Miss.'

'Would you prefer Evie?'

'No. I like Miss Cormac.'

Frank points to a high stool next to him.

'I'll be back later,' says Cyrus.

'You're leaving me here!'

'I won't be long.'

I sneak a glance at Frank, who is sharpening a pencil. He may look like a loveable granddad with his high-waisted pants and crinkly smile, but I don't have a good history with coffin dodgers like him. I'm not saying they're all bad – just the ones I've met.

'Shall we get started?' he says, leaning his elbows on his sloping desk. 'Tell me about the man you saw in the car.'

'I only glimpsed one side of his face.'

'I can draw him that way. How old was he?'

'Younger than you. Older than Cyrus.'

'Forties or fifties?'

'Forties.'

'Could you get a sense of his height?'

'He was sitting down.'

'Low in the seat or high in the seat?'

'High.'

'What colour hair?'

'Brown. He was wearing a baseball cap. His hair stuck out over his ears.'

Frank opens a book full of photographs of different faces, but the eyes and mouths have been covered, so I can only see their noses. Each photograph is captioned. Straight, convex, concave, wavy, upturned, snub, Roman, Grecian. I point to the upturned nose.

'Could you see any of his nostril?'

'No.'

Frank asks me about eyes and his eyebrows. The hairline. The forehead. He opens more pages, wanting me to pick out features that most closely match. He uses each of them as a starting point when he begins to sketch.

Sometimes I think I'm sure about a detail, but then I begin to doubt myself. Other features become clearer. His eyebrows were darker than his hair. And the arm of his glasses didn't sit snugly over his ear. I don't remember any tattoos.

'What about his chin?' asks Frank. 'Some people have square jaws, or pointy chins, or they might have two chins like me.' He lowers his chin to his chest, creating a roll of fat on his neck.

'Only one chin,' I say, 'but it wasn't very pointy.'

'A chinless wonder,' says Frank. 'Maybe he's posh.'

'Why do you say that?'

He waves off the question and continues working. After what

seems like forever, he shows me a partially finished drawing. I make him rub things out and start again. We seem to be going around in circles, swapping stuff in and out because I can't decide.

'This is how it works,' says Frank. 'Nobody expects us to produce a photograph. A likeness would be enough.'

'But I want someone to recognise him.'

'Yes, but it's very rare that a random member of the public recognises someone from a police sketch. We're doing this for his family and friends. People who might say, "Hey, that looks a little like Tom or Dick or Harry."'

After another twenty minutes, he shows me again. I'm even less certain than before. The sketch looks like an invented person put together by a committee rather than someone who is flesh and blood.

Frank suggests we move on to the second drawing, the man who I saw duck out through the kitchen. The questions begin again and we talk about hair, noses, eyes and ears. I move my stool closer and watch as Frank sketches a handful of lines on the paper and slowly fills in the features, using shading to create depth.

He chats while he works, talking about his three children and two grandchildren. I ask their names. I don't normally care, but I'd rather ask questions than be the one answering them. Frank tells me that he did a degree in fine art and wanted to be a painter, but his life changed when he got mugged one night walking home from the pub. Bleeding from a head wound, he was taken to hospital. While waiting to be stitched up, he asked for a pen and a piece of paper. He sketched his attacker and gave the image to the police.

'It was published in the local paper and the man's brother gave him up,' says Frank. 'That was my first collar.'

'How many criminals have you caught since then?'

'I don't keep count.'

I look at the new drawing.

'It wasn't really a beard. More like bum fluff on his top lip,' I say.

Frank makes the alterations.

'And his eyes were more hidden by his eyebrows,' I say. 'And his bottom lip was thicker. What do you call that bit up there?' I point to my own lips.

'The cupid's bow?'

'Yeah. It was straighter.'

Frank works on his own for another ten minutes, while I wander about the room and peer out the window. He has a family of Smurfs on the window sill, who look like they're dreaming of escaping across the parking area and into the distant trees.

'How about this?' he asks, turning the drawing to face me. My breath catches and I feel myself lean back as though trying to get away.

'That's him! The man at the bar.'

45

Cyrus

Cassie has been tracking Anders Foley's movements in the days before and after Maya Kirk went missing. Every mobile handset transmits a signature 'ping' that searches for nearby phone towers known as base stations. By measuring the time that it takes for these pings to reach a particular tower and be returned, it's possible to estimate the distance the handset is from the tower. If the signature 'ping' is picked up by a second tower, technicians can establish a general area; and a third tower will allow the signal to be triangulated, providing a more precise location.

'This is Foley's phone on Sunday evening,' says Cassie. 'He met Maya at the Canalhouse at seven-forty. They stayed for about an hour and then walked to the Lace Market.' She traces the route on a satellite map with her fingertip. 'It's about a ten-minute walk, up Middle Hill. They stopped at a bar called the Blind Rabbit on High Pavement and then went on to the Little Drummer, which is only three minutes' walk away.'

'What time did they leave?'

'The CCTV puts them in St Peter's Gate at ten-fifteen. Foley's van was parked here.' She taps the screen. 'From there, they drove to Maya's house, arriving at ten-fifty-six.'

She shows me the route they took to Hyson Green, pointing out Maya's house on the map.

'How long was he there?'

'Forty minutes, give or take. He left before midnight and drove directly back to his house in West Bridgford. His phone remained at that location until nine o'clock the next morning when he went to work.'

'What about in the days that followed?'

'Home. Work. Home again. He had IT call-outs, which the police are checking.'

'He could have left his phone behind at any of those locations or carried a second handset.'

'True.' She calls up a satellite map on which she has plotted every journey that Foley took using different colours to indicate the days. There are no unexplained routes or unusual patterns. Maybe Hoyle is right about an accomplice.

Cassie taps her front teeth with the end of a pen.

'This other missing woman – Daniela – if we tracked her phone, I could cross-reference her movements with Maya and see if there are similarities. Places they visited. Mutual friends. It may give us something.'

'They hadn't seen each other in years,' I say.

Cassie frowns. 'Are you saying they knew each other?'

'They went through nursing college together and worked at St Jude's.'

Cassie is distracted by something on screen. I wave my hand in front of her eyes.

'Sorry. Daydreaming. What did you say?'

'They were both nurses. They worked together.'

'When?'

'Eight years ago.'

'Is that important?'

'We don't know.'

On the corner of Cassie's computer screen, she has taped a photograph. A wedding scene. The bride and groom are surrounded by bridesmaids and flower-girls wearing matching dresses and floral headbands. Everybody in the image is smiling, except for one small girl in the foreground, who has burst into tears.

'That's not you,' I say, pointing to the bride.

'My sister. That's me there,' she says. 'I was the maid of honour.'

'You lost her recently.'

Cassie looks surprised. 'How did you know?'

'Dyson mentioned it.'

She brushes her fingertips across her sister's face. 'God, I miss her. My brother-in-law is a mess. I wish I could help him.'

'I could give you the name of a grief counsellor.'

'Does that actually work?'

'For some people, yes. It can depend upon what stage of the grieving process they've reached.'

Her voice drops to a whisper. 'Did you see a grief counsellor?'

'A long time ago.' I hand her a business card with my phone number. 'Tell him it helps to speak to someone who has experienced the same loss. It might help you as well.'

Cassie strokes the card with her fingertips and I change the subject, asking if Stephen Voigt is around.

'He'll be in the garage. I can take you to see him.'

We walk through a rear door and cross the parking area towards a prefabricated steel warehouse surrounded by bare trees. A train rumbles along a railway embankment, disappearing behind the roofline and reappearing on the other side. Inside the building, skylights create squares of brightness on the polished concrete floor.

Cars and trucks are dotted across the space, some twisted and torn apart by the force of impact. Forensic vehicle examiners are taking measurements, inspecting tyres, brake pads, speedometers, tachometers, on-board computers and engine wear and tear, as they piece together the last moments before each collision. What forces were at play? Who was to blame?

Cassie yells Voigt's name. A head appears from the far side of a Ford Ranger van, which is parked at the centre of a quartet of bollards threaded with yellow tape.

'Dr Haven.' His eyes are magnified by his round glasses.

'Cyrus. Please.'

I'm aware that neither Cassie nor I are suited up. Voigt is about to say something, but Cassie pre-empts him and takes me to a small kitchenette to the left of the main roller doors.

'I have work to do,' she says. 'Maybe I'll see you later.'

Voigt looks disappointed to see her leave. He unzips the top of his coveralls and peels them from his shoulders, letting them bunch around his hips, before filling an electric jug and flicking the switch.

'On Tuesday you collected a piece of rope from the evidence archives in the city,' I say. 'Have you tested it yet?'

'I gave that to Cassie. I'm still examining the van.'

'Out of interest – who asked you to collect it?'

'Dyson. Why?'

'A misunderstanding,' I reply. 'I went looking for the rope and found it gone.'

'Great minds.'

He has found two clean mugs and set them out on the table.

'What have you found?' I ask.

'Strands of Maya's hair – one on the headrest of the passenger seat and the other near the wheel arch on the near-side. We also pulled her DNA from the pocket of the passenger door.'

'Foley said she vomited.'

'That makes sense. He used bleach to clean most of it up, but he missed a small section.'

'What about Rohan Kirk's blood?'

'There were traces of blood on the steering wheel and the gear stick, but those samples were too degraded to confirm the origin. Bleach will do that.'

I can see why Foley is in the frame. Locard's Exchange

Principle supposes that the perpetrator of a crime will always leave something at a crime scene and take something away. Wherever they step, whatever they touch, unconsciously or otherwise, will bear mute witness against them.

Voigt has dropped teabags into the mugs before adding boiling water, adding a splash of milk without asking. He realises and apologises. I wave it off and take the mug.

'Is there a problem?' he asks.

'I keep asking myself why Foley took Maya back to her house. She was drugged, semi-conscious, helpless, suggestible. He could have taken her anywhere, but instead he took her home and put her on her sofa. He covered her in a duvet. He gave her a bowl in case she vomited.'

'He did more than that.'

'You're right, but why did he take her home?'

'Maybe he didn't set out to abduct Maya – not at first – but Rohan Kirk interrupted him. They fought. The old man died. Foley couldn't leave Maya behind – she was a witness.'

'That makes sense, until you consider what happened next. He took Maya somewhere secret. He kept her alive for more than two days. He shaved off her hair. He bound her in a very specific way. It wasn't accidental, or spur of the moment.'

'What's your theory?'

'That's just it – I don't have one.'

'Well, if you ask me, I think he's done it before,' says Voigt.

'Why do you say that?'

'He did such a good job cleaning up.' He stammers, suddenly, unsure about offering an opinion. 'I expected to find more blood in the van. I mean, you saw the crime scene. The killer would have been covered in blood – his hands, his clothes, his shoes.'

'You said he used bleach.'

'Yes, but do you know how difficult it is to remove blood? We have machines that can find traces on fabric that has been laundered dozens of times.'

'He changed his clothes,' I say. 'Maybe he borrowed some from Rohan Kirk's wardrobe.'

'We didn't find traces of blood on the stairs or the upper floor.'

'Then he must have brought a spare set with him, unless he left the house in his underwear.'

'There is another possibility,' says Voigt. 'We found traces of Rohan Kirk's blood on the kitchen floor and in the sink. What if he used the washer–dryer and laundered his clothes?'

'How long would that have taken?'

'At least an hour.'

That takes incredible nerve – to stay in a house with a murdered man and a drugged woman, while your clothes are tumbling in a dryer.

'You're quite good at this,' I say to Voigt, who grins self-consciously.

'You should tell that to Dyson. He thinks I'm a fuck-up.'

As if summoned by the mention of his name, Craig Dyson pushes a trolley through the roller door. He points at me.

'You're not supposed to be here!'

Voigt tries to explain, but Dyson talks over him. 'This is a secure area. Only designated staff allowed.'

'I was checking on the Maya Kirk forensics,' I say.

'Good. Write an email, make a phone call, send a carrier pigeon, but don't come in here without my permission.'

I want to argue, but I have no authority and Dyson's job is to make sure procedures are followed because any breaches will rebound on him. I empty my mug of tea into the sink and make my way outside, while Dyson berates someone else for not restocking the CSI kits.

Voigt follows me, looking embarrassed. 'I'm sorry about that. He's not usually so rude to people.'

'Only to you,' I reply.

He grimaces and glances skywards, as though searching for a sign or some warmth on a cold day.

'You know the biggest problem with this job?' he asks.

I could name a few.

'People don't trust the science any more. Back in the day, we had all these TV shows about crime scene investigators, which glamorised the profession, made us into heroes. But that only heightened expectations. Juries expect every crime scene to have DNA or fingerprints or fibres, the proverbial smoking gun.'

'And you think that's changed,' I say.

'Absolutely. I blame the pandemic. People started off listening to the health experts and the scientists, but slowly they drifted away. Some disappeared down rabbit holes and began believing in conspiracy theories and espousing quack cures. Livestock de-wormers. Anti-malarial drugs. Bleach. I could weep.'

My phone vibrates. It's a text message from Alissa, Daniela Linares' housemate. She can meet me at St Jude's when her shift finishes at three. Elias is due to arrive at four. I must be home by then.

Moments later, I'm back with Evie. Frank has finished two drawings.

'Miss Cormac was an excellent witness,' he says. Evie scowls, thinking he's teasing her. He's not.

The drawings are pinned to the desk. Frank is spraying one of them with fixer. The first shows a man in profile wearing a baseball cap and dark-rimmed glasses. It's a strange look, almost like a joke-shop disguise where the only thing missing is a fake nose and moustache.

Frank steps back. I glimpse the second drawing. Instantly, I recognise the mullet haircut and the poor excuse for a moustache.

'Who is he?' asks Evie.

'Paulie Brennan. Maya Kirk used to babysit him.'

46

Cyrus

Alissa Hussein is waiting for me in the foyer of St Jude's Medical Centre. She's wearing a cardigan over her blue uniform, which has white piping on the sleeves and collar. Her dark eyebrows bob up and down as she talks in a scattergun stream of questions and statements.

'Are the police looking for Daniela? I haven't seen anything on TV. They came to see me. I told them what happened. We shouldn't have left her. Harriet is beside herself. She couldn't face working this week. She's gone home to her parents' house. I hate being alone.'

I offer to buy her a coffee, but she chooses a hot chocolate, without the cream. We take a table in the medical school café, away from the noise of the coffee machine and the busy counter. Colleagues acknowledge her, but don't approach.

'None of us had been out on the town for yonks, not together,' says Alissa. 'I used to love going to the clubs when I was younger. Back then we used a fake ID to get past the bouncers. On Friday I felt ancient. The girls were so young and empowered.'

She fishes a marshmallow from the froth.

'Daniela wasn't going to come along, but Martyn, her boyfriend, was away on a rugby tour, so we convinced her to join us. We left home at eight, shared a pizza at an Italian restaurant and stopped at the Little Drummer because it was happy hour.'

'Did you see anyone you knew?'

'A few people. It was busy.'

'How did Daniela seem?'

'Good. Happy. Until the police arrived.'

'What do you mean?'

'They were showing photographs of Maya. Daniela grew upset. They went through nursing college together.'

'Did Daniela have much to drink?'

'We had a glass of wine at the restaurant and two cocktails. We bought the first round and the second arrived unexpectedly. The barman said we had a secret admirer. We thought he'd come over and introduce himself – try to chat us up, you know. We were checking out the guys in the bar, trying to guess who it might be, but nobody showed up.'

'How did this guy know what you were drinking?'

'He must have been watching our table. Is that important?'

'We think Daniela's drink was spiked.'

A shadow passes across her eyes.

'Who delivered them?' I ask.

'The manager – the one with the curly moustache.'

'Why did Daniela not go with you to the nightclub?'

'She said she needed the bathroom. The club was only two streets away and we thought we'd have to queue. Daniela told us to go ahead and she'd catch up. The bouncer let us straight through the ropes and we went inside. We were dancing and Harriet shouted Daniela's name in my ear. I sent her a text message and tried to call. She didn't pick up.'

'What time was this?'

'Midnight, maybe. I thought she must have gone home.'

Her voice shakes. She takes a tissue from the sleeve of her cardigan, as though preparing to cry.

'What happened when you got home?' I ask.

'Daniela's bedroom door was shut. I figured she was sleeping. Harriet and I were tipsy by then. I fell into bed and didn't wake until midday when Daniela's mum called because she wasn't answering her phone. I knocked on her bedroom door. Went inside. Her bed hadn't been slept in. I knew something was wrong. Daniela wouldn't stay out like that.'

I take out my phone and scroll through my photos, until I find one of Anders Foley.

'Do you recognise him?'

'The police were showing his photograph at the bar. Is he the one who took Maya?'

'We believe so.'

I show her another image – this one of Paulie Brennan.

Alisa studies it for a long while, pinching her fingers against the screen to make it larger.

She shakes her head. 'I don't remember.' Her eyes are shining. 'We should have waited for her, but we didn't know she was sick. We thought she was right behind us. If we'd known . . .' A sob chokes off the statement and she covers her face with her hands.

I understand that feeling. It has haunted me my entire life. What if I had pedalled harder? What if I hadn't ridden my bike past Ailsa Piper's house? What if I'd arrived home a few minutes earlier? Could have, would have, should have – nobody can change the past.

47

Evie

Elias is due at any moment. Cyrus isn't home and he's not answering his phone and I don't know what to do. I could hide and pretend that nobody is here. I could tell Cyrus I took Poppy for a walk or that I didn't hear the doorbell or that I was called to the school.

What happens if nobody is home? Would they leave Elias here or take him back to Rampton? I imagine them dumping him on the doorstep like an Amazon delivery.

Outside, a van is slowing. It parks beneath a tree. Two people get out. Oscar and Roland. The side door slides open. Elias is sitting on the bench seat. This time he has a suitcase.

They are walking up the path. Any moment they're going to ring the doorbell or knock. What am I supposed to do? Show him to his room? Make small talk? Hide the knives?

The bell startles me. I wait. It rings again. Fuck! I open the door.

'Special delivery for Cyrus Haven,' says Oscar. His gold tooth glints.

'Cyrus isn't home.'

'No problem. You know Elias.'

I want to say, 'Take him back,' but Elias is giving me his goofy smile, all chins and teeth. He's dressed in baggy corduroy trousers and a khaki shirt with press studs instead of buttons. There are old sweat stains under his arms, which have discoloured the material.

'Hello, Evie,' he says. 'How are you?'

I try to read something in his face but can't tell if he's being creepy or trying to be polite or if this is part of his training. They dump his suitcase in the hallway and turn to leave.

'Are you going?' I ask.

'Yeah,' says Oscar.

I follow them down the path. 'Is there anything I should know?'

'Like what?'

'Instructions.'

'He doesn't come with a manual.'

Smirks between them. Arseholes!

When I go back inside, Elias is in the kitchen, opening cupboards and drawers.

'Are you looking for something?'

'Just checking where things are kept.'

He is getting closer to the knives.

'Would you like a cup of tea?' I ask.

'I can make my own. Do you want one?'

'No.'

Elias fills the kettle. 'When will Cyrus be home?'

'Any minute. He popped out to the shops to buy some things. Milk.'

He has opened the fridge. 'We have plenty of milk.'

'Something for dinner.'

I'm standing with my bum against the cutlery drawer.

'What do you do, Evie?'

'I go to school. I work.'

'I'm studying too. I'm going to be a lawyer.'

Fat chance, I think. He's looking for a teaspoon. I reach

248

behind me and take one from the drawer. When he looks away, I slip a short-bladed knife into the waistband of my jeans.

Nursing his mug of tea, Elias continues opening cupboards. Reading labels. Looking at jars. Reciting ingredients. Maybe this is new to him.

'Do you have any Coco Pops?' he asks, looking at a box of cereal.

'Cyrus says they have too much sugar.'

'And he's the boss.'

'No.'

Elias begins arranging the jars and canned goods with the labels facing out.

'How long have you been living here?' he asks.

'A year.'

'Where were you before that?'

'A children's home.'

'Why?'

'My parents are dead.'

'And what – Cyrus adopted you?'

'I'm twenty-one.'

'You don't look it.'

You don't look like someone who killed four people, I want to say, but that's not entirely the truth. He looks exactly like one of those pasty-faced, overweight doughballs you see in TV shows about serial killers. Occasionally, one of them is handsome, like Ted Bundy, but most are like the creepy uncle you avoid sitting next to at Christmas.

Silence fills the room. Elias is embarrassed. I'm embarrassed. I want to hide in the attic.

'It must feel strange – being out after all this time,' I say, forcing myself to make conversation.

'Yeah. I barely recognise some of the streets. They knocked down the old cinema on Abercrombie Road and there's an office block where my old piano teacher used to live.'

'Can you play the piano?'

'Badly.'

He is adding more sugar to his tea. Four scoops. No wonder he's fat. He keeps talking.

'There are different makes and models of cars. And everybody is walking around looking at their phones – never taking their eyes off them. What are they looking at?'

'Messages. Instagram. TikTok.'

'I've heard of them – what are they?'

'Social networking sites.'

Elias looks at me blankly.

'You can post videos and pictures online. Stories.'

'Why?'

'Your friends will know what you're doing.'

'Why don't they just ask?'

How do I answer that?

'If you post something interesting you can get lots of likes.'

'What's a like?'

What is this – twenty questions?

'Ask Cyrus,' I snap and immediately feel guilty. Elias goes quiet and rocks back and forth, heel to toe.

'What are you going to do first?' I ask.

'I might make French toast. I used to love to cook. The French call it *pain perdu*, which means lost bread, because they use stale bread to make it. And the trick is temperature control – and not soaking the bread too long.'

This guy is seriously weird.

'It's the small things you take for granted,' he says. 'Like this.' He walks to the door and flicks the light switch up and down. 'At Rampton, I couldn't do that.' He looks at the ceiling. 'And there were cameras watching me everywhere I went.'

It was like that at Langford Hall, I think, but I don't tell him that.

He opens the fridge and chooses a carrot from the vegetable crisper. 'I couldn't do this,' he says, biting off the end and chewing noisily. A piece of carrot lands on the floor.

He carries his tea to the library and then the sitting room, where he turns on the TV and flicks through channels, leaning forward over his knees and thrusting the remote control at the screen.

'We have Netflix,' I say. 'You can watch lots of different movies and TV shows.'

'Like a normal TV?'

'Yeah, but there are more choices.'

Elias doesn't seem impressed. He points to the wireless speaker on the mantelpiece.

'It works with the TV,' I say, 'or you can stream music.'

'Where do you put the music?'

'It uses the home Wi-Fi.'

'Like radio.'

'Yeah. I guess.' I have no idea if that's true.

'Show me,' he says.

I take out my phone and choose a song. He is standing so close to me that I can smell his breath and his body odour. The music starts playing. He looks at the speaker as though I've performed a magic trick.

'Choose another one.'

I do as he asks. Celeste. 'Stop This Flame'. She sounds like Amy Winehouse.

'Make it louder.'

I turn up the volume. He closes his eyes and begins nodding his head and clicking his fingers in time with the beat. His body jiggles.

'Want to dance?' he asks.

'I don't dance.'

He takes a step towards me, reaching for my hand, but I back away towards the door. He tries again.

'Don't touch me.'

'It's only a dance.'

My back is pressed against the wall.

'I'm a good dancer. Mum taught me.'

'No.'

'I can teach you.'

'Stay away from me.'

Elias thinks it's a game. He is rocking from foot to foot, raising his arms, ready to put them around me. I pull the knife from my belt and point the blade at his chest.

Seeing the knife, he steps backwards. Shocked. I use that moment to slip under his arms and escape, through the door and up the stairs. Elias is calling after me, saying he's sorry and that he didn't mean to scare me.

In my bedroom, I lock the door, and push a chest of drawers across the polished floorboards, scratching the varnish, barricading myself inside.

Sitting on the bed with my back to the wall, I hold the knife and listen for his footsteps. Waiting for him to come.

48

Cyrus

My phone has been turned to silent. When I glance at the screen, I discover a dozen missed calls and messages from Evie, each angrier than the last. Elias has arrived. The prospect makes my pulse quicken.

I call. Evie picks up. 'Where the fuck are you?'

'I've been talking to one of Daniela's friends.'

'You should have been here.'

'Why? What did he do?'

'He tried to dance with me.'

I laugh, which annoys her even more.

'He won't hurt you,' I say.

'How do you know?'

'They've spent twenty years fixing him.'

'You told me schizophrenia can't be cured.'

'He's medicated.'

'Eighty per cent of them relapse.'

'Will you *stop* googling!'

There is another long pause. I can picture her, sitting on her bed, biting her fingernails, which are always chewed to the nub and raw.

'Have you found Daniela?' she asks.

'Still looking.'

'When will you be home?'

'On my way.'

I knock gently on Evie's bedroom door and call her name. I hear bare feet on the floor and her chest of drawers being pushed aside. A key is turned.

Her voice. 'You can come in.'

She is sitting up in bed, holding a pillow against her chest.

'Was all of that necessary?' I ask.

She gives me a shrug but no explanation.

I glance around the room. Right now, she's in her Goth phase, with a deep purple bedspread, black pillows and sepia-coloured wallpaper. Moving closer, I sit on the bottom corner of her mattress. There is a stony quality to Evie, something unforgiving and grey.

'Give him time,' I say.

'How long?'

'A few weeks, at least.'

She makes a huffing sound, which I take to be agreement, but could be my wishful thinking.

'Are you hungry?' I ask.

'Maybe.'

'I'll give you a call when dinner's ready – unless you want to keep me company.'

'No.'

Downstairs, I hear Elias laughing. He's watching an episode of *Friends*, with the volume turned up. He must think nothing has changed. Opening the fridge, I begin taking out ingredients. I search for a sharp knife to dice the onions. I find them in the breadbin. Either Evie has hidden them or Elias is messing with my head.

I hear a floorboard creak. He's in the doorway.

'I'm sorry I wasn't home when you arrived,' I say.

'That's OK.'

Pulling up a chair, he takes a seat at the table and tears a sheet of kitchen towel from the roll. He folds it in half and half again, making smaller and smaller squares.

'I think I should have Evie's room.'

'Why?'

'It's bigger.'

'She was here first.'

'I'm family.'

'And she *needs* one.'

Elias frowns, not understanding.

'Evie has been through more than you can possibly imagine. She's remarkable. Unique. And she needs someone to watch over her.'

'Why does it have to be you?'

'It could be you, too.'

Elias is about to say something but seems to change his mind. I open the fridge and take out two beers. Then I remember that he shouldn't be drinking because alcohol affects his medications. I put the bottles away. Elias has noticed.

'I used to do group sessions with guys who were alcoholics,' he says. 'Rampton had a programme for them.'

'I hope you're not suggesting I'm an alcoholic.'

'They were doing the twelve steps, you know. My case worker told me that I should do the same – make a list of the people I've hurt and make amends.'

'Step eight?'

'Nine.'

I tip the diced onions into the heated oil.

'I'm scared you won't forgive me,' says Elias.

'I've forgiven you already.'

'Have you? Really?'

'You're here, aren't you?'

'Everybody trusted me. Mum. Dad. Esme and April. What I did can't be undone. I can try to make amends for everything else, but not that. I wish I could bring them back. Every day, I pray for their forgiveness.' He has the fervour in his eyes of someone born again, yet I get the sense he's talking about events that happened to somebody else and he's puzzled about knowing so many of the details.

'I had a priest who used to visit me,' he says. 'He gave me a Bible and encouraged me to pray. He said that if I'm truly sorry for what I did, and if I ask for God's forgiveness, I'll receive his grace and be allowed to join them in Heaven.'

'Is that where you think they are?' I ask.

'Yes. Don't you?'

I avoid answering because I don't believe in Heaven, or Hell. And when I picture my family, we are all living in our little house, the twins sharing a room, Dad brewing his beer, Mum doing her yoga in the sunroom, and Elias and me kicking a football in the garden.

'You have every reason to hate me,' he says. 'And I have no right to expect anything from you – not friendship, or trust, or love. You said a lot of nice things to the tribunal, but it's just us now – you and me – in the kitchen of Grandma and Granddad's house. You can be honest with me. You can tell me what you really think.'

I fall silent, watching the spaghetti soften in the bubbling water.

'I'm not ready to talk about that,' I say.

After a pause, he clears his throat. 'I need to find some people. I have a list. I might need your help.'

'Who are they?'

'Folks who I hurt. Dad's old business partner gave me a job and I stole money from him. And when I was mowing lawns for the neighbours, I used to nick stuff from their garden sheds.'

'I'm not sure they'd appreciate seeing you,' I say. 'Maybe you should keep a low profile – at least for a while. You have to appreciate that many people don't understand mental illness and if they discover who you are – what you did . . .'

'You're worried about what they'll say.'

'I'm worried about you. If people knew . . . the media . . . the neighbours . . . I don't want you under pressure.'

'I should stay under the radar.'

'It's better that way.'

I drain the spaghetti in a colander, ready to serve, and move to the bottom of the stairs, looking up between the spindles.

'Evie! Dinner.'

49

Evie

Morning. Still dark outside. The radiators are ticking and clanking. The house feels different today than yesterday. Elias is the reason. He was up late last night, watching TV in the sitting room, flicking through the channels, laughing at ancient TV shows like *Seinfeld* and *The Vicar of Dibley*. And now I can hear him snoring in Mitch's old room – the one he used for two nights before being sent back to prison.

Cyrus is up already. I hear him in the shower and then on the stairs. I pull on my hoodie and Ugg boots and join him in the kitchen. He looks tired and there is the shadow of a beard on his cheeks. A coat with wide shoulders is hanging over the back of his chair.

'Where are you going?'

'Radford Road police station.'

'I don't want to be home alone with Elias.'

'He won't hurt you, Evie.'

'Yeah, well, I read about that guy who they released from a psych hospital and within two months he'd killed and eaten three people.'

'Is that according to Google?'

'Yes, but it's true.'

He changes the subject. 'Do you want sourdough toast?'

I hold up two fingers, meaning slices. 'Have you seen the sitting room? It's full of crisp packets and soft drink cans and old *Playboy*s that he must have found in the attic. You said he wasn't allowed up there. You promised.'

'I'll have a word.'

'I'm not cleaning up after him.'

'You don't have to.'

'What am I supposed to do?'

'Walk Poppy. Study. Look for another job.' He pauses and says, 'You could do me one favour. Elias needs to pick up his meds from a pharmacy.'

'I thought he wasn't supposed to leave the house.'

'He can go with you. I have to let Rampton know.'

Clearly, this is a part of me 'pulling my weight'. Maybe he's also testing Elias. We're like guinea pigs in some psychological experiment, or weird reality TV show. Put the psycho and the freak girl together and see who blinks first – only I don't think Elias would blink. He's like a snake. Cold-blooded and lidless.

'I'm busy today,' I say, not meeting his gaze.

'Doing what?'

'All of the aforementioned tasks.'

'Your vocabulary is improving.'

'Fuck off!'

Cyrus laughs. 'Do this for me.'

His eyes are kind and warm and lingering and I just want to hug him, which is weird because I don't usually like touching people and I'm frightened that my skinny body and the pimple on my forehead will repel him.

The toaster pops up. He shrugs on his coat. I catch him at the door and hold out my hand.

'I need cash for petrol.'

'What about *your* money?'

'I bought a car and lost my job; and I'm doing you a favour.'

He puts a twenty-quid note on my outstretched palm. I motion with my fingers, and he adds another twenty.

'When will you be home?' I ask.

'Early as I can be.'

'If I get murdered in my bed, I'm going to come back and haunt you.'

'You haunt me now.'

After he's gone, I take Poppy outside so she can do her morning business and scare away the squirrels. Elias doesn't appear downstairs until almost midday, smelling like he's drowned himself in cologne. He's wearing the same baggy corduroy trousers, but a different shirt.

'Why do you dress like a boy?' he asks.

'Why do you smell like a pimp?' I reply.

Elias cups his hands over his mouth and sniffs his breath. What a moron!

He sits at the table and asks if we have any bacon and eggs. I tell him we have eggs.

'I'd like two poached.'

'This isn't a hotel,' I say. 'Get your own breakfast.'

Elias cocks his head to one side like Poppy does occasionally when she doesn't understand a command.

'And clean up the sitting room. It's a pigsty.'

'Don't you have a cleaner?'

'Yeah, she comes in with the butler and the chauffeur.'

He recognises my sarcasm and gets a box of cereal from the cupboard. When he sits down his cuffs ride up, revealing his ankle monitor locked around his pale shin. Self-consciously, he hides it from me.

'I used to wear one of those,' I say. 'I was always escaping from the children's home.'

'Why?'

'I didn't like living there.'

'What happened to your parents?'

'What happened to yours?'

Boom! His face creases and I want to take the question back. Cyrus would call it a cheap shot, but I don't know what makes a comeback cheap or expensive or just plain nasty.

'I'm supposed to take you to a pharmacy,' I say, changing the subject. 'Are you ready to go?'

Elias takes a prescription from his pocket. 'I have an address.'

The Queens Medical Centre isn't far, but I take Poppy with me for added protection. She surrenders her usual front seat for Elias, who squeezes into Mouse, pressing his knees against the dashboard. Despite the cold, he lowers the window and holds out his hand, fingers wide, feeling the air push against his palm as we head along Derby Road, past Wollaton Park. Elias points out landmarks as though I'm new to the area, talking about places that served the best pizzas and fish and chips.

'I used to drive,' he says. 'Got my licence first time. Perfect score on my test.'

'Modest, aren't you?'

My sarcasm bounces off him.

'I was saving to buy a car. Had my eye on a Subaru Impreza. Nought to sixty in six seconds. What does this do?'

'No idea.'

'You must get good mileage.'

'If you say so.'

I take the exit onto Clifton Boulevard and immediately turn left, following signs to the hospital. As we pass a cluster of parked ambulances we give way to a police car. Elias goes quiet at the sight of it.

We reach the visitor parking area. I point to the sign that says *Main Entrance*. Elias doesn't move.

'You have to come with me,' he says. 'I'm not allowed to be on my own.'

'Are you going to run away?'

'No.'

'Well, I'll wait here.'

He has beads of sweat on his top lip. He licks them away.

'I don't need the medications today. I can come back another time.'

'Show me the prescription.'

He hands it to me. I crack my window and leave Poppy on the back seat. Elias catches up when I'm halfway across the parking lot. The automatic doors slide open and we follow the overhead signs to the pharmacy, which is on Floor B.

I walk to the counter, where a pharmacist in a blue medical smock has reading glasses hanging around her neck and a mole on her top lip. I explain that Elias needs a prescription filled. She glances at the form and back at Elias. I wonder if she can tell by looking at the prescription what's wrong with him.

'That will be fifteen minutes. You can wait or come back. There's a café in the foyer.'

We follow her directions, past an information desk, a florist and a gift shop. Elias sneaks a glance at two nurses who are walking past us. He looks away when he notices me watching him and does that same creepy licking of his top lip. It's freezing today. Why is he sweating?

Then I realise that he's nervous. He's not used to being in a busy place like a hospital. The café is the wrong choice. Instead, I find a bench hidden by potted palms. Elias sits with his knees together and head thrust forward, arms against his sides, fingers hooked under his thighs.

'When did you start hearing voices?' I ask, making it sound like we're talking about the weather, which is something I never do.

'When I was fourteen.'

'What did they say?'

'It wasn't a voice at first. It was a scarecrow man. He used to visit me at night. He had a hessian sack for a head and holes for eyes and he used to scratch on my bedroom window with his fingers.'

'That was probably branches in the wind.'

'Yeah, that's what my mum said. She asked Dad to trim the

tree, but the scarecrow man was still there. Eventually, he moved inside. I would wake and find him leaning over my bed, breathing on my face. I couldn't move or scream.'

'I've had dreams like that,' I say. 'The nightmares where you think you're awake, but you're trapped in the dream.'

I've had other dreams where the monsters were real, but he doesn't need to know that.

Somebody nearby laughs loudly. Elias flinches and wipes his top lip.

'One day he spoke to me.'

'What did he say?'

'"He is going to kill them."'

'Kill who?'

He shrugs. 'I thought he was talking about someone else. I tried to ignore the voice. I pushed it away. I told myself it wasn't real. But it started to follow me. I'd be at school, or mowing lawns, or down at the arcade, and suddenly, out of nowhere, I'd hear it. "He is going to kill them." It was always the same thing, like he was talking about someone else, but looking straight at me.'

'Did you tell anyone?'

'I didn't want them thinking I was crazy.'

'But you were.'

He is rocking slightly and his voice sounds groggy, like someone who hasn't slept in a long time.

'I tried to make it stop. I locked myself away. I drank. I smoked hash. I exercised. Once I didn't sleep for three days, but the voice kept whispering to me. It's funny how you get used to something like that. Instead of persecuting me, the voice became my friend. It set me tasks. Unspoken ones. They were small to begin with. Steal something from a shop. Cut myself with a knife. Shave off my hair. I began to wonder if my life would get back to normal if I did what he said. I just had to give up control. Stop fighting. Let him win.'

'Do you still see the scarecrow man?' I ask.

'No.'

'Do you hear the voice?'

'Yes, but he has no control over me now. I am different. Stronger.'

I get an odd queasy feeling in my stomach. It's not his answer that bothers me. For the first time, I can't tell if he's lying.

50

Cyrus

The atmosphere in the incident room has changed since my last visit. The celebrations have been replaced by disappointment and a faltering sense of desperation. With each passing hour, the chances of finding Daniela Linares alive have diminished, and some detectives have switched to recovery mode, expecting to find a body.

The task force has been broken into teams that are tackling different avenues of inquiry. Some are knocking on doors. Others are studying CCTV footage from traffic cameras and local businesses, trying to identify the car and driver that picked up Daniela from outside the Little Drummer.

Foley's poker-playing mates have each been interviewed and warned about perjury, but nothing has dented his alibi for Friday night. His phone records and social media pages are being searched, along with postings on message boards and possible links to radical incel groups.

Hoyle notices my arrival. He breaks away from a group of colleagues, signalling for me to walk with him, moving with less swagger than before.

'I wanted to apologise for the way I reacted at our last

meeting,' he says. 'I'm never at my best when I'm dragged out of bed.'

'I didn't take offence.'

Hoyle pushes through a swing door, holding it open for me.

'What about Paulie Brennan?' I ask.

'He hasn't been home. We're watching the house.'

'What does Marlene say?'

'She says we're harassing her family and has threatened to lodge a complaint.'

'Does that bother you?'

'Not in the least. You met Paulie. What did you make of him?'

'Below-average intelligence. Socially awkward. He hangs out with some dodgy mates.'

'Orlando Simpson and Rex Chande,' says Hoyle. 'They're members of The Blue Angels Motorcycle Club. Both have convictions for dealing.'

'Has anyone talked to Foley?' I ask.

'His lawyer is refusing us access.'

'Can you offer some sort of deal?'

'Not a chance.' We have reached the stairwell. 'There is one possibility. Foley's lawyer has agreed to a preliminary psych evaluation. I put your name forward.'

I don't know why Foley would trust me, but Hoyle must be running out of options. Unlocking a man's ego can be as simple as asking him to open a jar of pickles, or as complex as algebraic geometry, but a meeting with Foley is a start. If I can explore his state of mind, I can learn what psychological buttons might unlock his defences.

'One more thing,' says Hoyle. 'I have organised a TV reconstruction of Daniela Linares' last hours. I was hoping Miss Cormac might take part.'

'You want Evie on camera?'

'She'll be playing herself.'

'Will you blur her face?'

'Why?'

'Her identity is protected. Nobody is allowed to publish her name, address, or any photographs.'

'What has that girl done to get that sort of protection?'

He knows I won't answer.

'OK, but she wears the same clothes.'

Prime Time appears on the stairs, out of breath. 'Paulie Brennan has just been sighted. He's at Donington Park.'

I have never understood the appeal of motorsports. I don't discount the skill and bravery it takes to hurl a machine around a track at two hundred miles an hour, but calling it a sport is like saying that Neil Armstrong was an athlete when he piloted Apollo 11 to the moon.

From what I've seen – which is admittedly very little – winning and losing often comes down to the car rather than the person behind the wheel. All vehicles are not created equal. Then again, neither are yachts, nor polo ponies, nor football teams owned by oligarchs.

Donington Park is a circuit near Castle Donington in Leicestershire, about fifteen miles south-west of Nottingham. Today is an amateur track day, where petrolheads and hobbyists get a chance to test their skills on a circuit normally used by superbikes and touring cars.

Dozens of drivers are trackside with their vehicles, waiting for their turn. Paulie Brennan is somewhere among them. Police in plain clothes are moving into the crowd, trying to recognise him. Hoyle and Lenny are in the lower seats of the grandstand, scanning the onlookers with binoculars.

I watch quietly, keeping my opinions to myself. Like everybody else, I want to know what Paulie was doing in the Little Drummer when Daniela Linares disappeared, but this isn't the way to arrest him. He knew Maya, but there is no evidence he had any contact with Daniela. And his past acts of violence and criminal behaviour have been spontaneous or self-serving –

brawls in pub car-parks, or nicking stuff from freight yards and warehouses.

Daniela's abduction bothers me. If the killer is a sexual psychopath, he will be using these women to feed his fantasies, adding light and shade to events that he has already vividly imagined. In normal circumstances, Maya's death should have been enough to keep him satisfied for weeks, or months, but instead he has taken a new victim within days. That suggests a rapid escalation, or a different motive.

Hoyle is communicating with officers on the track via a two-way radio, but there must be two hundred people in the starting area and pit lanes. I hear someone shout and see a scuffle break out. People are scattering. Paulie Brennan is dressed in a racing suit, carrying a helmet. He jumps into a hatchback with a painted number on the door. A detective reaches through the driver's window and grabs the steering wheel, but the car accelerates along the pit lane, scattering the crowd, including a safety officer, who tumbles across the bonnet and bounces to his feet.

The Ford Focus accelerates into the straight, forcing another driver to brake hard and swerve out of the way. Paulie gets to the first corner, and steers across the apron, bottoming out and creating a shower of sparks.

Hoyle is yelling into the two-way, demanding the track be cleared. Organisers begin waving other drivers into the pit lane, until only Paulie remains on the track. The circuit is two miles long with a series of corners and chicanes, as well as two hairpin bends, where cars must slow down. This is where police and marshals gather, waving a red flag, signalling for Paulie to pull over. He ignores them and flashes past, grinning beneath his helmet. Raising his middle finger.

A police car pulls onto the track, giving chase, but that only seems to encourage Paulie. Now it's become a race. He roars along the straights, before braking hard, changing down through the gears, and steering the hatchback through each corner. Pedal down. More speed. Another circuit.

Safety cars are sent out, to try to slow him down, but Paulie toys with them, weaving back and forth, before ducking inside them under brakes.

'Don't chase him. You're making this a contest,' I tell Lenny. 'Let him get bored or run out of fuel.'

She looks at me helplessly. She's not in charge.

Paulie's hatchback roars past us again. Hoyle is arguing with the organisers, wanting them to deploy road spikes, but that's not something they have at racetracks.

From my vantage point, I watch five cars being positioned across the tarmac, bumper to bumper. This is madness. They should be setting up the roadblock at the slowest part of the circuit, not the fastest corner.

Someone holds up a sign, warning Paulie to slow down as he weaves through a snaking chicane, both hands on the wheel, arms straight, eyes on the road. He's in his element, driving towards a chequered flag. When he reaches the finishing straight, he accelerates, changing up through the gears. Hoyle is mid-track, with his arms raised, waving two red flags.

Taking a sharp line through the next corner, the hatchback bounces on the apron and fishtails as Paulie wrestles for control. At that moment, I imagine him looking up and seeing the cars ahead of him, straddling the track. He doesn't slow down. He wrenches the wheel and steers towards the advertising hoardings that decorate the fences. He thinks there might be enough space between the last car and the safety railings. He's wrong. I see a puff of smoke rise from the tarmac as he finally hits his brakes, but it's too late. Rubber squeals and the car slews sideways. People are running for cover.

The crash seems to happen in slow motion, the crunch of metal on metal, and the final image of Paulie, raising his hands as the airbag explodes into his face and his head snaps forward and then back and the windscreen explodes around him, and the track becomes a junkyard.

Track marshals are on the scene within seconds, spraying fire retardant foam onto the spilled fuel. Paramedics come moments later, but there is no saving Paulie, whose body is trapped in the twisted metal.

Hoyle is immediately on the phone to the chief constable. I can hear him using phrases like 'suicide by cop' and 'death wish', making out that Paulie Brennan chose to die rather than being questioned by police.

'We killed him,' I say to Lenny.

'He made his own choices.'

'He was playing a game.'

'He was resisting arrest.'

I know we're not going to agree. The police will close ranks, singing off the same song-sheet, and come the inquest a coroner will decide on death by misadventure. Another Brennan dead. A skid mark removed from the world as easily as the oil and foam being hosed off the track.

Even if Paulie was involved in abducting Daniela Linares, where does it leave us now? Where does it leave her?

'We follow the evidence,' says Lenny. 'We track her phone. We study the CCTV cameras. We identify the car. We investigate.'

I wish I could share her confidence, but I keep remembering the bondage marks on Maya Kirk's body, the rope corset designed to subjugate and humiliate. I picture Daniela similarly bound and gagged. Waiting for his return. Terrified he will. More terrified he won't.

51

Cyrus

HMP Nottingham is a Victorian Category B remand prison, built in the 1890s and modernised over the years with newer buildings that look like afterthoughts, squeezed into the available space. Prison reformers have long campaigned to have it shut down, calling it draconian and obsolete, but successive governments keep adding rather than subtracting to the numbers.

The reception area has regulations displayed on the walls, printed in different languages. No hats, scarves, hoodies, coats, jackets or gloves. No metal hair accessories, steel-capped shoes, ripped clothing, see-through tops, revealing blouses, miniskirts or short dresses. The banning of football shirts surprises me, but tribalism of any kind can be toxic in jail, where conflict must be dealt with before it boils over.

As I walk through the security check, the sniffer dog gives me a lazy wag of its tail. I am patted down by a separate guard, who makes me surrender my phone, watch and car keys, which are placed in a locker.

The visitors' room has rows of tables and chairs evenly spaced apart. Somewhere, beyond these walls, a warder will be fetching

Foley. I can picture him lying in a narrow cot, smelling the sourness of the air. The future is a scary business when you're accused of abducting and killing a woman. I doubt if Foley has slept more than a few hours each night, jerked awake at every fart and belch and rattling cough.

A yellow light flashes on the wall and the first prisoner arrives. After ten seconds another is allowed to enter. Each visitor is permitted a quick hug or a handshake, but no other touching is allowed, before they are separated across a table.

Foley appears, scanning the room expectantly. There's someone he hopes to see. It's not me. His expression changes, and he swaggers to the table, bigging himself up in front of his fellow prisoners. He's wearing prison-issue clothes, which are still creased from the packaging.

'Who are you?' he asks.

'I'm a psychologist. Cyrus Haven.'

'I don't need a shrink.'

'Maybe not, but you need a friend.' I hold up open palms. 'No notebooks. No wire. Just the two of us.'

'Mano a mano,' he says, his top lip curling. 'Why should I talk to you?'

'Your solicitor agreed to this . . .'

'That useless bitch,' he mutters. 'I've been stitched up.' He leans closer, speaking in a harsh whisper. 'I didn't kill that old man and I didn't kidnap Maya Kirk. Somebody out there is laughing, you know, because they got away with it.'

'You lied to the police.'

'That doesn't make me a killer.'

'Did you drug Maya?'

'Do I look that desperate? I can pull any bird I want.'

'Is that why you write fake dating profiles?'

'Everybody does that,' he scoffs. 'Women are the worst. Soft focus photographs, push-up bras, shapewear. You turn up expecting to meet Cinderella and you get the ugly stepsister. It's a game.'

I take two photocopied pages from my pocket – the sketches that Evie helped prepare. I slide the first one across the table, showing the driver of the car.

'Recognise him?' I ask.

Foley grunts. 'Prince Andrew? Harry Styles?'

I show him the second one.

'That's Paulie,' he says.

'How do you know him?'

'During the summer, me and my mates play basketball Sunday mornings at Victoria Embankment. Paulie used to play, until we told him to leave.'

'Why?'

'We have a no-dickheads policy. You can invite someone to play and if he turns out to be a dickhead, he gets booted.'

'And that was Paulie?'

'Yeah, he took the game too seriously. He elbowed Gazza in the face. Broke his nose. Bled like a stuck pig.'

'Who invited him to play?'

'Gazza. Serves him right, eh?' Foley grins.

'Did you ever see Paulie socially, out and about, at pubs or clubs?'

'Yeah. Occasionally.'

'What about on the night you met Maya?'

Foley pauses and scratches his nose. 'Would it help if I said yes?'

'Only if it's the truth.'

'Why? What's he done?'

'He died today in a car crash.'

Foley doesn't seem particularly concerned. I keep the drawings on the table, hoping for more.

'How did Maya seem on your date?' I ask.

'OK. A bit up herself, but she chilled after a while.'

'Who arrived first?'

'She did.'

'Anyone else talk to her, or buy her a drink?'

'No.'

'Anything unusual happen?'

'Like what? I mean, Maya asked me to swap seats because she saw some guy she wanted to avoid.'

'Did you see him?'

'Nah.'

'You said Maya was drunk. How much did she have?'

'Only three drinks, but she was slurring and swaying. That's why I offered to take her home.'

'When you left the last bar, was anyone hanging around – someone who might have been following her?'

'A driver pulled up. Asked if we'd ordered a car.'

'Did you see his face?'

'Nah.'

'What was he driving?'

'Took no notice.'

Foley finally begins to clock where I've been leading him. 'You think it was him? The driver.'

'Another woman has gone missing. She was picked up in the Lace Market on Friday night.'

'I was playing poker.'

'The police think you had an accomplice.'

'What! No!' He sits up straighter, leans forward. 'Does my lawyer know? She can get me out of here. Reasonable doubt, yeah?'

'Maya Kirk's DNA was found in your van.'

'She vomited.'

'Your semen was found at the murder scene and on Maya's dress.'

'I told you what happened. This is bullshit!'

He is shouting now. Guards are stirring. Visitors have stopped talking and are watching. Foley is jabbing his finger at me, spittle flying from his mouth. I tell him to be quiet, but he's on his feet, lunging at me.

'I'm being stitched up! You tell my lawyer she's fired.'

His fingers grip my shirt. Buttons pop. The guards are on him, wrestling him to the floor. Kneeling on his back. Dragging his arms behind him. Zip-tie handcuffs are looped over his wrists. Pulled tight. Chairs have fallen. Children are crying. I step back as they manhandle Foley out of the hall. I look at the other visitors and want to apologise. That's when I see Mitchell Coates at the end table. Our eyes meet and I see acceptance rather than sadness.

He's talking to a young woman. There's a resemblance. The eyes, maybe, and the peak on their hairline. A senior guard has arrived. Obese. Puffing. He wants to know if I'm injured and if I want to lay charges.

'He barely touched me,' I say dismissively.

'We have it on CCTV. We can charge him anyway.'

'That's up to you.'

I'm escorted from the visitors' room and pass close to Mitch's table. I make a show of searching my pockets and tell the guard that I must have dropped my locker key during the scuffle. He goes back to the table to look.

'How are you?' I ask Mitch.

He rocks his head from side to side, scratching at his cheek with two fingers.

'Evie didn't mean for this to happen.'

'We all make mistakes.' He nods towards his visitor. 'This is my sister Annie. She's driven up from London. This is Dr Haven – the guy I was telling you about.'

'Nice to meet you, Annie.'

'Are you going to help him?' she asks. 'He doesn't deserve to be here.'

'I'm going to try,' I reply, glancing at Mitch. 'Did you see the guy I was talking to?'

He nods.

'Ever seen him before?'

'No.'

'He's been charged with murdering Maya Kirk.'

'I heard it on the grapevine,' says Mitch.

'The police think Foley had an accomplice.'

'What's that got to do with Mitch?' asks Annie.

'Another woman has disappeared. Daniela Linares was picked up outside a bar in the city last Friday night. The police will want to know where you were that evening. You said something about emergency accommodation.'

'Yeah, but they didn't have any beds at the fire station, so I slept in the car park on Queen Street.'

'Can anyone vouch for you?'

'Yeah, but all of them are homeless and I don't know their names.'

'He shouldn't need an alibi,' says Annie, growing annoyed.

The prison guard is walking back towards us, having searched the floor beneath the table. I pat my pockets again and discover the locker key. 'Lose my head if it wasn't screwed on.'

The guard is unimpressed. He nods towards the door.

'Stay safe,' I say to Mitch. 'Nice meeting you, Annie.'

52

Cyrus

I drive into central Nottingham through misty rain that makes the wiper blades squeak against the windscreen. Traffic thins out as I enter Lower Parliament Street and pull into the Lace Market car park on Pilcher Gate. From there it's a short walk to the Little Drummer. Pushing open the heavy wooden door, I enter the warmth and hum of the bar, which looks bigger on the inside than from the outside.

The lighting casts the tables in a warm glow, making the place feel classy, even romantic, but most of the customers look like office workers who are grabbing a drink before they head home.

Cassie Wright waves to me from a table near a central pillar.

'When you offered to buy me a drink – I didn't expect it to be tonight,' she says, smoothing down her skirt.

'You look nice.'

'Thank you. You're late. I almost didn't stay. A woman drinking on her own looks sad or desperate.'

'You're not either of those things.'

'How do you know?' She smiles and pushes her hair behind her ears. 'Are you as clever as you think you are?'

'Rarely.'

She looks around. 'This is where Daniela Linares went missing.'

'Yes.'

Her left eyebrow arches. 'This is work, then?'

'Work and pleasure.'

'Mmmmm. OK. Dry white wine.'

The manager is easy to spot. Tall and skinny, he has a millionaire's moustache, waxed at the tips. Evie said his name was Brando, which sounds invented, or an affectation. When I reach the bar, he tosses a cloth over his shoulder and adjusts the rolls on his shirtsleeves, before moving towards me in a gangly, long-limbed way, like a baby giraffe learning to walk.

'What can I get you?'

'White wine. Something dry. And I'll have a Scotch on the rocks.'

He points to a selection on a shelf behind him. I choose one. 'Have the police talked to you about Friday night?' I ask casually.

A piece of ice slips from the tongs and bounces across the floor.

'You're not a copper.'

'I'm a forensic psychologist. I work with the police.'

'Yeah, well, I already told them everything I know.'

'Daniela Linares was sitting with two girlfriends at the table in the corner. You delivered drinks to them.'

'We only do bar service.'

'Not this time.'

Brando pauses. I can see that he remembers, but he wants to deny it, or block the thought.

'Someone bought them a round,' he says.

'What did he look like?'

'I don't know. A normal guy. The place was packed.'

'You can do better than that.'

'Forties. Shaved head. Your height.'

That doesn't sound like Paulie or Foley.

'What were they drinking?' I ask.

278

'A whisky sour, a Cosmopolitan and a daiquiri.' He smiles. 'That's my thing – I remember what people order.'

'You're like a Rain Man.'

Brando looks at me blankly. Sarcasm is wasted on some people.

'Did you leave the drinks unattended?' I ask.

'No.' As he denies it, I see uncertainty in his eyes. 'The police turned up. I talked to them. I was only gone for a minute.'

'Where were the drinks?'

'On the bar.'

I glance at the ceiling and notice a small CCTV camera tucked into the corner. The angle suggests that the staff are being monitored rather than customers.

'We had a few problems with one of our bartenders,' says Brando. 'Missing cash and bottles of booze. Officially, it's turned off because the staff complained.'

'And unofficially?'

Brando doesn't answer.

'Was it working on Friday night?'

He glances at the waiting customers. 'When I get a moment.'

Meanwhile, Cassie nudges my shoulder. 'A girl could die of thirst.'

'Coming now.'

I carry our drinks back to the table where we sit opposite each other. Cassie shifts on her stool. Our knees touch. She makes no effort to move. I take the opportunity to observe her up close. I look for some underlying feature or blemish that might detract from her good looks – lips that are too thin, or a crooked nose, or bad teeth – and while an absence of negatives doesn't necessarily make a positive, Cassie truly is beautiful. Yet behind the laughter and dancing eyes I can sense her sadness.

'Do you know this place?' I ask.

'I've been here a few times.' She motions to Brando. 'Did he make the cocktail for Daniela?'

'And delivered it to her table.'

'What was she drinking?'

'A whisky sour.'

'The lemon juice would have masked the taste of GHB.'

'Three different cocktails. Only one of them was spiked. If Daniela was the target, he must have been watching her.'

'Did anyone see him?' asks Cassie.

'No, but there might be footage.' I point to the camera.

She tilts her head. 'It's facing the wrong direction.'

'The drinks were left unattended on the bar.'

She makes a humming sound and sips her wine. 'You *are* very clever.'

'Not everyone thinks so.' I'm thinking of DCI Hoyle.

Cassie changes the subject and asks if I'm single.

'Yes.'

'Ever been married?'

'No.'

'How did you meet Evie?'

'I can't really talk about that.'

'Was she a patient?'

'No, but she needed my help.'

'Now I'm intrigued,' says Cassie, toying with a plain silver ring on her right hand. 'I think she has a crush on you.'

'What makes you say that?'

'The puppy-dog eyes are a bit of a giveaway.'

'That's too much mascara.'

I tell her how Evie has been trying to set me up on dates by faking a dating profile. Cassie thinks it's hilarious until I tell her that Evie swiped right on Maya Kirk, and they exchanged messages.

'That's cheeky – and dangerous.'

'I was almost kicked off the case.'

'OK, your turn,' says Cassie. 'What would you like to know?'

'I'm going to make observations.'

'OK.'

'You were married.'

'Who told you?'

'That ring on your right hand used to be on your left. It

doesn't fit since you swapped it over, which is why you keep checking that it hasn't slipped off.'

'Keep going.'

'You've recently grown your hair out – maybe during the lockdowns – and now you prefer it long. You've had back problems because you're quite tall and you're slightly pigeon-toed when you walk. You probably wear orthotics to correct it, but that's not difficult because you prefer wearing trainers and boots to sandals or ballet flats. Your shoulder bag is a senti-mental rather than a fashion choice. You put it on the chair next to you, rather than on the floor, which means you're carrying something valuable or important to you.'

Cassie's smile has slowly faded. I should stop, but I try to rescue the situation.

'I think you're quite shy, but you try to be confident, particu-larly when you're working with so many men who ignore your opinions or claim your good ideas as their own. You're grieving the loss of your sister but trying to hide your pain for the sake of others – your parents perhaps, or your brother-in-law – but sometimes that's impossible.'

Her features have changed. Hardened. Her knee is no longer touching mine.

'How do you know those things?' she whispers.

'This is what I do. I study human behaviour. Mannerisms. Body language.'

'Am I really that transparent?'

'No. You're quite difficult to read because you're very closed with some people and open with others.'

'But you barely know me,' she says.

I should never have started this.

'Most people do this subconsciously,' I say. 'We all look for clues in people's physicality, their attire, the way they speak, or act. Everything we do or say says something about us. Our age, grooming habits, clothing, vocabulary, accent, grammar, mannerisms, respiration, eye movements.'

'You were staring at me.'

'I was watching you, just like you were watching me, but I can explain what I see.'

Cassie shudders.

'I'm sorry. I didn't mean to upset you.'

She has finished her wine. I offer to buy her another.

'No. I have to go.'

She picks up her bag and squeezes past me, avoiding physical contact.

'I know we're not supposed to be talking about work, but did you test that rope?' I ask.

She looks at me impassively. 'What rope?'

'Voigt said he gave it to you. It came from another crime scene.'

She straightens her skirt. 'I've been busy on this case. Is it important?'

'Eight years ago, a woman was attacked in Nottingham. She had her hair hacked off, just like Maya Kirk, and her hands and feet bound with soft hemp rope. I want it tested against the rope used to bind Maya Kirk.'

'You think it's the same perpetrator?'

'The similarities are striking.'

We're interrupted by Brando. He props an iPad on the table and shows me the CCTV footage from the camera above the wet area of the bar. The angle is terrible, God-like, showing tops of heads and shoulders rather than faces.

Brando fast forwards and then slows the tape. We see him mixing the cocktails, adding ice, liquor and mixers. Shaking. Pouring. Something distracts him. He walks out of frame. This must be when the police arrive.

A man approaches the bar. He leans over, as though looking to attract the other barman's attention. I can't see his hands.

'That could be anyone,' says Cassie.

She's right.

'Isn't that Evie?'

At the edge of the frame, I see Evie holding a tray of empty glasses.

'Maybe he didn't drug the drinks,' says Brando. 'We had a needle spiking during the summer. A woman claimed that some guy stabbed her in the bum. Said she blacked out. Woke up next morning and found a needle mark.'

I remember there was a spate of similar stories around that time – and threats by women to boycott nightclubs and bars unless something was done to protect them.

'The post–mortem found no evidence of needle marks on Maya,' says Cassie. 'And it takes technical and medical expertise to inject someone with a drug.'

I replay the CCTV footage, pausing it every few frames, trying to glimpse the face of the man at the bar.

'Do you see that?' I say, pointing to the screen. For a moment, his reflection is visible in the mirror, partially distorted by the bottles. 'If we could enhance that . . .'

Cassie leans closer. 'We have software at the lab. I might be able to clean it up.'

53

Cyrus

The doorbell rings before anyone else is awake. Dressed in running gear, I'm about to clip a lead on Poppy and take her for some exercise. I open the front door. The reporter, Richard Holiday, has his hand raised ready to knock.

'Sorry about the hour, Dr Haven,' he says, touching his forehead, as though doffing an imaginary cap. 'Holiday. Associated Newspapers.'

He's wearing a rumpled grey suit that he might have slept in. He once spent two days perched in a tree to get a photograph of a grieving child, so a night in a car would be a small imposition.

'Do you remember me?' he asks.

'You're the tree hugger.'

He smiles at the joke. 'That was a long time ago.'

Poppy is sniffing at his shoes. Holiday tries to look past me into the house.

'I've heard whispers that your brother has been released from Rampton. Is it true?'

'No comment.' I begin closing the door.

He shoves his foot into the gap. 'I'll take that as a yes. How does it feel having him out?'

'Please get off my property.'

'Have you forgiven him?'

'He's a schizophrenic. You don't forgive a cancer patient for getting cancer or a disabled person for being disabled.'

'Can I quote you on that?'

'No. Fuck off!'

He is pushing at the door with his shoulder. 'Is he home? Perhaps a photograph of the two of you together. Brotherly love.'

'Get off my property.'

He holds up his phone and snaps a picture as the door shuts. From outside he yells, 'Do your neighbours know? I wonder how they feel about it?'

I go to the library window and watch as Holiday takes a photograph of the house and then walks up the path to my neighbour's place. Mr and Mrs Gibson. Brendan is a retired engineer who coordinates our local neighbourhood watch, liaising with the police to report any crimes. His wife, Julia, works for My Sight, a charity for the blind. They're about the age my parents would be if they were still alive. Now I can picture them at the head of the mob, carrying pitchforks and flaming torches, threatening to burn us out if we didn't leave town.

'Who was that?' asks Elias. He is standing on the landing, barefoot in pyjamas.

'Nobody.'

'It was definitely somebody.'

'A courier.'

'Where is the package?'

'It was the wrong address.'

I'm glad it's Elias and not Evie. She would have stopped me at the first lie.

'Are you going for a run?' asks Elias.

'I changed my mind.'

He follows me to the kitchen where he opens a cupboard and takes out a plastic pill box. He swallows six tablets with a glass of water. He will take another six in exactly twelve hours. Without them he'll lose his grip on reality.

'Are you working today?' he asks.

'Later.'

'I thought we might hang out. Go to the movies. Talk.'

'We can talk.'

He sits at the table and asks, 'Where are all the photographs? Grandma used to have dozens of them around the house – pictures of us as kids, growing up.'

'I put them away. Dr Baillie thought they might be triggering.'

He nods.

'How are you feeling?'

'Bored. I lie in bed. I listen to the radio. I watch TV. I stare out the window, counting birds on the telephone wire. I force my mind to go blank.'

'Don't you have assignments?'

'They'll never let me be a lawyer.'

'You don't know that.'

'Yes, I do.'

He scratches the hair above his navel. 'You've never asked me about that night.'

'I was there.'

'You probably remember more than I do. It felt like someone else was doing those things. That's why it took me so long to acknowledge what happened. I wanted to blame everyone else – the doctors, Mum and Dad, the drugs. That's what people do, isn't it? Blame everybody else because you don't want to deal with their guilt and their pain.'

'Yes.'

'For years I blocked it out. I pretended it was someone else – a different version of me. An alter ego, or a split personality.'

'What changed?'

'I don't know. Maybe it was the drugs. Maybe it was something in my mind. One day I had a sort of epiphany and started talking to people. Listening. Remembering. Forgiving.'

'Who do you have to forgive?'

'Myself.'

Elias must see the shock on my face.

'If I don't forgive myself, the remorse will consume me,' he explains. 'I was nineteen when it happened. I've had twenty years to learn that if you hold onto the pain and guilt it just keeps growing.'

He makes it sound so easy. For as long as I can remember, I have felt a vast weight resting on me, a sadness that has always been part of me yet doesn't belong to me. That's how I feel when I'm lying on the bench in the basement, holding the steel bar and weight plates off my chest so I can breathe.

Forgiveness and revenge are not opposing strategies or binary choices. Revenge can be empowering if the person who hurt you did so on purpose. But Elias didn't understand what he was doing. If I can forgive him, I can cast aside the weight, just like he has.

The doorbell rings again. This time I check the spyhole. My neighbour, Mr Gibson, is on the doorstep.

'Hello, Brendan. You're up early.'

'So are you,' he says. 'Going for a run?'

'Still deciding. Has Poppy been barking again?'

'No. Nothing like that. We had a visitor just now – a reporter from the *Daily Mail*. He said that Elias has been released from Rampton.'

'He's here for a few days.'

'Under guard?'

'He's recovered. A mental health tribunal has released him.'

Mr Gibson glances over his shoulder. Mrs Gibson is probably watching from their front window. She's a curtain twitcher, who seems to scowl disapprovingly at even the slightest change in the streetscape.

'As convenor of our neighbourhood watch, I think I should have been informed,' says Brendan.

'Why?'

'He's a . . . he's a . . . He's a convicted killer.'

'No. He was never convicted.'

'He killed your family.'

'His schizophrenia led to their deaths. A state of acute psychotic distress.'

'He was out of his mind.'

'Exactly. And now he's well again.'

Brendan begins to argue, saying residents should have been consulted. 'There are laws,' he says.

'No, there aren't,' I reply. 'You have no rights to be informed or to even ask about Elias's record or his health status. He isn't a sex offender or a paedophile. He's a schizophrenic and he's fully medicated.'

'Hello,' says a voice from behind me. 'What a lovely morning.'

Elias appears. 'Mr Gibson, isn't it? Lovely to see you again. I'm Elias.'

He holds out his hand and smiles disarmingly. The older man seems unsure of what to do. Prejudice clashes with politeness and the latter wins out. They shake hands.

'Your garden looks wonderful,' says Elias. 'I can't wait for the spring. What have you planted along the side fence? It looks like a climbing rose.'

'The Pippin,' says Brendan. 'It has a double bloom.'

'What colour?'

'Warm pink, with just a hint of orange on the petals.'

'I was only saying to Cyrus that I'd love to get a cutting.'

'Are you interested in gardening?'

'I did quite a bit at Rampton. They had a lovely garden. But I'm nowhere near as knowledgeable as you. I'd love to do something with our back garden. Perhaps you could give me some pointers.'

I can almost see Brendan's chest puff out.

'Having a dog doesn't help, but I could offer some suggestions.'

'That would be wonderful. I'm only here for a few days, but when I come back.'

'Yes. Right. Of course.'

'Give my regards to Mrs Gibson.'

'I will.'

The door closes. Elias grins at me. 'That went well,' he says.

Yes, but there will be more reporters coming and more neighbours knocking or gossiping. More rumours. More ghost stories. How long before local children are daring each other to ring the doorbell and run away?

Boo Radley has come to live with me.

54

Evie

The film crew has set up outside the Little Drummer. There are guys with hipster beards and girls in low-slung jeans and baseball hats, who spend a lot of time clipping lights onto tripods and hooking up cables that snake across the footpath. Each scene takes forever to set up and only seconds to shoot.

They have taken over the bar for the evening, filming indoors and outdoors, which must annoy Brando. I haven't seen him since he fired me.

Cyrus says this reconstruction is important because it might trigger people's memories and encourage them to come forward with information. He says that sometimes small details that seem inconsequential can prove to be the most crucial. I wanted to say that I'm a small detail and I've never been important, but he'd have some perfectly reasonable argument that made me feel selfish and even smaller.

DCI Hoyle is also here, walking around with a straight back and clenched buttocks like he's got a stick up his arse. I've noticed that he doesn't make eye contact with women when he talks to them. Instead, he looks past them, or over them. It could be nervousness or contempt.

A female police officer has been dressed up to look like Daniela, but the wig looks stupid and she's forty pounds heavier. If I ever go missing, I want them to choose someone hotter than me for the reconstruction. I know that sounds vain, but I don't want to look like a meth-addict or a baby-shaker. Cara Delevingne would be good, or that girl from *Emily in Paris*.

The police have found traffic-camera footage of the car, a stolen silver Prius, which was filmed about four streets from the bar. A day later, it was found burned out in a layby in Gedling. According to Cyrus there are more than two hundred CCTV cameras in Nottingham, filming intersections and public spaces. He said the local council hires people to sit in a room and watch them all day. I could do that. It couldn't be worse than those TV shows about room renovations, or fat people trying to lose weight.

'Everyone in position,' shouts the director.

I walk to the door of the bar. The Daniela lookalike gives me an encouraging smile. Someone holds a blackboard in front of our faces and claps his hands. The director yells, 'Action!'

We're supposed to recreate the moment when we left the bar, but it doesn't feel the same because it was darker and wetter that night.

'I have to put my arm around you,' I say to the policewoman. She leans on me so heavily that I almost fall over. 'I didn't carry her.'

'Sorry.'

Pedestrians are stopping to watch, taking pictures with their phones. They're probably wondering if this is some new TV drama, a cop show, and I'm some soon-to-be-famous actress. They might ask for my autograph. I used to practise signing my name, thinking I might be famous one day, and I wanted a signature with loops and swirls rather than my childish joined-up writing.

The Prius pulls up suddenly. Cyrus is behind the wheel wearing a baseball cap and dark-framed glasses. I open the back door and the policewoman crawls inside, slumping sideways. Overacting.

'Make sure she gets home,' I say.

The director yells cut. He wants a new camera angle.

'Did you remember anything else?' asks Cyrus, still behind the wheel.

'There was a tartan blanket on the back seat. And he had one of those air fresheners dangling from the mirror. It was shaped like a Christmas tree.' I can picture the scene more clearly now. 'His shirt had a collar and he wore a ring,' I say.

'What hand?' asks Cyrus.

'Left hand. Wedding finger. Silver. Plain.'

Hoyle interrupts, 'Then he's married.'

'Or it's part of a disguise,' says Cyrus. 'I think the cap and glasses were fake.'

They shoot the same scene again and this time the car pulls away. Everybody seems satisfied. A detective hands me a form to sign, which gives them permission to use the footage.

I look around for Cyrus to help me, but he's talking to Hoyle. Arguing. I move closer. Normally, I can't tell when Cyrus is angry because he doesn't raise his voice. If anything, he speaks more softly, making people lean closer and listen.

They're talking about the artist's impression that Frank drew. Hoyle wants to release it to the media.

'The only person who is likely to recognise himself is the driver,' says Cyrus. 'And if he thinks we're getting closer, he could panic and try to cover his tracks. That puts Daniela in greater danger.'

'We're running out of other options,' says Hoyle. 'I say we release the images and let him know we have an eyewitness. We appeal to him to let Daniela go.'

'And if he harms her?'

'He's going to do that anyway if we don't find her.'

I'm next to Cyrus, tugging at his sleeve. 'He'll know who I am.'

The two men turn to me.

'We won't use your name,' says Hoyle. 'And we're blurring your face.'

'Yes, but he knows what I look like. He saw me that night.'

Cyrus understands. He knows why I stay so quiet, why I want to be invisible, like a mouse in the walls.

After the film crew has packed up, Cyrus takes me to dinner at a Greek tapas place on Thurland Street. Our waiter is a young guy in a tight shirt and skinny-leg jeans. He asks me what I'd like to drink and I want to order something grown-up and Gucci, but I don't like the taste of alcohol.

'I can bring you a soft drink,' he suggests, making me feel like I'm twelve.

I order a rum and Coke.

'Am I going to have to drink that?' says Cyrus, after he's gone.

'Probably.'

'I saw Mitch today.'

My heart leaps. 'Is he out?'

'I went to the prison.'

'Was he angry with me? No, don't answer that. He must hate me.'

'He doesn't hate you, but the police still think Anders Foley had an accomplice and Mitch doesn't have an alibi.'

'Mitch wasn't driving the car.'

'I know, but the task force will look at him anyway.'

'He didn't attack Lilah Hooper. She didn't see the guy. She didn't hear his voice.'

'What did Mitch tell you about Lilah?'

'He said she was a nurse and that she looked after premmie babies, which was hard because sometimes the babies died, but that was part of natural selection. What does that mean?'

'Darwin's theory of evolution. In each generation, more offspring are born than can survive, but those who are fitter and stronger get to carry on and have more babies and pass on those traits.'

'That's brutal.'

'That's nature.'

Our drinks have arrived. I sip mine and immediately push it across the table.

'Is Lilah still a nurse?' he asks.

'Yes. Mitch said she was going to give it up because of some mistake at the hospital where she took the blame.'

Cyrus is staring at me. I can almost see his mind working. 'What sort of mistake?'

'He didn't say.'

He signals to the waiter. 'We have to leave.'

'But your meals are coming.'

'We don't have time.'

55

Cyrus

Melody Sterling peers nervously over the security chain.

'I thought you might be him,' she says, meaning her husband. 'He's not supposed to come anywhere near me, but he's been driving past the house.'

She unhooks the chain and leads us to the sitting room, where children's toys are stacked in boxes and playpens are resting against the wall, next to a teddy bear the size of a small pony.

Melody spies Evie. 'And who are you?'

'I'm nobody.'

'Oh, you never say that. Ever,' she replies. 'You are clearly someone very important because you're here with Cyrus. And he's a very clever man.'

'Evie is cleverer than I am,' I say.

'I have no doubt,' she replies, offering us the sofa. We've been whispering because Victoria is asleep upstairs.

'Has something happened?' asks Melody.

'You mentioned that Maya had left nursing after some sort of mix-up. What exactly?'

'Two babies were given the wrong drug. One died and the other became very sick. It was terribly sad.'

'Who was responsible?'

'There were three nurses on duty. None of them would say who made the mistake. They were charged with criminal neglect and one of them with manslaughter.'

'Was it Lilah Hooper?' asks Evie.

Melody's eyes snap open. 'Yes. That was her. The case was withdrawn. What's this about?'

'Could the third nurse have been Daniela Linares?' I ask.

'I only remember Lilah's name because it was in the newspaper. I was going through a box of Maya's stuff. I found a clipping.'

'Do you still have it?' I ask.

'It's in the spare bedroom.'

Melody goes upstairs. Evie wanders around the living room, picking up toys and rearranging them. She peers at some of the stick-figure drawings and finger paintings that decorate the walls.

'These are truly awful.'

'So were yours at that age.'

'How do you know? Maybe I was a prodigy.'

She retrieves a stray wooden block from a crack in the sofa. 'Do you ever want children?'

'I haven't thought about it.'

'Yes, you have.'

She's doing it again. It's like living with a mind reader.

'You're worried you might not be a good father,' she says.

'No.'

'Or that your kids might turn out like Elias.'

I don't answer, but she's closer to the truth.

After a beat she turns to study my face. 'Could you love someone who couldn't have children?'

'Yes.'

'You say that now, but you might change your mind.'

'That's possible.'

Another pause. 'You know that I can't have children – not after what they did to me.'

'How do you feel about that?'

Her shoulders lift and drop. 'I used not to care. Why bring a child into this fucked-up world?'

'And now?'

'What if a baby is the only way I'll ever be loved?'

'It won't be.'

'Do you love me?'

'Yes.'

'But not in *that* way.'

'In the best way.'

Evie smiles sadly. We have had conversations like this before and I have tried to explain to her that her feelings towards me are due to transference – the redirecting of emotions from one person to another because they represent what you desperately want, somebody who listens, or cares.

Melody returns with an old shoebox full of bric-a-brac – expired passports, postcards, photographs, lanyards, ticket stubs and receipts. She hands me a yellowing clipping.

A nurse accused of unlawfully killing a three-day-old premature baby and causing brain damage to another, has walked free from court after the case against her collapsed.

Lilah Hooper, 28, cried and hugged her friends and family as the judge instructed the jury that the prosecution had withdrawn from the case. Two other nurses, awaiting trial on charges of criminal negligence, were also acquitted.

The case arose after a mix-up in medications that occurred in the neonatal intensive care ward at the St Jude's Medical Centre in Nottingham, when one of the nurses mistakenly administered a dose of the wrong drug. One new-born died within hours, while another suffered permanent brain damage.

An internal investigation revealed that a pharmacy technician had stocked a cabinet with adult vials of heparin rather than Hep-Lock, a medication used to keep catheters open and flowing freely.

Judge Winston Davies, QC, instructed the jury to return a not guilty verdict against Lilah Hooper, who had denied the manslaughter of Oliver Rennie.

'In thirty-five years as a barrister and a judge I cannot think of a more tragic case,' Judge Davies said. 'My heart goes out to these families but also to the young nurses involved.'

Outside the court, a solicitor read a statement from the Rennie family. He said that his clients would be pursuing civil action against the hospital and the staff responsible.

A spokesperson for the St Jude's Medical Centre said the hospital trust was still considering whether the nurses would face disciplinary action or be allowed to return to work. The pharmacy technician had already been dismissed.

'Why was Lilah Hooper charged with manslaughter, but not the others?' asks Evie, who has been reading over my shoulder.

'Lilah was the senior nurse on duty,' says Melody. 'Maya was new to the unit. She didn't want to be a nurse after that. It broke her heart.'

My mind is rattling through the possibilities. Three nurses – the third one was almost certainly Daniela Linares. One attacked, one murdered, one missing – all linked to a joint tragedy. I've been looking at this from the wrong angle. The duck isn't a duck after all – it's only pretending.

56

Evie

'Where are we going?' I ask.

'I'm dropping you home.'

'But I want to come with you.'

'Not this time.'

'You think it has something to do with those babies.'

'Yes.'

We are driving towards home where Elias will be waiting, watching TV, eating snacks, wondering where we've been. He'll want to talk about a show he's discovered where people swap wives or get married at first sight. I don't want to be alone with him.

'Will you talk to Lilah Hooper?' I ask.

'Yes.'

'I thought that wasn't allowed.'

'This is different.'

Because there's one rule for you and another for me, I want to say, but that sounds childish when everybody knows there have always been two sets of rules – one for people like me and another for people like Cyrus. I don't mean men, although that's also true. I mean people who are respected and whose opinions are valued.

'I can show you where Lilah lives,' I say. 'And she'll be less frightened if I'm there.'

'I don't think that's a good idea.'

'I can tell you if she's lying.'

Cyrus seems to weigh this up as we turn into Parkside. We have reached the house. He doesn't stop. Instead, he turns left and left again, bringing us back onto Derby Road, heading east into the city. I have so many questions, but I stay quiet because I know that Cyrus is putting the pieces together. Eventually, I begin to fidget and sigh and make clicking noises with my tongue.

'What is it?' he asks.

'Why do some people find it easier to forgive?'

'What do you mean?'

'You've forgiven Elias for what he did, but you think there's someone who hasn't forgiven the nurses for what happened to those babies.'

'We don't know that's the reason.'

'But that's what you're thinking.'

Cyrus doesn't answer.

'You once told me that bearing a grudge was like mud wrestling with a pig. You both finish up dirty, but only the pig enjoys it.'

'Please stop quoting things back to me.'

'Why?'

'It's annoying.'

We've reached Portland Road. The lower windows are in darkness. I point to the buzzer. He presses. A light goes on. A voice crackles through the speaker. Sleepy. Anxious.

Cyrus holds up his identity card to the camera. 'My name is Cyrus Haven, I'm a forensic psychologist, and I work for the Nottinghamshire Police. I know it's late, but this is important. I need to ask you about Daniela Linares and Maya Kirk.'

There is a long pause. I can hear Lilah breathing.

'Who are you with?' she asks. I look up at the camera.

'You've met Evie,' says Cyrus. 'She's come to apologise.'

'How do you know her?'

'Evie lives with me, but this has nothing to do with Mitchell Coates.'

Well, that's not true, I think, but keep my mouth shut. We wait, wondering if silence is her answer. A siren sounds in the distance. A dog barks. Someone yells out a window. The door mechanism clicks.

Lilah is waiting for us. She's wearing a dressing gown over striped cotton pyjamas and is holding Trevor by his collar. He licks at my hand, remembering me.

Another small lounge room, this one lit by table lamps and smelling of dog. A sad-looking potted plant is almost leafless. Lilah takes the armchair, curling her feet beneath her. Cyrus sits opposite on the sofa, while I put a cushion on the floor where I can play with Trevor.

'This is about the babies, isn't it?' She takes a shuddering breath. 'I was going to come forward, but I was . . .'

She doesn't finish. I wonder what word she's missing. Frightened. Faint-hearted. Selfish.

'Daniela and Maya were the other nurses,' says Cyrus, wanting confirmation.

Lilah nods.

'When did you last see them?'

'Maya – not for years. I saw Daniela at St Jude's occasionally. I'm a theatre nurse now and she's in maternity. Have they found her?'

'The police are still looking,' says Cyrus, using his therapist voice, which makes you feel like you're being dipped in hot chocolate. 'I need to know what happened to the babies.'

Lilah picks at the polish on her toenails. 'It was a Sunday night. We were short-staffed. There were three new-borns in the neonatal ICU. Two of them were premmies and being kept

301

in incubators. The third needed a heart operation.' She pauses and takes an extra breath. 'Have you ever heard of Hep-Lock?'

'Explain it to me.'

'It's an intravenous solution which is injected into the IV catheter after the IV line has been inserted into the vein. It's designed to stop blood flowing back into the catheter where it can clot and prevent the flow of the IV medication. We use it a lot with premature babies.

'I sent Maya to get the Hep-Lock from the pharmacy cabinet. She came back with heparin – a blood thinner. The boxes were almost the same colour, light blue and dark blue, and the vials were identical. We administered the wrong drug – an adult dose, a thousand times stronger than a baby can take.'

'All three babies?'

'No, two of them.'

'When did you realise?'

'Babies are susceptible to heparin overdoses because of their weight, but the changes are quite subtle, so we didn't think anything was wrong until they started bleeding and had trouble breathing.

'I raised the alarm. The doctors arrived and tried to reverse the effects of the heparin, but it was too late. One baby was already dead and the other grew sicker. She suffered permanent brain damage.' Lilah's voice thickens. 'We didn't cover anything up. We told the truth to the hospital and the parents and the police – but we didn't reveal which of us had made the mistake.'

'Why?'

'Because it wasn't fair,' says Lilah. 'I took responsibility. I was in charge.'

'Did Maya administer the drug?' asks Cyrus.

'It doesn't matter. I should have checked. The pharmacy technician shouldn't have put adult heparin in the cabinet. But we were all so busy. Exhausted.'

'You were charged with manslaughter,' says Cyrus.

'The case was dropped.'

'What happened afterwards?'

'The families were furious. I don't blame them. The hospital had a disciplinary hearing. Maya quit. Daniela and I were suspended. I offered to resign, but they were short of nurses. They always are.'

'Surely the families sued?'

'The hospital settled. I wasn't called as a witness.'

Cyrus leans back and stretches his arms above his head. His shirtsleeves slide down his forearms, revealing a hummingbird and a house sparrow tattooed above his wrists. He glances at me. She's been telling the truth.

'How long after the case collapsed were you attacked?' he asks.

Lilah shoots a glance at me. 'What has that got to do with anything? You think I sent the wrong person to prison?'

'A jury did that – not you.'

Lilah shakes her head. Hair swings back and forth. 'Mitch attacked me.'

'But you're not sure,' I say.

Cyrus wants me to be quiet. He doesn't need to say as much. I can tell.

'You can understand why it's worth investigating,' he says. 'You, Maya and Daniela were all involved. You were attacked. Maya was murdered. Daniela is missing. Maya had her head shaved, just like you. Her arms were bound with rope.'

Lilah presses the palms of her hands over her eyes. 'It was Mitch. He had my earring . . . They found it upstairs.' When she shows her face again, there is a different emotion. 'Oh, God, what if I was wrong?'

'Let's take this slowly,' says Cyrus. 'Eight years is a long time to wait between attacks. The police are testing the rope used to bind you and Maya. If it matches, we'll know it's the same man.'

'What if it's not Mitch,' says Lilah, looking miserable. Before Cyrus can answer, she realises something else. 'Am I in danger? I mean, if he took Maya and Daniela . . .'

'He may feel that you've already been punished,' says Cyrus. 'But you should take precautions. Is there someone you can call?'

Lilah looks at her phone. 'It's after midnight. My mother would have a heart attack.'

'You can come and stay with us,' I say, glancing at Cyrus for confirmation.

Lilah hesitates, caught in two minds. She barely knows us.

'Or I can stay,' I say. 'I'll sleep on the sofa.'

I'm expecting Lilah to dismiss the idea, or for Cyrus to disagree, but neither of them says a word. Straight away I wish I could change my mind. Why do I care about this woman? Her evidence put Mitch in prison.

'I'll find you some pyjamas,' says Lilah, who goes to her bedroom.

When she's gone, I turn to Cyrus. 'Are you OK with this?'

'I think it's a good thing.'

'Why?'

'You can't always hide, Evie. Sometimes you have to show you're not afraid.'

'I'm not afraid.'

'Good.'

Lilah calls from the bedroom. 'I don't have anything your size.'

'A T-shirt will be great,' I reply.

Cyrus is still looking at me.

'Lock the door when I'm gone. In the morning, bring Lilah to our place. Wait for me to call.'

57

Cyrus

Silence in the pre-dawn. I have barely slept. I creep downstairs to the library and turn on the desk lamp. The pool of light reaches the mantelpiece and throws shadows on the walls. I look up, expecting to see a family photograph, but then I remember taking it down before Elias arrived.

The framed portrait was taken for a Christmas card when the twins were seven and I was nine and Elias fifteen. Mum made us wear matching sweaters with elves on the front and Dad has a Santa hat, tilted at a cocky angle. The only one of us not smiling is Elias, who participated under protest and adopted a defiant glare that he probably thought was rebellious, but just looks sulky.

Mum has a fixed smile and gritted teeth, having threatened to cancel Christmas if we didn't sit still and 'stop mucking about' because the photographer was costing money, even though she'd won the session as a lucky door prize at a school trivia night.

Unlocking my desk drawer, I take out two different photographs — one of Maya Kirk and another of Daniela Linares. I put them side by side on the desk. Light and dark. Blonde and brunette. Salt and pepper. Former colleagues. Nurses.

I am starting to understand this crime. The details have been floating in front of me like snippets from a film that needs to be edited into a story. The person responsible is no longer a mystery. I can see the world through his eyes. He's not a collector. This possession is about revenge, not ownership. It is about the yearning for a lost child; or a life that could have been.

Taking a large piece of paper, I concertina-fold it as though creating a road map that can be unfurled. On the first fold, I write the names of the three nurses. Maya Kirk. Daniela Linares. Lilah Hooper. On the second fold, I list the families: Rennie and Thompson.

Next, I create a timeline that begins with the tragedy at the hospital. Lilah Hooper was attacked seven months after the death of Oliver Rennie and six days after the manslaughter charges against her were dropped.

Eight years then passed before Maya Kirk was taken from her home. In that time, both families received compensation payments from the hospital, which settled without admitting liability; and none of the nurses were convicted of negligence or wrongdoing.

Although the world is naturally chaotic and unpredictable, there are cycles and patterns in nature that go beyond the passing of seasons and rise and fall of the sun; the petals of a flower, the notches on a pine cone, the Fibonacci spiral on a snail's shell, the fractals of frost crystals. There are countless examples of logic and order rather than randomness, but that does not mean that our fates are preordained.

Some people can see the world in patterns. In 2002, a middle-aged furniture salesman named Jason Padgett was attacked from behind and knocked unconscious as he left a karaoke bar. He suffered concussion and post-traumatic stress, but also, quite literally, he began seeing the world in a different way. Familiar scenes now had discrete geometric patterns superimposed on his vision. He saw fractals everywhere: in trees and clouds, in drops of water, in the number pi, or when he turned on a tap, or dipped his toothbrush. Padgett became a mathematics genius who could draw these fractals by hand.

As a psychologist, I look for the fractals in human behaviour. The things that are repeated or can be predicted. I can see one now. A man in his forties with a formal education to secondary level, and possibly a degree. Above-average intelligence, with strong geographical connections to Nottingham. He is a planner, who has made attempts to misdirect investigators and camouflage himself, hiding in plain sight. Some of the mistakes were genuine and others were manufactured to misdirect and deceive.

This is a man who has been frustrated at some point, who believes he deserves much better than life has given him. He has prepared for this, but not everything has gone to plan. When he slipped a drug into Maya's drink, he didn't expect Anders Foley to take her home. And he didn't realise that Rohan Kirk was in the house.

Foley didn't lie to the police about leaving Maya on the sofa. He covered her in a duvet and put a bowl next to the sofa in case she vomited. Yes, he took advantage of her stupor and masturbated on her dress, and stole underwear from her bedroom, but he didn't murder her father.

Somebody was waiting outside, watching him leave. He rang the doorbell. Maya struggled to her feet and answered. She would have seen her visitor through the reinforced glass, but she was groggy and disorientated. She turned the latch. He shoved her backwards. The door slammed against the wall, leaving a mark in the plaster. Her father heard the commotion and came downstairs. He interrupted the intruder, who panicked and picked up the closest weapon, the fire-poker. Blows rained down.

The killer was covered in Rohan Kirk's blood. Traces were found in the hallway, on the kitchen floor, and in the sink. He took off his clothes. He washed his face and hands. Then put his clothes in the washing machine and cleaned them, spending up to an hour in the house before taking Maya. That takes remarkable, almost sociopathic, calmness.

He took Maya to a waiting vehicle and kept her somewhere for forty-eight hours. Mortar was found embedded in her knees and paint flecks beneath her fingernails. It was somewhere old, an historic building, or an abandoned one.

I hear a creak on the stairs. Elias appears. He's dressed in baggy pyjama bottoms and an old T-shirt.

'Has something happened? Evie isn't in her room.'

I wonder how he knows, but her door is probably open.

'She stayed with a friend.'

He blinks at me. 'She doesn't like me, does she?'

'She doesn't know you.'

DCI Gary Hoyle has a regular court booked at the Nottingham Squash Rackets Club in Tattershall Drive. He plays with his brother-in-law, who is younger, fitter and a better player, but Hoyle makes up for his shortcomings by cheating. Whenever he's about to lose a point, he charges into his opponent, calling a foul. His brother-in-law doesn't complain. If anything, he seems to enjoy toying with Hoyle, missing a few easy forehands to make the score appear less lopsided.

I'm watching them through the glass wall at the back of the court. Hoyle waves enthusiastically when he spies me and tries to lift his game. Sweat drenches his T-shirt and runs into his eyes behind a pair of plastic safety frames. After another bodycheck and a mishit, he wins two points in a row and raises his arms in triumph. They shake hands and troop off the court.

'Cyrus, how nice to see you,' says Hoyle. Big smile. Sweaty handshake. He introduces his brother-in-law as Miles.

'This is our resident shrink,' he says. 'Careful what you say around him.'

Miles gives me a forced smile, before heading for the showers.

'I'm surprised they let you in,' says Hoyle. 'This is a private club.'

'I told them I worked for the police.'

'You don't carry a badge.'

'Not everybody does.'

Hoyle wraps every statement in a smile, but his eyes don't change.

'I left you a message this morning.'

'Early hours, by the look of it,' he says.

'Did you read my email?'

'Six pages. I'm waiting for the movie.'

He's heading for the locker room. I follow him through the swing doors into a dry area where a handful of men are getting changed. Hoyle peels off his T-shirt and drops it on the floor. His body is white and pale. A lone tattoo, inked along his forearm, reads: *I am not afraid. I was born for this.*

'Three nurses – all involved in the same incident – all targeted,' I say. 'Maya Kirk and Lilah Hooper had their hair hacked off. Both were bound with rope.'

'Lilah Hooper wasn't abducted,' says Hoyle. 'And we caught her attacker.'

'Mitchell Coates is innocent.'

'He told you that, did he? I saw him mowing your lawn. He was living in your house when we arrested him. You make very odd choices when it comes to lodgers, Dr Haven.'

Naked, he grabs a towel and strides towards the showers, his dick literally swinging.

'They were targeted because of what happened to the babies. The families were angry. You need to track them down. Interview them.'

'You described Maya Kirk's murder as a sex crime, but now you think it's an act of revenge.'

'I think it was made to look like a sex crime. The killer was trying to misdirect us.'

'Why now? Why does someone attack Lilah Hooper and then wait years before targeting the other nurses?'

'Something must have happened.'

Hoyle steps under the open shower. Water splashes on my shoes. I look away.

'Does my nakedness make you uncomfortable?' he asks.

'I'm giving you some privacy.'

'Is that what you call this?'

I go back to the locker room. His brother-in-law has gone. A few minutes later, Hoyle emerges, a towel around his waist. He begins getting dressed. 'I'm having Mitchell Coates transferred from HMP Nottingham to Radford Road. He was on parole when Maya Kirk was abducted, and he has no alibi for the night that Daniela Linares disappeared.'

'You're wrong about Mitch. You made a mistake seven years ago.'

Hoyle's features harden. 'I'm happy to entertain your speculations, Dr Haven, but if you begin questioning past convictions, you will have a very short career with the Nottinghamshire Police.'

Hoyle goes to a mirror and combs his hair, watching me in the reflection. 'You're an odd fish, Cyrus. You worked so hard to get the evidence against Anders Foley, and now you're working just as hard to find the evidence that will free him. Makes me wonder whose side you're on.'

'The truth doesn't have a side.'

Even as I say the words, I realise how trite they sound. Laughter explodes from Hoyle. He tries to apologise but he can't because he's laughing so hard. Other club members are drawn from the showers, smiling already, wanting to hear the joke. Hoyle waves them away.

'Please forgive me,' he says, wiping his eyes. 'I love your passion, Cyrus. I do. I think it's admirable. But you're looking for complex answers and ignoring the obvious ones.'

'That's not what I'm doing.'

'Of course it is. You're a psychologist. You look for hidden motives and buried secrets and strange perversions to explain human behaviour. But sometimes – most of the time – there aren't any. It's like Confucius said, life is really simple, but we insist on making it complicated. What you did – getting that footage from Melody Sterling – was brilliant – a feather in your cap – but you should step back now. Let me do my job.'

I am about to argue, but he stops me with the word 'enough', and slings his gym bag over his shoulder.

'If you really want to help the police, Dr Haven, go home and look after your brother. He's your responsibility now.'

'Elias is fine.'

'If it had been my choice, I would have kept him at Rampton for another twenty years.'

58

Evie

Lilah is one of those early risers, who bounces out of bed all sparkly-eyed and energetic. I'm the opposite. I wake slowly, as though I'm trying to creep up on the day, or worried I might scare it away.

'I made you a cup of tea,' she says, sitting on the end of the sofa. 'Would you like some breakfast?'

I cover my head with a pillow. 'I'd like another three hours' sleep.'

She waits for me to emerge. I hear Radio 1 Breakfast playing from the kitchen. Why are morning DJs so bright and chirpy and relentlessly positive? It's like Instagram for the ears. Everybody sounds prettier and happier and funnier.

Lilah is still sitting on the far end of the sofa.

'Are you working today?' I ask.

'Not until four. Normally, I'd go for a run, but I'm frightened of going out by myself and Trevor needs a walk.'

'I could come with you,' I say, before I get a new idea. 'We could collect Poppy and go together.'

Lilah likes that plan. I drag myself off to the bathroom and put on yesterday's clothes – the black jumpsuit, which I wore for the re-enactment. Now I feel overdressed.

Back in the sitting room, she's folding the bedding. We hold opposite corners of a blanket and bring them together.

'How do you know Dr Haven?' she asks.

'It's a long story and I'm not supposed to tell it.'

'Why not?'

'I spent most of my childhood in state care.'

'Did he adopt you?'

'No!'

'Foster you?'

'For a while, until I turned eighteen.'

'How old are you now?'

'Twenty-one.'

'You look younger.'

'Everybody tells me that.'

Pillows are plumped up and rearranged.

'Does Cyrus have a girlfriend?' she asks, trying to make it sound like part of the conversation.

'He doesn't want one – not right now.'

After toast and tea, we put Trevor in the back seat of Lilah's car where he moves from side to side to look out the window and occasionally sniff at my hair. Lilah drives even more carefully than I do, double-checking her mirrors and indicating well before she changes lanes.

At Parkside, she pulls over and parks beneath the plane trees. Fallen leaves cover the grass verge and footpath, creating a soft carpet beneath our feet.

She stops at the gate. 'This place is a mansion.'

'It belonged to Cyrus's grandparents.'

'My grandparents gave me nothing except achoo syndrome.'

'What's that?'

'I sneeze when I look at a bright light.'

'Is that a thing?'

'Oh yeah, just like ingrown toenails, big ears and rolling your tongue.' She rolls her tongue to show me.

I suddenly stop. Cyrus's car is gone.

'Is everything all right?' she asks.

'Cyrus's brother is staying with us.'

'Is he handsome, too?'

'No.'

I fish into my pocket, looking for my house key. I don't have it. 'We'll go around the back.'

I lift the latch and push open the side gate. I expect Poppy to be inside, sleeping next to a radiator, but somebody has locked her out. She barks aggressively, until she realises that it's me and goes crazy, dashing around the garden. Trevor joins the chase.

I tip over the headless garden gnome and retrieve the spare key.

'First place I'd look,' says Lilah, teasing me.

The kitchen smells of bacon and eggs. A greasy frying pan and egg-stained plate are unwashed in the sink.

'I'll get changed and we'll go,' I say, keen to get away, but Elias has heard us arrive and suddenly appears. He's wearing one of Cyrus's cotton shirts that's too small for him.

'Hi-ho,' he says, trying to sound jolly. He looks at Lilah, waiting to be introduced.

'This is Lilah. Lilah, this is Elias.'

'Hello,' he says. Is he sucking in his stomach? 'Cup of tea?'

'We're not staying.'

'Where are you going?'

'We're taking the dogs for a walk.'

'Can I come?'

'No.'

'Why not?'

I motion to his ankle.

Elias glances quickly at Lilah and away again. Embarrassed.

'Why was Poppy locked outside?' I ask.

314

'Oh, I didn't realise.'

He's lying, but I let it go and quickly run upstairs to change into jeans, a sweatshirt and my old coat. There are half-empty boxes on the landing and bulging bin-bags. Downstairs again, I ask him what he's doing.

'Cleaning.'

'Don't go into my room.'

'I wouldn't dream of it.'

We collect the dogs from the garden and Poppy leads us towards the park.

'That was weird,' says Lilah.

'Did he say something?'

'No. Why don't you like him?'

'I barely know him.'

'But he lives with you.'

'Only since last Friday.'

'Where was he before that?'

'Away.'

She knows I'm being secretive but keeps pushing. 'Why did you point to his ankle?'

'Did I?'

'You said he wasn't allowed to leave the house.'

'He's wearing a monitor because he's just been released from Rampton, the psych hospital.'

'My God! What did he do?'

'It doesn't matter.'

'Is he going to be staying long?'

'I haven't decided yet.'

59

Cyrus

The two men who meet me in the foyer of St Jude's Medical Centre are dressed in charcoal-grey suits, white shirts and silk ties. Both have a military bearing, and project their voices as though marshalling troops on a parade ground.

The older of the two introduces himself as Walter Farquharson, the hospital's in-house counsel. His colleague, who could be his son, only gives me his first name: Richard.

We talk in a boardroom which has a long table set out with a dozen water glasses, jugs of water, and pristine notepads with a pen centred on each. Their first questions are perfunctory. Did I manage to find a parking spot? Is the room too warm? Would I like to sit near the window? Everything appears scripted and stage-managed, right down to the choice of seats.

'How can we help you, Dr Haven?' asks Farquharson.

'I'm seeking information about an historic legal action against the hospital. One of your nurses was charged with manslaughter. The case collapsed.'

The lawyer appears surprised, although the only outward sign is the lifting of a grey unkempt eyebrow.

'Somebody has already called from Nottinghamshire Police requesting the same information – a detective chief inspector.'

'DCI Hoyle?'

'Yes.' The men exchange a glance. 'We're seeking instructions from the board of trustees before releasing any of our files.'

Clearly, they're worried about negative publicity.

'One of your nurses is missing,' I say.

'Which is highly unfortunate, but could be completely unrelated,' says Farquharson. 'It goes without saying that we'll do everything we can to assist the police, but her disappearance has nothing to do with St Jude's.'

'And if it were to be related?' I ask. 'And if the hospital was shown to have delayed or hindered police attempts to find her . . .' I don't finish the statement, but the implications are clear. 'Gentlemen, I'm not seeking to damage the reputation of your hospital. I want to find a young woman, who is possibly in great danger.'

There is a moment of silence. The men look at each other. The younger man speaks first. 'My name is Richard Hawkins. I'm the CEO of the St Jude's Medical Centre Trust. What is it you wish to know?'

I suddenly realise that he's the one in charge. Until now, he's been hiding behind the older man's gravitas, before deciding which way to jump.

'There was an incident eight years ago. Two premature babies were given the wrong medication. A nurse was charged with manslaughter and two others with criminal negligence, but the cases collapsed. The hospital was sued for negligence.'

'We settled both cases. One family received a lump sum payment of £400,000. The second case was decided twelve months ago in the High Court.'

'Why did it take so long?'

'We had to wait for the police investigation and the inquests and our internal inquiries.'

'That didn't take eight years.'

'The negotiations were sensitive in nature,' says Farquharson, who is choosing his words carefully.

'Why?'

'The Rennie baby was born at twenty-four weeks. His chances of survival were sixty per cent at best. He lived for less than three days. The hospital admitted limited liability and the settlement reflected our desire to compensate the family for the hurt caused.

'In the case of the little girl, Daisy Thompson, we knew that she would need round-the-clock care. She suffered from intractable epilepsy and cognitive impairment. We agreed to pay a substantial lump sum and index-linked payments to cover the cost of her ongoing care.'

'How much?'

'Three million pounds and an annuity of £250,000 to cover the cost of her future care.'

'Was her family happy with the settlement?'

'They agreed,' says the lawyer, as though it should be obvious.

Something is being kept from me.

Hawkins is more open. 'We were putting a price on a child's life. Nobody is ever completely satisfied. And given the circumstances . . .' He doesn't finish.

'What circumstances?'

The two men exchange a glance. 'Daisy Thompson died earlier this year. Pneumonia. Medical complications. It was very sad.'

Suddenly, it makes sense to me. 'You dragged out the settlement because you suspected Daisy would die.'

'That's an outrageous suggestion,' splutters Farquharson. 'We paid the family three million pounds.'

'Did you backdate the annuity payments?'

'No.'

'Which means the hospital saved two million pounds. That's money that could have been used to improve her quality of life.'

Hawkins is equally angry, his face turning a puce colour. 'Be very careful, Dr Haven. The board of trustees will not hesitate to sue if you defame this hospital.'

'What happens to the annuity payments now?'

'They will cease,' says the lawyer. 'As per the deal.'

'Another saving,' I mutter under my breath.

There is a knock on the door. A young man has a message.

'I have another meeting,' says Hawkins.

I suspect a signal was involved – a secret text message to arrange the interruption.

Both men get to their feet. Farquharson speaks. 'We reached very fair and equitable settlements with each family. The trust cannot be blamed for subsequent events.'

'What happened to the nurses who were involved in the mix-up?' I ask.

'One resigned. Two were suspended. And we dismissed the pharmacy technician responsible for putting the wrong medication into the ICU cabinet.'

'Lilah Hooper and Daniela Linares were re-employed.'

'They are both good nurses. Diligent. Caring. Given staff shortages in the NHS we couldn't afford to lose them.'

60

Cyrus

It isn't difficult to locate the Thompson family. A Google search throws up a local newspaper story about the settlement. It mentions a street name, Inglewood Road, and a suburb, Clifton. After that I simply knocked on doors until someone pointed me to the right house.

I'm at the front gate when I hear a voice.

'I thought I'd find you here,' says Lenny, stepping from her car.

'Are you having me followed?'

'I know how you think.'

'Daisy Thompson died eight months ago. That's the sort of trauma that could tip a person over the edge.'

Lenny glances up the path. 'You should leave this to the task force.'

'Hoyle didn't believe me.'

'You gave him no time.'

'He's convinced that Mitchell Coates is Foley's accomplice.'

'Or he's keeping his options open.'

I ring the bell and listen as two pairs of bare feet come thundering towards the door, racing to be first. Hands reach for the latch. Two breathless boys, aged about five, with tea-brown hair and pink cheeks, are blinking at us.

A woman's voice follows them. 'Don't you *dare* open that door until I get there.'

'Oops,' says the taller of the boys, who is wearing a Liverpool FC shirt.

Lenny holds a finger to her lips and motions for him to shut the door.

He does so. A few moments later, it opens again. The mother has pushed the boys behind her, telling them to watch TV.

'Orla Thompson?' asks Lenny.

'Yes.'

'I'm Detective Superintendent Parvel and this is—'

'What's he done now?' she asks.

'Pardon?'

'My husband. What's he done? Punched someone? Crashed his car? Walked into the wrong house?'

'Nothing like that,' says Lenny.

Mrs Thompson is looking at me, as though I'm familiar. She hears a noise behind her. The boys are still listening. She shoos them away and invites us inside, leading us down a long hallway to an open-plan kitchen and dining area, with picture windows overlooking a soggy garden with a plastic swing set and a bird feeder hanging from a tree. The kitchen looks new, with a large island bench and polished steel appliances.

Orla takes a seat. Thin and fair-haired, with sharp cheekbones and a narrow nose, she's wearing trousers and a white blouse, loose around her neck. The boys are wrestling or chasing each other upstairs. Something falls and breaks. She sighs but doesn't bother to investigate.

'They'll tell me if they're hurt,' she explains. 'Or if they're hungry, or if they're bored, but they never tell me they're dirty, or sleepy, or naughty.'

'Are they both yours?' I ask.

'Oh, God no. Leo is mine. Jamie lives next door. His mum and I take it in turns to give each other a break.'

'Where is your husband?' asks Lenny.

'We're separated.'

'When did he move out?'

'During the summer.'

'I heard about your daughter,' I say. 'I'm sorry for your loss.'

Her fingers reach for a small silver crucifix on a chain around her neck. 'God took her home.'

'I know this is a very personal question, but was Daisy's death a factor in the separation?'

Orla nods and lowers her eyes, using her sleeve to wipe at an invisible mark on the benchtop.

'We looked after Daisy for almost eight years. Twenty-four hours a day. She couldn't talk or hear and barely ever smiled. She was on a dozen different medications for seizures, body pain, spasms, acid reflux, constipation, you name it. It wore us down. When Leo was born, I worried that he'd grow up resenting us for spending so little time with him, because Daisy took up so much of our attention. I hope he doesn't hold it against us.' She sighs and smiles tiredly, before beginning again. 'I discovered the strangest thing when Daisy died. I learned that all I had in common with my husband was a sick child. Without her, we didn't have a marriage.'

'That must have been hard.'

She gives a little shrug of her shoulders.

'Does he still see Leo?'

'Of course. He picks him up from preschool two days a week and has him most weekends. He should have had him yesterday, but he cancelled.'

'Did he say why?'

'No, but he was drunk, which is another reason I left him. Mark has always called himself a wine collector – Pinots mainly. He calls them investments, but he drinks everything he buys and then moves on to whisky and port and whatever else he can find. He's an alcoholic, but he won't admit that. But I make sure he's sober when he comes to pick up Leo.'

She points to a small handheld breathalyser on the counter, which has a blowing tube on one side.

'Where is he living?' asks Lenny.

'This week? Who knows? Couch-surfing at some mate's house, most likely, until he wears out his welcome. I could call him, but he doesn't answer his phone on Mondays. It's his day off because he works most Saturdays showing properties.'

'He's an estate agent,' I say.

'Yes, but mainly he does property management.'

'You've renovated recently,' I say, admiring the kitchen.

'Thanks to the settlement,' she replies, taking no pleasure in the statement. 'We almost lost this place. We had to remortgage and borrow from family to pay for Daisy's care. I gave up work and we were surviving on whatever Mark could make until the hospital paid up.' Her mouth curls and eyes narrow. 'They dragged out the negotiations because they knew Daisy was going to die.'

'How did your husband feel about that?' asks Lenny.

'Bitter. We both did.'

'Did you blame the nurses for what happened?' I ask.

'It was an accident. I understand that. One of them wrote us a letter afterwards, saying how sorry she was.'

'Which one?'

'Lilah Hooper. She was in charge that night, but none of them took responsibility.'

'Did that make you angry?' I ask.

'For a while, maybe, but I'm a New Testament sort of Christian. I believe in forgiveness, not an eye for an eye.'

'Does Mark feel the same way?'

'He's not a Christian, if that's what you're asking. More an agnostic, but he's very passionate and headstrong. He gets teary when he hears the National Anthem, or when the Liverpool fans sing "You'll Never Walk Alone" at Anfield.' She smiles sadly. 'What's he done?'

'Maya Kirk was murdered twelve days ago,' says Lenny.

There is a flash of recognition in Orla's eyes. 'I saw it on the news. I thought it must be her.'

'And Daniela Linares disappeared over a week ago from outside a bar in Nottingham.'

Orla opens her mouth to respond, but nothing comes out. She tries again. 'And you think Mark had something to do with it?'

'We need to talk to him,' I say.

'He would never . . . I mean, he's not like that. He's a drunk, not a killer.'

Orla's defence begins to falter. Something breaks upstairs, followed by a cry of pain. A mother is wanted.

61

Evie

Lilah is a talker. A chatterbox. A stater of the obvious. She says things like, 'Doesn't the grass look green?' and 'Ducks have such funny walks', and she tries to catch the falling leaves, saying it's good luck.

We're following one of the paths through Pearson's Wood, past the lake and the deer conservation area, along the narrow tarmac footpath to the Nottingham Industrial Museum.

'I love this time of year,' she says. 'The air is so clean and it's not too hot and not too cold.'

'Like Goldilocks.'

'Pardon?'

'The porridge – not too hot, not too cold.'

She laughs and looks at me like I'm crazy, but not in a bad way. We're acting like we're friends, even though I'm much younger. I don't have many friends, and I hope I'm making the right facial expressions – smiling when I should smile. I should have practised in the mirror before we came out.

Lilah asks me if I have a 'special someone' and what I'm studying at school. I'd rather talk about her. She tells me about her family, which includes a brother and sister, who are both married with kids, which makes them the favourites.

'I'm the disappointment because I haven't added to the pool of grandkids.'

'Do you want them?'

'Kids? Yes. When I find Mr Right, or Mr Good Enough. I used to have a teacher called Mr Goodenough. We'd tease him by saying, "Do you ever feel you're not good enough, sir?"'

We stop and take photographs of Wollaton Hall, a big old mansion in the middle of the park, that was once probably owned by a duke or a lord and is definitely haunted. Lilah asks me why I think Mitch is innocent.

'Because he's telling the truth.'

'How can you be sure?'

'I can tell when someone is lying.'

She laughs, thinking I'm joking. I pull her to a park bench and make her sit facing me.

'OK, tell me something about yourself. Anything. Make it up.'

She thinks it's a game and plays along. 'At school I won a medal for Scottish dancing.'

'True. Try again.'

'My middle name is Penelope.'

'False.'

'When I was young, I tried to get rid of my freckles by scrubbing them with lemon juice.'

'True.'

She hesitates and softens her voice. 'My father has a mistress. I don't know if I should tell my mother.'

'You should tell her.'

'Are you saying it's true?'

'Yes.'

Uncertainty fills her eyes, and she looks exposed, as though she's stepped outside and discovered that she's not wearing any clothes.

'How . . . I mean . . . you're saying . . . that's impossible . . .' She can't finish, but she shuffles further away from me on the bench.

'Mitch didn't attack you. He left your door unlocked because you were always forgetting your keys.'

'I forgot them once,' says Lilah.

'More than that.'

Again, she realises that she can't lie to me.

'Trevor didn't bark. He always barks at strangers.'

'He didn't bark at me.'

'It had to be Mitch.'

'Why? He found you. He untied you. He called the police.'

'He knew that would make him seem innocent.'

'Or he *was* innocent.'

Angrily she gets to her feet and starts walking. 'I don't want to talk about this.'

'What about the other nurses – Maya and Daniela? Do you think Mitch attacked them?'

'Maybe that has nothing to do with what happened to me.' She keeps walking away from me. This is the reason I don't have many friends. It's not just that they lie to me – people do that all the time – but I'm not good at letting things go. I scratch at itches and pick at scabs and pull at loose threads.

As we circle back to the lake, Poppy spots a squirrel and takes off, ripping the lead from my hand. I call out to her and give chase. The squirrel scampers up a tree and Poppy circles the base, sniffing and barking.

When I get back to Lilah, she looks different. Pale. Scared.

'There was a man,' she says, pointing to the woods. 'He's been following us.'

'Probably some pervert.'

'No. I recognise him.'

'From where?'

'I don't know.'

I look around us, but the paths are empty. 'Where did he go?'

327

'He saw me looking and he ran off.' She points back the way we came. I take a few steps, but she calls out, 'No, don't go. Stay with me!'

'What did he look like?'

'He had a leather jacket, and he was bald, or his head was shaved.'

I wonder if I should call Cyrus. What would he do? Tell us to go home and stay there.

We exit through the western gate and turn along Parkside. As we near the house, I notice a van parked further along the road – a food truck. I've seen it before. Where? The hinged sides are folded down, and the cabin is empty.

Lilah is chatting again, asking about what I want to do when I finish school. I'm still thinking about the truck. I do that sometimes – look for things that are out of place. Veejay says I have an enquiring mind, but I know the real reason. I am waiting to see a face in the crowd that I recognise. Somebody from my past, who is looking for me.

62

Cyrus

TV crews and reporters have gathered at Radford Road, setting up lights and cameras in the conference room, checking the sound and the angles. There is a flurry of activity as Hoyle enters wearing his dress uniform, the dark trousers and white shirt with dark blue epaulettes threaded with gold.

'Ladies and gentlemen, thank you for coming. You will all be aware that we are searching for a nurse, Daniela Linares, aged thirty-two, who went missing from central Nottingham ten days ago. She was last seen getting into a car which she believed was a minicab or a rideshare lift.

'Yesterday evening we filmed a re-enactment of those events. The footage will be released to you today. We will also be providing an artist's impression of the driver provided by an eyewitness.'

The conference room lights are dimmed. Hoyle steps aside. The first frames show an external view of the Little Drummer. Hoyle gives a running commentary, setting the scene.

'It was a rainy Friday night. Nottingham Forest had played Blackburn Rovers at the City Ground, a five o'clock kick-off. There were fans on the streets in team colours. The Christmas markets had started in Old Market Square, but the tree hadn't yet been decorated.

'There were hundreds of people in the Lace Market area who may have seen Daniela that night, or the driver of the car, a silver Prius, which had been stolen earlier in the evening.'

Evie is in frame, standing on the footpath with the policewoman playing 'Daniela'. Both of their faces are clearly visible. Hoyle lied to me.

'Our actress is wearing very similar clothes to what Daniela was wearing that night,' says Hoyle. 'A halter-neck bodysuit with a suede, high-waisted skirt and strappy heels. This is the image of the driver. Our witness only glimpsed him very briefly from side-on, which is why we can't offer you a more detailed likeness, but it may trigger someone's memory. If you saw Daniela that night, or if you know the driver of the car, please call our Crimestoppers hotline, or the incident room. Any contact can be entirely confidential.'

'Who was the witness?' yells a reporter.

'A casual employee at the bar.'

'Is it true that Daniela was drugged?' asks another.

'I cannot confirm that.'

A third voice asks, 'Is there a link between Daniela's disappearance and the murder of Maya Kirk and her father?'

'Perhaps if you'd let me finish,' says Hoyle, but his refusal to answer triggers more questions.

'Could Anders Foley have taken Daniela Linares?'

'We don't believe so.'

'Did he have an accomplice?'

'That is one line of inquiry.'

'Did Daniela and Maya know each other?'

Hoyle would make a lousy poker player. 'I'm not going to conduct a running commentary on the investigation.' He raises his hands. 'Please. We have Daniela's mother here today, who is going to make a statement.'

I hadn't noticed Mrs Linares sitting beside the stage, flanked by Edgar and Monroe. Some people grow smaller in the spot-light, overawed by the attention, but she seems stronger and more determined when she steps to the podium, raising her chin as the camera shutters click in rapid-fire. She speaks without notes, but I know she's rehearsed what she's going to say.

'My daughter's disappearance is my worst nightmare and there are no words to describe my anguish. I know in my heart that Daniela is alive and desperately wants to come home. If you're the person who took her or if you know who's respon-sible, please call the police.' She pauses and looks directly down the lens of the nearest TV camera. 'And this is a message for my daughter, my dearest, my only child. On my last birthday, you asked me if the happiest day of my life was the day you were born. I said it was the happiest day *ever*. And the second happiest day will be the day that you come home.'

Her voice breaks, but she manages to get the last words out. Hoyle puts his arm around her and escorts her from the stage. The emotion of the moment seems to infect the entire room and the reporters have fallen silent. They have their story. Hoyle takes a few more questions before the news crews begin packing up gear, toting cameras and recording equipment.

As he steps off the stage, Hoyle is approached by a uniformed officer, who hands him an envelope. He tears it open and reads. The blood drains from his face. He looks up, searching the room. His eyes come to rest on Lenny, full of disgust and undisguised loathing.

'What is it? What's happened?' I whisper.

'Hoyle is off the case.'

'Why?'

'The Chief Constable believes the death of Paulie Brennan could have been avoided and has ordered an internal investiga-tion.'

'Who made the complaint?' I ask.

'I expressed my reservations.'

There is no sense of triumph or valediction in the admission.

Upstairs, detectives have gathered in the incident room, talking in whispers, as the news begins to filter through. Lenny summons them to gather around her. Soon they're two and three abreast, standing room only.

'DCI Hoyle is meeting with the Chief Constable,' she says. 'I'll be taking over the investigation. The focus is changing.'

Lenny pins a photograph of Daniela Linares alongside that of Maya Kirk on the whiteboard.

'Eight years ago, these women were nurses working in a neonatal intensive care unit at St Jude's Medical Centre. Two babies were given the wrong medication. Jolene and Patrice Rennie lost baby Oliver after three days. Mark and Orla Thompson had a daughter, Daisy, who suffered brain damage and severe medical complications. She died in March of this year.

'A third nurse, Lilah Hooper, was also working in the neonatal ICU. She was charged with manslaughter, but the case against her collapsed. I want her interviewed and put somewhere safe.'

'She's with Evie,' I say.

'Bring her in.' She turns to DS Edgar. 'We need to find the pharmacy technician who put the wrong medication in the ICU cabinet. The hospital has given us a name.'

Edgar nods.

Lenny looks at Dave Curran. 'What do we know about the families?'

'Mark and Orla Thompson separated in July, four months after their daughter died. Thompson has been staying with friends or living in Airbnbs and serviced apartments. He's an estate agent, who works out of an office in Hucknall. He handles the property management department, which means he has access to vacant houses and businesses.'

'I want a list,' says Lenny. 'Look for historic buildings, or places that are off the grid.'

Prime Time takes over.

'Patrice and Jolene Rennie sold their house in Nottingham

last January and flew to America in March for some sort of medical treatment. Rennie is a former soldier, who did two tours in Afghanistan, working as a medical support officer. He resigned his commission and retrained as a chef, before setting up a catering business that went under during the pandemic. The company still has a website, which hasn't been updated in almost a year.'

Lenny nods. 'Find out where they are now. The rest of you, focus on Mark Thompson. Talk to his friends, family, colleagues – anyone who might know his whereabouts. I also want searches of his social media accounts, credit card receipts and phone records.'

'Waiting for the warrant,' says Edgar.

I have stepped away to call Evie's number. She doesn't answer. I leave a message:

'The police want to see Lilah. Stay with her and call me.'

63

Evie

The cardboard boxes and bin bags have multiplied and are partially blocking the front hallway and the landing. I hear furniture being moved above our heads.

I shout up the stairs, 'Hey! What are you doing?'

Nobody answers.

I climb, leaving Lilah to put the dogs in the garden. The attic door is open.

'You're not supposed to go up there,' I say.

A head appears. Elias. Grinning. He has cobwebs in his hair. 'What are you doing?'

'I thought I might make this my bedroom.'

My throat begins to close. 'No! You can't! It's mine!'

'You already have a bedroom.'

'Put everything back. No! Don't touch anything. Get out!'

I push past him into the attic. The furniture has been moved – the wooden chests and boxes and old rugs and moth-eaten curtains. My cardboard walls have gone. My hiding place. He has forced the window open and swept at the dust, which is floating in the air as though suspended in water.

'A coat of paint and a bed and it's going to be nice,' says

Elias, who has no idea what he's done. 'I even get a view,' he says. 'Across the park. I was watching you and Lilah walking the dogs.'

I look at the window sill, searching for the collection of coloured glass, marbles, polished pebbles, and the button from my mother's coat.

'Where are they?' I ask, my voice shaking.

'What?'

'There was a button and pieces of coloured glass.'

'I thought they were rubbish.'

'Where are they?'

'I threw them away.'

'Which bag?'

'I don't know. One of them.' He laughs nervously.

'They were my things. They belonged to me.'

He gawks moronically.

'Show me where,' I yell.

'I can't remember. One of the bags.'

'In the hallway? On the landing? Where?'

I shove him aside and go down the stairs, tearing open the first plastic bin bag, which is full of bank statements, electricity bills and receipts. I rip open the next bag and find yellowing copies of *National Geographic* and crumbling school exercise books. I kick at a box. It topples over, spilling out old clothes including a mouldy army uniform and a box of military medals.

I only care about finding the button. It's all I have left of my mother – a small piece of something she wore. When I hold it in my fist, I can remember the sound of her voice and picture her face and feel her arms wrapped around me.

'What are you looking for?' asks Elias.

I'm so angry, I can't answer him.

Moving down the stairs to the hallway, I tip over more boxes and rip open bags, scattering the contents. I'm kneeling on the floor, using both hands to search. My phone is ringing. I ignore it and keep looking.

Elias has followed me. 'You're making a mess.'

I topple another box and scrabble through the innards, my eyes blurred by anger and tears.

'Where is it? The button. Which bag?' I scream.

He shrugs, grinning or grimacing.

'Fuck you!' I scream, thumping him in the chest. I want to rip out his eyes. I keep hitting him, but the blows bounce off. I aim at his face, connecting with his nose, and feel something break. He shoves me backwards with no effort at all and I slam into the wall, shaking the framed mirror.

He wipes his nose and licks blood off his top lip. I swing again, but he grips my wrist and his other hand closes around my throat and pins me against the wall. I keep trying to hit him, or kick him, but his fingers tighten, and my feet are no longer touching the rug.

His eyes are empty. Hollow. Unknowable. I can't see anger or pity or sorrow or empathy. My toes are scrabbling to reach the floor, searching for solid ground. My left hand is pulling at his wrist. I croak his name. I want to breathe. Just one breath. One mouthful. Air.

Elias's face is going out of focus. Blood runs from his nose, across his lips, staining his teeth. In that moment, I see the teenager who carried the knife. The one who heard the voice. The one who followed instructions. I am clawing at his wrist, trying to open his fingers. Losing strength. Slowing down. Light-headed. Dizzy. The last thing I hear is Lilah scream.

64

Cyrus

Unlike most people her age, Evie doesn't treat her mobile phone like an appendage. She doesn't spend hours glued to the screen watching TikTok videos, playing games, and DMing her friends. 'Because I don't have any,' she'd say, if I were talking to her now. I would if I could. She's not answering her phone.

A small doubt has begun to gnaw inside my chest, like a burrowing animal searching for safety. I tell myself that Evie would have stayed with Lilah. They probably slept in, or they've gone out for breakfast or to walk the dogs.

Edgar yells across the incident room.

'Thompson showed up for work last Monday with cuts on his face, smelling of booze. The boss sent him home. He hasn't been seen since.'

'Where's he been staying?' asks Lenny.

'Until two weeks ago, he was sleeping in a mate's spare room in Carrington but packed his bags after he almost set fire to the place. A towel fell onto a bar heater. I'm checking local Airbnbs.'

Dave Curran is pulling a page from the printer. 'Thompson manages a three-bedroom cottage near Newstead Abbey. Grade II listed. It's been empty for six weeks.'

'That's good enough for me,' says Lenny, grabbing her jacket. 'We leave in five.' She turns to me. 'Where is Lilah Hooper?'

'I'm trying to find her.'

'Should we be worried?'

'I don't think so.'

'Call me.'

Making my way downstairs, I pass through the custody suite and control room before reaching the holding cells. I deposit my phone in a plastic bag, along with my keys and credit cards. A sergeant unlocks the cell door. Mitch gets to his feet, with his hands against the wall, legs braced apart. He knows the routine.

'I'll be fine,' I tell the sergeant, who leaves us alone.

Mitch returns to the bench, without looking at me. Lying down, he covers his eyes with his forearm.

'You know what's funny,' he says. 'How you reach a point, when you say the same thing over and over and nobody believes you and eventually you start to wonder if maybe you're the one who's crazy.'

'You're not crazy. I've talked to Lilah. She's not sure any more.'

'Not sure?' he laughs, bitterly. 'How does that help?'

He's right. Even if Lilah changed her statement, it wouldn't be enough for a judge to overturn the conviction. And any appeal would take years, by which time Mitch would have served the rest of his sentence.

'Facts don't matter any more,' he says. 'I think they're like runners in a horse race. Some are favourites, others are even-money, or rank outsiders, but all of them can be beaten if someone manipulates the information or convinces the audience that everything is fake news.'

I can understand his pessimism. Mitch is living proof that luck doesn't even itself out, any more than it can be forced or predicted. It's like the old joke: How do you make God laugh? Tell Him you have a plan.

Mitch sits up, offering me half of the bench.

'So why are you here?' he asks.

'Checking up on you.'

'I'm not going anywhere.'

I lean my head against the bricks. 'On the night that Lilah was attacked, did you notice anything unusual?'

'I was asleep.'

'What about earlier?'

'Lilah went to work mid-afternoon. I took Trevor for a walk before it got dark. He was still a puppy back then.'

'Where did you walk?'

'The Arboretum – at the end of the road. On the way home, I bought a taco from a food truck and gave half to Trevor. He didn't like the jalapeños.'

The information vibrates inside me. It's like someone has hit a tuning fork and held it close to my ear.

'This food truck – had you seen it there before?'

'No.'

My mind reaches back, searching for other details. A neighbour saw a food truck parked on Beaconsfield Street on the night Maya disappeared. Patrice Rennie is a chef who set up a catering business that went bust during the pandemic.

'What's wrong?' asks Mitch.

I hammer on the cell door, yelling to be let out. As the door opens, I push past the sergeant and grab my phone from the counter before jogging up the internal stairs to the incident room. Many of the task force are with Lenny or knocking on doors, but a dozen detectives remain, searching databases, and studying footage from traffic cameras and private CCTV.

'Who is looking for the Rennie family?' I shout.

Prime Time raises his hand without looking up from his computer.

'Their home was sold in January.' He points to the screen. 'This is the last information I can find.'

It's an online news story from the *Daily Mail*.

The family of a desperately ill young woman hopes to raise £200,000 to help get her alternative treatment abroad. Jolene Rennie, from Nottingham, was just thirty-three when she was diagnosed with advanced bowel cancer.

Doctors advised her to start palliative care, but Jolene underwent twenty cycles of chemotherapy over the next four years. The disease went into remission but last October she received the devastating news that her cancer had returned and spread to the lining of her abdomen, her pelvis and her ovaries.

Specialist surgeons at the Royal Marsden Hospital in London decided that Jolene was unsuitable for surgery, but the family say there are multiple different treatment options abroad, which are not covered by the NHS.

Jolene's husband Patrice, a chef, has already sold the family's home in Lenton and hopes to raise the rest of the money by donations.

'In America, they are twenty years ahead when it comes to stopping this cancer,' he said. 'We're going to make every penny count and make Jolene well again.'

I look at the date on the article. It was published on 8 February.

'When did they leave the country?' I ask.

'In April.'

'Look for a death notice.'

Prime Time taps in a search. The single result is dated three weeks ago.

Jolene Phillipa Rennie (nee Wright), the much-loved wife of Patrice, daughter of Noel and Elizabeth, sister of Cassandra, sadly left us on Friday October 25, aged thirty-eight. She battled in every possible way, but now her suffering is over.

I call Lenny, but her line is busy. I'm about to try again when I get an incoming call from Dr Baillie at Rampton Secure Hospital.

'Is Elias with you?' he asks.

'No. Why?'

'The electronic monitoring service just sent me an alert. The GPS tracker shows that Elias left your address more than an hour ago. Can you confirm his whereabouts?'

'No.'

65

Cyrus

There should be a Murphy's Law or some corollary that relates to traffic – the more urgently you need to be somewhere, the slower the journey. The more roadworks, stop signs and red lights. The more little old lady drivers and men wearing lawn-bowling hats, and Sunday-school teachers, or any of those hackneyed clichés that nowadays seem to cause offence.

Evie still isn't answering her phone. I try Lenny. This time I get through, but she tells me to hold. I hear voices behind her – officers are being briefed. They have reached the cottage and found Thompson's car parked outside. An armed response unit is twelve minutes away.

Lenny comes back to me. 'Make it quick.'

'Patrice Rennie has a food truck. There was one spotted outside Maya Kirk's house on the night she disappeared. And Mitchell Coates remembers seeing a food truck on the evening that Lilah Hooper was attacked.'

'I thought Rennie took his wife to America?'

'Jolene Rennie died of cancer four weeks ago. It could have tipped him over the edge.'

'Where is he?'

'Prime Time has the task force looking, but I think I know someone who can find him.'

In the background, I hear a shout, 'Suspect identified.'

'That's him,' says Lenny, who is moving. Thompson must have emerged from the cottage. Someone else yells, 'Police! Hands in the air. Get down! Get down! On your knees.'

Lenny to me. 'Wait for me at Radford Road.'

'I can't. Elias has gone AWOL. His ankle monitor triggered an alarm an hour ago.'

'Where would he go?'

'I don't know, but I'm almost home now.'

'What about Lilah Hooper?'

'She's in the wind.'

Lenny curses and hangs up.

I've reached Parkside. The front door is wide open. I sprint up the path, yelling for Evie rather than Elias. What does that say? There are spilled boxes and ripped bin bags in the hallway. The contents are spread across the floor. Cast-off clothes. Magazines. Schoolbooks. Trophies. Sun-faded curtains. Ageing bedspreads. I can't work out if someone was robbing me or moving me out.

Poppy is barking from the garden. She's with another dog. Trevor. Lilah must have been here. Running up the stairs, I find more boxes and bags with their contents scattered across the floor. They've come from the attic. This was Elias, not Evie.

I try her phone again and hear her ringtone – a song from some Korean boyband with initials instead of a name. The sound is coming from the front hallway. I find the handset beneath a pile of magazines. My texts and missed messages are on the screen. I'm kneeling on the floor, staring at the phone, when I notice something shine from the pages of an open magazine. *National Geographic*. A droplet. I touch it with a fingertip. Smear it against my thumb. Oily. Dark. Blood.

Evie's car is gone. I try to tell myself that she and Lilah have gone shopping or to lunch, but Evie isn't a shopper, and she doesn't make friends easily and she wouldn't leave her phone behind.

I have an incoming call from Dr Baillie.

'Have you found him?' he asks.

'No.'

'Do you have any idea where he is?'

'None.'

'I am obligated to call the police.'

'I understand, but you said someone was tracking him.'

'The ankle bracelet sends GPS and radio signals. We use an electronic monitoring company in Manchester.'

'If I can get to Elias and bring him back to Rampton, will that count in his favour?'

'My advice is to leave it to the police.'

'I understand that, but he's my brother and I don't want him hurt.'

Baillie seems to take a moment to consider the request. 'I'll call the company and ask, but I warn you not to approach Elias on your own. If he has suffered a psychotic episode, he may not recognise you.'

He hangs up and I look again at the droplets of blood on the magazine. There are more on the rug. I notice dark scuff marks on the skirting boards. Someone small was held against the wall with her feet off the ground. Kicking. Fighting.

Family is a bond of blood and shared history, but how can two people who share the same genes be so different? There is supposed to be an eternal unbreakable bond between brothers. Family is family no matter what happens. Not any more. Not now.

I call Lenny. She's on her way back to Radford Road.

'Thompson is a drunk,' she says. 'We'll have to sober him up before we get any sense out of him.'

I interrupt her. 'Lilah Hooper and Evie aren't at the house. The front door was wide open and there were traces of blood in the hallway.'

'Where's Elias?'

'No sign of him.'

'Shit!'

My phone is ringing. I don't recognise the number. I put Lenny on hold.

Cassie's voice, 'Don't let the police kill him.'

66

Evie

The cold is leaking into my chest. It began at my fingertips and my toes and has slowly moved along my arms and legs, until I cannot stop my teeth from chattering. I tell myself I have been in colder places, darker places. I've been hungry and frightened and have listened to a man, my friend, being tortured to death. But I was always hiding, never held.

I call out, softly at first, 'Is anybody there?'

I listen to the sounds. Water dripping. A crow calling. A tree creaking in the wind. In the distance I hear traffic, or maybe it's a train, but no voices, or footsteps. No sign of life.

I can just make out the edges of a covered window because light is leaking through cracks where the nailed boards don't quite meet. And there is another strip of light beneath a closed door.

The last thing I remember is hearing Lilah scream before I blacked out. Squeezing my eyes shut, I try to recall something more, and another image flashes into my mind. Elias is leaning over me. His mouth is on mine. I taste blood on his lips and smell his sour breath and the scent of cologne.

Another image. Lilah on the floor lying next to me. I touch

her hand, thinking she might be dead, but her skin is warm. I press two fingers against her wrist, feeling for a pulse . . . she's alive. I try to remember more, but the cold keeps snatching the memories away.

Where am I? Sitting on an unswept concrete floor with my back to a metal pipe that rises to the ceiling. Ropes are wrapped around my arms and wrists. Another is looped around my neck. If I lower my chin it cuts off my air.

'I'm thirsty,' I say. 'Can you hear me?'

I listen. Nothing.

'I need to use the toilet,' I say, louder this time.

I wonder if Lilah can hear me.

'Hey! Are you there?'

If I'm alone, I'm going to shout this place down. I'd do it now, but it goes against my every instinct. When I was hiding in the secret room, a child in the dark, a mouse inside the walls, I couldn't make a sound. I tried to stop breathing. I could hear them calling my name, searching for me, ripping holes in the plasterboard walls, tearing up carpets and floorboards, over-turning beds.

Shuffling on my bottom, I see how far I can move. Only a few inches either way. I stretch out my legs, one at a time, sweeping them across the rough concrete. My toe touches something soft. I pull away, thinking it might be a body, but stretch out again. It's a blanket. I pull it closer.

Using my feet, I manoeuvre the blanket over my knees and then to my thighs but can't lift it any higher without my hands. The effort has warmed me up.

Footsteps. The door swings open and a shadow fills the frame. He has a torch that shines in my eyes. I turn my head away.

'Elias?'

67

Cyrus

Cassie is waiting for me when I pull up outside the Arncliffe Centre. She slips into the passenger seat and buckles her seatbelt, unwilling to make eye contact. I move off and drive the first few minutes in silence, waiting for her to speak. Expecting it.

'When did you realise?' she asks.

'The obituary called you Cassandra. Your sister changed her name when she married Rennie. Before that she was Jolene Wright. Patrice is the brother-in-law you were worried about. You said he was a mess.'

'I didn't think he'd do this,' she whispers. 'Until you told me Maya once worked as a nurse, I didn't even consider the possibility that she could be one of the nurses who . . .'

She seems to bite off the statement, swallowing the rest.

'What about Daniela Linares?' I ask.

Cassie doesn't answer.

'Where is Patrice?'

'He's been living in his food truck.'

'Where?'

'He moves around.'

'What about a phone number?'

'His mobile is turned off.'

'How do you contact him?'

'I can't. I've tried. The last time I saw him was at the funeral.'

She is hugging her knees, pressing her chin between them. I am driving into Nottingham, heading to Radford Road station.

'What does he want?' I ask.

'The truth.'

'He *knows* the truth. The nurses made a mistake.'

'They lied to protect each other.'

'They raised the alarm. They tried to save the babies.'

Cassie's eyes spark with anger. 'They killed Oliver. They were negligent. Somebody should have paid a price.'

'Like Maya?'

She stops and takes a deep breath. 'No. Never. Not like that.'

There is a pleading tone to her voice when she begins again.

'My sister was one of the kindest, warmest, most beautiful people you could ever meet. All she ever wanted was to meet someone like Patrice and have a family. When Oliver was born, it was like a dream had come true. I had never seen her so happy. And when he died, I had never seen grief consume someone like that.

'But she didn't complain. She didn't want the nurses charged. She didn't want to sue the hospital. All she wanted was another chance to be a mother. They tried everything. IVF. Homeopathy. Prayer. Acupuncture. Folk remedies. She slept on a hill in Dorset. She ate bird's-nest soup. Nothing worked. And then the cancer came. It was horrible. She disappeared, piece by piece, eaten away from the inside. What sort of God could be so utterly, utterly evil?'

She looks at me, wanting an explanation. I don't have one.

'Did you plant evidence to frame Mitchell Coates?' I ask.

'No. Never. Check the dates. I was still at university.'

'Who, then?'

'Hoyle.'

I take my eyes off the road for a moment to look at her face.

'Craig told me that Hoyle had done it before – taken material from a crime scene and planted it at the suspect's address, or in his car.'

'Why didn't Dyson say anything?'

'Hoyle was too clever to get caught. And nobody was going to question a senior officer without serious evidence. It would have been career suicide.'

'Dyson told you this?'

She nods. 'Hoyle thinks he's streamlining the process, not corrupting it. When he's sure of someone's guilt, he *finds* the evidence to convict them.'

'Mitchell Coates has spent six years in prison for a crime he didn't commit.'

Cassie goes quiet.

'The manslaughter prosecution against Lilah Hooper collapsed and two weeks later she was attacked. You must have suspected Patrice.'

'No. Never. He and Jolene were trying to have another baby. It didn't even enter my head.'

'Where is he? There must be someone who knows. Friends. Family.'

'Some of his old army buddies came to the funeral, but I don't know how to contact them.'

'You're covering for him.'

'No.'

'Voigt asked you to compare the rope used in the attacks on Maya and Lilah. Did you purposely avoid doing it?'

Cassie hesitates, as though debating how much to say.

'It's soft hemp,' she whispers. 'The same organic make-up and weave.'

'Did it come from the same source?'

'Yes.'

'When we met at the Little Drummer, you saw the CCTV footage from the camera above the bar. You recognised Patrice's reflection in the mirrors.'

Again, she doesn't answer. I can't tell if it's defiance or self-pity or embarrassment. Finally, she speaks. 'There's something else you should know. Ten days ago, there was a break-in at a pharmacy in Lenton. It looked like an addict, stealing methadone or opioids, but something else was taken. Heparin.'

'The blood thinner.'

'It's the same drug that killed Oliver.'

'How long have you known about the robbery?'

'Only since this morning.'

We're almost at the police station. My phone rings. I answer, hoping it might be Evie, but a perky-sounding voice with a Scouse accent introduces himself as Gary from EMS (Electronic Monitoring Services).

'You're looking for information about E645,' he says, tapping on a keyboard. I can imagine him holed up in some office block in Manchester, staring at a computer screen. 'The ankle monitor showed he left his designated address in Parkside at 11.26 this morning. Given the speed he was travelling, he was most likely in a vehicle. He drove north for twenty minutes and has been stationary for the past hour. Beech Avenue in Basford. The nearest cross street is Albany Road. His file has a red flag. I'm supposed to notify the police. Who is he?'

'My brother.'

'Is he dangerous?'

'Yes.'

68

Evie

I turn my face into the light, blinking at the brightness. The silhouette is the wrong size. The wrong shape. Not Elias.

He takes a metal folding chair from the opposite side of the room and spins it in his fist, setting it down backwards, so he can straddle the sides. Why do men do that – act like their balls are so big they need a chair to hold them up?

I remember what happened now. My memories float together to form a storyline, a three-act play, but it's not Shakespeare. Elias was leaning over me, breathing into my mouth. I thought he was trying to kiss me or kill me. I pushed him away and spat out the taste of him and called him a pervert and told him to take his filthy family-killing hands off me.

'Where is your friend?' he asked.

I remember Lilah screaming. 'What did you do to her?'

'Nothing. She ran away.'

The food truck was still parked on the corner, but now the awning was hinged up, the side door open. Gaping. Dark. I couldn't see a driver. I crossed the road and approached from the front. Crouching down, I looked beneath the chassis, between the wheels, but nobody was standing on the other side.

I suddenly remembered where I'd seen the truck before. The painted doors. The sombrero. The cactus. It was outside Lilah's flat on the day I met her. I was hungry and the driver said he wasn't open. I didn't look closely at his face because it wasn't important. I was looking for a taco, not a lie.

What was it doing outside Cyrus's house? I stepped closer, trying to peer inside, leaning through the open side door. I saw Lilah staring back at me from the darkness. Eyes wide. Mouth taped shut.

A hand closed over my mouth, cutting off my scream. My legs were kicked out from beneath me and I was lifted and thrown into the truck. I fought. Biting at fingers. Kicking at shins. I felt the needle prick my neck and heard the tape being ripped from a spool, across my mouth and my eyes.

Briefly, I glimpsed the man's face before the darkness closed around me. I saw the man who drove Daniela away. He is sitting opposite me now. No disguises. Not hiding any more.

'Who are you?' I ask.

'You can call me Rennie. What's your name?'

'Evie.'

'Are you a fair person, Evie?'

'Why?'

'I'm asking if you understand the difference between right and wrong?'

'Yeah.'

'Do you think people should be punished for doing the wrong thing?'

'I don't know what you're talking about.'

'Justice. Fairness. Accountability. Young people understand justice better than adults. Their minds haven't been poisoned.'

'I want to go home.'

'And you will, but first I need you to do something for me.'

He smiles without showing his teeth, but I know he's telling the truth.

'Did you kill Maya?' I ask.

'She got away and fell down the stairs. She was dead when I found her.'

Again, he's not lying. He stands up. I cower.

'I will not hurt you. I would never touch a child.'

'I'm not a child.'

'Good. I need you to be grown-up. You're going to be my judge and my jury.'

'I'm not going to judge anyone. Cyrus is going to find me. He's going to make you pay.'

'Who is Cyrus?'

'My friend.'

'Your boyfriend?'

'No!'

I say it too aggressively and he laughs. I want to wipe that smile off his face. Instead, I tell him to fuck off and call him the worst names, spitting them in his face.

'You have a potty mouth, Evie.'

'And you stink.'

The bald man folds the chair carefully before resting it against the wall. He leaves the room and I hear metal being scraped on concrete. Water sloshing. Footsteps return. The silhouette looks different in the doorway because now he's carrying a bucket.

'No, I didn't mean— Please. No!'

Filthy, freezing water slaps me across the face. The door closes. Darkness.

69

Cyrus

Gary is still on the phone, relaying information about Elias. Every so often, he puts me on hold while he talks to a colleague, or takes another call, checking on the status of a different parolee or defendant who has breached house arrest or curfew or bail conditions. The accused or convicted or blameworthy.

'I lost the signal eight minutes ago,' he says.

'Why would that happen?'

'Either he destroyed the tag, or he could be indoors, somewhere underground or behind thick walls.'

'Let me know if you get another signal.'

I type the cross streets into my phone, which is propped in a cradle on the dashboard.

'Who is Elias?' asks Cassie.

'My brother. He's been released from Rampton for a visit. He's wearing an ankle monitor.'

'I don't understand.'

'Evie and Lilah Hooper are both missing. I found my front door wide open. Evie's car was gone.'

'And you think Elias has them?'

'Or Patrice.'

Cassie seems to swallow her next question and we continue the journey in silence, heading south along Hucknall Road into Nottingham.

When we reach Beech Avenue, I drive slowly along the street, searching for Evie's car. To my left, a derelict building takes up almost an entire block. It is five storeys high, with large windows on every floor that are either boarded up or broken. The roof has collapsed inwards after a fire. I can see scorch marks above some of the windows and charred beams etched against the sky.

After circling the block, I pull over and glance at the factory, taking my phone from the cradle.

'Where are you going?' asks Cassie.

'To get a closer look.'

'I don't want to stay here.'

She joins me on the footpath. A gust of wind pins her coat against her body and the cold makes her eyes water. We circle the perimeter, which is surrounded by a brick wall and large iron gates. Using a low branch, I scramble up the trunk of a tree and sit on the wall, trying to get a better vantage point.

The factory looks out of time – a throwback to a different era when Nottingham was an industrial powerhouse. The collapsed roof has exposed the upper floor, revealing the skeletal beams and metal stanchions that once gave it support. Trees and shrubs have since germinated in the rain and sunlight, creating a dystopian rooftop garden of weeds. At the northern end of the building, a circular brick chimney rises above the rest of the roofline, having escaped the fire.

I scan the length of the building, studying the large rectangular windows, which are covered by sheets of plywood on the lower floors and shattered by rocks or heat on the higher levels. I can imagine local children telling stories about this place – convinced they have heard screams at night or seen ghostly shapes in the windows. That's what happened after my family died. Our house became the sort of place that children had nightmares about or challenged each other to ring the doorbell and scarper. It made drivers speed up and mothers clutch the hands of their children more tightly as they walked them to school.

Jumping down from the wall, I call Lenny. She's almost back at Radford Road.

'Patrice Rennie sold his house last year to pay for his wife's cancer treatment,' I say. 'He's been living in his food truck and hasn't been seen since his wife's funeral three weeks ago.'

'I'll put out a BOLO on Rennie and the truck. Does anyone have a photograph of him?'

I look at Cassie. She nods and begins scrolling through images on her phone.

'We'll send something through.'

'Who are you with?'

'Rennie's sister-in-law.'

'I thought you were tracking Elias.'

'I am. They lost the signal thirty minutes ago. I'm outside an abandoned warehouse in Beech Avenue.'

'The old Maville Works,' says Lenny. 'It used to be a lace factory called the White House.'

'It could be where Rennie kept Maya. Ness said it was likely nineteenth century.'

I have reached a set of iron gates. A padlock hangs on an uncoupled chain. I look across the asphalt forecourt, which glitters with broken glass. There is a loading dock with concrete ramps and parking bays. A metal fire-escape leads halfway up the building before stopping in mid-flight.

I lower the phone and turn to Cassie. 'You should wait here for the police.'

'Where are you going?'

'To get a closer look.'

After squeezing through the partially open gate, I crouch and run to the nearest corner of the factory. The foundation stone above my head reads June 29th, 1896. The sun is slanting through the trees, creating deeper shadows. Light catches a mirrored surface in the loading dock. A food truck is parked in one of the bays, partially hidden by rusting machinery.

Squatting on my haunches, I raise the phone to my ear. Lenny is still on the line.

'I think I've found Rennie.'

'Don't move. We're coming.'

70

Evie

As a little girl, I used to beg Agnesa to tell me bedtime stories. The scary ones were the best because I had an excuse to put my arms around her, pressing my head to her chest, feeling the vibrations of her voice.

One of my favourites was about three brothers who were building a castle out of stone. They worked all day, piling stone upon stone, but every night the walls would collapse. Eventually, an old man told them that they had to sacrifice someone so that the walls would stand. The brothers couldn't agree on whom to sacrifice, so they decided it would be whichever wife brought them their lunch the next day.

It was Rozafa, who was married to the youngest brother. When he explained to her the deal, she agreed to be buried in the walls of the castle, but she had one condition. She asked that they leave her right breast exposed so she could feed her new-born son, and her right hand to caress him and her right foot to rock his cradle.

I loved hearing that story even if I didn't understand what it meant. Maybe some fables aren't supposed to have a moral, or a message; or perhaps it's just another example of a woman sacrificing herself to improve the lives of men. I have been Rozafa. Trapped in the walls. Unable to escape. I'm there now.

The door opens. The bald man cuts the ropes from around my arms and tosses me a dry blanket.

'Come out, when you're ready.'

I climb slowly to my feet, rubbing circulation back into my wrists. I study the room, looking for a way out. It's some sort of warehouse with painted brick walls that are peeling and crumbling in patches, damp to the touch. I pull at the sheet of plywood that covers the window. It doesn't move.

I shuffle to the door and peer around the frame. The first thing I notice are the chairs and a table.

'That's where you sit,' he says. He tries to touch my arm, but I pull away, glaring at him.

My jeans are still wet. The metal chair is cold. He takes a rope and loops it around my arms and the back of the chair, tying it against my spine.

'Why are you doing this?' I ask.

'This is not meant as a punishment. It is your civic duty.'

'I don't know what that means.'

'You are going to sit in judgement.'

'I want to go home.'

'Be quiet now. Listen.'

The new room is much larger and lighter with painted metal poles holding up the ceiling. The floor is littered with rubble and broken panels of plywood and shattered glass. The large square windows are uncovered, divided into smaller panes, which are broken or missing.

The bald man leaves the room. I hear muffled groans and feet sliding across the floor. Daniela appears first. I barely recognise her because her hair has been hacked away, cut close to her scalp, making her eyes look enormous. Lilah is next. She must have fought harder because her shorn head is bleeding in places. Both have their mouths taped shut and their arms and chests are bound with rope.

Lilah continues to struggle, but Daniela shuffles to a chair and is told to sit. I try to make eye contact. She doesn't seem to remember me. Rennie goes to the table and unzips a sports bag. He sets up a camera and a small tripod, checking that Daniela and Lilah are in the frame.

Satisfied, he takes a piece of paper from the pocket of his jeans and clears his throat.

'Lilah Hooper and Daniela Linares, you are accused of murdering Oliver Rennie at St Jude's Medical Centre, Nottingham, on the sixth of February, 2013. You covered up your crime by lying to the police and to my family.'

Neither woman reacts.

'You have to let them speak,' I say.

'I don't have to let them do anything,' he replies. 'They have had many chances to speak. Each time, they told lies.'

'If I'm going to judge, I need to hear from them.'

'You will. But now it's my turn.'

He begins talking, but I'm only half listening. He mentions his wife giving birth prematurely and the baby being transferred to the neonatal ICU and placed in an incubator.

'We took turns to sit beside the crib. We touched his hand. We talked to him. We told him the life we had planned for him. The doctors said that Oliver was a fighter and had a good chance. I believed them. I thought our baby was in safe hands.'

Lilah is shaking her head. Daniela doesn't react. It's like her mind has broken off and taken her somewhere else.

'He was two days old when he was given the wrong medication. There were three nurses on duty. You were two of them. One of you went to the pharmacy cabinet and took out heparin rather than Hep-Lock. One of you didn't read the box. One of you didn't check the dosage. One of you filled the syringe. One of you injected the wrong drug into the IV line.'

'It wasn't done on purpose,' I say. 'It was an accident.'

'That's what everybody wants you to think,' he replies, 'but wait until you hear the rest of the story. I wish to call my first witness, Lilah Hooper.'

Lilah's eyes shoot up. Rennie steps in front of her and pinches the edge of the tape between his thumb and forefinger before ripping it away from her mouth. Her top lip is raw and bleeding. He does the same to Daniela, who doesn't flinch.

'Please, Mr Rennie,' sobs Lilah. 'It was an accident.'

He rolls the tape into a ball and tosses it aside, wiping his hands on the back of his jeans.

'Who was in charge that night?' he asks.

'I was the most senior nurse on duty,' says Lilah. She's telling the truth.

'Who administered the drug?'

'It was Maya.'

Now she's lying.

'Maya told me that Daniela administered the heparin.'

'No, it was Maya,' says Lilah, starting to panic. 'But it was my responsibility. I was in charge.'

'Why didn't you name Maya in your statement?'

'We were protecting each other.'

'You were covering it up.'

'We couldn't change what had happened.'

'You tried to make out that Oliver died naturally. You turned off his incubator and only turned it on again when his organs had failed.'

Lilah looks shocked. There's only one way that he could know a detail like that – Maya must have told him. She starts to stammer and shake her head. 'He was very sick. He was going to die anyway.'

'No! That is what the hospital *wanted* us to believe. He was a strong little boy. He was a fighter. That's what the doctors told us when he arrived at the ICU. You didn't give him a chance.'

'That's not true. We told them what happened. We raised the alarm.'

362

'After he was dead.'

There is a groan from beside her. Daniela raises her chin. Speaks. 'I made the mistake. Maya and Lilah had nothing to do with it.'

She's telling the truth.

71

Cyrus

I am not a patient person. I dislike the passivity of lingering. The ineptness. The helplessness. I know that Lenny is coming, but the cavalry doesn't always show up on time. In the movies, yes, but not in real life, which normally throws up near-misses, wrong turns, bad choices, and unexpected delays.

Once Lenny arrives, I will have no say in matters. She will bring an armed response team with all the latest technology. They will put drones in the air and aim microphones at the windows. Officers in body armour and helmets will go from room to room, with guns drawn, yelling the word 'clear'. That is how sieges are created and how innocents get killed in the crossfire.

From inside the factory comes a crashing sound that echoes through the stairwells. Something has fallen or been thrown. Cassie appears beside me.

'I told you to wait,' I say.

'Maybe we can stop this.'

I don't know if that's true, but I want to do something active, not passive. The tragedies in my life have always occurred when I've arrived too late to help or to change the outcome.

With Cassie behind me, we cross the pitted tarmac in a crouching run, reaching the first of four concrete ramps that make up the loading dock. A warning sign above our heads announces that trespassers will be prosecuted. I pause and listen, but the only sounds are bird calls and the distant horn of a train.

The food truck has been backed into a space between a quartet of concrete pylons that support the roof and the floors above. Approaching from behind, I avoid the mirrors in case someone is in the driver's seat. When I reach the rear of the van, I press my ear against the painted metal, listening for voices inside. Edging forward I pull myself onto the side-step at the driver's window and peer into the cab, which is littered with fast-food wrappers, coffee cups and plastic bottles of water.

My phone is vibrating. I answer the call.

'I picked up the signal again two minutes ago,' says Gary, 'but it only lasted a few seconds. It came from the northern end of the building. Maybe he passed close to a window.'

The nearest door is marked as a fire exit but has been barricaded or screwed shut. The next one is also locked. Cassie follows me as I walk along the western wall of the factory, pushing through waist-high weeds, nettles and blackberry bushes. Thorny branches tug at my coat and trousers.

Without warning, the ground opens beneath me. As I pitch forward, Cassie grabs my coat, hauling me back from the edge. Breathless, heart thumping, I stare into a brick pit overgrown with weeds.

'Don't do that again,' she says.

'Noted.'

She points into the shadows. 'There's a door.'

The stone steps are slick with moss. I pull aside planks and fallen branches, before wading into knee-deep water the colour of sump oil. A door is propped open by a broken beam. Ducking underneath, I squeeze inside, emerging into a large room with a ceiling criss-crossed by pipes. The broken concrete floor is covered in puddles and wooden pallets and rusting pieces of machinery. A chair. A pile of sand. Empty paint tins. Plasterboard. Tiles.

Cassie follows me, as I navigate through the rubbish, using my phone as a torch. We head towards the only other light, which is coming from a lift shaft that reaches to the upper floors. The lift cage has gone, but a rusty metal ladder, dripping with water, is fixed against one wall.

I can hear voices coming from above me. Male. Female. I test the ladder, pulling myself up and dropping again, making sure it can hold my weight. It creaks. The noise echoes up the shaft.

'I don't think it could take both of us,' I say to Cassie. 'You should go back. Tell DSU Parvel where I've gone.'

She glances at the ladder and reluctantly agrees. 'Tell Patrice . . .' She searches for the words. 'Tell Patrice that I'm here and I under-stand him, but he has to stop this. Tell him that I loved Jolene too and this isn't what she would have wanted.'

I begin to climb towards the voices.

72

Evie

The red light on the camera is still blinking. Rennie checks to make sure that it's recording and adjusts the angle. He steps closer and crouches to meet me at eye level.

'You have heard their confessions. They have admitted their guilt.'

'It was an accident.'

'Which they covered up.'

'I don't want to judge them. This is wrong.'

'They killed my son.'

'He was dying anyway.'

His hands are so low that I don't see his fist. He strikes me across the face, and I topple sideways, still attached to the chair, tasting blood in my mouth, sickly and coppery and warm.

Rennie seems to realise that he's been caught on camera. He picks up the chair with me still attached to it, setting it upright, apologising.

'You promised to be fair,' he sulks.

I blow hair out of my eyes and stretch out my lower jaw, moving it back and forth to make sure it's not broken. 'I didn't promise you anything,' I say, spitting blood onto the floor.

'My son was defenceless. He was an innocent. He deserved a chance. They were supposed to heal him, to keep him safe, but they gave up and covered up. They killed him.'

'No,' says Lilah, shaking her head. 'It was an accident.'

'You turned off his incubator.'

'He was already dead.'

'No! He was still alive!' He smashes his fist on the table. The camera topples. He curses and checks to make sure it isn't damaged. He adjusts the tripod and frames the two women in the viewfinder

'He didn't suffer,' says Lilah. 'It was quick.'

'Oh, that makes it OK,' says Rennie, sarcastically.

He has moved back in front of the camera.

'I didn't get to hold my son before he died. I didn't get to say goodbye. We didn't just lose a new-born – we lost the one-year-old he would have become. We lost the toddler and the three-year-old. He would have gone to school. He would have woken us every Christmas morning and birthday. He would have dressed up at Hallowe'en and had Easter egg hunts and written notes to the tooth fairy.

'Every year, on the anniversary of Oliver's birthday, we would try to do something unusual to take our minds off what happened. One year we went skydiving in Spain. Another year it was indoor climbing. Then, three days later, we'd visit his grave. We would talk about him and imagine what he'd look like now. Eight years old. Everything ahead of him. When I picture him, I see his mother – caring, clever, funny, good at practical things, hot-headed sometimes, passionate.

'We kept Oliver's memory alive, but the pain never diminished. And with every failed round of IVF, every miscarriage, every scalding disappointment, it grew worse. Do you understand what that's like?'

He looks again at Lilah and Daniela but doesn't expect them to answer.

'And yet we almost made it out of the vortex. Jolene had

come to terms with never having a baby of our own. We were going to adopt. We were on the list. But then the cancer came. I have never seen such bravery. She fought to her last breath. She gave herself a chance, which is something you denied Oliver.'

He pauses and wipes his eyes before moving slowly and picking up the heavy-duty tape. It screeches as he peels it from the spool. Using his teeth, he tears the tape and places it across Lilah's mouth. She is begging him and shaking her head.

'What are you doing?' I ask. 'They confessed. You got it on film. Let them go.'

He moves to Daniela, who doesn't complain as the tape is wrapped around her head. He pulls it under her nose to let her breathe.

He drags the same black sports bag from beneath the table and slides open the zip. Reaching inside, he takes out a clear plastic pouch. Inside are dozens of small glass vials with labels.

'You gave my baby the wrong medication. A thousand times more than the recommended dose. His brain began to bleed, and his organs shut down.'

'Lilah said he didn't suffer,' I say.

'Neither will they.'

He raises one of the glass vials and pokes a needle through the top, drawing the liquid into the syringe. I suddenly see what's coming.

I look at Lilah and Daniela, wanting some wordless explanation, but their faces are staring at the needle as he pierces another vial. A noise echoes up the stairwell from somewhere below. Rennie's head snaps around.

I start yelling. 'Help! We're in here!'

This time I manage to duck his swinging fist. The blow deflects from my forehead, but he comes again, gripping me across the mouth. I try to bite at his fingers, as he reaches for the tape and wraps it twice around my head, hissing at me to be quiet.

Getting to his feet, he reaches behind his back and pulls a knife from a scabbard that was tucked into his belt. He twirls the blade between his fingers like a juggler, before his palm closes around the handle.

'Wait here,' he says, as though I have a choice.

73

Cyrus

My phone is vibrating. I hook one arm over a rung and pull it out of my pocket, almost dropping the handset because I've lost the feeling in my fingers.

'I told you to wait,' says Lenny.

'I just heard someone yelling for help.'

'Male or female?'

'Female. It might have been Evie.'

'Where are you?'

'In a lift shaft between the second and third floors. They're somewhere above me. I think Rennie has Lilah and Evie.'

'What about Elias?'

'I haven't seen him.'

'Come back.'

'I'm close now. I can be your eyes and ears.'

'It's too dangerous. I don't want another hostage.'

'You're breaking up.'

'Don't do this, Cyrus.'

Lenny curses and begins issuing instructions. She wants a drone in the air and firearms officers on the surrounding buildings. I hang up and pocket the phone. It vibrates almost immediately as she tries to call me back. I'm climbing the final rungs towards an opening in the lift shaft.

Noise echoes from above. More muffled shouting. A male voice is yelling at someone to stay away. Elias answers, but I can't tell what he's saying. They're on the fourth floor. I'm on the third. The ladder won't take me any higher.

Shuffling sideways, hand over hand, I reach the opening and haul myself up and out of the shaft, lying on my back on the concrete floor, breathing hard.

On my feet, I examine my surroundings. This floor is even more cavernous than the basement, with metal pillars as thick as my waist spaced in rows, supporting a higher ceiling. There are old drums, broken tiles and mounds of scrap metal that throw shadows against the painted walls that are bubbling and peeling. An old sign says 'Tea-Room'. Another gives safety instructions.

I hear different sounds. Heavy items are being dragged across the floor. The noise bounces off the walls and I suddenly can't tell if it's coming from above or below me. Warily, I edge closer to an internal stairway, which is littered with cigarette butts, condoms and beer cans.

I peer up and down the stairs that twist back and forth. On the landing immediately below me there is an old washroom, with a broken toilet and a pipe sticking out of the wall. One cubicle door has been ripped off, while another hangs from a bent hinge.

I hear shouting coming from above. Suddenly, a forty-four-gallon drum bounces down the stairs end-on-end. I flatten myself against the wall as it misses my nose and continues tumbling. Moments later, a plank of broken wood drops silently past me and clatters when it reaches the basement.

I call Lenny. 'They're on the fourth floor.'

'Where are you now?'

'An internal stairwell.'

'A thermal drone has picked up five heat signatures.'

Heat means they're alive. Rennie, Lilah, Daniela, Evie and Elias.

'I'm waiting for a police chopper. I want to put an armed response unit on the roof,' says Lenny.

'He'll know you're here.'

'He knows already.'

'I'm going up.'

'You're not wearing a vest.'

'I'll keep my phone on.'

74

Evie

Pulling at the ropes around my wrists and arms, I try to wriggle free. The chair rocks, but I can't break loose. Rennie is somewhere nearby; I can hear him shouting.

Doubled over, I lean forward, putting all my weight on my toes. I manage to stand with the chair bound to my back and to shuffle a few feet like a hobbled turtle. Lilah is trying to say something behind the tape. Her eyes go to the sports bag and back to me. I understand what she means.

Rennie appears and crosses the room to the large windows, where he braces his back against the wall and looks out through one of the broken panes, cursing what he sees. He runs back to the stairwell.

'I know you're there. Don't come any closer or I'll kill them,' he yells.

After a few moments comes a reply. 'You don't want to do that.'

Rennie begins to barricade the door. He rolls a large drum into place and wedges wooden pallets and broken planks diagonally against the frame. He adds metal pipes and broken pieces of concrete and another drum, which sloshes as he drags it across the floor.

While he's distracted, I shuffle towards the table, bent forward, trying to stop the chair legs dragging on the floor. I bend even lower and manoeuvre my head and neck beneath the edge of the table. Bracing myself, I push up. The table lifts. I push again. It topples, helped by the weight of the sports bag. Tiny glass vials spill onto the floor, bouncing and scattering, but not breaking.

'What the fuck!' says Rennie.

I begin stamping on the vials, shattering them beneath my heels. Some of them spin away. Others refuse to break.

Rennie drags me backwards, hurling me onto the floor, still attached to the chair. I fall with my arms trapped beneath my back, crushed under the weight of my body. The pain makes my vision blur. I'm still kicking with my feet, trying to shatter the vials, but they're out of reach.

His boot swings into my stomach and air leaves my lungs. I fight to replace it, but I can't breathe. Maybe he's broken something inside me. Curled up on the floor, I suck in tiny gasps, drawing in dust, wanting to cough, unable to without air.

Rennie is scooping up the remaining vials. He continues filling the syringe, tossing away each empty ampoule. Satisfied, he turns and walks to Lilah, who knows what's coming. She bucks her hips and rocks her head, pleading behind the tape. He pinches the skin of her right forearm, searching for a vein, before plunging the needle into her skin, pushing the plunger until it empties. He goes back to the vials and fills the syringe again.

I hear the makeshift barricade begin to move. Someone is on the other side of the fire door, pushing against the broken wood and empty drums, trying to break through.

The needle slides into Daniela's arm and Rennie pushes the plunger, before tossing the empty syringe aside. He crouches between the two nurses.

'Heparin is an anticoagulant that causes the blood to thin, but you know that already. Oliver suffered internal bleeding, but you might be luckier.'

From within the stairwell comes an angry roar and someone

charges at the door. The barricade shakes and moves an inch. It happens again and again, and each time the door is forced open a little more. A hand reaches blindly around the frame, pulling at the wood wedged against it.

Rennie takes the knife from his belt. 'Stay away, or I'll kill them.'

'No, you won't,' says a voice. I recognise it now. Elias.

'Are you the police?' asks Rennie.

'No.'

'Why are you here?'

'I want Evie.'

Rennie looks at me. 'What is she to you?'

'She's mine.'

Rennie picks up the chair with me still attached to it. He shows me the knife, before he slices the rope and pulls me against his chest.

'I'm holding a knife against her stomach. Leave now, or I'll gut her like a fish.'

Elias calls my name.

I can't answer him.

Rennie rips the tape from my mouth. More pain.

'He's killing the others,' I yell. 'They're dying.'

Elias has managed to get his arm and shoulder through the door. Next comes his head.

'One more step and she's dead,' says Rennie.

Elias sees the knife and retreats into the stairwell. He sounds like he's arguing with someone, but I can't make out the second voice. I glance at Lilah and Daniela. Neither is conscious. 'He injected them with a drug. They're going to die,' I yell, hoping Elias can hear me.

There's no response.

'Are you still there?' shouts Rennie.

'Yeah,' says Elias. 'I'm getting my breath back.'

'You know I'll kill her if you come through that door.'

'I wouldn't do that.'

Rennie seems to find this amusing. 'Who are you?'

'Nobody important.'

'What's your name?'

'Elias.'

'Have you ever lost someone you love, Elias?'

'Oh, yeah.'

'Then you must know how it feels.'

'No. I didn't *feel* a thing.'

Rennie frowns, as though unsure he's heard him correctly.

'I watched them die,' says Elias. 'But I didn't feel their pain or hear their screams.'

'What are you – a psychopath?'

'People have called me that.'

'What people?'

'Psychiatrists. Psychologists. Therapists. Counsellors. They tried to make me better. Every day I'm still learning.'

'What have you learned today?'

'That I can't have the attic. And buttons are important.'

Rennie looks baffled.

Elias charges at the door. Another plank falls away. At that moment, I drop suddenly, twisting out of Rennie's grasp. He lunges at me with the knife, but I scamper to the side, bouncing to my feet. He lunges again, but I duck and skip away behind a metal pole.

Rennie curses. He tries again, but it is a big factory and I'm small and I'm quick.

Elias is still charging at the door, moving the pallets and metal and concrete. He puts half his body through the gap and braces his arms against the frame. Red-faced and eyes popping, he bellows and heaves the door further open.

Through a broken window I see a drone rise into view. Hovering. Filming. Rennie notices and changes focus. He crouches to pick up a half-brick, which he hurls at the drone. He misses and reloads, but the drone has already pulled away from the window.

Elias has almost broken through. Rennie yells at him to stay back. He returns to Lilah and Daniela. One has blood running from her nose and the other has vomited down her front. He kneels beside Lilah and puts his knife against her right forearm, slicing through her skin.

'No!' I scream.

He turns to Daniela and cuts her left forearm. I drop to my knees between them, using my hands to try to stem the bleeding. Blood is dribbling through my fingers, down their wrists, onto the floor.

Rennie grabs me and hauls me upright, holding his forearm across my throat and the knife against my neck. He pulls me backwards, away from the others, deeper into the shadows.

At the last moment, I glimpse Elias, who has broken through the barricade. His round face is damp with sweat, and he has brick dust in his hair. He bends and picks up a length of lead pipe, which he weighs in his hands. He looks at Lilah and Daniela, who are both unconscious. Then he turns and begins to follow us.

When he passes a pylon, he swings the pipe against it. The clanging sound echoes through the factory. He does it again at the next pylon.

Clang!

And the next one.

Clang!

And the next.

Clang!

75

Cyrus

Evie is screaming. I'm drawn to the sound, climbing as fast as I can, but the stairwell is full of broken wood and concrete and scrap metal. When I reach a partially open fire door, I force my arm through and then my shoulder, my head, the rest of me, scraping my chest against the sharp edges.

Lilah and Daniela are slumped forward in metal chairs with their arms bound behind them and tape across their mouths. Blood is running over their wrists and hands and is pooled beneath their feet.

I yell into my phone. 'I need paramedics. Bandages. Plasma. Two women. Bleeding out.'

'Where is Rennie?' asks Lenny.

'He's not here. I think he must have Evie.'

'Is he armed?'

'I don't know.'

'I can't send paramedics into danger.'

'They're dying,' I say. 'I need help now.'

I take off my shirt and begin ripping it apart with my teeth, creating bandages. I see a drone hovering in the window. Sound echoes through the building. *Clang! Clang! Clang!* It's coming from a distant part of the factory, perhaps another stairwell or the floor below.

Lenny is yelling at the paramedics to get moving. An armed response team is bringing them inside.

Lilah opens her eyes. I pull away the tape. 'Daniela first,' she whispers.

I do as she asks, wrapping torn cloth around Daniela's forearm and tightening the tourniquet to slow the bleeding. The bandage changes colour immediately. I keep wrapping, but it doesn't seem to make a difference.

I press my fingers against Daniela's neck, searching for a pulse. It's there. Barely. From below, I hear a battering ram breaking down a door and shouts of 'Clear!'

I take another strip of cloth and repeat the process, wrapping a bandage around Lilah's forearm, tightening it, and tying it off. I wrap my fingers over the bandages, squeezing as hard as I can, keeping pressure on the wounds. I'm kneeling in a puddle of their blood.

Lilah is still conscious. Mumbling. I can't understand the words. I lean closer.

'Evie. Find her.'

The clanging has stopped and the only sound I hear are the boots on the stairs, getting nearer.

I leave my phone on Lilah's lap. 'Keep talking. They're almost here.'

Lenny's voice. 'What are you doing? Stay together.'

'Go,' whispers Lilah, nodding her head in the direction they went.

I squeeze her shoulder and begin running into the shadows, passing through a forest of metal pylons that hold up the ceiling. Occasionally, one of them is scarred or dented by a recent impact, as though someone has left me a trail to follow.

I reach some sort of boiler or engine room that has machinery rusted into place between the metal stanchions. Old pipes that once carried water or steam are criss-crossing the ceiling.

'Elias? It's me,' I say. 'Where are you?'

The question bounces back at me from the darkness. I try different names – Rennie and Evie. The answer is the same.

Another exit. More stairs. These ones are clear of rubbish but reek of mould and fetid water rising from the basement. I descend, stopping every few steps to listen and look over the railing for some movement. Glass shatters in a muffled whop. It came from nearby. I follow the direction of the noise and emerge on a different level of the factory, which is darker because the windows are boarded up.

I reach some sort of canteen with a counter and a serving window. There are tables and benches coated in dust. A dented urn is still plugged into a wall socket. An extractor fan hangs from the ceiling by a single wire.

Something on the wall reflects the light. Liquid. Not water. Blood. The stain is shaped like a hand. I hear a gurgling sound, then silence, apart from my heartbeat.

'Rennie? It's over,' I yell. 'The police are here.'

The words echo and are smothered by the silence.

'I know about your son and your wife. I understand why you're hurting. I know what it's like to lose someone.'

Beside the serving hatch is a door to the kitchen. Inside, there are cabinets with broken or missing doors. Linoleum flooring. An industrial oven. Twin sinks. Blood snakes across the tiles, leading away from me.

I hear someone softly humming. Edging past the ovens and burner rings, I reach the end of a bench. I turn my head and glimpse the outline of someone, crouching in the corner.

'Rennie?' I ask.

The humming continues. The figure is sitting with his back to a wall with his arms wrapped around something. I move closer.

'It's me. Cyrus.'

The figure half turns, revealing his face. Elias. He cocks his head to one side but doesn't answer.

'Where is Rennie?'

Elias seems to be staring past me. I follow his gaze to another corner of the kitchen where I see the dark outline of a body lying crumpled on the floor. The head is resting inside an oven, while the torso lies across the hinged door. I move closer. My foot kicks a lead pipe. It rolls across the tiles.

Crouching next to the figure, I touch hair. Wet. A shoulder. Warm. I search for a pulse. None. I know CPR. I can save him. Rolling him onto his back, I tilt his head and prepare to give him mouth to mouth, but he has no face. Nothing recognisable. The beating did not end when Rennie stopped moving. It did not end when he stopped breathing. It did not end until Elias stopped swinging the lead pipe.

I retreat. Elias is still crouched in the same spot with his arms folded around his chest. He tilts his head like a bird staring through the bars of a wire cage.

'Where is Evie?' I ask.

He lowers his chin, and I realise that he's holding her. Her head is nestled in the crook of his arm, her face wet, her eyes closed. My heart stops. Breaks. I can't tell if she's alive or dead.

I moan and stifle a sob.

'Shhhhhh,' says Elias, rocking back and forth. 'You might wake her.'

Evie stirs. Her eyes open. Her head lifts. She reaches her arms towards me like a child swapping one parent for another.

Her head is against my chest. 'What about Lilah? Daniela?' she asks.

'The paramedics are with them.'

'Will they . . . ?' She can't finish.

'I hope so.'

Elias makes a noise deep in his throat. Toneless. Mournful. It may be acceptance, or disappointment, or grief.

'I guess this means I'm going home.'

76

Evie

The waiting room has a signed photograph of Princess Diana on the wall, which was taken on the day she visited Rampton in September 1989. Prince William would have been seven years old and Harry five. Agnesa wasn't even born then, but she would have married either of them. She wasn't fussy about her princes, not even the bald ones.

My fingerprints have been taken biometrically, along with my photograph, and proof of my address. Now they're searching my bag.

'You can't take this in,' says the guard. He's holding up a box of Coco Pops.

'It's only cereal.'

'There might be something hidden inside.'

Like what? Type 2 diabetes.

Cyrus is at the other security table. He looks at me as if to say, 'I told you so.'

'You can pick it up as you're leaving,' says the guard, putting the box on a shelf behind him.

Cyrus is waved through. He's carrying some superhero comics

and graphic novels, as well as writing paper and a deck of playing cards.

'What am I going to give him?' I ask, as we wait for our escort.

'You can give him this.' He hands me a photograph. 'I found it in the attic.'

It's a picture of two barefoot boys sitting in the bones of a treehouse made from planks of wood nailed across the branches. A knotted rope hangs down the trunk. The older boy has his hand on the younger boy's shoulder and the two of them are beaming at the camera.

In a different, parallel universe, those boys grew up and became men together. They were the best man at each other's wedding, and godparents to their first-born child. They argued about football and Brexit and Scottish independence even though both supported the same side. I would have liked to have lived in that universe, but perhaps Cyrus would be different if Elias hadn't done what he did. Maybe he wouldn't have become a psychologist and visited Langford Hall and met me. I wouldn't be here without him.

'Well, look who the cat dragged in,' says Oscar, grinning with his gold tooth. He doffs an invisible hat and bows. 'How are you, Evie?'

'Very well, Oscar. Thank you for asking.'

This has become our running joke, being extra polite to each other like we're meeting at a garden party at Buckingham Palace.

We follow him through fortified doors, along a covered path that intersects a large grassy lawn with raised garden beds at the borders. We pass an oversized chess set where the queen is missing her head and one of the bishops appears to be humping a horse. I know it's called a knight, but it will always be a horse to me.

Eventually, we arrive at an accommodation block, and are taken to a small lounge with two sofas and a low table and a bookcase full of board games and jigsaw puzzles. The furniture is bolted down, and a camera in one corner of the ceiling looks like a bulging eye.

Elias arrives and is patted down one final time before being allowed to enter the lounge. He grins and does a little jig, which makes his oversized body shake.

'You came.'

'Of course,' says Cyrus, but Elias is looking at me, not him.

'How are you?' he asks. 'Have you been well?'

'Very well, thank you,' I say, still playing the game.

'Sit down. Sit down,' he says. 'Not there. Here. This chair. You get a view. You can see the trees.'

Oscar has stayed in the lounge but is very good at blending into the background. Right now, he's playing draughts against himself.

Cyrus gives Elias the comics and graphic novels and other gifts.

'I brought you this,' I say.

As I'm passing the photograph across the table, I wonder if it's the wrong gift. What if it makes him sad, or brings up bad memories? Elias doesn't say anything. He's holding the picture in both hands.

'Where did you find this?' he croaks, his eyes shining.

'I can take it back,' I say.

'No. It's wonderful. Thank you.'

I want to say that he should thank Cyrus, but I'm selfish and it doesn't matter, and I know Cyrus won't mind if I take the credit.

'I also have these,' says Cyrus, giving him two letters. The envelopes have been opened and taped shut again by the security guards.

Elias opens the first, which is written on pale blue paper with a floral design around the edges. He smells the page, which must be scented. He reads slowly, pausing every so often to relay the news.

'Lilah is selling her flat and looking for a house to buy, somewhere with a yard for Trevor. And she might be able to come and visit me next month. Look, she included a photograph.' He shows us a picture – a selfie of Lilah and Trevor sitting on the front steps. Trevor has his tongue out, trying to lick the camera.

Elias opens the second letter.

'Guess what? Daniela is engaged. She and Martyn are getting married in the summer. They say I'm invited to the wedding, but they know I probably can't make it. Do you think I should ask Dr Baillie?'

'You should,' says Cyrus. 'And if you can't make it, I'll bring you some wedding cake.'

'I'll write back to them tonight,' says Elias. 'It's nice having penfriends.' He turns to me expectantly. 'Are you going to write to me?'

'I'm not very good with words.'

I get his sad eyes.

'I will keep coming to see you.'

'Even better.'

Elias grows quiet. 'I have something for you.'

I think he means Cyrus, but he's looking at me.

'Hold out your hand and close your eyes.'

Nervously, I do as he asks. His hand is twice the size of mine. He places something in my palm and closes my fingers over it. Even without looking I know what it is. My mother's tortoiseshell button.

'Where did you find it?' I croak.

'It was under one of the boxes.'

'You've had it all along.'

'I'm sorry. I thought it might bring me luck.'

It didn't bring it to me, I want to say, but I'm so happy I don't know whether to laugh or cry. I'll decide later, when I'm in the attic, hiding between the boxes, with the button on the window sill.

Wheels and cups rattle in the corridor as a tea trolley arrives. Oscar manoeuvres it through the door and Elias jumps to his feet, checking that we have enough cups, teabags, milk and sugar.

'I ordered us the carrot cake,' he announces. Another ritual.

And this is how we spend the next forty minutes, sipping tea and eating cake and making small talk, until Oscar tells us that it's time to bounce. Elias waves to us from the door of the lounge and watches from the window as we take the covered walkway back the way we came.

'Will he ever get out of here?' I ask.

'Yes,' says Cyrus.

I stop and tug on his sleeve, making him turn and look at me. 'Say that again.'

'One day Elias will be free.'

I nod, satisfied, and hook my arm through his, as we walk out of the hospital, into the parking area. For a fleeting moment I consider his answer and wonder if Cyrus has discovered a way to deal with my questions. Rather than lying, he gives me the sort of answers that have more than one meaning.

One day Elias will be free, like all of us.

77

Cyrus

Takeout Tuesday. Evie's choice. An Indian feast: butter chicken, beef korma, basmati rice, chapatis and lots of side dishes. She takes off the cardboard lids and puts spoons in the containers.

'You over-ordered again,' I say.

'No, she didn't,' says Mitch. 'And I'm paying.' He pulls a bottle of Prosecco from the fridge. 'I got a job today.'

'Doing what?'

'This big online gamer wants me to edit his Twitch stream and post them on YouTube. And he's recommended me to his friends. One of them has twelve million followers on TikTok.'

'That's dope,' says Evie, who clearly understands what he's talking about.

The cork pops. Mitch pours three glasses. Evie takes a sip and pushes her glass towards me. I drink twice as much when she's around.

Mitch was released from prison in the new year. It took that long for his appeal to move through the courts and for the police to withdraw their objections and offer no defence. There is still a question over possible compensation for wrongful imprisonment, but DCI Hoyle is denying that he planted evidence. The Chief Constable is standing behind him, fearing the repercussions if Hoyle goes down – the convictions that might have to be overturned, the men it would set free.

Cassie Wright has resigned from the East Midlands Forensic Services. One neighbour said she'd gone travelling. Another thought she'd moved to London. She has changed her phone and left no forwarding email and my two letters have been returned unopened.

The police considered charging her with withholding information about her brother-in-law, but Cassie denied knowing Patrice's whereabouts or having any prior knowledge of what he planned to do. The footage from the bar was inconclusive and there was nothing to prove that she delayed testing the rope that would have linked Patrice's crimes. I am not a believer in justice for the sake of justice, particularly when someone has already suffered enough. Three nurses were given the benefit of the doubt eight years ago. Now it's Cassie's turn.

The doorbell rings.

Evie answers it.

'You're late. We started without you.'

Lilah has come straight from work and is still dressed in her uniform. She has kept her hair short and has it pinned close to her scalp. She washes her hands, before taking a seat next to Mitch. They've been seeing a bit of each other these past weeks, walking the dogs, and going to movies or just hanging out.

'We're friends,' she says shyly, when dinner is over and we're cleaning up the kitchen. Mitch and Evie have gone to buy ice cream from Heavenly Desserts.

'Is it weird that I feel safe with him?' asks Lilah.

'Not at all. He found you. He called the police. He went with you to the hospital.'

'And I blamed him.'

'You made a mistake.'

'Which was huge and life-changing. He has every right to hate me.'

'And the fact that he doesn't – what does that tell you?'

'That I let a good one get away.'

There are voices in the hallway. Laughter. Mitch and Evie have raced each other up the path and into the house.

Lilah smiles. 'I'll get the bowls.'

THE SERIES SO FAR

Cyrus and Evie will return soon . . .